Chris Simpson lives and works in his hometown of Peterborough. A local businessman for more than forty years, he has always believed in the old adage that 'everyone has a novel in them' and set out to prove it. His works are always about ordinary people 'stepping up and doing right' rather than the usual secret agent, superman character beloved by so many writers.

It's About the Living is a prime example of this more-believable type of hero.

For my wife, Jillian Sarah Jane. All those late nights, but told you I could do it.

Chris Simpson

IT'S ABOUT THE LIVING

AUSTIN MACAULEY PUBLISHERS™

LONDON ∗ CAMBRIDGE ∗ NEW YORK ∗ SHARJAH

A CIP catalogue record for this title is available from the British Library.

ISBN 9781398402485 (Paperback)
ISBN 9781398402492 (Hardback)
ISBN 9781398402508 (ePub e-book)

www.austinmacauley.com

First Published 2022
Austin Macauley Publishers Ltd®
1 Canada Square
Canary Wharf
London
E14 5AA

Thanks to:

Lynton Towler, for the work and advice.
My sister, Susan, without whom this wouldn't have happened.

Most of all, Mr Russel Carter, who gave me the encouragement to continue when
I needed it.

Finally, David Hogg. He knows why.

Precis

The human species is dying, a murderous virus already released by ultra-green terrorists is spreading at an alarming rate. Antidote meant for the terrorist own use has been compromised.

Meaning that only the first experimental batch, barely enough for one thousand people is effective.

One package of this antidote, enough to allow about two hundred to survive falls into the hands of a very ordinary member of the public 'Charles Benford'.

With deaths already taking place and the clock running down, he has to decide whether to hand it over to the authorities or keep it to save those he chooses.

Realising that with only hours to go there would be no time to manufacture and distribute more of the vaccine, and so no James Bond moment. Benford decides to keep what he has and to play God.

Who to save and how to manage to do so when both government and terrorists will be hunting for him forms the first half of the book? Unable to trust even those whose lives he is saving, all of whom will desire more of the antidote for their own loved ones.

Benford while doing this has to also plan for the future of his community and try to anticipate all the other dangers they will have to face in the years to come.

The trauma of these choices and the way they are dealt with is presented in a series of snapshots of both victims and the odd person lucky enough to have a natural immunity to the virus (about a 1-20,000 chance). These snapshots continue throughout the book, presenting a look at life in a community rapidly falling back into a medieval existence.

This is a story of everyday people stepping up, or sometimes not, to fight for survival, at first against the virus and then for the dangers that the loss of electricity, gas and clean water brings.

Packs of wild dogs and other animals, poor sanitation and millions of unburied dead presenting their own dangers, and always the surviving terrorists who are determined to find and destroy the small community.

Benford, himself realising that scattered around the country there will be perhaps as many as 3,000 people with a natural immunity, who although having survived the virus will not necessarily survive so many other dangers and is determined to help as many of these as possible.

The story is one of courage, cowardice, tragedy and sometimes humour but more than anything one that reflects natural human behaviour at a terrible time.

Prologue 1

After the success of winning his second election and now understanding how to manage his PPS rather than the other way around.

Saturday afternoons, the PM declared were to be his private time, at least whenever possible. A time when he was out of sight of the press and more importantly away from the bewildering array of civil servants who wanted to commandeer those precious few hours for other things. Irritable things.

So he was more than mildly irritated when his wife called him away from watching the test match, because the health secretary was on the phone for him, and of course it being Al Coulson, it would have to be important.

"Alan, what is it?" Knowing the other man was no cricket fan, he made no attempt to hide his crotchiness at his own pleasure being disturbed.

"Good afternoon Prime Minister, I am sorry to disturb you, but I wonder have you caught the news from Hawaii?"

"No, what is it?" the PM was suddenly wary, there was something in Alan's voice that made his boss uneasy. Hawaii was the USA and that meant dealing with the Yanks.

His own personal relations with the American President had dipped recently, and he would prefer to have as little contact with the man as possible for a period. What was it about these people that they always came across so aggressively, even when they were supposed to be the main player of the so called 'special relationship'?

Reluctantly, he reached for the remote and switched the TV to the news channel. It took a moment for him to pick up the strand of the story and when he did, it sounded almost comical. Seemingly virtually, the entire population of the islands was going down with what sounded like incredibly bad cases of diarrhoea and sickness.

So bad was the outbreak that the state governor was at the point of asking the president for federal aid. "So what is it I'm listening from Alan, I doubt the cousins are going to be asking for any help or advice on how to treat an attack of the s—s." He really shouldn't be so offhand with Coulson, but the man always seemed to bring out bad behaviour in him.

The others reply was immediate and betrayed the speaker's excitement.

"Two things Prime Minister, firstly it's spreading, the bug I mean. It's spreading all around the Pacific basin, but it's going faster than it should. I've had Eric on from the world health, and he says it's impossible to spread at the rate that this is…" A pause and a change in tone followed before Coulson as though enjoying the drama added, "At least by natural causes."

The PM felt his heart sink at those last two words and immediately sensed what the other was thinking and voiced, "Terrorists?"

"That's what I thought and it's what Eric was afraid of." The speaker went quiet as he allowed the PM to gather his thoughts.

"So what are you telling me Alan, that Al Qaeda or Isis or whoever the latest bunch of bastards are, are making people s--t themselves now." He grinned to himself as he added, "Because they've been doing that to me for years." Reluctantly, mind racing as he made rapid plans, he turned more serious.

"Okay Alan, now you get your people on to this, I want as much info on this bug as you can. Find out if there have been any deaths or if it's felt they are likely. And you need to be quick, I'm calling a Cobra meeting for six pm, and I want some idea of what we might be up against by then. And mind, do it carefully, we want no leaks to the press, they'll make their own conjectures, but we don't need to give them any help." He replaced the phone, thought regretfully of the cricket match, damn Coulson, damn the Yanks and especially damn terrorists, turned the TV of and became Britain's Prime minister again.

Prologue 2

Slowly, very slowly, he eased the lid from the thermos barrel and placed it aside on the bracken. This was the third time today he had carried out this same process. Even before then, there had been plenty of practice sessions repeating the same operation over again and again. With constant rehearsing, he determined there would be no mistakes, come the real thing.

Of course, as with the earlier barrels, he at least had the reassuring knowledge that there was no danger to himself in the process.

Despite that comforting thought, and despite all those practice sessions, still his tongue licked his lips dry from concentration as he stared into the container. He felt no embarrassment at his nervousness.

Twenty-two years in the army had taught him that practice as many times as you like. When it's happening for real, the adrenalin still flows, the butterflies will still be in the stomach, and it would be an extraordinary man that could prevent hands from shaking at least a little whilst carrying out such a task.

Somewhere to his left, a moorland creature moved in the undergrowth causing him to start and peer cautiously toward the sound.

Belatedly, recognising the noise for what it was, he relaxed and wiped his sweaty hands on his trousers before continuing with the operation.

Pulling a pair of thermal gloves from his pockets he reached into the container and drew out the inner flask. A rime of ice had formed over the lid, and he brushed this off before unscrewing the cap and leaning aside as he removed it. The action was involuntary but given his knowledge of what was now pouring invisibly from the container was perhaps unavoidable.

Now past redemption, he sank to his knees staring at the empty vessel.

Was it empty? When you can't see or touch something, how do you know if it's still there or not?

He kept his vigil for half an hour, impervious to the sounds of the wildlife around him as they objected to his presence in their kingdom.

His eyes never leaving the thermos, his imagination was running riot as he thought of the death he had just unleashed on mankind.

Not just him of course, this was not just his act. Around the world hundreds of such containers had already or would be opened in a similar manner; six others in the UK alone, and their deadly contents also released. This is what he had wanted, why he had volunteered for this job and especially for this particular location.

He had waited for this moment for three years, he had visited the sites repeatedly, wanting to make sure that nothing would go wrong when the time came. Wanting even more to make sure that he was aware of every moment, he wanted to be sure that he would be able to remember every detail. This was something that no one had ever experienced before and would never, could never be repeated. He and a handful of others were doing something that was beyond belief, something that would change a world. He allowed himself a brief moment to think about some of those other people who even now would be bent over containers similar to his, releasing their contents and spewing death on to the planet.

He knew that most of the others were carrying out the deed as an act of vengeance, exulting in the pain they caused. Picturing in their minds the anguish of those people they hated as they were forced to watch their loved ones sicken and die and knowing that they themselves were inevitably doomed in their turn. That, the murderers claimed would be well-deserved justice, justice for a murdered planet.

That wasn't why Mike was here, oh he could find reasons enough for wanting revenge on society. If he felt the need to justify his actions, he could voice plenty, but he felt no such need. Mike knew quite simply that this was the right thing to do, he was helping the world to survive.

Possibly, even helping mankind to survive really. After all, if somebody didn't take action then human beings would be doomed eventually by their own rapaciousness. So Mike was doing the job he had volunteered for and was confident he would feel no remorse afterwards.

What he could not understand though, as he looked towards the village – the roofs of which he could just see in the distance – was if he so looked forward to it, why now did he feel as though there was something wrong, that he had missed something. Not mercy or anything like that, Mike didn't do mercy. No, this was something else and he couldn't figure it out.

It left him feeling uneasy and made him almost wish that he could rewind time and take back what he had just done.

Unable to decide what was bothering him, he shrugged his shoulders and abandoning the thermos bucket traipsed back to the village.

Chapter 1

It Begins

"Two one to us, ye'll see."

"Hey Ewan, what was the name of that bonnie redhead at the marquis arms?"

"No, it was 2014, I know it was cus it was our Ian's 21st." Snatches of conversation, similar to the kind that could be overheard in any pub in the country.

Of more interest to Mike Wilkinson was that between the two middle aged men stood at the bar a few feet from him.

"The six o'clock news reckoned there were thousands of dead in Hawaii already."

"Aye I heard, I've told the wife we're off to the doc's tomorrow for the flu jab."

"It's not the bluidy flu, I tell you, it's more like the plague." There was a touch of macabre triumphalism in the voice of the second local.

As though by forecasting doom for other people it would somehow allow the speaker himself to escape a similar fate. His mate was not to be so easily beaten, however. "If it gives people the squits and makes they throw up then it's the flu, or that's my way of thinking."

"It is insane I tell you."

The voices faded into the background as the landlady returned from changing barrels in the cellar and came across to serve him.

Flashing that winning smile that lit up an already attractive face was what Mike reckoned the reason for Maggie's bar being so popular among the sparse population of this remote highland village.

He had booked a room for two nights, enjoyed an excellent Aberdeen angus steak cooked to perfection by his hostess then after a shower had returned to the bar. This had always been part of the plan. Mike had used the first of his two syringes of antidote before releasing the last of the virus. So, freed of any personal risk from the murderous bug, his intention had been to stay and watch as the invisible killer commence its horrific work. He was interested, human behaviour had always fascinated him, and he wanted to see how people reacted to this, the most ultimate experience of all.

So, he sat in the bar and had listened to the chatter, watched as a young couple kissed and cuddled in the corner alcove and reminded himself that this was the last night when these people would ever enjoy themselves. By this time tomorrow, those who had not already died would be too ill to venture far. How would they feel, how would they react if he told them that? Kill him, yes certainly, but how would they deal with the knowledge regarding themselves.

That not only they, but also their families and everyone they knew were going to die within just a few hours and there was nothing anyone could do to prevent it. Would they just rant and rave, weep in each other's arms, or would they demand an explanation?

If they did, would they be able to absorb even a small understanding of why.

Of course not, how could they understand the need of what he and others were doing, and that if things went as planned, that man, the obscenest species ever to inhabit the planet would become all but extinct.

The pollution would stop, the never-ending rape of the planet cease, and the earth could maybe start to right itself.

This, this is what he had wanted, but as he watched Maggie bend to select a glass from the lower shelf, her skirt tightened across her mature but shapely bottom, accentuating the woman's curves, and arousing a natural interest in the watcher. He turned away embarrassed, in case she should see him perving and caught sight again of the young couple canoodling in the corner and felt confused and somehow lonely.

Did he really want these people to die? During all the planning and preparation he had felt no doubts, had volunteered for the deed, would have taken responsibility for other releases as well, if it had been feasible. So why the doubts now, Sanders who had recruited him to the organisation three years ago had said this might happen. Guilt, regret and doubts, he warned would be unavoidable. Mike had ignored him; how could Sanders know how he felt about the world and the people who lived in it. Sanders was just another intellectual who had jumped on the save the planet bandwagon because it was fashionable and would have jumped off it again as soon as some other cause became more popular.

Mike had seen it all before, socialism, human rights, animal rights, women's lib, religious tolerance, he had watched them, and a host of other causes become the crusade of the moment. But what did the likes of Sanders really understand about Mike's kind of life. Tucked away in their safe cosy worlds of salaries, pensions, and civil list rewards.

Sanders and his kind were protected and rewarded at every level.

Life for them offered the sanctuary of isolation from Mike's kind of realism. A sanctuary that allowed them to pontificate to others without risk or consequence to themselves.

They could choose to adopt the moral high ground and happily accept the plaudits for doing so, knowing that someone else would pay the price if they were wrong. Sanders and his mates were the type that would mouth of about a prisoner's right not to be tortured, they would insist on compliance of international laws and obedience of the rules of engagement. It never affected them if that prisoner had information that could save a squaddies life. Or that a young man would die because Mike and others like him were prevented from getting a piece of vital info out of the shit. Sanders hadn't had to listen to Fowgies screaming as his life blood ebbed away from the wound where his legs should have been. Or Tom Everett plead for his mother to help him as he attempted to shove his insides back into the cavity in his stomach torn open by a chunk of shrapnel.

Civvy Street was the same. It was Sanders's type again that had allowed Mikes mother to die on the streets. Died homeless because foreigners, the same foreigners that had tried to kill Mike, and had killed Fowgies and Everett, were given the homes built on the land his mother had been evicted from.

No, Sanders knew nothing, but Mike did, Mike knew about these things, he knew what a bunch of shits human beings were.

Kosovo twice, Northern Ireland three tours, first Iraq, second Iraq three tours, Afghanistan three tours.

Twelve times in all, twelve times he and his mates had spent months confronted by sudden death. Had watched as some of them had met the man with the scythe, listened as they screamed, and in their pain embraced even welcomed death as an escape from the pain of their wounds. Mike Wilkinson had witnessed the carnage caused by the bombings, burnings, and shootings, and listened to the hypocrisy of the politicians who had brought the violence about.

After all that, after the bombs and the bullets the army had abandoned him, had demoted, and then discharged him. He tried to return home but there was no home, Starlight, (his mother's adopted earth name) was dead. She had been turned off the small piece of land where she had somehow scrapped a living for twenty years and died on the streets of Glasgow.

Mike had stood by her unmarked grave and tried to picture her in happier times. She had been an earth warrior before ever the term had been invented. In earlier days, she had been called first a beatnik, then a hippy and finally a scrounger. She who had cared so much for people and the planet, had devoted her life to campaigning for the welfare of the earth.

Died reviled as a freeloader and waster, her life held as of no account.

Bankers and financiers had taken away her living, politicians, and industrialists her reason to live, and him? Standing there he could still picture her face as he told her he was going into the army.

Her only child was turning his back on the principles she held so dear and was entering an institution whose sole reason for its existence was to kill. She had turned away from him then, never answered his letters and refused to open the door to him when he tried to visit. They had never been reconciled. Embittered by a combination of guilt, both his own and his mother's treatment at the hands of 'them', he had bought a camper van and traipsed the country, his army pension financing his meagre needs. Now although in his fifties, he was still a striking looking man, and combining those looks with a certain hint of danger about him, he was still capable of pulling a woman when he wanted one.

Those, apart from prostitutes had come mostly from the tree hugging community. He had found himself drawn more and more to the natural world that his mother had loved so much, and he frequently camped with groups of likeminded earth warriors.

Arrested more than once, Mike had come to the attention of the security services, in particular of Phillip Sanders. They had met briefly years ago. Mike had spent most of his army career in the paras but had served four years in the SAS, before being RTUd as having been pronounced as psychologically unsuitable, something most people would have thought impossible for a member of that particular unit.

Sanders had been an under-secretary in the home office, and had been the political head, of an operation aimed against an Irish organised crime gang that was thought wrongly as it turned out to have links to the IRA. Nothing had come of the operation, but Sanders had noted the SAS sergeant, despite the man's surliness had marked him down as being potentially useful.

After arranging for the charges against Wilkinson to be dropped Sanders had courted him patiently for months, gradually sounding him out, before finally introducing him to the plot and offering him a role. Mike, although surprised by the man's hypocrisy, was excited by the idea.

Mistakenly assuming that his mother would have been all for the plan to save the planet from its human tormentors, he jumped straight in and had become one of the three chosen assassins for the UK.

Three years later, on a warm May Day, he had found himself crouching on a Scottish moor close to the community that had turned his mother out. A community that he still held responsible for her death. So, fate had come full circle. He had released the virus on their doorstep. A virus that would bring death not just to the village but to virtually all humanity. Mike and others like him would rid the earth of the murderous infection that was humankind, and inherit the world for themselves. They would know how to care for her, they would love her. They would live in small self-contained groups taking from the planet only that which they needed to in order to live. That which the planet could afford and nothing more.

Mother Nature would nurse her favourite child and restore its former beauty. The Garden of Eden would be reborn and this time, what remained of mankind would treat mother earth with the respect she deserved.

So Mike had bought death to these people, and he accepted that they all deserved to die. But as he watched Maggie Keenan's face, saw her looking around the inn, followed her gaze and saw people laughing, kissing, engaging in friendly argument and banter. He saw Maggie's face crease into that incredible smile again. Her eyes came full circle and she noticed Mike watching her. She caught his gaze and gave a slight nod of her head toward her collective customers. Her look seeming to suggest that all was well with the world. He dropped his head unable to make eye contact with the woman, then rose and hurried outside. His sudden departure confused the woman, causing her to wrinkle her brow and wonder what she had done to apparently so upset her guest.

Outside, Mike leant against the wall of the building and thought of the people inside and especially of Maggie Keenan. He told himself nothing had changed, that he still felt the same, but that wasn't quite true. Something had changed, it surely couldn't be just the woman. At his age, he was long past the time when a pretty face could affect him in that way, so why could he not stop thinking about her. She certainly did something for him, there was an aura about her that raised a man's mood just by being in her presence.

The sounds of laughter carried through the door and hung in the air, reminding him that the inn keeper had the ability to cheer not only him.

Listening to the sounds of her customers enjoying themselves, he knew that while he still did not want them to live, at that moment he no longer wanted them to die, and especially not Maggie Keenan. In that same moment as he accepted the truth of that, Mike Wilkinson felt himself to be somehow damned.

Chapter 2

Controlled Panic

He ran, desperate to be away from that awful place. His head a battleground, as the panic that sought to overwhelm him fought with that other part of his mind that was desperately trying to prevent his sinking into a paralysed torpor.

His physical progress was impeded by the large box he carried, that while not heavy, was bulky and required the attention of both his hands.

Even held this way, suspended as it was in front of him, he couldn't prevent his load bouncing relentlessly against his thighs and so making his progress difficult. Twice, he stumbled over unseen obstacles, the trips while serving to divert his mind slightly, also caused him to gasp at the efforts required not to fall.

Nevertheless, it was the events of the previous minutes rather than any physical exertion that forced him to a halt after only a few yards and crouch to throw up. A dry rasping heaving that left him feeling light-headed with foul tasting mouth and bruised stomach.

Panting, he rose slowly to his feet feeling every one of his nearly sixty years and tried to focus his mind as he continued his way to his car, walking now, as he tried to prevent the precious box fouling him again.

Think, he had to think, avoid panic, and think. Forcing himself to calm down, he concentrated on the situation. Help, he needed help, and he needed it now. He looked around him, here on the Leicestershire Nottinghamshire border he was in good farming country and knew there must be houses around somewhere, houses and people. Frustratingly, he seemed to be situated in a dip in the landscape, and this exacerbated by the surrounding hedges serving to block his immediate view.

Someone must be around though somewhere, someone, anyone. His phone, yes of course, but who to ring.

Sobbing, he tried to think exactly where he was, the emergency services would need to know where to come.

No! No bloody fool, think Charles think, you're still panicking, and you need to start thinking properly.

He fought an inward battle with his stretched nerves. What was it they did in films, count one Mississippi, two Mississippi or something like that? He tried it but was sure that he was wasting his time, or maybe not. The effort required to concentrate on how to concentrate seemed in fact to have helped as he opened the car door and nestled the box carefully onto the passenger seat.

Despite his shaking hands, he took the time to hook the seat belt around his treasure and checked to ensure its safety.

Closing the door he blew his cheeks out, leant against the car and took a number of deep breaths. He hadn't smoked for thirty years but would have killed for a cigarette at that moment. Instead, remembering a trick he had picked up when he had been quitting the habit. He simulated the act of smoking, raising his hand to his mouth and inhaling and exhaling as though in pleasure. The deep breathing helped him, calming him, and allowing him to think rationally.

Now, he realised that he had been wrong to think of seeking help. When what he really needed was to get away from here now, and without being seen.

A noise behind him startled him and he turned in fear to find a cow staring blankly at him from behind a hedge whilst slowly chewing her cud. He leant forward, placing hands on knees to support him, and panting as he looked at the bovine in the face. The peaceful satisfied look he received in reply was such an anti-climax to the last moments, that the absurdity of it calmed him enough to make him chuckle hysterically and helped him think more clearly. Even more importantly to realise that he must not be seen.

To be seen would be a disaster, if he were to be, the antidote, that life-saving precious antidote, for ownership of which four men had just died, would certainly be taken from him. The miracle, if that's what it was that had come his way and given him the chance to save his family would be gone. Someone else, someone with more gumption than he was currently showing would seize the god given opportunity of life, with both hands and take it away from him.

Now motivated, his brain finally gave instructions, *move Charles*, his actions heavy and mechanical he started his car and pulled away.

Then stopped, wait! Could he really do this? The enormity of what he was doing checking his actions. If he was to drive away now taking the antidote with him, no one else would have a chance. He looked at the car clock, according to

Roberts he could expect about another six or seven hours before the first deaths occurred, then a gradual escalation for a further twenty-four until, until, no he did not want to contemplate 'until'.

Fighting to stay calm, he tried to imagine how the scenario might go if he did attempt to hand the antidote over to the authorities. He would have to find a copper first, then what? He could just imagine the scepticism with which a young bobby would greet his story. Then again though, there was no denying the sickness that was sweeping across the country, indeed across the entire world since its start a couple of days earlier.

So, assume that he was believed, what then? Presumably, he would be taken to a police station to re-tell his story to a more senior officer, then no doubt again to someone higher still.

Somewhere along the line, the antidote would be taken from him and sent south to the capital. His story would have to be relayed time and again if not by him then by somebody. Presumably, chemists would be called to investigate and examine the antidote and to then run tests. Finally, the powers that be, would become convinced that he was kosher and would order the manufacture of more of the stuff. Useless! This wasn't a Bond novel, no one was going to save the world. There was no count down going on that could be stopped miraculously at the last moment.

The world was going to be destroyed. The process already well under way.

Any attempt to manufacture more of the antidote would be carried out against a backdrop of millions of people falling ill, and therefore would be unable to carry out their part of the work as the virus took a firm hold.

No, the authorities would have no chance; that kind of manufacturing and distribution took months to organise. Look at the palaver they had with the flu jab every year. No, the few short hours currently available to them would be like trying to extinguish a volcano by spitting in it.

So, eventually somebody at the top would appropriate the antidote and use it for those privileged few they deemed worthy of survival. He could bet that Charles Benford and his family would be long forgotten about at that point. So no, he wasn't about to surrender his families only hope of life.

But could he really just run away without giving others a chance. Just the thought of that and the consequences of doing so made him nauseous and caused his entire body to tremble. He raised his hands to his face, first cupping and then blowing hard into them, as though into a brown paper bag, trying to regain control both physically and mentally. He couldn't do this; he couldn't just run and abandon everyone else no matter how ineffectual his actions might prove.

Sobbing at the frustration caused by his own conscience, he cast another look around, still no one in sight. How much time had passed since those few violent moments had started?

It had seemed like hours, but he supposed that in reality probably no more than ten or fifteen minutes had passed since. Since! No don't go there. So ten or fifteen minutes, either figure was still a long time for a stretch of road to be this quite in a small country containing sixty million people.

Cursing at his self-imposed delay, he reached for the box and peered at the contents for the first time. His face registering his surprise at the sight of the tiny, loaded syringes inside. Given the importance of their contents, he supposed he had expected something more impressive looking.

Roberts had said the antidote was in two parts, the second to be to be taken 72 hours after the first. A quick count showed the top layer of syringes was divided into two hundred compartments, a few of which were empty, with another layer below that appeared to be identical. He rapidly selected two sets of the capsules and ran back to where Roberts and his dead companions lay. Even though the gesture was pointless, he had to at least make an effort to help others, if only for his own peace of mind.

Unencumbered this time, he was able to move faster, and it was the work of only a few seconds to secure the antidote onto Roberts bruised and battered corpse.

Those four capsules would surely give the same limited opportunity for the authorities to manufacture more, as if he had left them all the antidote behind.

It didn't really make him feel any better or more hopeful, but it was enough to allow him to justify his actions to himself. Then, while still keeping a constant watch, prepared now to flee if required, he used the dead man's phone to call the emergency services. Belatedly realising that he should have made this call later after he had left the immediate vicinity. If he was to be caught here now that would be a disaster, stop it! *Concentrate.*

Refusing to give his name, and now starting to panic at the amount of time he was losing due to his self-imposed delay, he garbled a message to the startled operator, remembering to include brief directions to his location, then taking a notebook and pencil from his pocket, scrambled a very brief note that he also lay on the corpse.

Afterward throwing the phone down, he turned to race back to his car. But spotting Robert's gun where Charles himself had thrown it only moments earlier, he paused long enough to retrieve the weapon, privately acknowledging that his omission in failing to have picked it up before was evidence of his panicked state. Forcing himself to stay calm at this further delay and overcoming his distaste for the gruesome task, he took the time to search Robert's companions and added another two pistols to the first.

Back at his car, he started the engine and pulled away, glancing into his rear-view mirror, still no one in sight. Had there been any witnesses at all? Had anybody heard the noise, and there had been plenty of that. If anybody had seen or heard anything of the incident, then the police could be on their way already.

He remembered hearing a policeman once say, "Somebody always sees. It's just a case of if they'll come forward." Had he been seen?

He was shaking badly now, think Charles think, think the worst, assume the police have been called and are already en route, and if they were, what about others, what about these conspirators. Whoever they were, they were obviously powerful people, lunatics they might be, but they would surely be powerful enough to have contacts within the police and security forces.

Either way, police, or conspirators, he must not be caught here or be traced. The consequences of that, no, don't even think about it. The fear was overwhelming now making his stomach churn again, twice the constant glances he gave the mirror spoilt his concentration and caused his car to veer dangerously. Concentrate, concentrate. He was driving as fast as he dared, turning left, right, anywhere, direction unimportant so long as it took him away from that place. How far away would he need to be, how many road junctions taken before he wouldn't be associated with those four corpses.

After a while, he became aware someone was crying and only vaguely realised it was Charles himself making the noise. A low primitive keening that gradually escalated to hard body racking sobs, the tears streaming down his face unchecked as the adrenalin that had kept him going until now gave way to shock. Until, finally estimating that he had covered enough distance for immediate safety, he pulled over and gave in to his misery.

Slumped over the wheel, Charles Benford reverted to his childhood as he wept, wanting nothing more than to feel his mother's arms around him, wanted to hear her reassurance that she would make everything right again. His weeping alternated with banging a clenched fist on the dashboard, shouting why! Why over and over, why. For perhaps ten minutes, he continued like this, overwhelmed by a darkness of mind that seemed unendurable. In the end, it was that same thought of his mother that saved him. Harriet Benford had been a strong woman who believed in doing one's duty and had brought her children up accordingly. It was this inbred sense of a duty to be done that now caused Charles to finally lift his head and suck in deep slow breaths along with a steadily decreasing number of sobs, he began the struggle to bring his shattered emotions under some control.

Come on Charles, come on. He was nearly sixty years old, a grandfather, a man respected in his local community. He liked to think that people looked up to him, asked his advice, and valued his opinions. Those same people would be amazed to see him like this. Even more importantly was the self-loathing he felt at his own weakness.

Crying like a baby, crying when this wasn't the moment for it, giving in to grief this way was wasting precious time, time he should be putting to a better use. Think, he must think, thinking is what he did.

He was a problem solver. He seemed to have spent his whole adult life solving problems of one kind and another. Anticipating them when he could, solving those he missed. He was proud of it, took delight in his reputation among friends of never being stuck for an idea. So think, that's what he had to do now think! Anticipate the problems and find a way to solve them however difficult. BUT THIS! This was so enormous, how could anybody. No he shouted inwardly; no he must think! Think, how could anybody think, but he must, he had to.

First though, he should get further away from the scene. Where? The A1 would be best and should not be too far away. Somewhere over to the east, he thought and hopefully not far, offering the anonymity of distance for a lone motorist. Which way was east?

Restarting his car, he drove on steadier now, and remembering his sat nav had a compass was able to join the great north road within only minutes.

He journeyed south for a couple of miles before parking in the first layby he came to. Then as the adrenalin continued to subside and his body adjust to the shock of the action he had just committed, he came over nauseous again.

Dashing out of the vehicle, he threw up repeatedly on the grass verge. Finally, feeling incredibly weak, he rose and surveyed the area. Was he far enough away from the scene for safety? Looking around he supposed that now his was just another car on a road containing thousands of others, giving him the anonymity he needed, or should have, Charles was no expert and he was aware that an accident in the early hours had left the southbound carriageway blocked some thirty miles to the north of where he guessed he now stood, but it seemed to him that the northbound traffic while flowing, was also not as busy as he would have expected it to be on a Monday morning, the start of the working week. It was he supposed a stark reminder if he needed one of the urgencies of his situation.

He flicked the radio on, every station a variant of the same horrendous story. Puzzled presenters and their guests all discussing the strange virus that starting in the Pacific less than 72 hours ago, and since the previous evening, first appearing in the UK was now sweeping the length and breadth of the country. It seemed that millions were dead around the world though no deaths were reported in the UK so far. But Charles knew with a sick certainty that Roberts had been telling the truth before he died, and that the deaths would start. The world really was going to end. Killed by a bunch of ideological shits who shared an evil dream. A dream that in their arrogant righteousness they had dared to put into a terrible reality. *Think Charles think.* Survival was the only thing that mattered now.

Recriminations could come later if there was a later that is, for now. Ignore the cause of the insanity and concentrate only on the now.

He had the means by which some people, his people at least could live, and if they were to then he had to concentrate and get the next few hours right.

But it was all so difficult. So difficult to even begin to think straight when all he wanted to do was yell at someone. Yell and Scream, why? Why do this terrible thing? By what right did these people think to play God like this? He had children, grandchildren, friends, neighbours.

What right did these maniacs have to just snuff out the lives of those people? The lives of seven billion people around the world, while they retained their own lives, and presumably those of their friends and families. How could these people decide that the lives of the ones that he and others loved were any less valuable than those they cared for, that is, if people like that were actually capable of really caring.

He was off again, *stop it, Charles! Concentrate.* He stood quietly for a while trying to clear his mind, calming himself, an inner voice telling him that despite his fears he could do this, he could save his friends and family, knowing that if he was to succeed, he had to get his head right, his anticipation, his planning all would need to be perfect. But it was so difficult. Charles Benford didn't know it, but his mind was in danger of a complete overload. So enormous was the situation he faced, the possible consequences of any mistakes he made, so traumatic! No, he couldn't do it.

Nobody could be expected to do it. It just wasn't humanly possible for one person in such a short space of time to think in any logical or organised way in order to make the right decisions. So despite his best efforts, his mind kept leaping about kaleidoscopically, one moment thinking of the immediate task of distributing the antidote, and the next concerning itself with how long they would have before they lost the utilities, or some other longer term problem.

His whole body shook, the ever-present nauseousness making him dizzy, and amid this physically debilitating assault there was always the distraction of why? Why the hell had they done this? With supreme effort, he centred on the one word: concentrate. *Concentrate, focus your mind, think Charles think.* He tried deep breathing, then counting slowly to a hundred.

A friend was into yoga, what was it she said about clearing the mind. He couldn't remember, but the diversion had helped, so he continued to think of other things. Inane thoughts competing with one another to present themselves, he'd had an electric bill arrive only days before, that wouldn't be paid now. On the other hand, he had recently paid the deposit on a holiday to Canada, which would be wasted. Stupid thoughts one after another, but it was working, the irrational humour calming him, his heart rate no longer thumping along like an express train. *Calm Charles, relax, breathe deep.* A range rover with blacked out windows all round cruised past and slowed down, although he couldn't see inside the vehicle, he sensed rather than saw the driver scrutinising him closely and slow further. Benford felt the start of a rising panic probably primarily due to his guilty conscience rather than anything else.

Then felt a surge of relief as the 4x4 suddenly pulled away as the driver presumably caught sight of the police patrol car coming down from the north behind him. The sole occupant of this latest arrival seeing Charles standing on the grass verge looked at him inquisitively and made to pull over. It took every part of Charles' self-control not to panic even further or to lower his face in guilty reflex. Instead, he smiled and simulated a stretching of the arms as he walked around to the drivers' door, giving a friendly apologetic wave as he opened it and took his seat behind the wheel trying desperately to intimate that all was well. Go, go he muttered under his breath as he fumbled for the ignition button. The officer looked hard for a long second, then deciding all was okay with the driver and presumably during this nightmarish morning used to similar occurrences checked over his shoulder and drove on.

Charles watched the constable leave then drew a deep breath in relief. The antidote and three revolvers were in plain sight in the front of his car. If the cop had stopped and seen either, then it could all have been over before he had even begun. His family would have been doomed to die along with all the others because he had been so weak and foolish. Concentrate Charles, time was passing, and he had so much to do.

Instinct told him to start the car and race home as fast as possible, and so make a start on administering the antidote.

Instead, the mini crisis of the policeman's appearance and his own successful handling of the situation had served to finally calm him somewhat.

Now his mind, used to years of solving practical problems told him that careful planning at this point would save him precious time later. Time was the key to this; lost time could never be regained. Any mistake, anything missed, even the most insignificant thing could prove fatal. So, he used what time he did have wisely. That also meant restraining his impulse to race home to his family at once and begin distributing the antidote.

Sound planning was vital rather than panicked reaction. He picked up a pen and paper and began to make notes and write down names. The thoughts occurring to him though obvious and frequently duplicating themselves, nevertheless served to continue to settle him down, and encouraged him in his efforts to rationalise and so slowly become able to think more objectively.

Thinking, thinking about the days to come but especially about the next few hours. Charles Benford liked to consider himself a realist who never made any attempt to fool himself about his own abilities.

He knew that he was very poor at weighing people up at first meeting.

So bad in fact that he used a rule that if he found that he liked someone on initial introduction, he would assume that person was going to turn out to be a bit of a plonker. While if his first impression was negative then he knew the individual would likely turn out fine. It was a rule of thumb that he had found proved correct more often than not.

But if his judgment was poor at first impressions then nature had more than made up for that shortfall by granting him an uncanny understanding of an individual's mind as he became better acquainted with them. From this, his ability to anticipate other thoughts and reactions had allowed him to manipulate people and events shamelessly, and Charles had been quite happily doing so for years.

That dubious ability he sensed would prove useful now. He realised that in the coming hours it would be people's immediate reaction to his story that would be critical. There would be disbelief, even with the news from around the world, lending authority to his story. People would still find it difficult to accept the real enormity of what was happening. When they did, the disbelief would be followed by fear, fear, and panic, and finally to relief as they came to understand that they were going to live.

That was when the most difficult time would come. Once they realised that there was a way out. Here, he glanced at the boxes of life saving syringes lying on the seat next to him as if seeking reassurance of their existence himself. At that point, everybody would become desperate for more.

They would all have loved ones that they would want to save, someone special. He cringed imagining the pleas, could hear them now, "Charles please just two more."

"Mum and Dad."

There would be sisters, brothers, "Please Charles, you know them, you've been to their house." He sighed even now steeling himself to resist. He tried to imagine what he might be prepared to do if the situation were reversed and someone gave him enough antidote to save his immediate family, but not enough for his sisters and their children. He was pretty sure that while he would be unspeakably grateful for what he had been given, he would do everything he could to obtain more, even including the use of violence.

He nodded his head in silent agreement that yes, if he had the chance to save the lives of those, he loved then he would be prepared to use violence even against the individual who had just saved his own life.

His thoughts flicked briefly to some of the people who would be on his list and knew to expect that at least some of them would behave in the same way as Charles himself would have done.

So that meant, he would have to be on his guard and manipulate the situations in some way that would allow him to keep total control of both people and situations.

He must create conditions whereby recipients would have to accept the limits he was setting. Accept them while not losing all hope for the future facing them. Morale would be important, he would need to make them concentrate on the fact that they and their immediate family were surviving, and that's what counted the most. As long as they had life, there would be chances to build a new world for their loved ones. Give them the belief that there would be a tomorrow. Well, a tomorrow for them at least, but who was them? Who would he save, he looked down at the box containing the antidote?

A quick count revealed that there were 191 sets of double capsules and three singles. If he doubled two of those up – and they looked as though they were the same as the others – there would now be enough of the antidote for 192 people. That established, he started jotting down names.

Writing furiously for several minutes at a time then lifting his head to recollect a name or remember how many children someone had.

All went well for a few minutes, his own children and grandchildren numbered fifteen, while his sisters Liz and Debbie would need twelve and eleven respectively. He had even managed to prepare his mind to deal with Stephen's situation and allowed another nine capsules there.

He continued in this vein for about ten minutes, listing names of relatives and close friends, until after writing down the name of a favourite uncle who was over 90 years of age, he realised he could not justify the inclusion. Then as it dawned what that exclusion would mean, he dropped the pen in horror. He stared at the list in his hand, slowly realising that this wasn't so much a list of who would survive, but of who would, by their very absence on it die. Realisation hit him like a brick.

How could he do this, it wasn't his, wasn't his what? Wasn't his job, wasn't his right, wasn't his duty, wasn't his place to decide who would live and who would die. Those 192 capsules said it was someone's job, and he had possession of them. He also had family who he wanted to live, so get on with it, it is what it is. Sick to the stomach, he tried to put the problem of his uncle to one side with the promise that he would face that decision later.

But now his mind was totally dominated by the issue of exclusions.

People, friends, relations who for various reasons ought not to be a priority. Some by reasons of health, others by a lack of any life skills that disqualified them from inclusion on his list, and in doing so therefore, disqualified them from life.

He couldn't do this! How could he decide something this monstrous? Who was he to say that a road sweeper or bin man was less than, say a brickie or motor mechanic? Was a loving and treasured parent less than a doctor or scientist? A bin man could have all sorts of less obvious talents.

It wasn't Charles Benford's place to value one life above another.

That was exactly what these insane psychos thought they were entitled to do and not something he wanted any part of. The incredible responsibility of his situation hit him now properly for the first time. It was as though a kind of fog had been surrounding his mind before, allowing him to be at once both aware of the position he was in and yet protecting him from the full implications of it. Now he realised belatedly, that in claiming ownership of the only lifesaving capsules in the country – like it or not – he had assumed the power of not just the giving of life but of both life and death. There would be no way of passing the buck, no excuses, no one to share the blame with him. As names occurred to him, he would either choose to save that person's life or he would allow them to die. Dress it up any way he liked, and that is still exactly what it would amount to.

For today, Charles Benford had been granted the ultimate of all power. He could if he chose, revenge past slights, or reward kindnesses received. Friends could be rewarded with life, enemies sentenced to die. How on earth could anyone cope with that and stay human or even sane?

The thoughts continued to swirl around his brain, chasing each other at bewildering speed, never giving him time to settle on one issue before another one came along, confusing him. People, problems, places, all demanded his consideration each claiming priority for his attention.

He knew that by rights, and given enough time, he should be looking at saving scientists, surgeons, engineers all sorts of artisans and experts.

But this was reality, and his list of acquaintances did not include those kind of people. He did a quick count of the list of names he had been jotting down, eighty-five so far. Eighty-five people who would live beyond tomorrow night because he had included their names in his little black book. What was wrong with him that even at a time like this he could find gallows humour in the irony of that? He looked again at those names and noted guiltily that the lucky eighty-five were all either friends or relations.

But what choice did he have, he could only save people he knew, because theirs were the qualities he knew, and yes, people whom he could hope to manipulate into accepting the handover situations he imposed.

He certainly had no intention of sacrificing his own family and friends for the unknown qualities of strangers. Besides, as he looked again at the eighty-five names he had written down and again attempted to judge their worthiness for inclusion on his list, he saw they included carpenters, mechanics, electricians as well as a number of teachers, nurses and a couple of wpcs. All types of people, good people, honest people. Who could say their right to survive was any less than others, simply because those others boasted a higher IQ or a place higher up the social scale?

No, he would reserve twenty to thirty places for people like doctors, farmers, and their families, perhaps even a vet. Assuming that is, that he could find any of those in the time available.

But for the most part, he would continue to look among his own circle for those whose attributes he felt could be used or adapted to help the chosen few in their efforts to survive. He had continued to write as he thought and was up to ninety-six now and starting to flounder slightly.

It was so difficult to concentrate on this when other concerns, not as immediate but just as important, kept flitting through his mind.

Electricity, gas, clean water, sanitation, sixty million unburied bodies giving off all kinds of deadly diseases. With the aid of the antidote they would survive this virus, but there would be a host of other dangers queuing up to threaten his chosen survivors.

Problem after future problem would occur to him, only to disappear as another took its place, thoughts unbidden, confusing him, blocking his mind making concentration difficult, and even more pertinent preventing him finishing his list. Above all, there was Stephen. Enough! He threw the notebook down, realising that all this, the listing of names and pondering future problems was just his way of deliberately avoiding the taking of irrevocable action and so selecting the coward's way out again.

No, stop with the excuses and get on with it. He could think further about the list as he drove home. Right now, if his family and others were to survive, he needed to start taking that real action. And for the sake of his own battered morale he really did need to do it right now. "Come on you fool; take that first step you'll feel different when you've made a real start."

With that muttered thought, he traded the pen and notebook for his mobile. The first calls he made were to his sons Niall and Robbie.

Both physically younger versions of himself, short and stocky with thinning hair, in their cases, only just starting to turn grey but completely so in his own. They had both inherited not only his physical appearance but also his stubborn independent streak and the same stolid refusal to accept adversity without fighting back.

Having made the calls and given a number of instructions that caused his sons to pause audibly, he allowed himself a quick grin wondering what a shrink would make of a relationship between father and sons. That, having listened to what he had to say, and his subsequent requests allowed both sons to accept the situation he outlined without any real question. The trust between the three of them had always been high, but even Charles marvelled at their almost bland acceptance that if dad said the world was about to end but that he had the means to save them, then that's what would happen. Maybe, the hysteria was back but he laughed aloud at the thought of both sons now trying to explain the same thing to others as they attempted to carry out his instructions. As he drove, he was impervious to the glorious May sunshine that warmed the countryside around him. The rolling fields of green on which spring lambs gambolled, and the colours of the wild flowers they shared their fields with would normally have enthralled him.

Today was so out of place in what was happening to the world around them, that he noticed nothing as he continued to formulate his plans.

His thoughts were interspersed with occasional phone calls to some of those on his list. His sister, Liz, was one of several people with children living in various parts of the country. If they were going to have any chance of survival they needed to start traveling now, before the sickness overtook them, assuming it wasn't already too late. That last thought made him step on the accelerator even harder than previously.

Thinking of Liz, again produced another unpleasant thought for him.

She would want another five capsules. Some years ago, she had unofficially adopted a young family of five. Mum and Dad and three young children, all five of whom suffered from multiple and bewildering illnesses. Liz had taken them under her wing and really did regard them as a part of her family. For his part, he had never taken to them in the same way and now realised he would have to decide their fate.

Even as the thought occurred to him, he knew immediately that those same bewildering illnesses and lack of any skills in either parent ought to exclude them from inclusion on his list.

He put the thought away from him, cursing himself again as a coward, knowing that by ignoring the issue he was attempting to take the easy way out.

35

But he couldn't bring himself to face excluding them either, so for a second time, he chose instead to just ignore the problem.

His inability to face that decision for the moment brought his attention back to the now. In particular, the problem of those living some distance from his home in Peterborough. Trying to explain the true but complicated situation and convincing them he wasn't drunk or dreaming would have been impossible or at least have taken far too long.

He was also probably paranoid but having watched so many films and read so many thrillers, he was afraid that the conspirators would have contacts within the security services and especially within GCHQ.

He knew that inside those premises, computers monitored the millions of phone calls made every day. Knew that those same computers could be programmed to listen for certain words or phrases. These machines could even now be waiting for, "I have an antidote that can save you," or something similar, anything that might indicate his possession of the sole means of survival. It was this type of intelligence monitoring that had prevented a number of terrorist attacks over the years or so, the public were led to believe. And what about the government, had anybody there known about the existence of this quantity of antidote prior to his telephone call of earlier. If they had, then surely the security services would have been hard on Reynold's tail.

Benford suddenly felt very alone and very vulnerable. In a moment of clarity he saw himself as a he truly was. A near sixty-year-old, overweight man that had dropped into a situation that he was in no way suited for.

For a brief second, he thought again of driving to a police station and allowing somebody else to bear this awful responsibility. Perhaps, if he removed just enough antidote for his own immediate family, he might be permitted to keep it, but that would mean the deaths of so many others that he loved. *No, stop this,* he had set out on a course of action, and he would see it through all the way, and in doing so save his friends and family in the process.

With huge effort, he forced himself to drop the negative thoughts and to concentrate on being positive. Telling himself that on reflection it was probably too soon for the authorities to be aware of the situation, and that urgency dictated that he had to risk making those type of calls now before they did become aware.

If the calls to his sons had been easy enough, the next ones he made were anything but trying in as few sentences as possible to convince people that the sickness sweeping the earth actually heralded doomsday, no matter what assurances the government were issuing to the contrary, it wasn't easy. To then add that he had the only antidote in the country and that if they wanted their sons and daughters to be safe, they had better get them moving now, required the work of genius. He struggled through four such calls and then a mixture of the difficulty involved, and some residual paranoia of eavesdropping decided him not to risk any further use of his phone that might involve the mentioning of antidote or pills etc. Instead, he settled for a period of intelligence gathering as he drove, requesting information about doctors, vets, chemists, and farmers, He was seeking names, age groups, any knowledge regarding their marital status and children and especially addresses. His enquiries were met with little success, his friends and relations already preoccupied by the mysterious illness that was affecting many of their families, had little time for what must seem to them a rather trivial request. Eventually, he gave up, instead concentrating now on getting home as fast as he could. Hoping that his sons would have started to carry out his instructions before awaiting Dad's arrival. He needed to save time somehow. A glance at the clock, 11:47 am.

If the conspirators were correct in their estimates, there was a little over 28 hours before virtually everybody on the planet who hadn't taken the antidote would be dead. But how long did that give him to administer the medication before the sickness was irreversible. Every radio station he tuned into was still speculating on the mystery illness that was now known to be worldwide. It was thought that tens of millions were dead around the Pacific, but so far there were still no confirmed deaths reported in the UK at least, so how long?

If the A1 Road had been quiet, Peterborough was quite the opposite with plenty of both pedestrian and vehicular traffic about. Although, he sensed an air of aimlessness about both. Drivers pulling over to shout questions of pedestrians, who in turn were stopping one another for a short conversation. Charles guessed that people were demanding where they might obtain help or advice for their sick. Passing a bus stop close to his home, he recognised a young couple, not friends of his, in fact he had never spoken a word to them but had simply seen them about the area in recent years. Both were always well dressed, he in collar and tie and she in long skirts, and never seeming to have their own transport. Charles had tended to assume that from their dress and demeanour the pair were probably Jehovah witnesses or something similar.

Now seeing them stand hand in hand as they waited patiently in hope of a bus actually arriving against all the odds, they looked like the perfect couple. On impulse, Charles pulled over on the opposite side of the road and looked across at them. It made no sense but if he didn't help them, this pleasant looking couple, whose very appearance seem to represent everything good with the world, they would be dead by tomorrow evening.

Surely, such a clean-living couple like these were the type worthy of saving, if not them then who?

His right hand went to the door handle as his left reached toward the box on the passenger seat. Before he could either speak or grasp the antidote, he spotted two more people walking towards the bus stop.

An elderly lady first, who he recognised as living around the corner from Charles himself. The other a stunningly attractive young woman whose name again he had no idea of but had seen around the area with her husband in recent months, and who now seemed to be appealing for help from the joey couple.

His head dropped, what could he do, he couldn't continue now. It would have been difficult enough trying to explain his tale to the couple and then offering the antidote to them were they alone. Now these other two people had appeared, no it was impossible.

Reluctantly, and feeling both confused and sickened and for some reason slightly foolish, he slammed the car door shut, started his engine, and sped away. Leaving all four people looking after him in puzzlement.

Charles was gagging as he drove, knowing that in driving away he had just sentenced all four to die. Was this how it was to be? Would people's lives depend on things as slim as that? Another couple arriving at an unsuitable moment meaning that all four would die. Yet again, Benford was aware that he was failing dismally in his self-appointed role of leader.

With both his uncle and Liz's five adoptees, he had been cowardly to face the decisions he knew he should make. Now he had let another four people die, simply because he hadn't acted decisively. So far then he had allowed ten people to die and saved no one. Well done, Charles, you're a natural superhero. With a sickening sense of self-loathing, he accepted the truth that from somewhere within himself he was going to have to find some inner courage that he had failed to show so far, if he was ever going to do what was needed.

Still cursing his lack of that courage, he indulged in his habit of blowing his cheeks out in an attempt to relieve stress, and with tyres squealing around the last corner, yelled in triumph as he spotted a number of cars, including both his sons' vehicles drawn up outside Niall's home.

Obviously, they had both been busy and had carried out his instructions while he had been driving. Just the knowledge that he would now have the support of both them and Jilly, that he was no longer alone in this fight for life, gave him renewed hope. He paused to wipe away the last of his tears, promising himself as he did so that they were the last he would shed until this was over. From now on, he would steel himself to do what had to be done, whatever the cost.

His grandson Sean, a sturdy four-year-old ran to meet him as usual, and that was enough, just the sound of his laugh was like a breath of fresh air and gave Charles the new sense of determination that he so badly needed. He would find the inner strength somehow, they would succeed, they would survive. He would not allow his family to die. Whatever needed to happen for them to live was going to happen, no matter what it took.

Chapter 3

The Nightmare Begins

Natasha pulled herself to her feet, she felt drained and listless, had done so all morning. She needed to get up, needed to get on, but it would be so much easier for her if only Kieran wasn't so poorly.

His constant crying was really getting on her nerves, making her own condition feel so much worse, and resulting in a lot of fist clenching from the young mother.

Nevertheless, despite her fast-rising blood pressure, the sight of her two-year-old in distress coupled with her own inability to comfort him, brought forth a wave of sympathy for him. Though it did nothing at all to alleviate the sense of utter helplessness she felt.

Why hadn't the doctor arrived yet? She had phoned the surgery four times. The first time the receptionist, and how she hated that condescending bitch had tried to get her to bring Kieran to the surgery.

They had argued for several minutes before the cow had accepted that Tash warranted a home visit. Since then, she had made more than a dozen calls, all either without reply or only to find the line engaged.

Bracing herself, she struggled through to her son's room, his cries had diminished somewhat, only to be replaced by a fierce sucking at his dummy as the child sought solace from his discomfort.

From experience, she knew that if she left him alone there was a good chance, he would cry himself to sleep, a sleep that might hopefully last until the doctor arrived. Tash closed the door quietly and returned to her armchair, she desperately wanted a hot drink but felt too weak to make the effort required.

The young mother closed her eyes, perhaps if she rested now, she might feel better later. A cry from the bedroom woke her, and she glanced immediately at the clock, "Oh no Kieran, please." It had only been ten minutes since she had sat down, no wonder she still felt so tired.

A further cry from the bedroom told her that any hopes of Kieran sleeping further were gone. Wearily, she rose and entered her child's room while heaping wicked imprecations onto the heads of doctors and receptionists.

Chapter 4

Canterbury

"So, what do we do now? I knew we should have sent someone other than those three muppets, and why the hell were they there anyway, do we know what they were up to. Are we even sure they had the antidote with them, and if they did, where the hell is it now?"

The speaker paused in his tirade and glared at the older man. He had never liked the suave pretentious pratt and was making no attempt to show otherwise.

The object of his dislike, a rather distinguished looking sixty-year-old, turned away from the window that overlooked Canterbury cathedral, the spiritual home of the church of England and took his time replying.

In part because he enjoyed the hostility he aroused in Crispin, regarding the younger man as nothing more than a thug, if somewhat more intelligent than the average of that breed. Also in part because he was still planning his proposed course of action as he spoke. The dislike and contempt he felt for the other man clearly showing as he did so.

"We stay calm, and we use the resources we've been given. I suppose we are lucky that most of them are gathered at this Selby Manor, so at least we can mobilise any assets that we need." He pursed his lips, sipped his coffee appreciatively then continued.

"Well, some of them are going to have to go into the office today after all." "As for why they were so far of their course, I don't know, I've told you what the police told me. We know they picked the antidote up and the local plod say that there was supposed to have been four syringes of antidote left with the bodies, but there weren't any. The note with the message written on it was there and somebody, presumably the same individual that had telephoned the Peterborough police claimed the same thing. So obviously, a fifth person or persons were present and made off with the antidote. Now the fellow who made that call and left the antidote or didn't leave it but meant to, probably intended doing so as a salve to his conscience, and that tells me that he or she is an amateur."

He paused slightly, not at all sure that Crispin was following his line of thought or was the best person for this task. His natural insolence and a tendency to rely overmuch on violence, made the younger man, though extremely capable in most things, unpredictable for Sir Harmers comfort. Although, he reflected, Crispin's readiness to become physical would no doubt have its advantages later. That is, if they were able to locate both antidote and the thief who had stolen it. He took another sip of coffee before sitting down and continuing. "We play it like this. One, we use the local police. They of course, are already pursuing their own enquiries visiting every house, every farm and every building in the vicinity, trying to find out who the fourth corpse was, my guess, he will just turn out to be a local farmer or something similar."

He spread out an ordnance survey map as he spoke, "According to this, there isn't much in the area, so they'll start central and fan out for say, a half mile radius." He paused for breath still gathering his thoughts. "Personally, I don't think that will get us very far, so secondly, Nigel contacts GCHQ and briefs them on what they are to listen for. He will need a cover story for that, but you can leave that to him." He half smiled at memories long past, "He's an old pro at that." "Let me finish," he raised his hand to silence the younger man who had attempted to interrupt his flow. "Thirdly, if you look at the map you can see the only real main road in the area is the A1. Now apparently there was a nasty accident on the southbound early this morning and a large section of it has been closed off ever since. Probably contributes to why Roberts and the others were where they were but doesn't explain why they were so far of course to begin with, or so far behind time. Anyway because of absences caused by the virus, police diversions were slow being set up. That means drivers have been largely finding their own way around the pile up and getting back on the A1 wherever they can.

"There we have been lucky. Apparently, there are a lot of traffic cameras along that stretch because the locals are carrying out a survey so it's all being videotaped. Bertie Mears," he named one of their fellow conspirators, "should be able to get traffic police on to that. He is to look at both north and southbound lanes. Try to spot anything that joined from a side road, say ten miles in either direction. Of course, the locals will also be trying to sort out tyre tracks to work out what type of vehicle we are looking for, but we both know that time is against us for that kind of thing. So I think, you had better go up there as well and take a couple of our people with you. I mean from the department he qualified not from the list, obviously you'll need to take those that appear the fittest, though how long anyone will remain like that for, who knows. Once you're in the area just stay loose somewhere, we don't want local plod knowing you're around. As soon as we get anything, I will let you know directly and call the locals off, so you can move in. Remember also that we might be asked to lend a hand with any official investigation regarding these missing syringes that they failed to find with the bodies. If and when someone gets around to mounting an investigation that is, and if they do, it's not going to have the time to amount to anything is it."

His head angled to one side in question, challenging the younger man to suggest a better idea. Crispin had nothing to offer but that did not stop him criticising others. "Where do you suppose all this local manpower is going to come from, half the population haven't turned in for work remember? And even if we find whoever's taken the antidote, they will have used it by the time we get to them."

The heavy sarcasm not only failed to hide the younger man's nervousness but also irritated his senior who snapped. "Of course, I remember, I remember that a bunch of idiots dreamt this whole effing nightmare up. I remember that it was a similar bunch of idiots that put a so-called plan into operation, apparently without orders, and without ensuring that the effing antidote worked correctly and was actually available. I also remember the air traffic control dispute; can you imagine that! An air traffic dispute as the world is dying. That sent the package containing what little there was available to Scotland. And most of all, I also remember," his voice unusually for him rose to an angry yell, "that without it, you and I are dead men along with everybody else, including my daughter who is already feeling ill. So I suggest that you pull your finger out and find whoever's got it." He paused again and then in a more conciliatory tone added, "Look Crispin, think about it for a moment. Nobody could have known about Roberts' change of route. Until yesterday morning, we didn't even know ourselves that anyone would have to go and fetch the damn things. So this person or persons are opportunists, they've come across this situation purely by chance. Prior to today they would have had no knowledge that this was going to happen, no chance to plan anything, no chance to select a list of survivors. Now they have suddenly been given a chance to save their own lives and those of nearly two hundred other people. Imagine what that would be like, if you were in their position, who would you save?" The question being rhetorical, Crispin made no reply and the knight continued. "It's going to take time for him or them or whoever, to first of all absorb the truth of what's happening to the world, then decide on what he's going to do with the antidote. Before even attempting to decide who's to be saved, and then he still has to actually distribute the antidote, and that in itself will be tremendously difficult. Also remember that two identical ampoules are required over a 72-hour period so that even if we miss the first distribution but manage to get just the second ampoules, we can still save half of our people, and frankly I don't give a monkeys for the majority of them anyway. So get yourself up there and let's do what we can."

After the younger man left, Sir Harmer rose and crossed to the fire. It was a reasonably warm spring day, but his secretary knew her boss enjoyed looking into the flames when he needed to think, and had arranged to have it lit. At any other time, he would have found looking into the fire relaxing, not today though. Today, they were just flaming. He sighed heavily. He had a bad feeling about this one, the organisers, whoever they were and however much he would have willingly killed them himself. While they were obviously clever scientists, they were also totally incompetent in every other way.

As far as he could ascertain there had been no central control, no real plan, no timetable, no reliable distribution network and evidently, no effective security.

As a result, there had been too many cock ups, too much bad luck for them and not enough for the worlds security services.

Sir Harmer Evans was among the most experienced heads of intelligence departments in the western world and understood only too well what it takes to make even the best plans translate into a successful reality, and this one stank. He sighed again, yes, a very bad feeling.

Chapter 5

Gathering

Sean was excited, he sat on the stairs waiting to see what would happen next. More people were arriving, a group of five this time; parents with two girls and a boy. All three somewhat older than Sean by five years. There had been similar groups calling ever since he had come home after his daddy had taken him out of school. And every arrival had presaged a period of explanation from his father. What of, Sean wasn't sure, but the result was the same every time. He could see that the visitors disbelieved his daddy at first and asked lots of questions, then the ladies in the group would start to cry. His mummy and the other ladies in the house would join in, while the men would start using a lot of bad language. Finally, his daddy would raise his voice and restore order.

Sean himself alternated between excitement one moment and then as the visitors became upset, their palpable fear communicated itself to the child and he would try to seek out his mummy or daddy. But every time he did, they would pass him over to his sister Affricas care. She was currently standing with her ear to the lounge door trying to hear what was going on. Affrica was twelve years old and considered herself very grown up.

Sean knew that she even had a boyfriend, though Affy herself would have denied it. Right now, she was most offended that she had been excluded from the conversation that was going on in the room.

Convinced that if their eldest sister Endia wasn't poorly in bed, she would have been allowed to attend with the adults. That was because Endia was, as she never stopped pointing out to her siblings, seventeen years old and was soon going to be off to somewhere called uni. But today had been so eventful already that Sean was happy enough to just wait and see what would happen next.

The day had started normal enough, he had gone to school as usual, though his best friend Tommy wasn't there, and a lot of other children had been absent as well. Ms Mortimer had said there was a germ about, and that lots of people everywhere were poorly that day. She said that there would be no school tomorrow or the next day until people were feeling better. Then a while later, his daddy had arrived and taken him out of class. Before leaving, Daddy had spoken to miss Mortimer and told her that the school should close, and everybody should go home. The teacher had agreed with Daddy but said she couldn't just send the children, some of whom were feeling sick home on their own. Their mummies or daddies would have to collect them, and then she had started to cry.

Seeing their teacher break down in front of them had upset the other children, and the whole class had given way to tears. At the sight of the weeping frightened children, his daddy had closed his eyes and tipping his head back taken a huge breath before pulling Sean hard by his hand saying, "Come on, we have to go." His voice had been ever so strange, and Sean had been sure that his daddy had tears running down his face, leaving Sean more frightened than he had ever been in his life.

Things were just as strange when they arrived home. Nanny Sally was there with his uncle Robbie and three other huge fierce looking men. They all had great bushy beards and long straggly hair. He had seen one of them before and knew that his parents didn't like him.

The other two were complete strangers to him but Sean knew instinctively that his parents would be no keener on them either.

Certainly, the sight of all three staring down at him was unnerving to the child, making him seek protection behind his father's legs. Where peeking from behind his human barricade, Sean waited to see what else was going to happen on this strange day. He wasn't left in suspense long, first nanny Jilly arrived then his daddy's friend Stewart with his wife Amanda and their daughter Susie. Sean didn't like Susie very much; she was twelve years old and would normally claim to be too old to play with him.

Today was different, she came straight across and taking him by the arm led him into the rear garden demanding, "What's going on, my school was closed today, then dad came home from work at dinner time and said we were to pack suitcases and come down here. Are we going on holiday or what, because I'm supposed to be going with Jackie Cunningham to Ibiza in August? I've been saving up for it for ages and I do not want to waste my money on a holiday with you."

Sean shrugged his shoulders and pulled away from the girl whose anger was alarming him, "I don't know, but I don't want to go on holiday with you either."

Sean stuck his tongue out defiantly at the girl as he spoke. They were saved from further bickering by Affy's appearance. "Grampa Charles has just arrived," she announced. That was enough for Sean, he adored Grampa Charles and Nanny Jill, associating them with trips out to the seaside and other exciting places, always accompanied by lots of fun and laughter, and of course ice creams and Mc Donalds or KFCs.

Today though, he was even more pleased to see Grampa for another reason. One of the big men who so frightened him, kept taking a bottle from his pocket and drinking from it. With every drink he took, his voice seemed to grow louder, and Sean knew that some of the words he was using were naughty, the youngster had seen his mummy and some of the other women looking across at the man and talking to each other with their hands across their mouths. Sean knew that other men seemed to do what Grampa asked them to and had heard people call him boss. He knew that meant Grampa was important or something, and hoped the big man knew that as well, and that Grampa could stop the man from shouting like that. Grampa had behaved strangely though, he had hugged Sean and Affy tightly and kissed them both but had made no attempt to play with or tease either of them, then he had simply walked across to the big man and quietly taken the bottle from him. Luckily, the big man must have known that Grampa was boss because he had given the bottled up without saying a word, not even complaining when Gramps had tipped the bottle up to his own lips and emptied it down his throat.

When Gramps had handed the bottle back to him, the man had looked at it, then at the older man's face and just shrugged. Then Nanny Jill had scooped Sean up and taken him and Affy into the garden calling for Susie to follow. By the time nanny had allowed them to go back in, Grampa had gone and taken two of the big men and Uncle Robbie with him.

Then his mummy had given him a sweet, and while he was concentrating on taking the paper off it, his nannies, both of them had ganged up on him, and while one held his arm, the other had jabbed a huge needle into it.

When he screamed and tried to resist, Nanny Jill told him off good and proper, speaking to him in a really cross way, and using a voice that she normally used only when she said Grampa had had too much whisky. So, Sean had had his jab and suddenly everybody wanted to hug and kiss him.

Eventually, the child fell asleep where he sat, and he was carried up to bed by both his grandmother's. Having tucked him in, Sally glanced up at her ex's second wife and asked quietly, "Will he have a future?" Then more urgently, "Please tell me there is going to be a future. He's only five, his life can't be over at five. Him, Affy, Endia, please tell me it's not so, there has to be some hope, please."

Jilly reached out a compassionate hand and embraced her, the two of them had not always got along well for obvious reasons, but she was a kindly woman and could see her predecessor needed support. "I don't know Sally, I really don't," and there were tears in her eyes as she spoke. "But you know Charles, and what he is like. He got us this antidote, how I don't know, but it's here and he seems to be following a plan of sorts. Like you and everybody else, I'm terrified of what's happening and of what happens next. But if anyone can get us through this, it will be Charles." She placed a hand on Sally's arm as she spoke in an attempt to add a reassurance, she was far from really feeling.

How could she speak her own worries about her husband, she had seen the strain in Charles' face? She knew better than anyone the degree of resourcefulness that her husband possessed at his best. She also knew the over confidence that he had in his own abilities at times. There was as well the knowledge that her husband was close to sixty, no longer the young man who could work fourteen-hour days for weeks on end. In recent years, he had relied more and more on Joey and the others to do most of the physical work. Now he seemed to think he could turn back time and command the health and fitness that he had once enjoyed.

As for this task, he was involved in selecting those he chose to survive, those chosen to live and so by default at least those who would die. And she had seen the anguish in his eyes as he resolutely refused to discuss those selections with her or anyone else.

Then he had departed to commence delivering the antidote to the chosen ones. She could only begin to guess the emotional strain that must involve and dreaded the effect that such a trauma could have on his health.

But there was another more insidious worry that was bothering her. She knew her husband well and knew that for years he had pretty much had his own way in life. It wasn't that he was selfish, Charles Benford was the most generous man imaginable, and it was because of that generosity that he tended to get his own way so much.

Nobody ever wanted to disappoint Charles because he never disappointed them. He was always patient and understanding, always ready to forgive, always prepared to go the extra mile, not just for friends, but for perfect strangers. So people who knew him felt obliged to act the same way toward him. But nobody can control events all the time and occasionally Charles did not get his own way. In these instances, he never lost his temper, never let his disappointment show, and never really bore a grudge, more importantly, he never let go. If he hadn't achieved the result he wanted, he would just go at it from another direction. Time and time again, no matter how long it took or how much it cost, Charles would just keep trying in a calm but obsessional way. That was what worried Jilly at this moment. Charles was, she knew, trying to do the right thing, he had wrestled with his conscience and come up with a list of names that he would try to save, and therefore those who he would allow to die. How he had managed to make those kinds of decisions was beyond her imagination and probably beyond anyone else's. She also knew that he would want to continue to do what he thought was correct, but what would happen when others disagreed with his decisions. Jilly shook her head in an attempt to prevent her thoughts becoming blacker.

Whatever happened, she would continue to support her husband and just trust in the God that she knew Charles at least believed in, that they could somehow muddle through.

Chapter 6

Early Deliveries

The man she was thinking about was at that moment knocking on yet another door. He had been doing it all afternoon and into the early evening and was feeling the strain mentally if not physically. He drove his body on by constantly reminding himself that he was delivering life.

You gave somebody the antidote and they lived. Huh! If only it was that simple, but Charles had known it wouldn't be. He had started at his sister Liz's home. He and Liz were twins and as most twins are, the two were extremely close. After his wife and children, Elizabeth had been the first person he called from his car earlier.

Liz had children living away and had needed to arrange to meet them en route to save precious time before the virus took too deep a hold and prevented travel. Charles insisted that she and her husband Phil should use a syringe there and then while he watched, careful not to hand over any more of the antidote until they had both done so. Then still avoiding the inevitable, he spoke to her first about Stephen. Their younger brother was somewhere in the mountains of New Zealand alone 'finding himself', he called it, after yet another, was it six now, divorces. "E mail him Liz, tell him to stay where he is, if he gets the e mail, and if the area he is in is as isolated as he says, maybe he can survive. Tell him," Charles continued, "I have rung his family and they are on their way; I've got enough antidote for all of them." Only then did he pass on another ten syringes enough for her immediate family, two daughters, a son, and their children. Liz looked at the capsules in her hand did the maths, and then realised her brother's intention. "Charles five more surely, please."

The other had continued to avoid making the decision until actually counting the ampoules out, and even then, still mentally refused to face it head on.

Instead, leaving things until the last minute, he had simply stopped counting at ten. So, as his twin started to protest, he was already striding away having anticipated her appeal. "Liz I can't." But she was running after him, unable to believe what her brother was intending.

"Charles, please you can't let them die, please." She had reached him now and was pulling on his arm. "Charles, they are my family, Charles please. I would have gone without, you know I would, please Charles."

But now, Martin and Cliff two of the big men who had so frightened his grandson performed the job that they had been included on his list for, and gently but firmly pulled her away. Her husband Phil, running to his wife's side pushed the two brothers away from her and took Liz into his own arms, while glaring wildly at everyone else.

Checking quickly to ensure that Liz while distressed was unharmed, Charles slipped into the open door of Robbie's car, and his son forewarned slipped the clutch and drove off before his bereft sister was released.

His two minders followed in a separate vehicle, leaving Liz collapsed on the ground in tears. Inside the leading car, father and son sat in silence.

Robbie giving his father sideway glances could see the pain in his eyes, and only now began to understand the implications of what they were about. He looked again at his father's stony face and felt the tears forming in his own eyes.

The quartet had dropped Charles' own car and mobile phone at his home, hoping that if he was somehow traced by the conspirators or anybody else for that matter, he might create a temporary dead end for them by using his companion's cars and phones. It wasn't much of a ruse. But together with using Niall's home as a base, and Niall's house actually belonged to his common law wife and was registered in her name. It was about all he had been able to think of without losing too much time, and in this business of being hunted, time at least was on their side.

The conspirators, presumably as vulnerable to the virus as anyone else would become weaker by the hour, and less able to pursue him, or so he hoped.

After Liz, they called at his elder sister Debbie's home, this visit being smoother than the last. Debs was six years older than Charles and Liz; their parents having been blessed with half a dozen children. Hugh the eldest had been killed on duty in Northern Ireland back in the 70s. Eddie had died in an accident at work only weeks later, leaving Debs as the oldest of the remaining siblings. Because of the age difference, Hugh, Eddie, and Debs had tended to mix together as had Charles Liz and Stephen. The deaths of the two older brothers had left Debbie slightly isolated within the family, and consequently to her immersion into one of her own. She had married young and had two children and five grandchildren, all of whom were on their way to her home and would receive the antidote. She kissed her brother goodbye and watched him disappear out of the street, then continued to stare after him in deep thought. There had always been something immature about Charles, she thought. He was ever ready to have fun, or to create minor mischief.

He loved nothing more than to play with his grandchildren or pull an adult's leg. He also suffered somewhat from an inflated ego, crediting himself with abilities that while they might be glimpsed occasionally by others, were all too often missing in everyday life. Mostly because of his refusal to take anything too seriously. Unsurprisingly, there was no joking or anything like that about him today, but there was also more than just a new seriousness about him. There was something else different.

It showed in the way he carried himself, and more so in how he had spoken to her. He had an authority about him that she knew he possessed when dealing with others, but that was usually absent when talking to his own family members, especially to her, his older sister.

Today, he had taken charge so naturally, giving his older sister instructions in a way that he had never done before, and then departed as though certain that his wishes would be obeyed. Looking after him now.

She thought back over the last fifteen minutes and mused, "Little brother it's taken you nearly sixty years, but I think you might finally be growing up."

So on to the next family on his list, each case slightly different from the others, but tactics were always the same. In order to keep problems to a minimum, he tended to drop a substantial number of syringes off to one address, usually the parents, and then leave it to them to distribute it further to their family members.

On arrival at each drop point, he would do the talking first, spelling out the conditions that he had decided he must insist on; conditions that meant those receiving the antidote would be tied to Charles and the small community he planned for at least fifteen years.

Having gained their agreement, and under the circumstances there had been no arguments from anyone. He would then make the prime recipients take the antidote, and only then pass on the remainder, just enough for the recipient's immediate families, while ignoring the pleas for more.

When those pleas became too vociferous, Cliff and Martin would do their bit as gently as they could. While Charles took the cowards way out and did a runner as fast as possible, the sheer size of his ex-brothers-in-law were enough to prevent pleas for more of the antidote turning into any physical attempts to take any extra by force.

Fear for his own family had tempted Charles to make those members his first calls. Nevertheless, he could not ignore geography and incorporated other visits en route accordingly.

So it was not until mid-afternoon that he was able to drive the ten miles north to call on his sister-in-law Peggy and her family.

Jillys sister and her husband, Harry, had three sons and a daughter all grown up and married with a family of their own. Charles had allocated sufficient antidote for the whole extended group and had expected his in laws to behave pretty much as others had. There was initial relief and even euphoria for a moment as they realised that their families would be saved, followed almost immediately by horror as the full realisation of what was happening to the rest of mankind set in.

Up to this point, according to the media, it seemed the public in general had clung to the vain hope that this virus would be like other previous frights. Such as bird flu, aids, and mad cow disease etc., and would not be the widespread killers that was at first supposed by a press always looking for the sensational. So, Charles was surprised that as he explained about the antidote,

Peggy looked at her husband totally distraught and collapsed in tears. Harry took his wife in his arms and held her to his chest, looking over her head he addressed his visitors in a broken voice, "Alice," their only daughter, "and her family are all on holiday in Turkey and had been uncontactable all day."

Charles own face looked as though he had just been hit by a hammer. He could imagine his in laws emotions only too well. To have the means of saving your family offered and then to realise that for some at least it wasn't possible. The cruelty of such fate was beyond belief. He wanted desperately to spend time with the couple and offer his support but knew that he was still racing against the clock. Robbie had come over and was desperately trying to suggest ways and means of getting his cousin Alice and her family home.

"Private jet dad, whatever the cost might be it doesn't matter. Nobody's going to be cashing any cheques."

Distressed, Charles ordered his son back to the cars, pointing out that it wasn't going to happen. They now knew that Turkey had been hit by the virus nearly a day ahead of the UK and was already in meltdown.

Nobody was going to be flying in or out of Turkey ever again. Steeling himself to ignore the pain on Harry's face and shaking him forcefully by the shoulders to concentrate – the others attention upon himself – he continued to give instructions to his brother-in-law regarding their other family members.

Suggesting that Harry call his sons to his home to take the antidote, and that they should all meet with Charles the following morning in the car park of the Castle hotel, similar instructions were being given to all the recipients of the syringes. As he spoke, Peggy had gathered herself together and she and her husband conferred briefly, before turning to face Charles. Peggy acted as spokesperson for the couple, "Charles, thank you for this and we will take the antidote for the boys and their families, but Harry and I do not want any for ourselves. We are both in our mid-sixties, not perhaps particularly old but we have had a happy life until now." She took a deep breath, straightened her stance then continued,

"Charles we would sooner you gave our antidote to someone younger. That you are saving the boys and their families, is more than enough for us. We feel that we cannot justify depriving others, perhaps people younger than ourselves of a chance of life, especially in view of Alice and the boys."

Husband and wife both lifted their heads in defiance and looked at their would-be saviour in the eye as she finished speaking. A full minute of silence passed. Charles seething inside, made no attempt to hand over the antidote as he fought to control his temper. In the past hours, he had made himself draw up a list of intended survivors. In doing so, he had felt like he was acting as both judge and executioner. He had tried to convince himself constantly and not always successfully that he was trying to choose wisely and not just saving those people close to him.

And he had suffered as he had made his selections, fully aware of what omission from his list meant for those unfortunates not to make it on. People he knew personally, people he liked were going to die along with their wives and children because he hadn't chosen to include them in his numbers. He knew that from now on for however long he lived, he would see faces in his sleep. Faces of the people he had allowed to die and especially those of the children. As they drove from one address to another, he had too much time to think. Faces, faces of people who in that first frantic hour had escaped his attention, but who now haunted his every free moment. Parents begging him to save, if not them, then their children. He heard them, "Please Charles, you know we would have given you at least enough for your grandchildren, please you can't let Henry die he plays with your Sean. Charles please, I beg you."

Their cries deafened him, tore him apart, tempted him to change his mind a dozen times, but somehow the sanity of his original choices clung on. Afraid of perhaps eventually giving in to some form of emotional blackmail. Even more afraid of the consequences he would have to face when he had to remove someone who was already on the list in order to accommodate anybody new.

On his way to Harry and Peggy's he had scrawled a brief note of the addresses they still had to go to. Passing it on to Robbie with orders to stick with the schedule no matter what his father might say later.

Now having run his nerves ragged in making his choices, Peggy was arguing with him, refusing to accept those decisions so painfully decided on.

Whatever her reasons Charles nerves were in no state to cope with disagreement. He wanted to rave at her, threaten her, cajole her, make the two of them bow to his will. But somewhere inside him a warning voice told him that anger wouldn't work here. If his in laws were to be saved despite themselves, he would have to calm himself and find a way to be more subtle.

He used every ounce of concentration he could, as he tried desperately to think of what to say to them.

He knew that in everyday life he was a convincing talker, usually able to sell himself to potential customers or persuade people to his point of view.

But a situation this heavy was different and he was close to panic as he thought of what it meant if he failed to persuade the couple to change their minds. How could he ever face Jilly again if her sister died when he had managed to save everybody else.

Finally, taking a deep breath and then blowing out his cheeks, an inherited family habit that he was prone to whenever he was under pressure or had something that he rated as being of particular importance to say.

So it was with a huge lump in his throat that he addressed the couple that he held in such high regard.

"Look Peggy, I have given this a great deal of thought. Today I am deciding who lives and who dies, and that is something that I know I'm not fit to do, but it's down to me and I have done it, and I have tried to do it as wisely as I can. Right now I feel like the loneliest man in the world, I want to weep buckets, I want someone to just hold me, I suppose I want to turn the clock back fifty years or more and have my mother hug me and tell me that everything will be okay." He licked lips dry from tension. "But it's not going to be okay, is it?" He lifted his head that had dropped as he spoke and now looked at the couple with what he hoped was steely defiance.

"That's not going to happen, we both know it and that's my self-pitying indulgence over with. Now what I need you to understand," there was a new and authentic determination in his voice as he spoke, "is that the choice of life and death is for today only. Tomorrow and in the days and years to come there are going to be hundreds of other dangers facing whoever survives.

"Dangers that there are no magic pills for, no antidotes. I don't have time to list them all and I know that you and Harry are perfectly capable of thinking of them for yourselves. Whoever is left alive after all this, they are going to be fighting for survival every day, and frankly I doubt the ability of a lot of them to cope. You two on the other hand are amongst the most resourceful people that I know, and your courage and integrity have always been beyond reproach.

"You're giving a fine example of that now by refusing to take the antidote for yourselves. It's that resource and bravery that I need from you now.

"You have experience of life; you have a depth of knowledge that only comes with that type of experience. You're from our era of people who live life in reality and not via computers and video games, we have lived and learnt about lives lessons. You're respected and trusted by those who know you. If the people are to survive, if your sons and their families are to survive, they will need the type of experience, knowledge and yes even the example of what your offering to do now, that you two provide. I won't blackmail you into taking the antidote." As though in an effort to prove his words Charles passed the syringes over as he spoke. Then continued, "But I do need you," there was another significant pause before he spoke again, this time in a lower almost a whispering voice.

"I'm frightened Harry, I know it's immodest of me to say this, but I honestly do not know of anyone better equipped than me to do this, but I am still frightened and I need you two, and people like you." As he finished speaking, he held out his hand containing two more of the syringes. "Not for you and Peggy's sake, not even for your sons, but for me, Harry, I need you, I need you both please, I can't do this alone, I have to have help." The last word was spoken with such intensity that Harry was forced to look the question at his wife, who finally gave an almost imperceptible nod of her head and reached out to take the antidote.

Minutes later and feeling much relieved Charles and his entourage were on their way again already running late for a rendezvous with his brother's children and their families. Despite his quiet elation at having persuaded his in laws to join his growing band. Charles sat with his head in his hands and breathed deeply. Despite his success, his in laws news while obviously devastating enough already had added yet another personal trauma for him.

Harry and Peggy's tragedy meant that there would now be four sets of the antidote unclaimed. Like it or not Charles would once again have to decide who to allow to live. The very thought of this business of selection for a second time around seemed somehow dirty, and Charles could feel the familiar nausea rising again as he contemplated it.

Nevertheless ignoring the situation wasn't an option and his thoughts immediately flew to Liz and her adoptees. After only brief consideration and for the same reasons as before he knew he had to reject them again.

He tried convincing himself that his decision was correct but couldn't escape feeling as though he was personally executing the little family all over again. That fear compounded even more now by the suspicion that it might be just stubbornness on his part that prevented him from including them. If that was the case, he knew their faces would join all those others that would haunt his dreams for the rest of his life.

Next to him Robbie was aware of his father's emotional state and guessed the cause. Robbie as the younger brother, and part of a loving family had always been somewhat protected from the harsher realities of life. After leaving school he had worked with his father for a few years before going off on his own as an odd job man cum bouncer. So that again his life experiences had been different to most young men of his age.

As he had grown up, he had also inherited his parent's cheerful disposition that rarely wavered whatever the stress. When the small group had set out on their mission to deliver the antidote Robbie had just got on with the job without giving it any really deep thought. He would drive where his father told him to go and do what he was told to do. Had he been asked for his thoughts on the mission, his opinion heavily influenced by the dozens of action films that he was slightly addicted to would probably have gone along the lines of seeing the quartet rather as heroes.

People were dying until the four of them arrived and then were saved as a direct result of their visit, simple really.

Somehow though that wasn't how things were panning out. Of course he was as aware as everybody else of what it meant to be one of those not chosen to receive the magic elixir. That wasn't Robbie's fault, and it wasn't his father's either. Robbie was one of those lucky people who could stand aside from tragedies. He could sympathise with the victims of earthquakes and the like and would contribute to relief funds. He had even gone on sponsored runs and walks to raise money for that sort of thing. Though each time it was because some girl or other had enlisted him to do so. But none of the dramas were down to him and he wouldn't beat himself up over them.

What he hadn't reckoned on though as they had set of on their mission was the way that everywhere they visited seemed to have a drama of its own that he hadn't expected and now the worry for his father was obvious in his voice.

"Dad, I'm not sure about this, somehow you have to be able to share the responsibility, you're tearing yourself apart here, and you can't keep doing it." Charles turned blank eyes to him without speaking, to Robbie it seemed as if there was an ethereal aura around his father. An Aura that was somehow taking him to a different place and time to Robbie, placing him in a world of his own.

The silence lasting for fully two minutes as though the older man was struck dumb before he whispered, "Thanks Son, but let's just get on."

Despite the weakness of the whispered reply, the tone of Charles voice left little room for further argument.

Chapter 7

Natasha Two

A sharp rapping on the front door woke Natasha, who glancing quickly at the clock as she ran to the door, realised she had slept for more than two hours. That was two hours without checking Kieran, and she desperately wanted to go to him first, but the knocking came again loud and urgent.

"Alright, alright I'm coming!" she shouted fumbling at the door catch.

Bloody doctor, she thought, *takes hours to arrive then can't wait thirty seconds while the doors answered.* "Thanks for coming, doct–" her greeting was cut short, it wasn't her doctor standing in the doorway.

Instead, she saw a middle-aged woman who was leaning against the wall of Tasha's porch gasping for breath. She was tall with straggly shoulder length blonde hair, some of which was hanging down her face, with what appeared to be specks of vomit adhering to the strands. There was more of the same forming a dry crust around the woman's mouth. Her clothes bore the evidence of a fresher eruption and from the stain on the front of her jeans, she had evidently wet herself, or worse.

Natasha drew back alarmed. She vaguely recognised the woman, knew that she lived on Tasha's own estate. They had nodded good day to one another several times without ever actually speaking. "What do you", "Help me," they both spoke together, then promptly ceased as the woman's body was suddenly racked with another vomiting fit. The hand she put over her mouth in an attempt to stop the eruption proving entirely inadequate and her body distorted in pain. The sight of the woman's distress twigged something inside Natasha. She slammed the door shut in the woman's face and ran to her son's room shouting his name. Opening the bedroom door the smell hit her first, then she saw his pale little face amid all the vomit and screamed, "Kieran, no, god no, please." She

61

bent and lifted her son's body from the cot grasping him to her chest and sank to the floor with him sobbing her grief.

Chapter 8

Sterry Brown

"Get out." Crispin Sterry Brown turned in his seat to look at Paul Bunt who opened his mouth to protest against being ejected from the vehicle.

"I said get out." The order was more forceful this time, and left Bunt in no doubt as to what would happen if he hesitated a second time. Crispin was not renowned as a tolerant person, and today he seemed especially hyped up. The two of them accompanied by Steve Cherry, a fellow operative that Paul had worked with on several occasions had left Canterbury several hours ago. Circuiting the M25 they had headed north on the A1.

After the M25, which strangely given the circumstances had as usual been teeming with traffic the A1 was strangely quiet. Once, on the great north road the remainder of the journey had been fast and incident free. The paucity of other motorists allowing Crispin's vehicle an easy progress.

Under normal circumstances, the journey would have represented a welcome break from the ceaseless hours of watching CCTV tapes that had been his main duties in recent weeks. But not today, Paul a married man with children was concerned about his family. Consequently, he ignored the passing countryside of the shires and instead paid close attention to the radio. Combining his listening to a variety of supposed experts, with constant use of his mobile phone to his contacts in an attempt to obtain updates on this strange bug that for the second day running was dominating the media that morning. Worried about his family, Bunt had tried to quiz his companions for any information they might have about the possible cause of this plague or whatever it was.

The thing had struck with such bewildering suddenness that when he had left his home earlier that day, there had been only vague reports of thousands, possibly even millions of people, dying around the world.

During the day, those reports had grown increasingly alarming, and then had come confirmation that it was indeed the same virus that was now striking people down in Britain.

Now it seemed the first deaths had started. Shaken at the speed that this 'plague', as he thought of it, seemed to travel, he had checked in with his wife several times during the day and had at first been assured that despite being severely frightened she and the children were fine.

Bunt had sat quietly after that trying to assess the situation. He couldn't conceive the idea that the world was dying, but obviously a lot of people were going to do so. In which case, what should he do to protect himself and his family? The countryside speeding past his window offered no contribution to his dilemma, and he continued to sit in quiet meditation.

Shortly after they had joined the A1 at the South Mimms roundabout he had phoned again this time unsuccessfully. Since then he had tried again repeatedly but always to no avail. Increasingly concerned, he had attempted to call friends and neighbours.

Disappointingly, only two of his calls had been answered and both of those by individuals who were obviously feeling unwell themselves.

Each had apparently only picked up the receiver because they had been hoping for a call back from their GP. The disappointment in their tone when they heard Paul's voice instead was obvious and both made excuses to hang up before he could request them to check on his own family. As he watched the Cambridgeshire countryside flash by and listened to the local radio reporter steadily growing more hysterical by the minute, he had thought of asking Crispin to be dropped off at the nearest rail station so that he could return home himself, assuming that is that there were any trains running now. As he debated the question, he was aware of Steve Cherry discussing their current mission with Crispin. That man's replies had, as always, been abrupt and hardly encouraging of further discussion. Nevertheless, Paul had formed the opinion that whatever their objective was, it had some sort of connection with this plague. After mulling it over, he decided he might be protecting his family more effectively by staying with Crispin and awaiting developments, as he looked at the back of the younger man's head and thought of some of the things Crispin was reputed to have done.

He felt pretty sure that whatever might one day kill his companion it would not be something as ridiculous as excessive crapping however lethal.

Then half an hour ago, Bunt had started to cough repeatedly, the coughing quickly leading to a feeling of nausea by that time they had pulled into services just north of Norman cross and were apparently awaiting further information. Paul, aware that Crispin would not keep anybody with him who he felt was a liability, had tried to hide how bad he was feeling by making frequent excuses to leave the vehicle. Citing toilet breaks or buying refreshments from the only outlet left open in the services.

He took advantage of these intermissions to throw up in the loos and to gulp down a variety of medicines and tablets from the limited stock the newsagents carried, then attempted to cover his foul breath by a combination of rinsing his mouth in cold water and a plentiful supply of extra strong mints.

In the front of the car, Crispin Sterry Brown was becoming more irritable by the minute. Never a patient man, he knew that he needed information very soon if he was to have any chance of locating the possessor of the antidote before whoever had it had disposed of it all. Paul Bunt's attempt to hide the symptoms of the virus had not fooled Crispin for one minute.

He was well aware that sooner or later they would all fall victim to the bug, so wasn't surprised by Paul's condition, and was also aware that possession of the antidote was their best, indeed only hope of survival.

It was that knowledge that he decided that he might be better off without his companions. The virus besides being airborne was also transmitted in a variety of ways including physical contact. He reasoned therefore that he must have already contracted the bug and staying isolated in the car wasn't going to save him. But without this pair of wankers irritating him with coughing and constant whinging, he might last a few hours longer than he was likely to if he allowed the prats to stay with him.

That meant of course that he would lack back up when and if the call came, giving him the name and address he was so desperate for.

He reasoned one against the other and decided that an absence of back up was of no consequence. Crispin having complete confidence in his own ability to deal with any number of lucky chancers that the person he was looking for so obviously was.

All he required was an address, once he had that, whatever antidote the thief had left would become Crispin's.

That, of course, would be after due retribution had been collected against the person or persons who had not only upset Crispin's own plans but also threatened Crispin's life by stealing the syringes.

Chapter 9

Middle Deliveries

The meet with Stephen's children had been arranged for the car park of a McDonald's restaurant to the west of the town. The place itself was closed and the doors locked, but strangely half a dozen cars still littered the parking area without any sign of ownership.

There were nine expected in the party and all had arrived safely, having driven down from Lancashire in convoy. Kelly and Graham were Stephen's only children despite having been married six times; they were themselves parents of five children between them. All were tired and feeling the early onset of the virus. The four adults beside themselves with worry about the fate of both their own parents and their spouses' families, not to mention what was happening to their own families.

Such was their state that Charles decided it was pointless trying to explain everything to them and so turned instead to Chris Porter. Chris was Stephen's son in law, an ex-boxer turned builder, and himself built like a brick outhouse.

Charles had anticipated problems with Chris and had planned for it, accordingly, carefully coaching his accompanying trio on how to handle the big fellow at the handover of the antidote.

He had also hinted to Chris that there could be trouble obtaining the gear as Charles had put it and asked the younger man to bring his two shotguns with him.

Chris had done as requested and handed both weapons over to his wife's uncle without suspicion. Charles paused to load both before passing one each to Robbie and Martin.

Then leaning back on his car, he explained more fully the garbled instructions he had given his niece and nephew over the phone.

Afterward handing over the antidote, and only now did it register with Chris that this was it. These few syringes, one each for his wife children and himself would be all they were getting.

He watched as his brother and sister-in-law and their family received their own quota as well then looked at Charles questioningly. Chris had two brothers, a mother and father, nephews, and nieces. During the trip down from Lancashire, he had convinced himself that this miracle cure or whatever it was that his wife's uncle had promised them, would be in good supply. That he had been instructed to bring his wife and children with him, was he assumed simply to ensure they as Charles' relations would receive the antidote in good time. Then he hoped he would speed back up to Lancashire with more for the rest of his family. It had never occurred to him that there would be no more of the antidote available for him. It was also obvious the way Charles had spoken, giving instructions for them to join up in the morning with other survivors, meant that there were other capsules available. As the situation and what it meant for his family dawned on him, he made a grab to retrieve the shotguns.

Robbie, while himself a former bouncer knew he was no match for the former professional had somewhat nervously anticipated this situation and was ready for it.

Bringing the barrels of his just acquired shotgun down sharply on Chris's grasping fingers, making the big man wince in pain and withdraw his hand, before levelling the weapon at him and speaking, "I'm sorry Chris, really sorry. Don't!" he added warningly seeing the dangerous look in the big man's eye.

Martin, whose reactions were somewhat slower than Robbie's belatedly raised his own gun to point at the same target causing Chris to pause.

Charles, having jumped aside as soon as Chris had moved repeated Robbie's words as he went first to the visitors' cars, removed the ignition keys and threw them into the neighbouring bushes before retreating once more to his own vehicles. Driving himself this time, as Robbie kept his cousins' husband at bay with the gun until they had put a safe distance between them, leaving a stricken Chris, arm held by his wife in nominal restraint, mouthing obscenities and staring with hate filled eyes after them, before hurtling into the bushes in a vain attempt to retrieve the discarded car keys.

After leaving his niece and nephew, the quartet moved immediately on to the next addresses on their list.

Each new visit starting in similar ways to the last, but quickly developing into their own particular dramas. By now the virus or whatever its name was, had really taken hold. People struggling to open their doors to his urgent banging looked pain racked and smelled of vomit and occasionally faeces. Despite this or perhaps because of their visual reminder, Charles still insisted on recipients answering his questions.

Questions aimed at obtaining information on doctors, vets, and farmers.

He wanted to know anything they could tell him regarding ages, families and addresses of any they knew.

The householders both understandably tetchy at his persistence and feeling so unwell themselves, became euphoric if bewildered as he explained about, and passed on the lifesaving syringes. Then as realisation dawned that his questioning meant that more of the antidote was available but was going to other people. Like Chris they would ask for more, demanding, cajoling, pleading until again his trio of minders would extricate him amid many tears and even the occasional threats.

Threats that the sight of the shotguns kept as just that, threats, and nothing more. Gradually, though Robbie sensed a slight lifting of his father's spirit as they made progress.

Every call they made saving another handful of lives and giving hope where before there had been none. This new lightening of the mood lasted only as far as Graham and Dawn Porters. Graham an engineer had been close friends with Charles during their younger years, while the latter unknown to Graham had been more than friends with Dawn.

A blazing row between the two lovers that had ended the affair had also eroded the friendship more than a decade ago. Nevertheless, theirs had been among the first names to be jotted down on Charles' list.

The couple had two sons and a daughter, all three of whom had children of their own. It was like Harry and Peggy all over again, Graham and Dawns youngest child, their daughter Gemma was on holiday abroad with her partner Philippe.

For Charles, it was as though he had walked into a wall, his knees visibly buckled, his hand stretching out to support himself against the brickwork of the house. "Mason," the name was said as a question directed at Graham. Mason was Gemma's 18-year-old son. "He's staying with us, he didn't want to go with his mother, she agreed he didn't need to go with her, but he wasn't allowed to stay at home alone." Graham had spoken as he held his wife to him in an attempt to comfort her. There was movement behind the couple and Mason himself appeared wondering what was going on in his grandparents' doorway. Charles who never coped well with emotional situations couldn't bring himself to face the boy. More especially he had to avoid meeting Dawn's eye, there were so many things to say here none of which could be spoken about or be allowed to spill out at this time, however much he desperately needed to.

He pulled Graham to one side and handed the antidote over, mumbling instructions for the morning mixed with inane words of sympathy. As he left, his route back to the car took him past Dawn and her grandson.

To avoid having to meet the anguish in her eyes, he shouted to Robbie, barking orders to start the car, and receiving puzzled looks from his son who had left the engine running ever since they had arrived. All the time, he could feel the woman's eyes boring into the back of his neck but how could he bring himself to look at her.

For nearly forty years, she had always been there for him no matter what.

Even during the past ten years, there had been occasional phone calls and coffee mornings, keeping him abreast of both Dawn and her families' happenings, especially of Gemma's and Mason's.

Yet, despite his promise that he would never let her down, now when she needed him most, when he needed her as just as much, all he could do was abandon her.

Taking his seat, Charles barked an address to his son, and they drove off followed closely by their pair of minders. Neither man spoke much, each nursing their own dark thoughts.

Robbie not for the first time was puzzled by his father's behaviour toward Dawn and the anguish in Charles' voice as he gave his directions. He supposed that his father's preoccupation was a combination of his friends' tragedy regarding their daughter and the renewed stress of again having to choose who would receive the antidote no longer reserved for Gemma's family.

That thought, though at the back of Charles mind was only a secondary issue. More importantly, he was working out dates, just as he had done hundreds of times before. Thinking back to that first time in the Bull Hotel as two young people started out on an illicit affair. He knew what the answer would be the same as it was every time. If Dawn had fell that first time, then Gemma could be his daughter, but was she? Charles had been asking for years, badgering, cajoling, even threatening.

Knowing as he did so that Dawn would never take any threats from him seriously. In their affair, she was the dominant one, she who had initiated it, she who set the pace. Dawn controlled the whole relationship, the only time in his life that Charles willingly allowed anybody to do that. He had actually enjoyed the situation, had found it amusing, certain in his own mind that he could take charge any time he needed and that he was simply basking in the luxury of having someone else call the shots for a change. Of course, he was wrong, Dawn had retained her dominance and always avoided giving him a straight answer, now he knew she never would. Dawn's treatment of him had always veered strangely between being a lover, to that of a younger brother, now he was sure she would treat him as the latter and seek to protect him from the hurt of losing a daughter.

"Dad, where are we off?" Robbie's voice brought him back to the present. Concentrate Charles concentrate, why the hell should he, what was the point. Death was winning everywhere he looked, everywhere he went it seemed death either followed him or beat him to it. He looked again at the names on his list. Too many fifty- and sixty-year-olds, not enough younger couples. He had picked the oldies because they knew so much more than the younger ones, they had skills picked up over their lifetimes.

Skills balanced against age, and he had chosen so many of the oldies, was hat a mistake, did it even matter. He was tired and wanted to give up.

They were as good as dead any way. This f------ virus was only the start, there was going to be so many dangers ahead of them, and all anybody else cared about was to have more of the antidote. No thought of what he was going through, just condemnation for not giving them more. He had tried, God knew he had tried, but all he had in return was death. He heard somebody give a loud snorting sob and realised it was himself, causing his son to turn toward him in alarm.

Robbie's obvious concern jarred him back to the present, Robbie, Niall Jilly and all the others, they were alive. Sean and his sisters were alive, and it was his job, his duty to keep them that way. What a fool he had been, indulging his misery in such a futile way. If any of his family had done such a thing, he would have slapped them silly. If his mother had ever caught him doing so, she would have disowned him for ever.

He sat up straight and squared his shoulders in preparation. Then giving further directions he put all further thoughts of Gemma and Dawn to the back of his mind and concentrated instead on the job in hand.

He needed to select someone else to receive the antidote that was now so tragically available. Somewhere, someone else would now be lucky enough to live at Gemma's expense, at possibly his own daughter's expense.

With massive effort, he forced himself to concentrate on his duty. He needed to decide on who else he should save. He was sorely tempted to just give in and allow Liz to have the extras she wanted. At present, she was never going to forgive him for allowing her foster family to die when he had possessed the power to save them. Quite apart from that, the thought of the hurt he was causing his twin, and the way that hurt would affect their future relationship was in itself painful to him.

But no, surely, he had to make reasoned decisions. If he didn't, if he allowed emotions alone to rule his choices, then how would he justify those decisions in the future. No, he had to do this properly, and he told himself he should have faith in Liz. His sister had always been the most sensible one of the two. Of course, she would be torn by this, and the hurt would last forever, but surely eventually she would come to understand the mental trauma her twin had gone through during these hours.

So, he would do the right thing and choose those to survive purely for the good of the community or at least he would attempt to. For the sake of his own future sanity, he had to convince himself at least if no one else, that the selections he was making had been made for the right reasons.

Earlier after Harry and Peggy's tragedy, and entirely unbidden thought of some kind of a reserve list had occurred to him. Possible substitutes in case of any more tragedies. The idea had at least the appeal of saving him from the anguish of having to choose which new people to survive every time something went wrong.

Despite that attraction, he had rejected the idea in disgust as he thought of the new horrors of what creating such a list would involve.

It was awful enough deciding who to include as it was. To then have a reserve list of people, presumably, in some sort of descending order who were just waiting for a tragedy to happen to some unfortunate third party in order to provide themselves with an opportunity to survive.

That idea was just too obscene even for this, the obscenest day the world had ever endured. Eventually, as before, when he couldn't bring himself to face a decision at the time, Benford simply moved it to the back of his mind for attention later.

Chapter 10
Mid Deliveries

Malcolm and Joan Ward's home was next on his list; the couple were long-time friends of Charles' and had three children. Two of them, older boys both of whom had returned to their parents after failed marriages. It was the third child Wendy who had come along later in her parent's life and was only fourteen, who threw a spanner in Charles' plan this time. For a change the whole family seemed to be in good health, with no one yet complaining about the familiar symptoms of the killer bug. But when Malcolm led Charles into the lounge, there were six people gathered in the room watching the horrific story breaking on the news instead of the five he had expected.

Jean Paul Corbieire from Bourges was visiting his friend Wendy on a school exchange visit. The French boy was looking so miserable and forlorn like something out of a silent movie, that under different circumstances he could have been amusing. As it was, Charles heart went out to him, to be so young and away from home at this time didn't bear thinking about. Did this make the boy lucky or unlucky. Whichever, Charles knew he would have to include the youngster among his survivors. What would he have done if there had been no spare capsules, no! He wouldn't allow his mind to go there. Concentrate, Charles concentrate.

He smiled at the boy in an attempt to reassure the youngster then drawing Malcolm to one side he finished giving his instructions and departed, leaving the unenviable task of explaining to the French boy – that he would never see his own family alive again and as to why it wasn't possible to save them – to his friend.

The quartet moved on, while they had been about their business the afternoon had passed into early evening and all four men were aware that time was against them. At every home they called at, the deterioration in the health of the occupants was plain to see. The four men themselves were now in danger of becoming over exhausted.

Not by any physical exertion but simply being drained by the continual emotional strain of their work. Even the two big men, a pair not usually noted for sentiment or imagination had been forced to wipe away an odd tear during some of their more traumatic visits.

None more so than when they called at Clive and Heidi Greaves, both schoolteachers and parents of three children. Robbie had insisted on his father sitting this one out and knocked hard at the door trying to instil a sense of urgency in the occupiers by the sharp rat tat tat. Eventually, a haggard Clive opened the door by barely an inch barking, yes, what! The tragedy this time was little Chelsea Greaves, the four-year-old had died minutes before the arrival of the mercy mission. This latest blow was felt all the more because the Greaves home had been the last address on the list of Charles' scheduled calls. He sat slumped in his seat, aware that had they been about their business faster than young Chelsea could still be alive. A minute saved here another there, or if they had altered their route slightly and visited the Greaves earlier then things might have been so different.

"There's something else as well dad." Robbie was fighting hard to prevent the nausea he felt at the families' tragedy, as he continued. "Clive's father was there, he moved in with them a week ago, what could I do, I had to include him in place of Chelsea." His voice was miserable as he added, "He's in a wheelchair dad, I know he can't pull his weight but what else could I do. I couldn't give the others the antidote in front of him without giving him any as well."

Robbie had spoken loudly to penetrate the wall of misery that he was afraid was building up around his father and determined to try to divert his attention to Robbie himself by inviting recrimination.

It partly worked, "Don't ever let me hear you denigrate someone like that again Robbie, that's not how you were brought up to be. I've met Clive's father and he's a very clever man, he'll earn his keep. And you're right you couldn't have excluded him, but don't underestimate anybody just because of a disability, usually what you lose on swings you gain on roundabouts." The thought of Liz's adoptees crossed his mind and the way he had excluded them because of their various illnesses and added hypocrite to his own shortcomings before looking at the paper in his hand with loathing. Why had he placed the Greaves so far down the list, he knew they had children and should have made sure he was here earlier.

Chelsea's death was down to him and at some time in the future the same thought would occur to the child's parents, and they would also rightly blame him. How could he ever look them in the face again? Robbie had nothing to blame himself for except misunderstanding.

As for his own guilt, looking down the list of calls he couldn't see any obvious gap where he should or could have made it here any earlier, but knew that one way or another he ought to have done so.

Once again, to save his sanity he forced himself to switch his thoughts to the immediate future and away from what didn't suit. Enquiries had given him the home address of his own Doctor an Asian woman, Dr Showandra. It was to this address they now headed; Charles still desperately trying to clear his mind of a four-year-old girl who in his memory was always smiling or chuckling when he had played games with her.

Earlier in the evening, the traffic had at times become chaotic as people had continued to seek help from any quarter that occurred to them, but now there was a significant lessening of both vehicles and people. Until that is they arrived at the home of Ursula Showandra.

Here there was a crowd of some twenty or more people besieging her front door, all apparently intent on obtaining help, medicine, or just advice. A couple even begging the doctor to accompany them to their homes to attend a patient.

Nobody appeared to be threatening violence, indeed most of the visitors seemed to sick themselves to even think about it. Nevertheless, the doctor herself looked extremely frightened as she tried to convince the crowd there was nothing, she could do for them, pleading that her own family were also affected by the virus. Claiming her own son and daughter were both almost comatose and that she was powerless to even aid them.

As if in an attempt to prove her words, she suddenly bent over and started to heave as a jet of dark evil smelling vomit exited her own mouth, forcing those people immediately in front of her to back away in alarm. Charles determined not to lose another of his intended survivors, organised his minders into a small phalanx and pushed their way through the protesting but still non-violent mob.

Benford himself seized the protesting woman and bundled her inside the house, while Robbie and the other two turned to face the crowd. Robbie advised them to go home, drink lots of salt water and lie down to rest. Drawing himself upright, he tried to inject a tone of confidence into his voice in an attempt to give an impression he knew what he was about.

But the stooped shoulders of those few members of the crowd that did trudge away showed they had little faith in this young fellows' abilities as a doctor.

The remainder stood around apathetically, occasionally pleading for the doctor to come to the door again, but with the trio carrying shotguns and baseball bats there was still nothing that amounted to anything more than verbal pleas.

Inside the house, Charles brushed aside the woman's queries of who they were and what they were doing in her house, then poured a glass of water and passed it to her to swill her mouth and rid the taste of vomit.

Still, without offering any explanation, he produced the syringes and ordered her to inject herself with the antidote. Something about the man – who, while she couldn't name him, she thought she recognised as a patient of hers – seemed reassuring. And so, too exhausted to argue she obeyed somewhat reluctantly while he explored inside the house. Taking it one room at a time, he discovered first, a young man who he guessed to be in his early twenties lying on a bed and groaning miserably.

Then, following a series of gagging sounds coming from further down the landing, he came across a girl, perhaps slightly younger than his first find, kneeling in her own soil with her head draped over the toilet bowl.

Now, he met a new problem; Charles had never thought of himself as particularly squeamish but found that he couldn't bring himself to use the syringes on the two youngsters himself.

Back at Niall's, Jilly had carried out all the injections, while during the deliveries they had been making, the recipients themselves had taken responsibility for it. Fortunately for them both, the teenager herself had no such qualms and realising the man was trying to help her, roused herself enough to help him administer the antidote to both herself and her brother, then also to another young woman in the en suite of the master bedroom, again found lying with her head draped over a toilet pan.

Charles aided both the girls to their own rooms and instructed all three to clean themselves up and dress as soon as possible, before he himself returned downstairs to the doctor.

Showandra had stopped vomiting but looked terribly weak and seemed to have picked up a cut to her forehead which had bled freely down one cheek. Charles helped her to the bathroom, as she somewhat warily asked again who he was and what the syringes contained. Charles having seen the rapid deterioration in the people he was meeting and knowing he was running out of time, was desperate to move on. Now, absolutely determined to avoid another Chelsea Greaves, he again answered the Doctors questions fairly brusquely. A glance outside showed that despite the people that Robbie had persuaded to leave, the crowd had once again grown and now looked to a number more than forty.

It seemed that people unable to get a response from surgeries and health centres were growing increasingly desperate to obtain help for their families. They were obviously tracking down doctors – and unknown to Benford – nurses and even chemists to their homes, anyone who it was thought could offer help. It seemed fair game.

Showandra was now pulling on his arm demanding answers to an avalanche of questions: what this miraculous cure was, who was he and these other people, was he from the government, what was the government doing about distributing more of the antidote, question after awkward question.

Realising that the doctor's sense of doing the right thing combined together with the gathering crowd outside, might threaten his mission, Charles decided that despite the urgency he could not afford to leave the family here. So, he gave the shortest possible explanation to the woman liberally combined with threats against her and her family, then softening his tone, urged her to prepare her family to leave. It took a further twenty minutes during which time Charles took a mobile call from his son in law Kevin to whom he promised to send extra antidote.

Finally, the little family were ready, and the four men once again formed a small phalanx with the doctor and her children at the heart of it.

As the quartet attempted to bundle the four of them into their vehicles, the crowd realising they were about to lose any hope of aid from the doctor now grew hostile. Several of the fitter looking men were blocking the path leading to the cars. Charles determined not to injure anyone and afraid that his ex-brother in laws would panic and overreact pushed his way to the front of his group and holding a shot gun across his chest strode purposely forward. Robbie took station behind him with another shotgun held in a similar manner, while the brothers with the bats in their hands flanked the doctor and her family just behind the leading two.

Faced with the threat of the guns those members of the crowd immediately in front of father and son gave way; unwillingly allowing the group to reach the vehicles. Ignoring the continued muttering Dr Showandra and her children were bundled into Robbie's car, who was under instruction to take them to Niall's house and to then re-join his father later.

As an afterthought, Charles still worried about a possible hunt for himself. He relieved the doctor and the other members of her family of their mobiles, to prevent their contacting the authorities, and sent instructions to Niall that he should send as many of his people as he could home with instructions to meet at the Castle hotel in the morning. Further, he suggested that those people who could not go to their own homes for whatever reason should instead go to Niall's friend Stewart's house.

Stewart lived in a village to the north of the town, and Charles' hope was that this move would be enough to confuse or even delay any pursuit.

Eventually, an increasingly harassed Charles, having given his instructions to everybody, pushed on with his remaining two companions.

Dr Showandra had given him the address of one of her fellow practitioners, a Dr Stephen Lamb, who was aged about thirty-five and was married with two children, and with a third on the way. Again, that terrible macabre humour that he seemed unable to control surfaced with the thought of, "Oh good, might get two for the price of one."

Oddly enough, after their last experience, when they arrived at Lamb's the street was quiet with little sign of life in any of the half dozen houses in the small close. Here they found that oddly, so far only the doctor himself had been taken ill, although his wife claimed that she had just started to feel slightly nauseous herself. The antidote was administered, and Mrs Lamb seeming a far more practical woman than Showandhra had been, was both grateful for the antidote and not minded making a fuss about who, what or where it had come from.

The trio were again able to move on. As they did, the weather that had been warm and dry all day and on into the gathering evening now gave way to a torrential downpour. The rain fairly bouncing off the car bonnet deafeningly loud and making visibility difficult.

Charles still doggedly refusing to let his mind dwell on little Chelsea Greaves and having enlisted medical help, had now turned his attention to recruiting farmers. He remembered a TV programme he had seen a year or so ago that claimed the average farmers age was a startling fifty-eight.

That was much older than he wanted, he had hoped for someone more in their mid-thirties, reasonably experienced but still young. However, he didn't really know any farmers himself and the only one he had worked for in recent years was he guessed in his mid to late forties, and the two of them hadn't really gotten along all that well.

Nevertheless, knowing no one else and since neither of his companions had any better suggestions, they headed toward Warren farm.

The sheer force of the rain was making visibility even more difficult for driving and no one saw the young woman who staggered into their path until it was too late. The cars impact flinging the girl into the air with a sickening thud, and her body landing half on the road and half on the pavement with blood pouring from her head, and legs bent at what seemed an impossibly obscene angle to her torso.

Martin who had been driving reached her first, bending over her, and as he did so repeat over and over, "I'm sorry, I'm sorry I didn't see you," then recoiled as the woman screamed her agony. Appalled at all the blood and the noise of the woman's pain, he stumbled away protesting his innocence to anyone who could hear, "I didn't see her, she just stepped out. I didn't see her, it's not my fault, I didn't see her."

Charles meanwhile had reached for the latest mobile they were using and inanely dialled 999 requesting an ambulance. A harassed operator allowed him little time to speak before interrupting to point out that she had no ambulances or drivers, "There is nothing," she shouted several times.

"Nothing, don't you understand nothing." Through the hysteria, the sound of her sobbing could be heard as she spoke more quietly this time.

"I'm sorry, A&E have got queues of hundreds of people waiting and we have so little staff left, I'm sorry you will have to bring her in yourself."

Charles started to protest but was cut short again, "I cannot help you, why don't you understand, there's something going on. Something awful is happening in the world, I don't understand what it is but it's terrible and I just can't help you." And still half sobbing she broke the connection.

Already appalled at his own stupidity in contacting anyone in the emergency services, albeit not the security departments Charles turned back to the injured woman; though not a particularly skilled first aider, he had been on a couple of courses years ago and knew enough to realise the woman was dying. Moving her was obviously out of the question. The coward within him wanted to get the brothers back into the car and just drive away, anything to avoid yet another liability that he couldn't do anything about but knew he couldn't do that.

He looked around for help, inspiration, anybody, wanting desperately to abdicate responsibility of what would happen to her. A couple of passers-by looked but did not linger in the pouring rain, too intent on their own problems to have time for someone else's.

Finally, he yelled at the brothers to return to the car, both looked at him uncomprehendingly and he screamed at them, repeating himself, "Get in the effing car." Grateful to be out of it, both obeyed quickly. Martin in particular looking relieved to be turning his back on the screaming woman.

As a boy, Charles Benford had been with his older brothers when they had found a blackbird mauled by a cat. The bird had a broken wing and leg, and lay flapping its sound wing, feebly trying to get away from the humans now approaching it. Both brothers and their friends had agreed that the bird needed to be put out of its misery, though nobody was in a hurry to volunteer for the job. Eventually, lacking a volunteer, the small group decided to move on and leave the bird where it lay allowing nature to take its own course. Charles, a mere seven-year-old among a group of teenagers had wandered off with the others only to turn and run back to the stricken creature. Seizing the bird in one hand, he took the head in his other and twisted hard. Afterwards, Hugh and Eddie had eased the tiny corpse from their little brothers' hands and wiped away his tears.

Perhaps, ashamed of their own behaviour, they had lavished praise on the boy for having the courage to do what they hadn't been able to.

For himself, Charles never forgot the warmth of the bird's fragile body in his hands or the beating of its tiny heart, more awfully, he never forgot the sensation of holding a living thing in his hand and it watching him helplessly as he forced its tiny life to an end.

Likewise, he had also never forgotten his mother's words when she was informed of his actions. Of how 'very proud' she was of her son for 'doing the right thing'. Basking in that praise, the boy had promised himself that he would always continue to do that, though he was only too well aware that as he matured, he had frequently failed to live up to that particular promise.

Now, as he looked down at the young woman lying in a puddle of blood and rain, he knew what he had to do. He spoke to her, addressing her, but speaking for his own benefit and dimly aware that she almost certainly couldn't hear him above the sound of her own continuing screams of pain. "I'm sorry, I can't do anything else for you." She paid no heed to him, too wrapped in the misery of her own pain to register anything else.

Charles sank slowly to his knees by the woman's side, and now this close to her, he realised that she was more of a girl than a woman, probably not even as old as his granddaughter Endia. Slowly, his hands feeling like lead, he used the fingers of his left one to pinch her nose together and placed his other tightly over her mouth and pushed down, preventing the girl from breathing. For the first time since the accident had occurred, her screams now stopped; she opened her eyes and lifted her hand to his in a feeble attempt to stop him.

Charles tears mingled with rain drops ran freely down his face. He continued to apply the steady pressure while still sobbing, "I'm sorry, I can't do anything else. Please don't look at me like that, please I can't do anything else for you, oh look away, please look away, please don't look."

His entreaty failed, and to avoid having to return her stare the man closed his own eyes instead, still managing to maintain the steady pressure on her face.

Eventually, after a lifetime, her initial struggles gradually slackened, then while still staring at him, the girl unexpectedly lowered her hand and lay still, seemingly accepting the inevitable.

Charles felt her body relax and now opened his own eyes, while at the same time thinking that it was all over, he released his grip on her as his shoulders slumped in blessed relief only to suddenly meet the gaze of the girls own pain filled, but still very much alive eyes. Recoiling in horror, he half rose to his feet, before realising his mistake. Now, rattled more than ever, he again looked longingly towards the car. There was no one about, the two brothers were in the vehicle looking determinedly away from the appalling scene, if he chose to walk away now, leave the girl to die on her own, no one would ever know, no one would ever blame him.

Desperately he licked lips – that despite the rain, felt dry – while gauging the distance to the car. Less than thirty feet, it would be so simple, just run and go. The other two would be just as pleased to leave as he would be.

They would never say anything, would never even mention it again. It would take only seconds to cover those ten yards, ten yards and then he would be free of this horror.

He rose to his feet to leave, then with an almost animal like grunt of despair, he sank again to his knees, and replacing his hands on the girls nose and mouth reapplied the pressure. Now, unable to break eye contact, he squeezed steadily while whispering quietly to himself, "Die, please die, oh please die, please." Again her body relaxed slightly, but this time he maintained his hold but leant over her and whispered tenderly into her ear, "Go to sleep darling, just go to sleep and the pain will go, please sleep." It seemed to take hours, before just like the blackbird more than half a century earlier, and for the second time that day he felt a body go limp as its life force departed at his hands.

When it was over, he cradled her head in his lap apparently oblivious to the fact that he sat in a puddle of bloody water. As his body rocked backward and forward in time with his gabbling and crooning, he alternately begged both her and God to forgive him.

"She looks bad, you won't get no ambulance for her, no ambulances today for anyone." The words making him jump came in the almost unintelligible sing song high pitched voice of loony Tom.

Tom was two- or three-years senior to Charles, as children the older boy had at first frightened Charles and his friends, making them scream and run away every time he appeared.

Later, the fear grew into an ignorant contempt for the slow thinking Tom who was treated awfully by the unthinking youngsters. As they progressed into their teens, the cruel treatment stopped but there was still no real understanding of what was actually wrong with Tom.

So, the simpleton as most people called him or at least thought of him even if they did pretend otherwise, became a familiar sight around the area. If Charles saw him in a pub, perhaps because of a sense of guilt at his earlier treatment of him, he would occasionally stand the other a drink, but like most people he found it too hard work to give Tom what he required most, friendship. For years, Tom had pushed a two wheeled cart around the area containing a variety of what he considered his treasures, though to others it appeared to be no more than other people's unwanted rubbish. Whatever they were, he never seemed to actually do anything with them other than transport them around.

So it was Loony Tom who now broke into Charles trance, "Is she dead," he peered closer as he spoke ignoring the rain pouring down his face.

"Yes Tom, she's dead."

"You won't get no ambulance nor burial man, not today, you won't." Tom shook his head as he spoke, "Things are bad, nothings working."

"Tom," Charles pulled himself together enough to bark loudly. "Tom, I need you to help me, I need you to bury her, will you do that for me. You can take her to the building site behind your house there are some footings there dug out, put her in there and cover her over, will you. I don't want her left out here for ever."

As he spoke, he removed a fob watch and an expensive looking pen from within his pockets and handed them to Tom, "Bury her for me and you can keep these."

The other man looked longingly at the treasure being offered to him. "I won't be in trouble with Pasha, will I? He's told me to keep off the site, and he won't like me burying people there, not without asking him first, he won't."

"You just tell him Charles said it was okay." He had no idea who this Pasha was, but it wouldn't matter anyway, and he didn't like the idea of the girl not receiving some kind of burial however primitive. Loony with another look at the pen and watch nodded his assent and the two of them lifted the girl onto the cart, Charles then turned away to re-join his minders. As an afterthought, realising that Tom had looked unaffected by the virus, Charles yelled after him, "Tom meets me at the Castle hotel in the morning around nine, will you do that, do you know where the castle is?" And receiving a wave of assent in answer, the trio drove away.

Chapter 11

Sir Harmer's Story

Sir Harmer Bolton was dying, and he knew it; the sickness had started an hour ago and would he knew grow progressively worse. A fit young man would be dead within 40 hours of the first attack of retching, he was neither as young as he looked nor as fit. Thirty-five years ago as a young field agent, Sir Harmer had been shot in his stomach and was it not for the skills of a sympathetic East German doctor he would have died of his wound. As it was, he had been left with what he described as a 'blasted growling gut' and a proneness to catching any stomach ailments going. As a result, he guessed that he had no more than eighteen hours to live, unless that is Crispin Sterry Brown got a result soon. He was surprised to find that he didn't really mind his passing nor even the manner of it, just a regret for Becky and the pain his death would cause her.

But she had TC now and would cope with his help, well she would again provide that Crispin located the capsules in time.

That wasn't proving easy, Charles Benford need not have worried about phone security. Around the world seven billion people were attempting to use telephones to call for aid and using every combination of words and syllables possible to do so. Even if GCHQ had been operating at peak efficiency, the staff would have had a job to track down anything he was saying. Sir Harmer lay on a beautiful chaise longue in his office and awaited his own hour of judgment with the same calm dignity that he had shown throughout his life. At a relatively healthy sixty years of age, he could have reasonably expected another twenty years or more of life.

Twenty years of enjoying his family, his lovers, good food and fine wines. For months, he had been claiming an intention to retire before the coming winter and had really meant to this time.

He owned an 18th century cottage, high above the Italian resort of Sorrento overlooking the bay of Naples, a place that held so many wonderful memories for him. But that had been another life, an earlier life, a life shared with Alicia his wife. Beautiful caring Alicia. They had enjoyed eight years of married life together before she had died in a motoring accident. The best of those years had been spent at the cottage, the place becoming more of a home to the young couple than the London house had ever been.

The cottage once belonging to a local landowner had been virtually destroyed during the allied advance up the Italian peninsula in 1944.

Sir Harmer's father, a captain in the guards had spotted the place and after the hostilities ended returned to buy it. His premature death only a few years later had meant the place being abandoned for a couple of decades.

Sir Harmer had inherited it, and he and new wife Alicia had visited during their honeymoon. His bride had been enchanted by the whole area, unspoilt as it was by tourism at that time, and the two of them had spent most of their holidays after that working to restore the place.

Both had loved every moment of their time spent there, the work though hard was rewarding, and so therefore pleasurable. It was here their only child Rebecka had been born twenty-four years ago, here that Alicia had miscarried a son just weeks before her own death and here that Jacquline had seduced a middle aged and still grieving Sir Harmer a decade later. But all of that had been before this madness, before he had allowed himself to be seduced a second time, seduced on this occasion by an idea, rather than a pretty French girl. Now it seemed that idea was about to kill him, his daughter, his now ex-lover and virtually every other man, woman, and child on the planet.

He grinned mirthlessly, vanity that's what was killing him. His name was included on a list of people intended to live. A list that said his genes were considered to be among a select few worthy of life, of being saved while mankind was destroyed. Oh! How that inclusion had affected him, thrown his normal good judgment aside and dictated his course of action from that point on. Of course, it hadn't been that simple, he himself had never been part of any conspiracy. Until two days ago, he could not with certainty have even named anyone else as a conspirator.

He just knew of the existence of a list of names. A list that contained his own and his families' names, and he knew with certainty that none of those were part of any plot. So presumably, others whose names appeared on the list may have been equally blameless.

It was a strange, distorted plot anyway, more a concoction of ideas and wishes than anything else, the imaginings of dozens even hundreds of minds.

It had started after the Second World War, a decade and a half before Sir Harmer was even born. The so-called MAD strategy (mutual assured destruction) that had driven the cold war nuclear race had also been applied to the development of chemical and biological weapons. The military of countries around the world insisting that 'if they've got it, we have to have it' had resulted in the manufacture of weapons so disgusting they defied words to describe them. Anthrax perhaps the most famous of them was not even amongst the deadliest half dozen. There were some who even claimed that the aids virus had been unleashed on the world as a result of one such experimental programme running out of control. But first had come Professor Thadeus Eickes paper.

In the late 50s, the professor, a world leader in demographics and an ardent conservationist had written a paper for the United Nations that had since come to be known as the doomsday paper. In it he argued that the world's population – four billion in the fifties and sixties decades – would reach five billion by the turn of the millennium (it actually reached more than six).

He also produced figures to show that this rising population would have exhausted the world's natural resources before halfway through the following century. Most of his claims, especially the more extreme ones had since been rubbished or at least shown to be inaccurate; this coupled with Eicke's habit of never using just one word – if twenty would do – had meant that very few people had waded through the more than two thousand pages that made up his paper. One who had was Brian Russell, a noted if eccentric historian and another keen conservationist, who after reading Eicke's material was inspired to add his own submission. In this he suggested that nature had habitually culled the human population of the planet by regularly producing a series of devastating diseases every three to four hundred years. Citing as evidence not only plague in the 17th century and (perhaps, the most terrible of them all) the black death in the 14th, but many other earlier outbreaks that had occurred including those around the turn of the first millennium, as well as the seventh and fourth centuries AD and there was some evidence of others occurring even earlier.

Politicians, he claimed had also repeatedly helped natures work along with a series of disastrous wars and pogroms. He quoted as examples not just the fifty million that had died in Hitler's war, coupled with another thirty million in the first truly global conflict earlier in the century. To these were added the likes of Stalin's purges, accounting for perhaps forty or fifty million.

Before that the Taiping rebellion in China had claimed another thirty million. Genghis Khan, Pol pot, Tamerlane, the Mfecane in Africa, Aztecs, Incas and Mayans, the Europeans expansions into the Americas, events everywhere in all countries and continents Africa, Asia and the Australia's had all added to the total. It seemed that every inhabited continent, and every century had played its roll in trying to limit the rise in human numbers.

Until now! Russell claimed that advances in medical science, coupled with determined efforts from the politicians (aided no doubt by the spectre of annihilation) to avoid major wars meant that the world's population was now rising unchecked, that this rise would, as predicted by professor Eicke would exhaust the worlds resources if not by 2050 then still within a frighteningly short space of time. A well-researched and argued work was then spoilt by Russell showing his true colours as a racist and bigot; with his contention that the only way to avoid Armageddon was a mass sterilisation of anybody of whom Russell disapproved. Basically, that amounted to anybody who was of a different race or of different politics to Russell himself.

Both of these papers would eventually pass Sir Harmers desk and were routinely filed away under whatever heading Ms Reynolds labelled as rubbish.

That's where they would have stayed if some years later a Dr Varone in Milan had not been arrested for drunk driving. Among the papers found in his car were the details of what at first were thought must be the plot for a film or book. Closer inspection showed that however fantastic the idea, the papers really did relate to a conspiracy aimed at controlling the world's population. Among the papers, covering virtually every country in the world were endless lists of names. These names, evidently of people who it was intended should be exempt from enforced sterilisation. The list covering the British Isles included the name of Sir Harmer Evans, then simply plain Mr Evans, and a rising star in British security.

His own inclusion on the survivors list was not held against him, as virtually everybody of his rank or social standing in British society were also included among the names.

Careful security checks on the names failed to show anything incriminating for any of those included on it, they were it seemed more in the way of a wish list than a membership roll.

Again, the incident would probably have been filed away as just another farce except for two things.

The first being that the various wish lists showed an amazing knowledge of not just the politicians of those countries but also of scientists, artists industrialists, journalists etc., basically the leaders of all aspects of society and the establishment in each country mentioned. So extensive was the knowledge shown in the assembling of these lists that the information could only have been supplied with the collusion of a number of senior people in those countries.

Secondly, Dr Varone was assassinated whilst still in police custody in what could only have been a very professional hit.

Taken together, the two things meant that despite protestation of time wasting by people such as Sir Harmer himself, the conspiracy had to be looked at more closely.

Independent Investigations by the British, Americans, French and Israelies produced an understanding of the plot but no arrests. It seemed that the conspirators had simply rehashed Brian Russell's idea of mass sterilisation with no mention of how this was supposed to come about other than a vague suggestion of some kind of chemical inducement.

Sir Harmer and the other named individuals on the lists along with their families and dependents were to be exempt from this treatment.

The listed fortunates were then to nominate others who would also be exempted, these nominees would in turn suggest more names in a growing pyramid. Until, in the case of the UK some three to four million of a population of sixty million plus would eventually be included among this sexual elite.

This, it was supposed, would bring about a 90% reduction in human numbers within two to three generations without the need to shed any blood. French investigations also produced a collective name for the conspiracy, 'the Utopian league', with no mention of how the plotters had intended to administer chemicals or presumably antidote, or indeed of how they thought to avoid retribution from the worlds various governments.

Sir Harmer once again had the whole thing filed away as rubbish, but now the thing stuck. There were lots of interested parties in all aspects of the idea. Military commanders the world over would love to be able to reduce any potential enemy's manpower. Again the proponents of the MAD strategy insisted on parity or better. Industrialists, while claiming to abhor the whole idea of such chemicals, nevertheless wanted their companies to be the ones collecting the research and development cheques for the work and the manufacturing of them.

Whilst around the world, the racists that exist in every society exulted in the idea that they might be able to prevent inferior races from breeding. It never seemed to occur to them that they themselves might be classed as the inferiors by most of mankind.

Over the next years, snippets of information continued to reach Sir Harmers ears, and small seemingly innocent comments would be made to him while attending a variety of social occasions, parties, conventions, the theatre, and worst of all Glyndbourne. Comments that by themselves were of no import but that had or could have a double meaning and would be accompanied most annoyingly with a knowing look, a look that would be quickly denied if challenged.

Then, recently Crispin Sterry Brown had started to find excuses to hang around the department, he would engage Sir Harmer in private conversation and as soon as possible turn to the topic of 'the Utopian league' probing for any progress in the investigation of the organisation.

For his part, Sir Harmer gave nothing away, simply insisting that the whole thing was rubbish. He had little real hope that Crispin even if he knew anything more than Sir Harmer himself would give anything away. That young man, with his almost obsidian eyes was too well trained for that.

But the older man possessed tremendous body language reading skills and was convinced that Sterry-Brown was far better informed than himself on this particular subject.

Then there were the E mails, a half dozen of them over the last few months. Sir Harmer's private e mail address was known to only a small number of friends and family and he had changed it once as a test, but still they continued to arrive, mailed from a different country each time and from locations that left no clues as to the sender. The tone of the missives was as if from an associate, a confidant even; they claimed the plot was making progress. Assured Evans that he and his daughter were still included on the proposed list of survivors, highly valued in fact and that they should be prepared to act on short notice. What that act was supposed to consist of was not disclosed. The e-mails annoyed him, they seemed to hint that the sender or senders (as it seemed to him that there was a noticeable variation in the styles of some of the e mails) was firmly of the opinion that the Knight was in some way obstructing the investigation, and that he was doing so in order to shield the plotters and hence earn his place on the list. It wasn't the assumption that annoyed him so much as a nagging but growing doubt at the back of his mind that the assumption might be correct. Was he impeding the investigation, he had ridiculed the whole idea at every turn, and was sure that he was correct in treating it with contempt?

But if the idea was so foolish then why were some of the world's most respected security services treating it with least seriousness. France and Israel in particular were pressing for international co-operation to identify the plotters. Israel, he supposed was understandable but France! So was he deceiving himself, should he be trying harder, assigning more resources to the investigation, perhaps appoint a dedicated team headed up by a top Scotland yard detective? The Israelis had done something very similar and produced nothing concrete, only a vague rumour that the recent urge among some of the world's richest people to suddenly give huge parts of their fortunes away was somehow tied into the plot. Even Becky had commented that the sudden largesse shown by some of these people seemed to suggest that they were trying to save their collective consciences. But just how this spontaneous bout of charity was tied into Utopia nobody knew.

Then suddenly, it was too late, just three days ago an E mail arrived, a chemical was ready (no hint as to what), there was only weeks to go (for what), and he should be ready to go to a location that he would be advised of with very little notice. But only Sir Harmer, his daughter and her fiancée were now to be included. If he had treated 'Utopia' as a joke before he didn't now. Intelligence services around the world saw to that, but still only rumours, nobody had definites. Yet there was an uneasiness amongst the professionals that he had never in nearly forty years in the security community experienced before.

Everybody sensed something was going to happen, but nobody had any idea what. Arrests were made in a number of countries as security forces rounded up a variety of suspects. Ethnic minorities around the world complained as their young people were taken in for questioning on the flimsiest of excuses, still nothing, until a bare 40 hours ago, first over in Hawaii hundreds then thousands of people fell ill with what seemed to be a particularly virulent and severe form of diarrhoea and sickness. Within hours other Pacific islands were reporting similar cases followed quickly by Korea, China, and Japan. In the countries affected, hospitals and health authorities were quickly overwhelmed, doctors and pharmacists left helpless by the speed of the virus and its seeming imperviousness to the assortment of drugs being thrown at it.

People at the World Health Organisation were nonplussed and appealed for people to curb travel plans in an attempt to slow progress of the virus. In New Zealand, the opposition leader called upon the Prime Minister to ban all flights in and out of the country. North Korea threatened nuclear war on anybody and everybody, but plainly had no more idea of what was going on than anybody else. Among all this, Sir Harmer received a call from Steve Hinks an American industrialist, among his other interests Hinks was an arms manufacturer. Consequently, the two men had met half a dozen times over a period of years. Gradually developing a loose but valued friendship based mostly on a mutual liking of good malts and fine cigars.

There was no bonhomie about Hinks' call on this occasion, his voice was thick with emotion and constantly broke down. He garbled like a drunken man with every sentence preceded by the American slurring.

"I'm sorry, I'm so sorry. You've got to believe me I never, never meant this, I'm so sorry." It took a deal of effort but eventually the knight coaxed more information out of the fellow. There was a conspiracy, always had been since the time of Varone, but a very loose one.

Hinks himself knew only a very few names or that's all he would admit to. A chemical had been developed, as before it was supposed to induce sterilisation of all but the chosen few, perhaps twenty per cent of the world's population.

Hinks only role in this along with many of the world's richest people had been to help finance all the research and planning required.

They had been lied to; they weren't saving a world; they were killing one. There were dissident elements within the plotter's community – possibly several different groups – each of whom were following their own aims. The chemical they had manufactured was designed to kill rather than sterilise, and to kill fast.

Only those destined to receive the antidote – less than a half of one per cent of the seven billion of the world's population – were intended to survive. Stockpiles of both chemical and antidote were already distributed around the globe ready for the word to go.

Then someone had panicked, a minor conspirator in Hawaii had been arrested on a drug charge. His companions unaware of the minor nature of the arrest and afraid of retribution if he talked, forestalled any such by releasing the chemical early and themselves taking the antidote thinking that by taking such drastic action they could prevent any effective police activity.

As they had hoped, this started a chain reaction around the world, as the individual groups of plotters realised that once started, there was no going back, and the chemical was released haphazardly around the globe.

The ineptness of the plotters was now shown by two acts of sabotage against them. Firstly, by an explosion at the plant manufacturing the antidote, then with the discovery that the antidote that had already been manufactured had itself been tampered, rendering the ampoules useless.

Only the original test batch it seemed was immune from the interference. A batch of this, enough for two hundred people was now underway to the UK. Meanwhile, panicky efforts were being made to manufacture more of the antidote.

Though Hinks was convinced that enough of the chemical had already been released worldwide to ensure global genocide before any significant amount of the lifesaving antidote could be both manufactured and distributed.

An ongoing air traffic control dispute had ensured the cock ups would continue by the diversion of the antidote to Scotland. Three men had been dispatched to collect the precious cargo. Guy Roberts had been one of the plotters, the other two had been Evans own operatives, neither of whom knew anything about the plot or the package they were instructed to guard with their lives. What had gone wrong after that, Evans could only conjecture about. Whatever it was, Roberts and his companions had been way off course and hours behind schedule when they had met their deaths.

Before he could speculate further the telephone rang. As Ms Reynolds who had been feeling ill had been sent home some hours before, so he answered it himself. The caller spoke for a little over a minute giving a name 'Charles David Benford', an address and a brief outline. Hanging up the knight stood pensive for a time before somewhat reluctantly reaching for his mobile. A call to Crispin Sterry Brown, and this Charles Benford would be dead within seconds of meeting that lethal young man. Before he could make the call, his office phone rang again. It was a longer conversation this time at the end of which Evans simply said, "Thank you for letting me know," and hung up.

He poured himself a large malt, his favourite Balvennie and downed it at one go. He refilled his glass and returned to his couch without making the call to Sterry Brown.

His daughter was dead, his beautiful, golden haired Becky, except she would not have been beautiful when she died. Earlier that day, he had watched as a fellow mandarin had died of this 'plague', as he thought of it, death had come to the victim only amid a lot of pain. Constant vomiting and bowel movements had seemed to be the main symptom, but to a degree of both that Sir Harmer had never witnessed before. The victim had first emptied his stomach, then continued with a horrible dry rasping that brought forth first a bloody froth then eventually tissue. To Sir Harmer it had seemed as if his friend was attempting to literally heave his insides out. The idea that Becky had died that way without at least having his comforting presence was beyond bearing.

He tried to turn his thoughts away from this nightmare scenario. For himself, he was ready to die, ready to join Becky and Alicia. At the thought of his daughter, his mind wandered again. Becky was dead before her life had really begun. She was to have married shortly. Her fiancé was a professional footballer who had captained England on several occasions.

How proud Becky had been when she had introduced the tall, good looking sports superstar to her father. How proud again when they had sat together at the new Wembley and watched him lead out the national side.

How could he tell her that he disliked the young man, considering him to be a braggart and a bore.

Now she was dead. Sir Harmer sighed deeply, and thought of a man called Charles Benford, wondered if he had a daughter and if he had, how far would he go to ensure her survival. Would he ignore every code, every moral he had ever believed in to protect her? He looked again at the telephone; no he would not call Crispin. Becky was gone and he would soon be joining her; this Benford person could keep the antidote and allow his own selections to survive, for now. Much good it might do them, Evans allowed himself a bitter grin and muttered, "Stupid f...k, I wonder if you have any idea of what you're facing." He poured himself another large malt, drank it in one go and poured another, then opened the bottom drawer of his desk and withdrew his old service revolver.

Automatically breaking it open and checking the load before retaking his seat on the couch, whisky in one hand and his own means of death in the other.

Chapter 12

TC

He paced up and down the small room, glancing occasionally at the body of his fiancée and grimacing as he did so. In the last few hours, his emotions had run full circle. He perhaps had never really loved Becky, could probably never love anyone other than himself, but he had liked her, was happy to be marrying such a beautiful and charismatic girl. Just as important, he knew she was an incalculable asset to him. TC was the boy from a council estate who had made good. His football skills had earned him fame and fortune and had given him the cash to buy whatever he liked. And he liked expensive things, fast cars, jewellery, and women, especially women. For the latter, fame was so useful. Nowadays, he was recognised wherever he went, and could actually pull women by just a look and a nod toward the door. He had tried it for a bet the first time, found it wicked and repeated the stunt any time he felt like showing off in front of his mates. Of course they, 'the girls' he pulled were as some would put it 'of a certain type', but that didn't matter to TC it was still great, something that others, lesser mortals than he could ever hope to do.

Then along had come Becky a society girl and the daughter of Sir Harmer Evans, a knight of the realm and some kind of a big prick in the civil service or something. A father and daughter who had given TC what his money could never have done, access to the upper classes. With Becky on his arm another world had opened up to him. Now, it wasn't just sycophants and hangers on that sought his company, now he mixed with viscounts, right honourable, Sirs, Lords, the lot. It appealed to his vanity that now he hung out with not just with his fellow internationals in various sports but with society's best. The birds he pulled now when Becky wasn't around spoke with a plum in their mouth and were a different class to the groupies he was used to. Although, he noticed happily they were just as dirty in the sack. If he realised that his new contacts, including the girls who allowed themselves to be pulled, looked down on him and sniggered behind his back, he didn't care. He was content to know that he made more money and was more instantly recognisable than any of them stuck up snobs.

For TC that was what really counted, money and fame. Three months ago, he had proposed to Becky and been accepted as he had known he would be. That had been a brilliant time, the newspapers had gone overboard about the society girl and the football superstar. The couple had even made the first item on the news at ten. There were constant interviews for TV and magazines, never a day passed that there wasn't a photo of them in some newspaper or other. Their marriage was to have been the wedding of the year with even minor royalty invited, then just hours ago, his world crashed. Becky's father, who TC sensed didn't really like him had called at the luxury penthouse he shared with her. The story Sir Harmer related had blown TC's mind, he couldn't get his head around what this meant. Everything was going to end; everyone was going to die. The world as he knew it would no longer exist. Once he realised the older man was deadly serious, he had almost shit himself in fright; that had been followed first by denial and finally by a limited form of acceptance. After that everything else happened in a sort of fog, TC only vaguely aware of what was happening around him. First, her father, then Becky herself had shouted instructions at him, pulling and pushing him at times, getting him ready before shoving him into a car and driving to somewhere called 'The Manor'.

Of course, he hadn't been able to deal with it. How could anyone really understand what all this would mean?

Everyone dead, no football, no TV no Man Utd or Chelsea everything gone. Try as he might, he just couldn't get this understood. The only thing that had registered with him was that he was to be saved.

He, TC, had been chosen to survive, he was Becky's fiancé, and her father had the means to ensure that his daughter and her fiancé would live – not that TC was too surprised about that. After all, he was TC, a premiership footballer, a favoured person. Of course, he would be wanted in any new society. TC was not the type of person who could imagine a world without TC in it.

So he had gone to The Manor with Becky and waited for the antidote that was to save them. Instead, the phone calls had started, a problem of some kind, there would be a delay. Nothing to worry about it was being dealt with. TC had sat shaking in a chair as it went on around him only half understanding what it all meant. At some point, he remembered Casey his older brother and his family, and supposed that he should be trying to do something for them. What? He thought about it but what could he do, he didn't have the antidote, he was only getting some himself because of who he was. Well alright, because of who Becky was or rather who her father was. Either way, he couldn't possibly get any more. He was halfway to belling Casey and explaining the sit to him before it occurred to him that it might not be the right thing to do. Casey would be sure to be uptight and might even suggest that TC give his own antidote up to one of Casey's kids. No, that would be a daft idea, but there was a part of him that wanted to tell someone, anyone that TC was going to survive this.

There was something about this place, these people that made him feel small made him feel unimportant. He was an international footballer and captain of England, yet some of these nobs seemed to look down on him.

So, TC badly wanted to prove to someone that TC was still the man; before he could do so Becky had become ill, coughing at first, then spewing up in a truly disgusting way and finally was unable to control her bowels.

What type of person crapped themselves in public and allowed the stuff to run uncontrolled down her thighs?

He couldn't marry her now, every time he looked at her, he would see her like this, frightened, pathetic and covered in shit with not a trace of the society girl she was supposed to be.

Time passed and still the antidote had not arrived. Becky had deteriorated fast and eventually died a couple of hours ago after vomiting blood and tissue and fouling herself ever more frequently.

It was disgusting, the smell and the indignity of it; by that time TC couldn't bear to be near her. The smelly pathetic heap who laid on the floor screaming in her agony bore no similarity to anyone he knew and certainly not to the girl he had asked to marry him.

Worst of all, the other people in The Manor and Becky herself had seemed to expect him to look after her, the others all being concerned with their own problems had no time for his.

For the first time in years, TC didn't have an agent or a manager to arrange things for him. After a nightmare hour, TC made an excuse and left the room, failing to return until standing outside the room with his ear to the door he could hear nothing. Gingerly, he had entered the room and found her dead. TC fled the scene and had wandered The Manor aimlessly.

Nobody he met wanted to talk to him or even offered sympathy. The majority of people already feeling unwell had taken the advice of the medical staff and were sitting quietly in order to conserve their strength, while nervously continuing to await the arrival of the antidote. The fog was clearing now and as it did reality set in, that antidote TC was now afraid would never arrive. He was convinced of that with the awful certainty that only a true coward knows. If it did fail to arrive then TC would die along with everybody else.

That could not be, it could not happen, it shouldn't be allowed to.

It wouldn't be right. It was, it was, he couldn't think what it was, but someone had to do something.

He was already feeling sick, and amid his fears recognised that as the first symptom of the illness.

TC had returned to the room where Becky still lay unattended and stared down at her. This was so unfair, he was rich and famous, he had everything to live for. He was different to others, those little people, those prats who week after week paid their hard-earned money to pay to watch TC and his mates. Oh how he despised those little people.

Sometimes, he would lay in the bath and work out how many of them it took to equal his wages. His total income last year had been over fifteen million, so at an average wage of say twenty-five grand a year it took about six hundred of the little people to equal him. It usually gave TC a hard on just thinking about that.

Now it meant nothing, he was going to die along with everyone else and not even all of TS's vast fortune could do anything to stop it. He screamed aloud in his rage and lashed out with his foot at his fiancés body. In some way this was her fault or her fathers or anybody's, but not his and it wasn't right. It wasn't right that he should die, he was TC, he was famous, an England captain, he couldn't die, somebody should do something.

The tears rolled down his cheeks as he looked again at the smelly heap on the floor that had once been Becky, beautiful, sophisticated Becky. The football superstar fell to his knees in front of the corpse then allowed himself to slump sideways so that he laid alongside her. He put his thumb in his mouth and burying his head into the lovely blonde hair, wept like a child.

Chapter 13
Niall's Night

Lewis Barnet was bored, he leant against the wall of Niall's lounge waiting for the next family to arrive. When they did, he would lurch upright and scowl at the visitors, who already shaken at the events that were destroying their world would then be overcome by relief as they began to understand that they were going to live. These people were never going to be a problem to Niall with or without the presence of Lewis.

The youngest brother of Charles' first wife, Sally, Lewis had been left behind to act as one of Niall's minders, while his two brothers accompanied Charles and Robbie in a similar role on their journeying's.

Charles and Sally had both been teenagers when they first met. She had two younger brothers Cliff and Martin. Cliff, the eldest, was four years Sally's junior and Martin a further four behind him. Ten years later they were joined by baby brother Lewis. Being older than the boys it had been easy for Charles to dominate first the two then later all three brothers as they grew up. Although, as they reached maturity all three had grown into strapping young men well over six feet tall and weighing in excess of 120 kilos, all dwarfing Charles by six or eight inches and close to 30 kilos.

Despite the difference in size, Charles had still managed to maintain his domination over the brothers by a mixture of stronger personality combined with his occasional employment of the boys whenever they were between irregular jobs. A case of who pays the piper naming the tune. When his sister's marriage to Charles had broken up, Martin, who because of his size was the leader of the three had become embittered at what he thought was his sister's shabby treatment by her husband and had given Charles a hard time. He became a nuisance in a number of ways, constantly seeking to test or undermine his ex-brother-in-law at any and every opportunity.

Charles for his part had put up with the provocation for more than a year, until finally tiring of the other antics, had laid a trap for Martin. Borrowing a light van that his target wouldn't recognise, Charles waited down a quiet rural road that Martin used as he push biked to and from his current work. Hiding crouched in front of the parked van, Charles shoved a metal poker into the spokes of Martins front wheel as he passed his hiding place. As his machine came to an abrupt stop, the rider had sailed over the handlebars and landed heavily on the tarmac. Charles had emerged fast from his position of ambush and before his unfortunate victim could recover, had stood on his victims' hands to prevent his movement then proceeded to beat him with a cricket bat. In an attempt to avoid incriminating bruising, he chooses to strike only the soft and fleshy part of Martins body repeatedly.

A day later it was the turn of Cliff the eldest of the trio to experience a taste of Charles revenge. Arriving at Cliff's place of work in a timber yard, Charles had chased the younger man around with a baseball bat, making sure that he never actually caught up with his target, then had allowed himself to be brought to a halt by Cliff's workmates who tried to calm him down. Charles pretending to give way to their pleas explained, "That thing over there has been abusing my son, and I'm going to beat the crap out of him." Since both claims were totally untrue, he had then allowed himself to be ushered away by the works foreman who pointed out that the office staff over the way had been able to see what was happening and would have undoubtedly called the police. Obviously sympathetic to Charles aggrieved claims, the foreman urged him to leave at once. Pulling him aside, he looked knowingly in Cliff's direction and muttered audibly that he and others in the yard also had young children. Turning, he gave Charles a meaningful glance and nodded his head toward the exit.

Charles was quite happy to leave, content in the knowledge that his former brother-in-law was finished at his place of work. The two incidents had caused an obvious rift for a period but had nevertheless left Charles as the top dog on those few occasions that they did meet, and eventually necessity had seen the brothers once again in his periodic employment. Lewis had been too young to have been involved in any of this and was the only one of the three who had never really been employed by Charles. So his contact with the older man was minimal and had left Lewis looking at Charles' relatively diminutive if powerful frame, wondering why his brothers allowed themselves to be so intimidated by him.

It was to these three then that Charles had turned to for help in distributing the antidote. Deciding that this alone would justify their places on the list of survivors and confident that although the brothers did not live up to their tough appearance, they nevertheless looked the part for his needs and would help him to control most of the difficult situations he anticipated facing.

Upon receiving his father's first phone call that morning, Niall had ignored the formers advice about not using telephones too much, but only to the extent that he would send a text message to those people whose help he needed in distributing the antidote. Then, only if he failed to receive a reply within minutes, would he phone and in terse voice suggest the individuals to check their messages. After making those first brief calls, he had taken his children out of school before returning home in time to greet his first visitors. Although, his father had left him two of the handguns that he had taken from Roberts and his companions, Niall had no intention of shooting anybody. But accepting his father's argument that the best way to prevent situations from arising was a show of strength, Niall had recruited further back up from both his brothers in law Kevin and Dean. To these he added his father's foreman, Joey, a very handy and streetwise 26-year-old, and his own close friend Stewart Wright. As he sent his texts, Niall had suggested that only one adult should call to collect the antidote and then return to their families with their treasure. Perhaps, because parents were reluctant to leave a sick child or their spouse this idea was rarely followed, and it was more usual that an entire family would arrive at his home.

Inevitably, once the visitors had received the antidote and they had had a few minutes to absorb the fact that they were going to live, thoughts would turn to their other loved ones and the possibilities of obtaining more of the lifesaving syringes. When these incidents arose, Niall who while sympathising with their various requests was unable to accede to any of them, obviously refused. Just as obviously none of the visitors were willing to accept this negative response and would try every method, they could to cajole even a little more of the magic potion out of him.

Frustrated and annoyed at what he saw as ingratitude, even though he understood where they were coming from, Niall after a time simply resorted to giving the petitioners the name of the next families as they arrived with the suggestion.

"If you can persuade one of them to give up any of theirs and agree to die, then sure you can have any they don't want," he added, "because that is what you're asking, when you ask for more, you sentence someone else to die." Unsurprisingly, there had been no takers. Instead, as the newcomers arrived to receive their allocation, those desperate for more were hoping against hope that perhaps someone might refuse theirs.

Perhaps on religious grounds, or maybe because their requirements had been miscalculated. They would remain at Niall's home, leaning against the walls for support as they watched for each new arrival. When that happened, bent heads would raise and watch silently as the needles were injected. As the last ones disappeared, the heads would drop again while they awaited the next group still hoping, clinging to the feint possibility that a family, any family might fail to arrive and so leave a small surplus that they could lay claim to. Even Niall's closest friend Stewart who was supposedly there to lend his physical presence to Niall was busily practising his arguments as to why he should be given a further allocation of three for his wife's parents and sister. Niall, knowing that Stewart himself was a lone orphan had not thought about Amanda's family. But aware that his friend was withdrawn wasn't sure why. He was allowed little time to ponder Stewart's anxiety. Having instead to deal with a series of mini crises. The first of which was Tom Sanders, Tom ran a scrap yard and a secondhand car sales outlet assisted by his three sons and a daughter, all of whom were built in a similar mould to Tom. A two metre, 160 kg giant. The whole family were into anything to do with motors of all kinds and could perform minor miracles in keeping even the sorriest looking vehicle on the road. Charles had allowed sufficient antidote for ten people in order to cover Tom's children and grandchildren. A generous enough figure, but he was well aware that the mechanic came from a large family that included numerous brothers and their families and would undoubtedly want far more of the syringes than Charles was prepared to part with. Aware of this, Niall and his father had deliberately risked leaving it late in contacting Tom in the hope that the big man would be weakened by the virus and so relieved at having an opportunity to save his own family that he would be less liable to offer trouble in trying to obtain more. That the big man and the one son who accompanied him to Niall's home were both suffering from the virus was obvious. Tom himself needed to lean against the doorjamb to support his huge frame. The two of them listened as Charles' instructions were relayed to them, then as they understood the full implications of what they were being told, Tom grabbed Niall's arm in his huge hand and leaning toward him asked desperately, "Is there any more of this Niall, I've got other family. If you could get me more, I'd be grateful lad." Niall pulled his arm free and explained that there was no more, intimating that Tom was receiving the very last of the antidote. Rebuffed, the big man pulled himself up to his full imposing height and glanced beyond Niall into the younger man's home where other people could be seen and heard talking, eating, drinking, and living. "But there was more," Tom managed to inflect both disbelief and condemnation into the words. At that moment and on cue, Joey appeared in the doorway alongside Niall. While nowhere near as tall as the older man, Joey was well built, young and fit.

He also had one of the pistols Charles had left behind, stuck ostentatiously in his waistband. "Hi Tom, best get those syringes back to your family as fast as possible. Charles sends his regards and says he will see you tomorrow at the hotel," he paused, then added significantly, "The Boss also said two other things."

Here Joey looked directly into the giants' eyes as he spoke, "He said to ask you how much antidote would you have sent him if things had been reversed. He also said to tell you, this isn't about the dying, it's all about those that will live, and you and yours are going to live Tom." He had kept his eyes fixed firmly on Toms who was still looking very undecided on whether or not to accept the situation. The barb about how much antidote Charles might have expected from Tom if their situations had been reversed had struck home. The two were not exactly friends, they just carried out an amount of business at times and Charles had known that the other man would have been unlikely to have even thought about him had the other man been in possession of the antidote.

Nevertheless, his body language made it clear that Niall's visitor was still debating whether to try and take more of the precious life saver by force when Jilly took a hand. She had been listening carefully from behind the door and with perfect timing suddenly shouted as if panic stricken, "Sean will you please put that gun down, it's not a toy." Then in an angrier tone as if directed at some careless individual. "Who left these guns lying about again, I told you to keep them out of the way of the children." As she spoke, she had grabbed Sean and put her hand firmly over her grandson's mouth blocking his protests that he wasn't touching any gun and couldn't even see one.

But her ruse had worked, Tom had heard the words and worked out that there were more firearms on the premises and looking at Joey and Niall there were men to use them. He nodded reluctant acceptance to himself and muttered to

Niall, "Tell your dad thanks, I'll see him tomorrow." Then father and son walked heavily away from a very relieved Niall.

The relief lasted only minutes and was interrupted by a loud knocking on his front door. His invited visitors with the exception of Tom had been following instructions and coming to his rear garden entrance, so Niall was on his guard as he answered the incessant rapping, wondering somewhat warily if it was the big fellow, perhaps feeling a little better and returning intent on trouble.

Instead, Ralph Williams, a neighbour from next door was stood leaning against the door jamb and so was another who was visibly suffering from the effects of the virus.

Williams ran his eyes up and down Niall's body, plainly noticing that the younger man was looking fit and well, in direct opposition to his own appearance. "Niall, help us please, my whole family is ill." Williams paused to gulp and clear his air way, talking was obviously difficult for him, the effort it took seeming as if it would drain the last of his strength.

"I saw you're having a lot of visitors," he finally gasped out. "I thought, I thought … perhaps you've got something that helps, please Niall I… I think, … I think the kids might die if they don't get help soon. … Oh shit I can't breathe, … I can't get hold of a doctor… or anybody. Nobody wants … to help us, …I tried to take them down to casualty, but you can't get…… you can't get anywhere near the place. There are thousands waiting down there. Oh…please Niall help us, please you're our last chance."

The effort proved too much for him and he slumped to the floor. Niall called over his shoulder to his brother-in-law Kevin for help and between them they picked Williams up and carried him to his home. Neither man felt able to face the trauma of what they might find inside the house and settled for laying Ralph, who now seemed to be coming round just inside his door and departing quickly before anybody still able to walk inside the building could come out and trouble their consciences still further.

Neither man spoke as they walked back, both severely troubled by the experience. Niall wasn't losing anybody in his immediate family, although his wife, whose parents lived abroad was certain to lose both, and was currently both trying to call them while at the same time mourning them.

Kevin, married to Charles' and Jilly's only joint child, was somewhat younger than Niall and was an only surviving son. His parents were included on Charles' list and had already taken the antidote. So, both men were very much aware of the miraculous position they were in and felt the guilt that is often associated with survivors of tragedies.

As they approached Niall's driveway a small girl about five or six years old stepped from behind the Leylandi bush that marked the extent of his property. The youngster was in tears and the stains on her clothing indicated she had contracted the virus. She seemed unable to speak and simply stared at the two men in mute appeal for help. Before either man could speak, a car pulled up alongside of them, another of Niall's expected callers had just arrived. Kevin glanced between the arrivals and the small girl, and making his mind up asked his brother-in-law if he knew where she lived. "I don't know any names because they've not been moved in long, but they live in the house with the merc in the drive."

Niall nodded his head in the general direction that the spoke of. "Okay well, if you see to these people, I'm going to take her home," as he spoke Kevin picked the child up and strode of. The house he now approached looked to be a three-bed semi with what in the growing dark appeared to be a well-kept front garden. The drive led by the side of the premises to a garage and a side gate to the rear garden. The gate was wide open as was the back door that led into the kitchen. Here, at the rear of the home it seemed that every room was bathed in light. Still with the girl in his arms, Kevin stepped gingerly into the room shouting, "Hello anybody about, hello, I have your daughter here." With each word spoken he had advanced another step inside and now found himself in a hallway with a set of stairs to one side of him and a closed door to the other. Opening the latter, he fumbled with his free hand to find a light switch and immediately registered the room was empty of life. Turning the light back off, he reluctantly made his way a step at a time up the stairs, pausing halfway to shout, 'hello' again. He could not have explained why he was so unwilling to enter any of the upper rooms, other than an inner dread as to what he was going to find.

From the toys scattered everywhere, the room the first door he opened into was obviously the child's he still carried in his arms.

As soon as he started to open the second door, he knew his fears were well founded. The stench of vomit mingled with that of voided bowels was overpowering and made him gag despite himself. Here again the light was already on illuminating a pathetic sight. The child's mother lay dead in the arms of her husband. He was sat on the bed with his back supported by the wall and because his face was turned away from the door, at first glance looked as if he might still live. Leaving the girl outside the room, Kevin crossed to the couple and checked both occupants for a pulse, the disappointment at a lack of one in either parent left him sickened. Unable to bear either the sight of the tragic scene or the appalling smells any longer than was necessary.

Kevin closed the door and lifted the girl into his arms hugging her close as much for his benefit as hers, they re-trod the stairs below. Returning to the kitchen, he ran a tap and washed the child's face as best he could, then seated her on the kitchen table.

She had still never spoken a word and now man and child faced each other in mutual silence for several minutes. Finally, he fumbled in his pocket searching for the numbers of the various mobile phones his wives' father was using temporarily and entered the digits for the first of them. It took three attempts before Charles wary voice answered, "Hello, who's this?"

"Dad, it's Kevin," In as few words as he could, he explained his situation finishing with the words, "Dad, I've got to have another set of antidotes, I can't let her die dad. I mean it, whoever goes without, I have to save her, please dad." He gulped and continued, "Look, obviously I don't really mean to let someone else die, but I can't let her die dad, I just can't. If you could see her, you'd know what I mean."

Kevin and Charles' daughter had been childhood sweethearts having met on their first day of starting school at five years old and had been together with only one short but bitter break ever since.

Consequently, he had known his father-in-law for a long while, and from a young age they had always got along well enough, and for a time Kevin had even tentatively called him dad. That had stopped when the break in his relationship with Kelly had occurred and had never re-started when he had got back together with her. It was the use of the word now, as much as the tremble in his voice that informed his father-in-law of the intense emotional state he was now in. Kevin couldn't see the tear in his father in laws eyes and would never know the immense pride that Charles felt as he heard Kelly's husband championing a child's right to life. "Take her back to Niall's, Kevin, I am sending Robbie back in a few minutes with some passengers one of whom is a doctor. Robbie will bring extra antidote with him."

"Thanks, dad."

Kevin would have kissed the man if he had been in front of him but was silenced as Charles who was rarely impressed by anything for long interrupted him, "Don't thank me yet, the girls' an orphan now, so guess who and his wife are going to be her new family. You should save your thanks for ten years or so until she's grown up, if she's anything like you lot, you'll be cursing not thanking me," he joked. "Bye for now."

The phone went dead as soon as he finished speaking, leaving Kevin and his new daughter looking at each other's tear-stained faces in silence.

Chapter 14

Deliveries Late Evening

In the car, the three men shaken by the events of the last few moments of the girls' death were silent. Cliff, the elder but weaker brother was in a complete state of shock and was sat staring wild eyed and with his whole body shaking uncontrollably. Martin the younger of the two, who had no idea of their next destination but whose self-preservation instincts had kicked in realised that they needed to be away from here. Starting the car, he drove aimlessly around the streets awaiting instructions from his ex-brother-in-law but afraid to ask for any.

Precious time passed, Charles was in a little better state than Cliff, and sat quiet in a world of his own, re-living the last, what was it fifteen to twenty hours, and especially the last few moments in time.

So much had happened, a whole world had passed on and to Charles it seemed to have happened in a series of jerky horror sketches.

Discovering the plot and obtaining the antidote, the torture and death of Roberts and his accomplices, the nightmare of selecting the names of those chosen to survive and even worse having to reject others. That later thought conjured Liz's face, as he refused her the five extra syringes she so desperately wanted. The tragedies of Harry and Peggy, then Dawn and Graham, the death of little Suzy Greaves, now the murder of this woman, and he did not kid himself about that. He had murdered her, yes, she had been in pain and would undoubtedly have died from her injuries.

But he had ended her life prematurely, and murder, however well intentioned, was still murder.

In fact, the acceptance of this knowledge seemed to help him.

In later years, Charles would see the death of the unknown girl as his defining moment.

When he thought back over the day and of his own actions during that day, he realised what he had always known, had at times even boasted about, but until today had perhaps never really understood the importance of was that despite his outward bonhomie, the hail fellow well met act that he did so well, underneath that, he had a deep sense of duty and responsibility. A sense so strong that he always had and would always do whatever was needed to be done and would do it at whatever cost to himself.

Reassured and comforted by that self-knowledge, he forced himself back to face the present.

But now again, that terrible mix of humour and hysteria of which he was so ashamed surfaced involuntarily with the thought that, "You wait nearly sixty years to kill someone then do two in one day." A former lady friend who fancied herself as an amateur psychologist, had once told him that this macabre sense of humour was simply a defence mechanism that anybody who worked in the emergency services would recognise, and he shouldn't worry about it. Charles accepted that her diagnosis was probably correct but was still appalled at himself and his insensitivity.

However, with an effort, he pulled himself together and was eventually able to give Martin directions, and only then noticed for the first time that the big man was as messed up over the woman's death as he was himself.

He sought for the right words to convince the driver that the accident had not been his fault, only to discover it was fear of the law as much as the girls' death that was worrying the other two. Not bothering to hide his contempt, Charles assured the brothers that there was no possibility of them ever being held accountable for tonight's events, and only when both were at least outwardly composed did they continue to the farm.

As the trio pulled into the farmyard, they were greeted as always on farms by what seemed a whole pack of barking dogs.

Charles had never been afraid of man's best friend and indeed usually got along well with them, so he spent precious minutes making a fuss of the pair of border collies and a black Labrador that bouncing about him prevented his reaching the door of the house. He didn't mind the delay, guessing that after all the barking, the farmer if he was still fit enough to do so would not take long in investigating who his visitors were.

He was right, the back door opened an inch or so and a woman's voice asked rather shakily, "Yes, what do you want?"

Charles left of fussing the dogs and moving to where the woman would be able to see him clearly said, "Hi, remember me, I helped Greg Moore carry out a barn conversion for you a while ago."

The door opened wider and a rather wan looking woman in her late forties peered closer at him in the now fading light, "Oh yes, Charles, isn't it? I remember you." Her voice faded away as she saw the state, he was in. His clothing soaked and blood stained didn't inspire any reassurance, and she continued in a very unsure voice. "What are you doing her? I'm afraid we are all down with this bug that everybody seems to be getting. My husband went down with it first, he's in bed now and I don't think I should disturb him really." Her politeness and the apology in her voice seemed almost comical in the circumstances and brought a rare smile to Charles face as he, as briefly as possible, explained his mission to the woman. Her face expressed first irritation at their intrusion, then turned to a guarded disbelief and finally she sobbed in gratitude as he handed over the six syringes, he was told she needed for the household and attempted to leave.

Bunty Dawson wasn't having any of that; these men had appeared from nowhere like three drowned rats, one of them covered in blood and who despite his bravado was plainly at the end of his tether and had brought with them a miracle.

The farmer's wife had had no idea what was happening to their world, but she wasn't stupid and had listened closely to the radio and TV all day as the traumatic events had unfolded. She had known in her heart that her family were going to die but Bunty was both a Christian and a regular churchgoer and digging deep into her faith had never given up hope.

When she had heard the car pull up outside, she had prayed that it would be the doctor or nurse, for whom she had been leaving messages all day. The slight sense of alarm she had felt when saw three strangers piling out of the vehicle had been swamped by the disappointment that the visitors were plainly neither of the hoped-for medics. Then, despite their appearances it seemed the three had brought salvation with them, and her family would be saved after all. In that miracle, Bunty saw the hand of her God.

So, now she insisted that the men come in and allow her to fix them up as best she could with dry clothes and a hot drink before allowing them to leave. Chafing at the delay, Charles nevertheless welcomed the much-needed food and drink and even more the dry clothing however ill fitting.

The sight of his ex in laws struggling into clothes intended for a man considerably smaller than the two brothers caused the trio an all too brief but welcome moment of humour.

Minutes later, Charles and his minders left the farm with another address to visit. This one supplied by the farmer's wife, who kissed his cheek and thanked him for the lives of her family. For his part, Charles was not sure whether he should be disappointed on finding out that two of the precious syringes were for Bunty's mother and father-in-law who lived with them, and both of whom were in their early seventies, or if he should be pleased at gaining the vast experience of the couple who had spent their entire lives in farming. As there was obviously no chance of getting the antidote back, he chose to accept the situation with as much grace as possible and the trio continued on their way.

It was less than a half mile drive to Mallard farm, and the three men turned into what could have passed as a plant hire yard rather than a farm. There was both agricultural and construction machinery of all types and sizes on show, and even in the failing light Charles could see that it all looked clean and well kept, speaking volumes for the owner. The farmer who answered the door this time was forty at most, and again was visibly suffering from the virus along with the three other members of his family. One youngster, a boy of about eight looked so badly affected his breath was coming only in huge rasping gasps. Charles was so moved he broke his questions first rule and handed over the antidote at once with only the briefest of explanations.

Having watched the farmer administer the antidote to his family, Charles questioned Tom Bradby as to which vets he used, and was at first elated to find that not only was the farmer's daughter a trainee vet herself and currently living at her parents' home but was also given a name and address of the vets Bradby used. It was just at that moment the farmers' wife came in and hearing the address exclaimed, "Oh Frank as well, that's wonderful." Something about the way she said it made Charles suspicious, while a single look at Bradby's face told him he had every right to be.

Bradby nevertheless showed defiance, "Alright, he's not a vet he's my brother, I had to try you can't blame me for that surely." As he finished speaking, he changed from defiance to pleading, "Look he's also a bloody good carpenter and joiner, and when dad had the farm, he used to help out until he left home, so he knows a lot about this business as well." His face became even more earnest, "Please, he really would be useful to you. You wouldn't regret it I promise you."

He stopped speaking and looked hopefully at Charles to see what effect his words may have had. "How many in his family?"

"Four."

Charles calculated fast, if he gave up another four, that would leave him with just nine syringes, surely enough for a vet and his family, but was there any one he had missed out. He had now covered everyone on his initial list that he had been able to think of but what if he had forgotten someone.

That particular thought set of a fresh sense of panic, what if he had forgotten someone?

It would be easy enough to do so given all the things he had had to think about today. If he had slipped up and then remembered someone who should have been on the list, only to find the antidote all accounted for, what would he do then. He supposed he could keep four or five doses back just in case, but against that, a joiner, especially a joiner who had farming experience as well ought to be an asset and worth a place. But what if he had missed someone! Once again, the full weight of his responsibility hit him, at the same moment, he caught sight of the farmers smiling face and mistook friendly reassurance for smugness.

As he stared at him, the farmers face changed before his eyes into that of a pain filled girls, and he saw again his own hands clamped over her mouth and nose, killing her. The dreadful hallucination combined with the pressure of the diminishing number of syringes available to him brought both panic and anger to him and made Benford trip out.

Since Martin had taken over Robbie's job of driving him around, Charles had adopted responsibility for one of the shotguns. Now without warning, he swung the weapon two handedly in a vicious arc smashing the shotgun into the farmer's shoulder which then bounced upward to collide with his face, opening a nasty gash in his cheek and knocking the man to the floor where he lay dazed.

His two minders, their own nerves already frayed, gave in to their herd mentality and without knowing or asking why rushed to join in, kicking and punching at the unfortunate farmer. In their enthusiasm to inflict punishment, their larger frames pushed Charles to one side, which luckily for the farmer brought Benford to his senses in time to call the brothers off their prey, leaving all three men panting heavily.

Charles' sub consciousness had enjoyed every second of the short burst of violence coming as it did, as a release of all the pent-up tension he had been under for the last 14 hours, and he now advanced on the prostrate farmer allowing the twin barrels of the shotgun to rest against Bradby's chest.

The farmer's wife had screamed as her husband had been attacked and yelled, "No, please, leave him alone, please he meant no harm, please."

And moved to stand protectively over him. Tense seconds passed during which no one moved, the only sound coming from the brothers continued rasped breathing before a panting Charles spoke in a clipped tone. "If I give you the four for your brother, you will have to deliver them to him yourself because I'm running out of time. Now, I want the name of your vet and if you f--k with me again, I will kill you." As he spoke, he removed the shotgun from the farmer's chest and then quickly, and viciously jabbed it down again, forcing a grunt of pain from Bradby. Even without that demonstration of a readiness to violence, his eyes and voice convinced everyone in the room that Charles Benford meant every word that he said.

"Thanks," Bradby, his mouth swollen, and bleeding spoke with some difficulty and kept his eyes already starting to puff up alarmingly lowered. "Look, I can give you the name and office address of the vets practice, but I don't know where he lives honestly."

"Tom," his wife interrupted, the relief on her face palpable that her husband was still alive, and now from the sounds of it likely to remain so.

"When you phone him of a nighttime he still answers on the same number, call him and ask for his address." Even as she spoke the woman was picking the phone up and referring to a list of numbers evidently kept by the side of the machine in case of emergencies and dialled a number.

She left it ringing for several minutes before reluctantly accepting that she wasn't about to get an answer. Charles appeared to have relaxed somewhat and passed the gun to Martin who having been impressed by his own and the others demonstration of violence, now held the weapon with more confidence and looked even more intimidating than previously.

Taking the address from the farmer, Charles told the woman not to bother with the phone and instructing the family to be at The Manor hotel the next morning for 9:00 am he left. He didn't share his plans with the farmer or his wife, but he had decided he would call at the vets practice and break in, certain that the man's address must be on record somewhere on the premises.

With the time now fast approaching eleven pm and with the flow of traffic there had been earlier now starting to thin out, they made fast time to the vet's office.

This turned out to be just a converted and extended house in a residential area. Nevertheless, Charles didn't hesitate to break a window and entering the premises despite the alarm that blared out. At this point, Robbie re-joined them having been given their location over a mobile and informed his father that Niall had decided not to vacate to Stewart's for a number of reasons. Charles somewhat irritated at his instructions being ignored, busied himself opening desk drawers searching for anything that would show an address of the vet. "Shh," Robbie held up a warning hand quieting everyone, "someone's upstairs," as he spoke, he advanced to the bottom of the staircase and spoke in as reassuring a voice as he could manage, "Hi, don't be afraid we are here to help you. I'm coming up alone so don't go hitting me on the head or anything okay." The speaker advanced as he spoke and now the scared white face of a young woman showed over the balcony.

"Please don't hurt us, my husband and daughter are both ill and I think my friend and I have both caught whatever it is as well. If you're clear of it, you should keep well away from us." Robbie continued to advance slowly while keeping up assurances that they were here to help and asking who her friend was. "Maria she's Spanish, she's a veterinary student, she's staying with us over the summer." Below stairs, Charles swore silently, his worst fears had come true, he had just thought of two small groups of people he had missed and for whom he would need six capsules if he was to save them, were he to distribute four here he wasn't going to have enough for everyone.

Strangely, the certainty of this knowledge rather than the previous fear that it might happen, served to calm Charles. If he couldn't do anything about a particular situation then it would just have to be lived with, end of conversation.

With this acceptance, Charles made this latest decision of who would live and who would die with much less anguish than his earlier ones had caused him. He needed these vets so they had to have four capsules, the other two families were a childless couple and a family of four, the parents of whom had skills that he realised he was going to need so they would get antidote for four. The remaining capsule he would leave to chance.

Minutes later, having left Robbie to look after the vet's family, Charles and his two minders were speeding toward his home.

Charles now droves and turning into his own road, parked some hundred yards from his house. His car was parked outside where he had left it and the house was in darkness, the only one in the street that was, but it was not to his own home he now headed.

Howard and Lesley Backus were both freelance computer programmers who lived with their two children a half dozen houses from his own.

He liked both parents and children, but they weren't relatives of his, and while they were friends they weren't particularly close their names had not at first occurred to him.

He excused himself with the thought that it was probably the type of work they were involved in that had caused him not to register the family in his mind. He had been preoccupied with the need for physical work skills rather than those involved in IT. At first sight, those particular accomplishments were hardly likely to be needed in the world they would wake up in tomorrow.

As the day had progressed, Charles whose mind was rarely inactive, had used the time he spent as a passenger in the car thinking and planning for the future, and contrary to his earlier opinion had become convinced that there would be a great deal of work for at least one computer whizz kid in their small community. He felt his spine really tingle as his brain registered the fact that the lives of this little family had hung on these two little things. First, on the number of syringes left available, and then on his change of opinion as to the usefulness, not of themselves but of a computer. He made a very strong effort not to think about the people who wouldn't be receiving any of the antidote now as a result of that.

Especially, the couple he had just passed over in favour of the IT family. A couple in fact, who he had known for a lot longer than he had the Backus family.

He succeeded in banishing the black thoughts for now but knew that the darkness of them would return in his quiet moments.

On arrival at their destination they found that Lesley Backus was suffering from the virus as were both children, but none of them seemed to be in a terribly advanced state yet, while husband Howard was only just starting to feel slightly sick.

Charles supposed that the families well known isolationist lifestyle may have delayed their contracting of the virus and noted it as a ray of hope for his brother in New Zealand. If isolation was protective, then Stephen living in such a remote area might have a chance. The Backus were family injected with the antidote and instructions were given, including a request for the adults to commence work immediately on the tasks he gave them. The exhausted trio continued to Niall's home.

Chapter 15

Sterry Brown Hunting

Having reached his decision, Crispin Sterry Brown ordered both his companions from the car and left the service area, driving north a mile or so, then pulling over into a layby to continue his wait alone.

That wait continued for less than an hour, before eventually growing ever more restless and needing to be doing something, he drove to the site of Roberts' death some forty miles to the north and west.

Police tape surrounded the site, but he failed to see any attendant members of the constabulary and guessed the virus accounted for that.

The bodies had gone but there was no sign that forensics had spent any significant time here, again no doubt due to the virus.

A short survey of the area convinced him there was nothing new to learn here without an entire team doing a fingertip, and that wasn't ever going to happen now. There were half a dozen farmhouses all within a half mile radius of him, but it required only the most cursory of visits to see that they amounted to nothing. Increasingly frustrated, he returned first to his car and then back to the service area where he had dropped the other two.

The place was now deserted but strangely unlocked, and there was no sign of his former companions. So after a brief search of the facilities and finding the electric still on, he made himself a coffee and a sandwich, then read yesterday's papers as he decided what his next move should be.

Evening was turning into night now, a reminder – if he had needed one – that time was growing ever shorter.

It was now that Crispin became convinced that he wasn't ever going to get the call he was waiting for. Whether it was a failure of detection or a betrayal by Evans who had never been a real part of the conspiracy, he could only guess at.

But he knew with a burning certainty that if he didn't initiate action himself that he would just be left here to rot.

By then he had also had to leave the car twice to throw up and had accepted that he was himself now heavily infected by the virus.

Some months earlier, he had witnessed at first hand, both the effects of the virus and the amazing speed at which the antidote worked.

The selected victim (a vagrant who had been pulled of one of the back streets of Mexico City and forcibly injected with the virus), had appeared to be only an hour or so from death.

His recovery after receiving the first injection had been remarkable, vomiting had first slowed then ceased entirely.

Within a couple of hours colour had returned to the patient's face, and he had been eating within a further eight. Dosage of the antidote required the patient to take a second but similar capsule within forty-eight hours of that time. By then the vagrant had looked better than he probably had in years, it had seemed almost unfair to then have to kill the fellow.

Nevertheless, Crispin had watched unmoved as the unfortunate chap had been led away presumably to be rewarded for his enforced heroics with a bullet in the back of the head. Now, sitting in his car and feeling the virus taking a firm hold of his body, Sterry Brown knew he had to get hold of the antidote within the next few hours if he was to live, and Crispin had every intention of living. He tried to ring a variety of contacts, starting with Evans, and receiving no answer. From Sir Harmer, he had moved on to other security operatives. Just how deep a hold the virus had established on the population was driven home to him when after trying more than twenty numbers he had struck out completely. Even home numbers remained unanswered, people either too ill to lift a receiver or possibly having fled to country homes in a futile attempt to outrun the virus. At this point, his phone had bleeped to warn him his battery was low and throwing it down in frustration he referred to a map. Having visited the site of where Roberts and his companions had died, there was something puzzling him about it, and he thought he had just realised what it was.

The scene of the incident was forty miles to the North and in a different county to where he was now, with large well-equipped police stations at Nottingham, Newark, and Grantham all of which were much closer to the scene than Peterborough. Yet it was from the latter that the search for whoever had the antidote had been organised from. Why from Peterborough then, he knew that it was possible that this could have simply been as a result of the ravages the virus had caused to police numbers. But why would Peterborough have been hit with fewer casualties than anywhere else. No, that didn't make sense there had to be some other reason. In his mind, he went back over again to the conversation he had had with Harmer Evans.

Now, he really thought about it, he was sure that the original call from the thief informing the authorities of what had happened had been made to Peterborough. The question remained why to there, why not to one of the other closer stations. Consideration of the riddle brought only the one obvious answer. The thief had called the Peterborough number because that was the number, he or she either knew or had in their phone contacts.

That would probably also mean that that was where he was, and Crispin was sure it would be. So it was to Peterborough's Thorpe Wood police station he now made his way to.

His journey took him down urban parkways and while driving these, he met a new phenomenon. The A1 had seen only light quantities of traffic since this crisis had started. These local carriageways were the opposite. As the population fell to the virus, the victims sought help anywhere they could.

Doctors, hospitals, chemists, and the police were all inundated with calls from the frightened public. The emergency services as always made heroic efforts to cope with the influx of pleas they were receiving, but themselves short staffed due to the effects of the same virus were soon overloaded. Unable to obtain any real promises of help and becoming increasingly desperate, people took to the streets. Driving themselves or their loved ones to hospitals, doctor surgeries etc. even to the homes of friends and relatives, anywhere that they hoped could offer help or protection. These journeys were being made by drivers who themselves were suffering the early onset of the deadly bug and found themselves frequently having to pull over to empty their stomachs and occasionally bowels. Crispin passed at least two vehicles that were parked on the hard shoulder their drivers' doors open and the unfortunate driver slumped unconscious or dead on the seat. Their open doors forced other drivers to swerve wide around them causing traffic to slow, and as the momentum of the delays increased, it created small jams. These interruptions to his journey did nothing to calm his temper. A temper that flared again as he arrived at the police station and found a mob of more than two hundred people besieging the reception desk.

This was being manned ineffectually by a pair of policewomen and a grizzled sergeant.

Crispin elbowed his way toward the front and attempted to catch the veteran's eye.

Sergeant William Coombes was a man of thirty years' service, and recognised a 'suit' when he saw one. Stepping away from the counter, he opened a side door and beckoned Crispin through into the Station, with only a perfunctory glance at his Id card. The veteran himself looking and feeling like death warmed up, explained that there was only one detective left on duty in CID. "Actually," he added as they walked together to the plain clothes section, "we had less than forty men report for duty this morning from a shift of close to a hundred and twenty." He pondered for a moment before adding, "And something like half of them have since gone of home, either ill themselves or because they were called to a dependant who was."

The young detective to whom the sergeant handed him over was obviously overwhelmed by the day's events and visibly suffering from the early onset of the virus. His forehead was perspiring heavily, and his hands were constantly fluttering up to his mouth to cover tiny staccato burps. It had been an awful day for Terry Dawes, the youngest DC in the county had been one of only five detectives who had turned in for duty that morning. He had found it difficult to work any of his cases, partly because of how he was feeling but equally because all anybody wanted to discuss was this virus currently sweeping the country.

As the day progressed, his attention was further diverted by the crowd of frightened and angry people who virtually held the station under siege all day, seeking help or advice on how to protect their families. Then around midday the DCI who was supposed to be on leave had turned up in a right flap. There had been, what the DCI would only describe as an incident on the Lincolnshire or was its Leicestershire, Nottinghamshire border; the way he felt at the moment made concentration difficult.

Anyway, wherever it was, as a result of the incident, they were now looking for a vehicle that was believed to have been at the scene.

For Terry that had meant an afternoon studying traffic tapes without success. His concentration was broken on three occasions, when he had been called to help out in reception to quell mini riots caused by the now slightly smaller but still significant numbers of the public, still hoping for police aid where the medical world had failed them.

On each occasion, after some sort of order had been restored, he had gone back to his viewing. He never knew who had discovered it or even how, but suddenly they had a car and then a name. Terry himself was not privy to knowledge of either. The DCI himself passing the info on to the brass in London. After all the hoo-ha had died down, the DCI had wasted no time slipping away, to be followed shortly after by the rest of the shift.

Before leaving, the DCI had asked Terry as the fittest looking left on duty to stay on until a relief could be found for him. Now to have this highflyer from intelligence thrust on him was just unfair. Crispin was demanding an update on an incident, that although Terry knew had taken place, had no idea of what that incident was, or where or even when it had occurred. When he informed his visitor that he was sure they had had a result but didn't know what it was his unwanted guest insisted on Terry ringing his superior. After several attempts to do so it was obvious the DCI wasn't taking calls, or else was another one doing a runner in an attempt to escape the virus. Either way the phone remained unanswered, and this 'suit' seemed to be getting more p----d by the minute.

Eventually, the youngster under pressure from Crispin showed the older man into the DCI's office who then ignored the young detectives' presence and started to systematically search the room. The DCI was evidently somebody with Spartan tastes, the only furniture consisted of a six-drawer desk on which sat a surprisingly old computer. In one corner were stood two filing cabinets, again very old, the only other furniture in the room were two chairs and a waste basket. In common practice within the force the chief inspector normally cleared all paperwork away before leaving his office. Today, perhaps as a result of the unfolding crisis he had left a pile of work out on the top of his desk. Crispin started on these, inspecting every piece of paper in turn, looking for an address, a name, anything to give him a lead to the possessor of the antidote. Moving on to the desk drawers, he leafed through a pile of notes suddenly stopping and going back to the previous one he had just discarded. In his hurry, he had almost missed seeing it, but there in one corner of a sheet of paper torn from a notebook were eleven digits that he recognised as Sir Harmer Evans direct line telephone number.

Underneath this there was a car registration number and the name, Charles David Benford accompanied by an address. Even the usually unflappable Crispin couldn't refrain from a brief cry of triumph as he gripped the note in both hands and pushing past Terry Dawes left the room. Sergeant Coombes was still busy in reception when Crispin once again burst in, and ignoring the people clamouring for the sergeant's attention, demanded, "Charles Benford does that name mean anything to you?" Coombes took a moment to adjust his mind to the demand.

"Charlie Benford, yes I know him vaguely, sort of a friend of a friend. I can't imagine him being involved in anything very serious. Charlie's a bit of a legend in his own mind if you know what I mean, calls himself a property developer but is really more of a jobbing builder. Arthur Daley meets Del boy type," his voice trailed off as Crispin had already turned his back on the speaker and headed for the door. Coombes watched him leave and gave a small shake of his head as he muttered, "Spooks, even now, still playing effing spooks," before turning away to shout at yet another member of the public who was vomiting all over his floor. The sergeant looked at the chaos around him, dozens of frightened people still seeking advice or help from what was left of his small staff, who were themselves terrified of what was happening to their world. He decided he would give it till midnight and if anyone was still on their feet then he would send them home. For himself, he intended to remain here until the end, he had always joked that he would have to be dragged out of the station feet first, now it looked as if that was going to be true. He paused for a moment then reflected the way it was going that it was highly unlikely that anyone would be around to drag him out.

For some reason, the idea that his body might spend eternity in the nick was both amusing and somehow appealing, and he turned back to the waiting public with a totally inappropriate grin on his face.

It took Crispin a further half an hour to make his way to Benford's home, as he drove, he couldn't help but notice that the local traffic while just as busy as before had now been joined, despite the late hour by large numbers of pedestrians; those lucky enough or perhaps unlucky enough not to have yet gone down with the virus, and were now wandering around apparently aimlessly in not just one's and two's but in sizeable groups as well.

Crispin had no interest in them or what they were doing, though the unbidden thought occurred that now as mankind approached their doom, human beings were behaving as any other animals do when frightened.

Herding together looking for support or a lead from anywhere and yet ready to run at the first alarm. He turned the final corner into Benford's road and exclaimed exultantly when he immediately spotted the car he was looking for. He parked some 50 yards further down the road and made his way quietly to his quarries home. The building, 1980s types three storey town house showed lights in both upper and lower storeys, and curtains were left open on the middle floor in what he guessed was either the lounge or a bedroom.

He looked carefully up and down the road, while most houses were still bathed in lights, he could see no signs of pedestrians down here in these narrower streets.

There was a passageway a few yards further down the road that evidently led to the rear of the houses.

Crispin made his way down here carefully, the moon being bright enough to not just show him the way but in turn to also silhouette him if anybody were looking. At the back of what he worked out was Charles Benford's house was a seven-foot-high wall with a single gate. He tried the latter only to find it locked, and so climbed over the wall, the fact that he took three attempts to achieve this comparatively simple thing was ample warning to him of his fast-deteriorating condition.

He made his way through a well-kept vegetable garden to the rear of the house. Again there were lights on and curtains open at all levels of the accommodation. Crispin crouched behind a bush and studied the house carefully. There was no sign of life in any of the rooms and he finally decided that Benford and his family had almost certainly left hours earlier. Probably at the time expecting to be returning later as normal. The lights were no doubt on a timer, and he supposed that the man had left his car here and was using another vehicle. Maybe afraid of exactly what had happened, and his own vehicle being traced.

He broke a window as quietly as possible and entered the house. A quick search revealed there was no one home, and that as he had thought timer switches controlled the lights. More importantly, there were a great many personal belongings still laying around in every room.

Crispin actually felt a small degree of elation. He had come to accept that without back up from Evans or some other Intel agency he had no chance of discovering where Benford might currently be. Even if he did manage to find out, he would probably lack the physical stamina to pursue the thief. None of that mattered now, the clothes and other effects in the house undoubtedly meant that Benford was coming back. There were photos, certificates, jewellery etc., he and whoever lived with him would want these personal things.

He picked up a framed photo from the mantelpiece. The picture showed a man and woman possibly in their late forties and he wondered idly how old the photo might be. It was unimportant anyway but looking at the somewhat overweight couple he was convinced, yes, these two would come back for what they regarded as their family treasures, those things that represented their very lives and when they did Crispin would be waiting for them. He located the mains box and turned the electric of plunging the whole house into darkness. His eyes would become accustomed to the dimness within minutes, giving him an advantage over anybody entering the premises from without. Then he took up station in an armchair that allowed him to cover the front door whilst being out of sight of anyone looking through the windows. He placed his pistol on the chair arm and made himself as comfortable as his condition allowed.

While he accepted probable defeat in his search and realised that by the time the occupants of the house returned, the precious antidote would undoubtedly be long gone, thus sealing Crispin's own doom. If that should be the case, then Benford and whoever was with him would pay with their lives.

Because whatever happened, infected or not he would hang on to the very last thread of life, to kill the man or men who were responsible for Crispin's own death.

Chapter 16

Niall's Later Night

It was after Kevin had returned to Niall's home with the girl that Lewis Barnet flipped, most of the other occupants of the house had gathered in the lounge around the child as they listened to Kevin's story.

Lewis not interested, noticed that Joey had left both one of the guns and the box containing what was left of the antidote unguarded on a chair.

Jilly's pretended remonstrance with Shaun regarding gun safety seeming to have left no impression on Joey's thoughts.

Lewis had spent the last few hours becoming ever more perplexed. In his own slow way, he had gradually reached some of the same conclusions that Charles Benford had realised in those first few moments after gaining possession of the antidote.

While others were terrified of what was happening and of what the future might hold for them, Lewis had at first sensed opportunities. He thought first of money banks, building societies anywhere that held cash would all be vulnerable to him and his brothers. They could be unbelievably rich and at no risk to themselves.

It was several minutes before it registered with him that money was never going to be needed again, and at first, he still could not quite accept the fact. He would think about it time and again, trying without success to imagine some time or situation when he might need money in the future.

The concept of being able to accumulate more money than he had ever dreamt of and yet of not being able to spend even a penny of any such wealth was just too difficult to comprehend. When he did finally give up on that one, he switched his mind to consumer goods. If money was going to be of no benefit to him then he could concentrate instead on those things that money would normally buy. TVs, computers, mobile phones anything he wanted was his. He mentioned this to Joey who looked him up and down slowly before leaning toward the others ear in an exaggerated confidentiality and whispered, "Where do you suppose the TV programmes, or the electricity is coming from. Or who do you think you are going to be phoning or e mailing, sorry mate face ache, tweets blogs, LinkedIn and everything else like that are gone forever." And he turned away grinning at the big man's dumbfounded scowl.

Cars were next on Lewis' mind and here he was certain he was okay. He could have any car he wanted, just walk into any car sales place, pick up a set of keys and away, no law, nothing. He grinned to himself; he was right about this at least. There would be no law, no need for insurance no car tax nothing. He tried to think where a Ferrari dealership was and failed, alright a Lamborghini, a Bentley, a Range Rover anything, he would try them all.

Once started he was on a roll, fags, no cigars, booze not beer but whiskey, whiskey like Charles drank, malts, no to hell with that, he'd drink nothing but champagne. A Lamborghini and bottles of champagne that would pull the girls. And that's when Lewis realised the real problem that had been nagging away at him. Girls, he had watched as dozens of people had called at Niall's home, all of them in family groups or in couples. The only singles he had seen were like him, males. He didn't know Charles destinations, but he would be willing to bet his calls would all be to people in similar situations as those coming to here. That stupid old man had slipped up. There would be no single women, what about people like Lewis and his brothers. Alright, the other two were no oil paintings, and except for an odd night in the company of a whore had little contact with women. But Lewis did, oh he had never had a steady relationship, in fact he rarely managed a third date, but he still liked girls and wasn't keen on a future without the possibility of having one. What would be the point of fast cars and champagne, nice clothes, anything he wanted if there weren't any women about to impress. No, Charles had slipped up and Lewis began to both panic and at the same time began to see hurried opportunities.

There were two girls on the estate where the three brothers lived, two absolute stunners. When drunk, Lewis would leer at them and occasionally call out to them, causing both to cross the road whenever they saw him coming and generally ignoring his very existence.

But not now, if Lewis appeared with the means of saving their lives, he'd bet they would put out quick enough. There would be no more ignoring him, oh no, Lewis Barnet would be the number one. Why stop there, he knew plenty of other girls, well not actually knew them, not knew them to speak, but knew where they lived, knew which ones he liked, which ones he would offer to save, as long as they understood the situation that is. Niall saw the movement out the corner of his eye. "What are you doing Lew, leave the gun alone."

But it was too late, snatching up the weapon Lewis pointed it at the room in general, "Stay back Niall I don't want to hurt you or anybody else but your dads slipped up. I'm taking these last syringes. I told you stay back," he shouted the last words to Joey who had tried to inch closer. "I will shoot, I'm warning you." Lewis' shrill voice betrayed the nervous tension he was under, prompting Niall to reach out a warning hand to motion Joey to remain still. Reluctantly, the younger man complied, but his very stance betrayed his urge to fling himself at the big man and beat the crap out of him. Niall meanwhile attempted to persuade the would-be thief to put both the gun and the antidote down and not be stupid, he might as well have saved his breath. Lewis ignored his nephew while continuing to menace the room with the weapon before backing toward the kitchen behind him to where the rear door was and escaped with his treasure.

Later, when Charles was talking to his son, he would ask, "So, the idiot pointed a gun at and threatened Jilly's family, while she was stood behind him in a kitchen full of dangerous implements." Charles shook his head in mock disbelief. "He's a braver man than me then. She's like a mother bear where the family is concerned. So what did she actually hit him with?" Despite the trauma of the night's events, Niall had allowed himself an all too rare grin as he recalled the picture of Jilly in her rage.

"Do you remember that wooden chopping board you bought us years ago, it's about so square," his hands moved in description, "and so thick. She welted him twice across the head with that. I think she would have carried on and killed him if Joey hadn't managed to get it away from her. Fortunately for Lewis, Robbie arrived about then with your lady doctor. She seems nice by the way, and she patched him up, but he was left with a bloody sore head."

After Lewis' attempted revolt and the arrival of Robbie with Doctor Shawanda's family, the return of Ralph Williams begging for help, though might have been thought of as an anti-climax was anything but. Williams should have been dead; his mouth and clothing was blood caked and his breath was coming only in dry rasping gasps that plainly took every ounce of the man's strength. As before, he leant against the door post, his pain filled eyes holding Niall still, as his neighbour somehow gathered the last remaining dregs of energy to make his plea. "Niall please, not for me or Judy," the words came out in broken jerks, "The kids, please Niall," his eyes flickered briefly toward the door leading into the lounge. "You've got something, you're going to survive, you, your friends, please Niall, just the kids. Don't let them die, please." Tears slid down his face as he slid slowly to the floor, his eyes never leaving Niall's own while he continued to mouth heart-breaking pleas for aid.

For his part, Niall stood transfixed, horror struck. For just a second, he wished his father had never won possession of the f------ antidote. What, how, his head was spinning, he couldn't begin to think. Williams wouldn't stop looking at him, the man might even be dead, but his eyes still stayed on him in mute plea for his children. Niall no longer knew what to do, every fibre of his being ached to rush around to Williams' house to help the man's children, but his head told him it was impossible.

Seeing her stepson's distress, it was the level headed Jilly who with an effort, shook off the last dregs of the emotions that her run in with Lewis only moments earlier had caused her. Now again, she took command of another terrible situation. Taking Niall by his arm and leading him into the room, she instructed the ever-faithful Joey and Stewart Wright to carry Williams home. "Don't go inside the house just take him inside the garden gate and leave him there. Remember Joey that whatever is happening in that house is going to happen and is happening in millions of other homes tonight and there is nothing we can do to prevent it, nothing at all." As she spoke, she stressed the word nothing while reaching out to touch Niall's face in reassurance.

Then raised her voice to ensure everyone present would hear what she had to say. "Listen to me all of you, don't beat yourselves up about any of this, this is not something that's our fault, some bunch of mad men caused all this, not you, not me, not Charles. We're just trying to survive. That's all, and for anyone else, everyone else, all we can do is pray."

Chapter 17

The Cabinets Goodbye

"Gentlemen, thank you all for your efforts, you've all worked very hard in a fight that it seems was probably hopeless from the start. I think it's time now that we should all go home, and each make our own arrangements. I do not believe that anything is going to happen now in time to save the day. There is simply too much to do, and no resources to do it with."

As the surviving members of the Cobra committee filed out, a number of them plainly distressed, and all pausing only long enough to shake his hand. The PM watched them leave and allowed himself a few moments to reflect on the last fifty-eight hours since that first cobra meeting on Saturday evening.

Fifty-eight hours that's all it had been, yet so much had happened in that short time.

Medusa, the name he had himself given to the killer virus, had swept across the world at an incredible rate. From the first outbreak in Hawaii on the previous Friday evening, it had taken just a little over two days for the first cases to be diagnosed in the UK.

In those two days, he had spoken to twenty-eight heads of government and countless experts, trying desperately to find a way of dealing with this nightmare, to no avail; thanks mainly to the Americans and the Israelis they had gained some knowledge. They now knew that there had been a plot or rather plots to cull or wipe out the world's human population. The immediacy and the breath-taking scope of the threat meant that the world's governments had co-operated with each other in a way that had never been seen before. But not until it was too late. They had discovered some names and where they had, they managed to make some arrests.

Intensive questioning had added further to their knowledge. The questioning for the perpetrators had in most cases been followed by summary executions.

The world's leaders not prepared to allow the murdering c---s to survive their victims, simply for want of a fair trial.

Not that there had been many arrests, most of the plotters had planned their own survival based on what had turned out to be faulty antidote, and so were dying along with the rest of the world.

Some of the faulty antidote had been found and having recognised it for what it was, chemists set to work to break down its chemical components in the hope that they might be able to work out what was required to bring it up to a working level.

Here, as in everything else they attempted they would come up against the same problem, Medusa herself. Key individuals were too often dead, dying or already too ill to work. It seemed impossible that he who was the head of government of one of the world's leading nations, a member of the UN security council and the G8 group of countries with the fifth or was it the sixth nowadays largest economy in the world and a nuclear arsenal, yet he couldn't even save the lives of his own family.

The PM had never and would never hear the name of Charles Benford.

Had he done so and known his story, he would have acknowledged that Benford had been correct in his assessment that there was just not the time to achieve anything.

The first deaths in the UK had occurred around noon on Monday. Oddly, despite the very best medical attention the PM's two youngest children had been amongst the first to die, leaving just his eldest son, Jeremy, as the sole survivor of what until then had been regarded in the press as the epitome of a happy British family in the twenty first century.

After that tragedy, it became impossible to concentrate on matters properly and the deputy PM had fill in for him for a time. His own sense of duty however kept him going to some extent. He still attended all the remaining Cobra meetings, noting sadly as he did so the gradual fall in attendances as Medusa struck ever harder.

He still listened to but did not hear, did not take in, every word that was spoken at these meetings.

The Yanks had, it seemed, picked up a rumour that some genuine antidote had been sent to the UK, and had apparently arrested the pilot of a plane that was supposed to have carried it up to Scotland. If that were true, then the antidote had disappeared soon after without trace. Police and the security services had been unable to find any evidence other than that a plane had landed. The aircraft had apparently been met by three men, none of whom were recognisable and that was it. The cars plates were false according to Sir Harmer Evans, the only man who might have made sense of the puzzle.

It was on the veteran security chief that the PM had placed his real hopes of survival. Even that slim hope had been erased when Sir Harmer had apparently blown his brains out some time Monday afternoon or evening.

That news followed soon after by the even more bitter knowledge that the Knight himself had been partially responsible for the disaster. Exactly what role Evans had played in the affair wasn't known for sure but that he had sold out was it seemed indisputable.

That was another puzzle, after the security chief's death it emerged there had been an incident somewhere more than a hundred miles to the north of the capital. A phone call and a note indicating that the caller had left some genuine antidote for the authorities to find. A flickering light of hope in the gathering darkness. That slim hope had again amounted to nothing. Had it been just a cruel hoax, there had been no sign of any antidote where it was supposed to have been. The first young copper to have arrived at the scene had been suspected of having sequestered the lifesaving antidote. Rough and forceful questioning had elicited nothing, and when the young bobby himself had died from the disease, it seemed he had probably been truthful in his denials.

Harmer Evans also appeared to have known some information about the missing vials, but if he had then he had withheld any such information from the government.

Would finding even just the small amount of antidote mentioned, have made any difference. Probably not, now they would never know.

Sighing the PM stood, straitened his tie, and left the room. He would return to his wife and surviving child. Mary had promised that she would somehow keep both of them alive until his return. In his hand, he held the capsules given to him by Dr Anelka; that the doc had assured him would allow their passing to be together and less painful than otherwise.

Chapter 18

Prison

There had to be a way, there must be a way, something, anything.

For the hundredth time, he looked around the cell in desperation. There must be something he could do, a way out of here, there must be a way out of this somehow.

The panic took over again and returning to the window, he yelled for help over and over at the top of his voice. Banging on the glass ineffectually, screaming and sobbing alternately, until his throat rasping, he fell quiet and sank to the floor in despair.

Stephen Letman was going to die; he knew that now and he was frightened. Frightened in the way that only bullies can know. The fear gripping his stomach caused him to dry retch, then raise his eyes upward to a god he had never had time for and whisper, "Help me, please help me," then curling himself into a foetal position on the floor he cried himself to sleep.

When he awoke it was daylight, but was it was still the same day or had he slept through the night and the world had passed into another day.

That was a big part of the fear, the unknown. He had never been a clever man and had never needed to be. Even at times, he took pride in his ignorance of what was going on in the world. As he often quoted, "I don't know what's going on out there and don't give a shit anyway. That way I don't have to worry about anything except where the next drink is coming from, and unlike you lot I won't have a heart attack and die young."

But now it was ignorance that was the worst part of what was happening.

What was going on, where was everybody, when would he get fed again, what time was it, what f-----g day was it. Oh f—k! Someone comes, someone, anyone but someone come and tell him what's happening.

A period of time ago – and again he had no idea of how long ago that was– everything had been normal. He had been serving his time for the neglect of his girlfriend's baby and of causing its death by shaking it and causing brain damage. Arseholes the lot of them, the kid had just kept crying didn't matter what you done, it just kept crying. So, what was he supposed to do, she'd been worse than useless at looking after it? So he'd shook it trying to shut it up. He hadn't meant to kill the kid, course he hadn't but it had happened.

That had meant that while inside, he had to keep his head down and spend long periods in his cell, with the other inmates knowing him for what he was and despising him for it.

That contempt had led to two serious attacks on him and to his voluntarily living in what amounted to solitary confinement.

Then something started to happen outside, and he had no idea of what it was. Jackson, the trustee who delivered his dinner – always spitting in it just before he handed it through the trap to him, while making sure that while Letman could see what he was doing the CCTV would be blinded by the trustee's back – had said there was some kind of killer bug around and everybody was going down with it. Jackson had been almost gleeful about it, confident that he who enjoyed excellent health wouldn't be affected by it. The trustee had refused to answer any other questions or more probably didn't know anything else. So had just taunted him as he left yelling, "You'll get it and they'll let you die, they'll just leave you in here and let you rot, just what you deserve you c---" and walked away, cackling to himself all the way down the corridor.

Since then there had been nothing. No food or drink, no contact of any sort, even that turd of a trustee hadn't returned.

There had been some noise though. His cell was above the yard but from his small cell window he couldn't see down into it. He could hear sound though and some time ago, how long, again he couldn't tell, there had been the noise of what he thought was a riot.

He had been really scared then. If there was a full-blown riot and the prisoners had gained control of his part of the prison, he had a good idea of what the other inmates would do to him.

Nothing! The noise had lasted for about two hours before gradually dying away into what had sounded like weak calls for help, then silence.

How long ago, that's what bugged him the most. Oh, he was hungry and thirsty, but it was this ignorance of time that was really getting to him.

Why had nobody come to him, he was sure that at least two days had passed since his last contact with the trustee but was it more or was it only hours. His water had run out a while ago and shouting for help had only resulted in a sore throat. What the hell was happening, there had to be someone about. For the umpteenth time, he went from cell door to cell window, shouting the best he could.

Nobody would come, nobody would hear. Stephen Letman was one of the few to have a natural immunity to the virus, and very little good would it do him.

Chapter 19

End Deliveries

It was as they drew up outside his son's house that Charles finally decided where he would use the last of the antidote. A few doors from his son's lived a young West Indian couple with a daughter slightly older than his grandson Sean.

Had he thought about the family earlier, he would probably have included them on his list. The father, Dwayne Rooney was a toolmaker and one of those really gifted people who can turn their hands to all types of practical jobs. Rooney himself opened the door looking gaunt and close to death. The householder had hoped the knocking at his door had meant that medical help had finally arrived and explained that his wife and daughter were both sick but still alive. Nervously embarrassed at the awful thing he was inviting the other to do, Charles briefly filled Rooney in about the antidote.

Then calling upon every ounce of inner strength and determination he possessed and offering no apology or explanation for there being only the one dose available, he placed the single syringe on a coffee table and suggested that Rooney might want to use it for his daughter's survival.

Promising that if he did, then Charles would take responsibility for the child and have her brought up within his own family circle.

Understandably, it took time for what Charles was saying to sink in, then as he absorbed Charles explanation and understanding dawned, Rooney broke down, looking unbelievably at the older man and began begging for more of the antidote, throwing himself on the floor at Charles' feet and pleading through the tears streaming down his face, offering anything and everything if only he could have more of the lifesaving syringes.

Now more embarrassed than ever, the older man having assumed that Rooney would be like Charles thought he himself would have been in the same circumstances. The survival of the man's child would be the most important thing in the world to him. Instead, the spectacle of Rooney grovelling, and pleading sickened him, and drove him to leave.

He left the syringe on a coffee table instructing the man to pull himself together, give the antidote to his daughter and walk her down to Niall's house after saying their emotional goodbyes.

It still took time to pull himself free of the younger man's hands and it was with huge relief when he was finally outside of the house. Now he leant against a tree in the garden, the rain that had been intermittent for the past hour had finally stopped. The night air was warm enough that his borrowed clothing that had become both damp and uncomfortable had started to dry out on him. "Must call at home and get some fresh clothes," he muttered to himself as he listened to faint sounds from the house and reflected on the last few moments. It had been, he supposed, pretty stupid of him to think that Rooney or anyone else for that matter could have just accepted what he had suggested calmly. Come to that, he couldn't now believe that he had actually suggested the idea, and it was, he guessed, evidence of how emotionally drained he had been by the last hours that he had done so.

"Charles." He looked up as his name was spoken. Jilly had come looking for her husband. Having heard from Martin and his brother of some of the nightmare the trio had been through, she knew he would be in need of her support. Husband and wife hugged, and Jilly assured him that all members of their family were safe and accounted for.

Movement in the house roused them, and hearing the door starting to open and Jilly not wanting to intrude on what would be a heart-breaking moment between parents and child, moved into the darker shadow of the tree. Only an ashen faced Rooney emerged, walking zombie like toward them. "They're dead, they're both dead," he looked at Charles as tears streaked down his face. "I, they're both dead," he repeated in a barely audible voice that broke between sobs.

Jilly emerged from the shadow's intent on offering comfort to the man who understandably looked and sounded completely desolate.

Rooney put his hands up to ward her off, crying, "No, it's, it's my fault. I was so frightened, I didn't want to die, I, I couldn't help myself, I didn't mean to, but I didn't want to die." As he finished speaking, he broke down and sank to his knees alternately sobbing and begging forgiveness.

Jilly looked up at her, husband her puzzled face betraying her emotions. "Charles, does he mean..." she couldn't bring herself to finish what she had started to say. Shocked! Shocked and horrified beyond all belief at the very idea of what she feared the man had done.

Her husband meanwhile had crossed to Rooney and holding him by both shoulders shook him violently. "What have you done, what have you done, you injected yourself, didn't you?" He answered his own question in fearful disbelief.

Rooney's tear-stained face looked up from his kneeling position in mute confirmation. Looking down at him, Charles head swam with picture after picture. Rooney's daughter as he had last seen her laughing with Sean, Liz's face when she realised there was to be no extra antidote for her extended family. His sister-in-law telling him her daughter was abroad, Peggy's face was replaced by Dawn Porters informing him that Gemma, possibly his own daughter was also away and so would die. Above all, a girls agonised face with his own hands suffocating the life out of her.

The horrific images were chasing themselves one after another through his mind. Then he looked again at Rooney, a man who had just allowed his wife and daughter to die, possibly even killed them himself in order to save his own life and wanted nothing more than to smash his fist into the man's face time and again. Wanted to beat him to a bloody pulp, wanted to release all of his emotions, his terrors of this day in a torrent of violence on this cowardly worthless piece of shit of a man. As he stared at him, Jilly emerged from the house having ran inside as soon as she realised what Rooney had done. "They are dead, both," her voice was high pitched verging on hysteria as she spoke. "Charles, I think he…" she couldn't finish what she was going to say, just stared dumbly at both men in horror.

Charles with almost superhuman effort brought himself under control, breathing slowly, deeply, telling himself this was just another test, another obstacle to be overcome. In that, he was right. He didn't know it then, but this was just that, another obstacle that he had to face down and deal with in his acquiring those leadership qualities he was going to need to call on in the coming years, and one that he would have reason in the future to be glad that he had managed to overcome. Helping the man to his feet and taking a huge breath, Charles addressed both Jilly and Rooney. The former still staring sheer loathing at the other.

"Right listen, listen well, this stays between us. Dwayne, your family was dead when I arrived," he shook the man again. "Do you understand, they were already dead?" He looked at the man still shaking him like a doll until his victim was able to meet his eye.

"Yes, dead," the two words spoken as a whisper.

"I hope so, Dwayne, because there are men in that house," he nodded toward Niall's as he spoke, "who would kill you if they knew what you have done, do you understand me?" This time his glance extended to include his wife as well, who nodded her own understanding.

"Okay then, both of you pull yourselves together, we still have a lot to get through tonight, remember they were dead, and we will never speak of this again, alright. Jilly you go on, I need to speak to Dwayne alone." Jilly paused, concerned about what he might be planning, Charles met her eyes and gave the merest nod to indicate she could go, that he planned no harm and was confident that the much larger and fitter younger man represented no danger to him either.

After his wife had left them, Charles suggested the two men sat on a nearby garden wall. Somewhere to their left, a cat wailed and was answered from further away, bringing an almost ridiculous sense of normalcy to the night. "Dwayne, I can't begin to understand how you are feeling right now." He paused for several seconds, stuck for the right words to use to this man, then, "But I do know that in the coming days and years we are going to face all kinds of dangers. We will be at risk from all kinds of threats, and we will have need of men who have all kinds of skills and resourcefulness. What I'm trying to say is that while it seems improbable at the moment, there will be plenty of opportunities for you to, if not actually forgive yourself for today, at least to atone to some extent." Resting his hand on the man's shoulder in what was supposed to be a gesture of reassurance, Charles was well aware that his words had sounded inane and were unlikely to be of any help to the other. But he had very little else to offer, and pulling the man to his feet, together they walked toward the morrow.

Chapter 20

Stefan Tustanowski

"Peiter come, we need to be going," Stefan Tustanowski looked toward the kitchen door awaiting his son. Stefan felt unwell, his stomach and bowels both churning painfully, and recognised the onset of the same filthy disease that had killed his daughter in law, Peiter's wife.

Sarah lay on the bed she had shared with her husband until the virus had struck her the previous morning. Father and son had tried to save her, but like millions of others were discovering that doctors and indeed any other form of medical help were simply unavailable.

Disappointed but determined to save her they had tried to get her to A&E, that had proven equally unsuccessful. It was impossible to get anywhere near the hospital by car. So, while Pieter had stayed with his wife, his father had left the vehicle to investigate on foot. Only to return more than an hour later to report that it wouldn't matter how serious anybody was, it made no difference. There were so many others just as serious already waiting for attention that there was no hope of getting aid in time to be of any help.

Eventually, Sarah, in great distress and constantly throwing up and finally fouling herself had insisted they take her home and nurse her there.

Arriving home, the two men had tried everything they could to save her. In desperation, Stefan had even cooked up a vile concoction that he claimed was his grandmother's remedy for everything, from a hangover to a cure for food poisoning, but to no avail. In great pain, Sarah had died an hour ago. Died, death, neither word was adequate for the way that their lovely Sarah's life had ended.

A horrible combination of disgusting gut-wrenching vomiting, and awful bowel evacuations. Despite their love for the woman, it had been difficult to hide the disgust that both men felt at the nauseous sight and smell that this filthy plague caused as it ravaged its victims.

When it was over, they washed Sarah's pallid body tenderly and laid her on the bed in her wedding dress. Peiter had knelt by her side, weeping, and promising to be reunited with her shortly, that was when the room lights had started to flicker.

Stefan a power station worker for more than thirty years had recognised the cause as a drop in the amount of power coming into the house and the reason for it and had come to a decision.

Going into the bedroom, he had helped his son to his feet and explained that they must go into work. Pieter had looked disbelievingly at his father then shaken his head in mute refusal.

They had argued for a few moments, Pieter despairingly pointing out to his father that his wife had just died and not only that, but it also seemed the whole of mankind was surely about to follow her.

They themselves were already complaining of feeling unwell and both men recognised they were suffering the same symptoms that had killed Sarah. So what was the point of going into work, the world was dying, and the dead would have no need of electricity. His father had stubbornly refused to accept that terrible verdict. Stefan's father had come to Britain as a child well before Hitler's war, and there in the sixties had met and married Mathilde, Stefan's mother. Three years later she gave birth to a son, and they had named him for her dead father.

As a child, growing up within the local Polish community Stefan had mixed with children the majority of whose parents had escaped the camps; some fleeing for their lives before the advancing panzers, others who had come over as members of the free Polish forces. None of them in the safe and comfortable style of the Tustanowski family.

Stefan, listening to the stories of their adventures, tales that he could never share had somehow come to resent the tame way that his own family had arrived, as economic refugees. To a young boy, there was nothing heroic in following a trade, or in the pursuit of money. As a result, Stefan had always felt ostracised by his grandparent's actions in fleeing to the UK.

Ignoring the fact that their foresight had probably saved all their lives, including the as yet unthought about, Stefan's.

He grew up desperately wanting to be a hero of some kind, wanted to feel a part of what he saw as other members of the community's adventurous past. When he was old enough, he had tried to join the army but failed the medical, so had been forced to watch as others, some of whom were known to him fought in places like Northern Ireland, the Falklands and then the various Islamic terrorist wars. He married in '89 and Pieter the only child had come along the following year.

Three months later, his wife dropped dead at his feet from a blood clot on the brain, leaving Stefan as a single parent.

Though now a man with the tremendous responsibility of fatherhood, Stefan had still continued to want to be a hero, not realising that as a single working parent that's just what he already was.

But the same lung condition that had prevented his enlistment into the army had also counted against him in his efforts to join the police and fire brigade, then even his last resort the Territorials had refused him.

Fate had then come to his assistance, he'd been to the pub, unusual for him who normally preferred to drink at home alone. But it was the anniversary of his wife's death, and depressed, he had felt like getting drunk He had smelt the fire first, as he walked unsteadily home. Then turning a corner saw a woman standing outside a house from which smoke was pouring, screaming for someone to rescue her children. An inner voice told Stefan to act, but instead he stared open mouthed at the sight of flames and smoke bursting from the shattered windows. Finally seeing him, the woman grabbed his arm and begged him to help her.

Belatedly galvanised into action, he had shambled to the front door, opened it and had been knocked of his feet by the blast of flames and hot air that met him. He couldn't believe the intense heat that stripped him off his eyebrows, singed his clothing and hair, and forced him to retreat from the nightmare.

No films or books had ever described the real terror of a blast of heat like that. The pain, the fear, it was unimaginable, nobody could brave that. Holding his hands in front of his face, he turned and ran. The woman's cries calling him back echoing behind him.

Stefan had never come to terms with his actions or rather his inaction of that day. Unfairly convinced himself that he had acted as a coward, and so decided that he didn't have what it takes to be a hero. Instead, he threw himself into his work at the power station, seeing loyal duty to his employer as some kind of substitute for his lack of heroism.

Years had passed and Pieter having attended university had come to join him at the new gas fired plant, that had made Stefan proud especially with his son having the qualifications that would and did get him early promotion.

His second wife had died from breast cancer four years before, and Pieter and his then fiancé Sarah had come to live with him. Approaching sixty, Stefan had now looked forward to grandchildren and old age fully content.

But then this filthy evil disease had struck the world and claimed Sarah as a victim. Not just Sarah, this thing was greedy and wanted Pieter and Stefan along with the billions of others.

They could not save themselves, he knew that, accepted it even. But he would not accept that everybody would die, there would be survivors, there always were. His people had survived the camps just as they had survived other pogroms around the globe for centuries. The world had survived all kinds of disasters and horrible events. It had survived the terrible Black Death; he had learnt that at school in history. He had liked history and had even visited the village of Eyam in Derbyshire where the inhabitants had behaved as heroes. Though confusingly that seemed to have been a different plague, but that didn't matter, some of the villagers had survived that's what counted, and most of all he had liked the way that ordinary people had coped with whatever had been thrown at them. Whether it was invasions of Romans or Normans, raids from Viking warriors, or plagues, people survived, and they would do so this time. Stefan could not, would not envisage that the entire species would die. People would survive and they would need electricity to do so.

The government would be making plans, he had watched films, knew that there was something called COBRA, not the snake cobra but a committee of clever people that met and dealt with crises.

It was just a matter of time, engineers in white suits would eventually arrive at the power station and take over the operation. They would know what to do and would ensure that hospitals and care homes, places like that would receive the electricity they needed.

But that would take time and it was up to Stefan and Pieter and others like them to provide that time. The two of them would go into work, they would keep the power station running. By the time, the virus bit deeper they would have jabbed the switches open, isolated levers, do whatever it took. Pieter was clever, he would know what to do. Whatever it was, they would do it, somehow, they would leave the station running for as long as was possible after their own deaths.

Pieter had continued to argue for a while but eventually worn out by a combination of emotion and the onset of the virus, he had looked lovingly at his father, pulled himself to his feet and loyally accompanied him to work.

They lasted a further twenty hours, despite throwing up and fouling themselves repeatedly, they worked like slaves. When they were ill, they would help one another to their feet, look at each other and pull faces at the stench, then laugh. A laugh that perhaps bordered on insanity, but a laugh that acted as a release of some kind and that showed their love and affection for one another as they again continued with their self-imposed task.

Pieter had suggested that they should concentrate on supplying power locally, feeling that to try and contribute to the grid would be beyond their abilities. That would have to be left to someone else to do. They would have to settle for doing as much as they could for the people of their own town.

Despite Stefan's lung condition, it was the younger fitter Pieter who fell first. His father missing him for a few moments eventually found him in the toilets lying in his own dirt.

He cradled his son in his arms for a few moments before, unable to carry him, dragged him out into the works canteen. There laying him out as lovingly as possible in the circumstances on a dining table.

Next, he pulled another table over and situated it alongside the first, intending it to become his own repository in due course. He gave a last look at his son before returning to work for a further hour.

At one point, he thought he heard vehicles outside and struggled to the door to look hopefully toward the road a hundred yards away. But if there had been anyone there, they had passed straight by. Stefan Tustanowski died that Tuesday evening at 6:45 pm, one of the last to do so from the initial plague. There would be no medals for the two men, they would never even receive a proper burial, and no one would ever know about the heroics performed by father and son.

But Charles Benford's survivors would be forever grateful for the electricity that lasted for hours longer than they could have expected and had given them sufficient time to lay in the supplies that they would need in the coming months.

Chapter 21

Jannine Danes

Jannine Danes slumped forward, allowing her head to loll onto arms that were crossed and supported by her dining table. Her sobbing had stopped and her breathing gradually slowed to almost normal as she sat slowly, sinking into torpor.

How long she sat immobile she never knew, it didn't matter, nothing mattered anymore because there was nothing. For Jannine, the nightmare had started less than two days ago, just two days, is that all it was, that surely wasn't possible. Just forty-eight hours before her life was normal, the world was normal and her family were all alive and well.

Oddly, her husband had fallen ill first and that was wrong in itself. Tony was big and strong, although perhaps filling out slightly as he reached his mid-fifties. He jogged daily, played golf twice a week and cycled everywhere he could. Yet, this filthy disease had lain him on his back within hours. They had been up town, his annual bonus paid out in time to celebrate his promotion. Shopping in the west end, a nice restaurant was followed by a show. How lovely it should have been; then back to the hotel not a terribly expensive one but nice and she had brought her black negligee with her, the one Tony liked her in. She had planned a special treat for him as well and had giggled all day as she remembered the bit in fifty shades that she had in mind and imagined her husband's face when the time came.

It never did, nor the restaurant and show. They had shopped pleasantly for an hour or two when without warning he had been taken ill for the first time, vomiting uncontrollably in the street followed by a desperate rush to the men's room with a diarrhoea attack. They had raced home, Tony wrapped in a car blanket acting as a nappy. En route she had called for the doctor, this early in the onset of the plague it was still possible to get through to the surgery, and Dr Forbes, a family friend had promised to call round later that day.

That never happened and the surgery phone was never answered again. She tried to nurse her husband herself, using dio calms and anything else she could think of all without success. She was just never allowed to really give him her best attention. Instead, was being constantly interrupted by the next incident in the endless nightmare that life became for her.

Firstly, James her youngest son came home from his office early, apparently suffering from the same bug as his father. Caroline trailed her brother by only minutes. Jan had barely settled them into bed with sick bowls when the phone started, it was her father, now nearing eighty beside himself with concern for his wife.

Like his daughter, despite repeated attempts he had also been unable to get through to their doctor. He asked if Janine could call round to the surgery or go to the chemist for him, he couldn't leave her mother in the state she was in. Equally reluctant to leave her own family, she called Jonathan, her eldest son, only to learn that he was himself busy looking after his own wife Alice and the children, both of whom were also desperately ill. Johnny had been about to call his mother himself to ask what the hell was going on in the world and to request her help convinced that he was himself coming down with the bug.

Jannine, it seemed was the fittest in the whole family. After a serious but hurried con flab with a very weak but bravely determined Tony, it was decided that Jan would have to visit the others and see what she could do to help some or all of them.

Making her three patients as comfortable as possible and promising to visit Johnny as soon as she could, she called at her parents first, her route took her past both surgery and the adjoining pharmacy. Queues outside the doors of both stretched way back down the street, with hundreds gathered around, all clamouring for help, for themselves, for loved ones, for neighbours. Clearly there was no aid to be had there. Shaken at the evidence of just how bad this thing was, Jannine continued to her parents and let herself in announcing her arrival shrilly as she entered, so as not to frighten the elderly couple.

Both parents were in their bedroom, her father also suffering the now all too familiar symptoms. The room stank of vomit, and it was plain neither of the elderly couple were capable of clearing up properly and certainly unable to look after themselves, let alone each other. At her wits end to know what to do for best, she washed both of her parents clean, then made up a drink of raw egg and milk, an old remedy her mother swore by for diarrhoea. She was barely finished attending them when her mobile rang. Tony sounded really awful, his voice frighteningly weak and his speech broken, as though every word he uttered was forced from him.

Good man that he was though it wasn't himself he was phoning for, it was Johnny who needed her. Alice had died in his arms moments ago and between the sobs racking his body, he had managed to get across to his father, he was afraid the children were also close to death. Johnny had wanted to get them into his car and attempted to get them to hospital but wasn't up to it himself. He had broken of the call at that point unable to continue. Tony had tried to leave his sick bed himself without any success and becoming desperate, urged his wife to help their son, even though it meant leaving her parents and the rest of the family without any assistance for the moment.

Shocked and devastated, Jannine had still hesitated, she had sensed something in her husband's voice, did he think that he didn't have much longer himself and typical of him wanted her to attend their son rather than for the two of them to be together at this time as he would really want.

Tony had said he had tried to go to Johnny himself and hadn't been able to. Jan knew what that really meant was that Tony had dragged himself out of his sick bed, determined to help his son, only to find that no matter the wish, he was just too weak to do any more or go any further. So, was now probably laying on the floor somewhere unable to move or possibly even unconscious Caught between her husband and their two younger children, her parents and her eldest son and his children, Jannine was terrified, she wanted to scream in both terror and frustration but found herself unable to utter any sound, her mind and body close to a massive panic attack.

What was happening to her, to her family, it was only hours ago that everything was fine, her family fit and well. After the celebratory trip to town that had ended so disastrously, they still had holidays to look forward to and her own birthday, a special one this year. Now this, for the hundredth time that day, Jannine Danes tried to wake herself up.

Desperate that this nightmare should be exactly that, just a nightmare. How long she sat in a daze she would never know, a groan from one of her parents finally decided her. She couldn't help all of them, couldn't be with all of them so would do as duty demanded, do as she know Tony would want her to. She kissed and said goodbye to her barely conscious parents, all three of them aware that they would never see one another alive again, then forced herself to leave. As she drove, she begged and prayed to a god she had ignored for years, promising a different life from now on if only he would allow her family to live. "Oh let her wake up! Please let me just wake from this f-----g nightmare."

Arrival at Johnny's brought fresh horrors, her son was plainly close to death and too weak to be of any help to her. The children sat either side of their father dressed only in soiled underwear, both looked barely conscious. Johnny reached out a trembling hand to her and tried to speak.

Instead a vile smelling vomit erupted from his mouth that seemed to be comprised horrifyingly of blood mixed with what looked like lumps of raw meat.

Despite herself, Jannine leapt away from her son in an attempt to avoid the awful mess. Then instinct took over and she embraced him tightly as she felt his life force ebbing away, his eyes locked on hers in a heartbreak appeal for a help that she couldn't give him. Afterwards, she wanted to just sit and hold her son to her but was denied even this.

Cries of pain and terror coming from the children's rooms cut that short and thrusting away the pain of her loss, she struggled to her feet and went to them.

She didn't need any medical knowledge to know that both were beyond any help she could give them. Alice lay on her bed eyes closed, only the faintest rise and fall of her tiny chest betraying any sign of life. As she looked down at her, the child's eyes opened and she whispered, "Nanny, I'm frightened, please hold me nanny, make me better." Choking back her sobs, Jannine lifted the girl, who felt so light and frail and crushed her to her breast as she carried her into her brother's room. She planned to lay with them both on the bed hoping to comfort them until, until? She couldn't bring herself to finish that thought. Her mind would go no further than that, she would lay with them and love them to the end.

She was cheated of even that. This awful thing had no mercy, regardless of age or sex or emotions. The virus was all about death, a death that was to be brought about by sickness and diarrhoea, and nature took its course. Both children's tiny bodies were racked by repeated attacks of the now all too familiar vomiting that again included blood and flesh, leaving both children weaker by the minute and in great pain.

The sheer helplessness that she felt was the worst thing, the children frightened beyond words and in their terrible agony screamed constantly, crying for the help that she couldn't give.

Jannine felt she was going mad; she knew now all too well that this wasn't the nightmare she had so desperately wanted it to be. She was never going to awake from this, instead fate had decreed that she was doomed to watch her entire family die around her and be unable to do anything to stop it or even to ease their pains.

Eventually, that part of the nightmare came to an end in a welter of blood and faeces, Alice lasting only minutes longer than her brother. Afterward, Janice rose wearily to her feet totally bereft and incredibly weak, too used up to even cry any more.

She knew it would be no good going back to her parents, both would be dead, and besides she wanted desperately to be with Tony, to feel his strong arms around her, arms that she knew wouldn't now be able to hold her that way ever again.

But just his very presence would help, she had to be with him at the end.

She drove home through streets that were indescribable, people wandering aimlessly looking for a help that wasn't there and yet most of them strangely silent as though they didn't have the strength to talk.

Instead, friends or strangers would look at each other almost vacantly and seeing only the others pain or helplessness move on.

Opening the door of her home, she called for Tony but received no answer, she paused momentarily, bracing herself for what she knew the silence must mean. They were in her bedroom; Tony must have used the last of his strength to bring his family to where they could be together before laying down with them. Janice sat down beside him ignoring the stench and held his hand. There was still a warmth to it indicating that she may not have missed him by much. She didn't weep, she was past that. Instead, just sat there for a long time her thoughts wandering back over their life together. The children, grandchildren so many wonderful memories, and now all gone, only her left. That paused her, she hadn't thought about it until now, why she was alive. Everybody was dead or dying, yet Jannine didn't even feel ill. Her heart was breaking, eyes and nose sore from her weeping and butterflies churned her stomach with the day's events, but she wasn't physically ill.

Why? Why had she been spared, it didn't make sense. Tony and Johnny at least were so much stronger than her, always doing their keep fit stuff and watching what they ate.

So why her, what was special about her, she didn't want to be alive, not if all her family were dead, it wasn't fair. She didn't work out or anything, didn't watch what she ate, in fact had packed on a lot of weight in this past year. So why was she exempt, it was all so wrong, so wrong.

She looked about her, there was some medications in the cupboard but nothing that she thought would do what she wanted. She looked at the bath, remembered reading that the ancient Romans would sit in a hot bath and slash their wrists. She wasn't sure she could do that and besides she wanted to be with Tony when she died. Eventually, she worked out a way of achieving that. Going into the kitchen she turned the gas taps on full, opened all the doors between the kitchen and bedroom then sat on the edge of the bed. Picking up the telephone, she called her parents' house knowing that there would be no reply, but the answer machine would be on and she felt that she needed to say good bye to someone. She spoke to the machine telling her parents how much she loved them, of how happy her life had been until today and of what her dreams had been for the future, and she told them what she was going to do next and asked them to forgive her.

Then she lay on the bed alongside her family with the box of matches in her hand and waited.

Chapter 22

Chris Simpson

The operator who took Benford's call from the scene of Roberts and his companions' deaths. Informing her of the four doses of antidote he had left behind balanced on Roberts' battered corpse. Was herself already feeling the effects of the deadly virus?

Perhaps it was this, or maybe it was the garbled stammering of Benford's message. Either way, there was an insufficient sense of urgency in the first response of the police. Consequently, it was another twenty-five minutes before the first constable arrived at the scene, by which time two other calls from people in the vicinity had been made reporting the deaths of the four men.

But even before these events took place, an out of work chef had discovered the bodies.

Chris Simpson, like so many others that day had woken that morning feeling unwell and assumed it was the alcohol from the previous night causing the fluttering in his stomach and bowels. His usual remedy for a hangover was a brisk walk and having only recently been reunited with his two German shepherds, he had set off with the intention of doing a couple of miles.

As fortune dictated, man and dogs arrived almost immediately after Benford's departure. Simpson was recently returned from the states where, yet another business idea had flopped badly.

This time, a takeaway selling traditional English dishes had gone tits up. It seemed that bangers and mash, and a variety of stodgy puddings failed to impress the New Yorkers enough for Chris to earn the millions that he yearned for.

Returning to Britain, he had rented a country cottage, bought a couple of Alsatians, and decided he would become a breeder of highly trained guard dogs. The fact that he knew nothing about animals, kept losing them and had failed to notice that the dog was neutered, and the bitch spayed, heralded the start of another failure.

But this time, it wouldn't matter, Chris not only found the bodies, but he also found the antidote together with the brief note that Benford had left behind balanced on Roberts' corpse.

Chris may not have had the best business brain in the world, but he was quick enough when it came to surviving. As he walked the dogs, he had been listening to the news of the virus that had travelled around the world in less than three days, and that since yesterday evening, had arrived in the UK.

As he registered that the queasy stomach, he was suffering from was almost certainly the virus, Simpson had gone into a panic and had been trying to think of a way to stay alive. Convinced that nothing, no matter how lethal could kill everybody, everywhere. It was he was sure just a case of finding a way to either avoid catching the damn bug, and it seemed he might be too late to manage that. Or failing that then of beating the thing. So having absorbed Benford's note, he realised far quicker than the writer had, the various implications this led to.

The principal one being that there was no way the authorities could hope to make any more of the antidote in the few hours remaining to them.

So this was it, the only available antidote in the country. Although as he thought about it, obviously whoever had left it here with the bodies must presumably have had more. That thought combined with the presence of the four dead, prompted his next move.

Pocketing the syringes, he called the dogs who for once actually obeyed him and left the scene – if not at a run at least as fast as his dodgy bowel would allow him.

Arriving home out of breath, he called Kerry, his long-time long-suffering girlfriend. He was trying to save her life so why did the damn woman have to be so difficult. Kerry was at work, had struggled to get in despite not feeling well, only to find that she was the only PA in the company to have done so, and cursed herself for her misplaced loyalty. Not that many of the partners had arrived either but those that had all seemed to think that she was there to serve them alone and not for work. "Kerry, can you get hold of a doctor. Kerry, can you nip to the chemist, can you call my wife and see how she is."

Now she had Chris, according to him her 'boyfriend' instructing her to just walk out and go to him. "He could save her life, there was a killer bug and he just happened to have a miraculous antidote, the only available stuff in the country."

Insane totally frigging insane, and she couldn't make up her mind whether she referred to him or herself. Three times he called her sounding more desperate every time and finally yelling down the phone.

"Look your stupid bint, haven't you been listening to the news, aren't you even feeling a little sick yourself. You just said half your firms not at work. WAKE UP, the world's dying, now just walk out, don't tell anybody where you're going, just walk out and come straight here, DO IT."

That really wound her up, her and Chris had always been a bit on and off at the best of times. He had happily cleared off to the states without her and she hadn't really missed him. Instead, she had sort of drifted into an affair with Ron Appleton, his supposed best mate. Unfortunately, Ron was married and wouldn't leave his family. So, on Chris' return she had took up with him again but still continued the affair with her lover. He was just so much more exciting than Chris and sort of sophisticated. Now she was being told to do something crazy that if Chris had got it wrong, she would lose her job. Damn the man, why couldn't it have been Ron calling her, if he said come away with me the worlds ending, and I can save us she would probably have believed him and certainly wouldn't have hesitated to go with him anyway.

But Chris? Well, this wouldn't be the first time he'd come up with some ludicrous idea that never even came close to reality.

Fortunately, for both of them Chris's calls were made minutes before GCHQ had been primed by Sir Harmer Evans as to the kind of phrases they should listen out for. Equally lucky for Kerry, her bosses suddenly vomiting all over his office floor and seemingly expected his PA to clean it up. Combined with, the afterthought that in that last call of his there had been something in Chris's voice, something different to normal; the two things together finally convinced her he was deadly serious and decided her to do as he instructed.

Grabbing her bag and jacket and without a word to anyone she left the building and drove to her boyfriend's cottage in a daze.

Kerry had a family, mum, and dad, two brothers and a sister and five nephews and nieces, all of whom lived over in Coventry; so far since this bug thing had started, she hadn't called any of them. It just hadn't occurred to her that they might be in any real danger. This was just another bug, surely Britain had a health service. There must be a cure for this there always was. What did Chris mean he had an antidote, where from, how come there wasn't any more. Why wasn't the government doing something? Why didn't the TV people know anything about an antidote? A thousand and one questions came to mind but not a single sensible answer. None of this made any sense and if she lost her job because of Chris's nonsense she'd? What, well she'd think of something to do to him.

Chris wouldn't allow her any time, as soon as she arrived, he bundled her into his car overriding her objections to being treated in this way and having released the dogs to run free drove away.

They covered thirty miles in as many minutes, then spotting a sign for a country park turned in and parked the car in a secluded bay.

Twenty minutes later, Kerry was out of the car and throwing up in the bushes. This time not as a direct effect of the virus, they were going to die, her family, parents, brothers and sister nephews and nieces all of them. Everybody, all around the world everybody was going to die.

It wasn't possible, Chris had got to have it wrong, but the proof was there in front of her, it was there on the radio that worked on some stations but not on others. It was there in the antidote now coursing through her veins and already making her feel a physical if not mental improvement.

And it was there with the man sat in the driver's seat of the car she had arrived here in. Chris Simpson was he really to be the last man on earth.

If he was, did she want to spend forever with him, well the rest of her life anyway, a twenty first century Adam and Eve! Hardly.

That passing thought wasn't encouraging either. Chris was okay and could be funny in small doses, but Tarzan he wasn't.

Wait though, from what little he had told her about his finding the antidote. Others would survive this, but who were they and where were there, more importantly were they dangerous to her and Chris, or maybe they could be a source of getting more of the antidote. Movement within the car showed that Tarzan was getting restless waiting for her, and sure enough a second later came the shout, "Kelly, are you ready, we ought to be moving on."

She popped a mint into her mouth to try and remove the after taste of vomit and walked toward him. Her mind made up about one thing at least, "Yes, I'm ready to go, and the first place we're off to is Coventry to see my family."

Chapter 23

Wilkinson Saves Maggie

Wilkinson was growing desperate, it was Monday afternoon and unknown to him more than 400 miles to the south, Charles Benford was delivering the antidote to his chosen people.

At the Bonnie prince inn and guest house in the cairngorms, Maggie Keenan was in the loo throwing up for the third time in an hour. Mike knew what that meant and gave the woman six to eight hours of life. A life that he did not want to end. He had watched her last night, had stayed in the bar until the last punter had left. He had watched as she worked, as she talked, as she laughed, watched as she brushed the back of her hand across her head to wipe away a bead of perspiration. Smiled to himself as she repeatedly gave a slight shake of her head to rid herself of a stray wisp of hair that would insist on falling back over her face.

He had wanted to say something to her, had been so drawn toward her, had wanted her. It might have only been his imagination, but he even sensed that his advances would not be unwelcome.

That was last night, today was vastly different. Today Maggie Keenan was dying, he could hear her now, retching her life away with her head hanging over a toilet bowl. Dying because he had killed her, her, and everybody else. As he listened to her now the guilt was overwhelming.

He wanted to tell her what he had done, wanted to tell her that this was all his fault and apologise for it, wanted her forgiveness. But more than anything he wanted her to live. He had spent the last hours trying to work out how he could save her and knew there was only one way. He had thought hard, thought of the consequences, and was prepared to do what was required. It would mean the death of two more people, but he had killed before, in Iraq, in Afghanistan, and he had just helped in the mass murder of seven billion human beings so what was the lives of two more people to him.

He would gladly kill two or two hundred, two thousand even just to give this woman one more hour of life. No, two more deaths weren't what was preventing him from saving her, nor the act of telling her what he had done. The deed had needed doing, the world required saving and though he was sorry for her inclusion in the numbers, he still felt justified in the deed. No, what was holding him back from acting now was that he knew she wouldn't understand the necessity of what he had done, and if she didn't understand then how could he bear the thought of the look in her eyes. The depth of loathing she would give him when he explained his role in the saving of the earth.

Wilkinson nearly left it to late, when he had finally taken the second of his two syringes and pushed it into Maggie Keenan's arm, he estimated she had been less than an hour from death with specs of blood already starting to appear in her vomit. It would still be a matter of luck as to whether she would suffer any long-term damage, but there was little he could do about that now.

He had carried her into a bedroom cleaned her up with flannel and towels, then forced her to drink water that she hadn't wanted. In her delirium, she fought against him; afraid that anything she took into her stomach would cause her to vomit again and dreaded that body racking heaving that felt as if her entire insides would burst from her mouth.

Eventually, she slept. Wilkinson, who now needing two more doses of antidote and would have liked to have headed south as soon as possible.

He was forced to recognise that the woman needed to restore her strength before she would be up to the six-hundred-mile journey, so he reluctantly had to let her rest.

His mind was still in turmoil, it was he who had released the virus that had so nearly killed the woman and indeed might still kill the pair of them. He had carried out the deed willingly enough at the time and still did not really regret it, but within hours a tiny seed of doubt had crept into his mind and had grown steadily since. He still accepted the necessity of his actions, it was just some of the consequences that now bothered him, prompting the wish that it had somehow been possible to make the virus more selective Realising that he would also need rest if he was to tackle the long drive south later, he laid down fully clothed next to the woman. Lying there and able to feel the warmth of her body, hear her now less strained breathing, he felt an inner peace descend, a calmness that he had not known since the opening of the last of his thermos buckets thirty hours earlier.

She woke in the night and found him sleeping alongside her, his presence alarming her at first until dim memory returned. Unable to untangle her thoughts, she continued to lay still until sleep once again returned. When she awoke a second time, he was gone but she could hear movement within the flat she occupied above the bar separated from the guest rooms only by a fire door. Then the delicious smell of bacon cooking roused her to movement. She was starving and supposed that was natural after the way her stomach had emptied itself yesterday.

Thoughts of yesterday prompted her to pick up the remote and attempt to switch the TV on, needing information of what was happening to her world. Nothing happened and she shook the remote trying again and again before crossing to the telly and pressing the manual button. Again nothing, puzzled she tried a light switch, nothing.

Now alarmed, she ran from the room and headed for the stairs aware that Wilkinson had emerged from her kitchen and was calling to her. She ignored him, continued on her way downstairs, slid the bolts on the front door and yanking it open ran up the street.

Behind her Mike Wilkinson cursed, returned quickly to flick the gas hob of where a pan of bacon and eggs sizzled enticingly and dashed after the woman, afraid of losing sight of her.

Maggie Keenan was one of three sisters, the eldest Catherine had emigrated to New Zealand years ago, the youngest Dilly lived with her husband and three children, a scant two hundred yards from Maggie's inn.

It was to hear she ran and here where Mike found her sobbing over the five vomit and faeces stained corpses. He pulled her away and held her talking quietly, soothingly, combining the words with stroking her hair as he attempted to calm her.

Later in her flat, he ditched the long cold pan of breakfast and served up some bread and cheese instead, insisting that she ate something before he would answer any of her questions. When he did, he gave her the story that he had thought up during the night. He was an intelligence agent sent by the government who knew of a terrorist plan to release a killer virus onto the world. It was known that an individual was heading for the highlands, and he was supposed to have intercepted the man. Obviously, he had missed him and the b....d had released the virus. Fortunately, an antidote had been found but and there were problems with its manufacture. The story was weak and full of holes and would not stand up to any real questioning, but it was enough to persuade her to get moving. Though, that involved carrying first her sisters and then the rest of her families' bodies to their beds where she planned to leave them until she could arrange burial.

Listening to her, Mike was sure that she had not really understood what he had been telling her, until that is they went into the rear yard of the Inn. Here Maggie kept a few hens, she looked at them for a moment in thought then entered the coop and expertly caught each of them in turn and wrung their necks. He was prepared to help but sensed his interference would not be welcome. After the woman had finished, she looked at him with the last bird still in her hand and shrugged. "Normally, I would ask Alistair to feed them. I guess that won't ever happen again."

He said nothing and waited while she packed a small bag, then in afterthought strode off toward her sisters again. He followed her afraid that whatever she was intending now was going to take up more of their increasingly precious time, these delays were starting to irritate him now. She ignored anything he said and the impatient looks he gave her, instead she made her way to the rear of the premises. As soon as they opened the yard gate a dog could be heard barking. The sound coming from a brick built shed at the far end of the garden.

Maggie opened the door and a large bundle of fur bounded out and jumped at her, then chased around her in circles all the while keeping up a nonstop barking. She shouted a name repeatedly that sounded like Dalglish until the animal finally sat still and she reached down to fondle its ears. "He comes with us," the words were spoken flatly and left no room for argument. He settled for asking, "Dalglish?"

"Named for Scotland's greatest ever player," she replied simply.

The dog took up station in the rear of Wilkinson's BMW loaned to him by Sanders for his mission to the north. Before the woman took her seat, she gave a final look around the tiny village, with a small Tarn on one side then a view across the moor where he had released the killer bug to the distant mountains. The area was picture postcard beautiful. The man once again had to drop his head afraid to catch the woman's eyes in case she saw the guilt they contained.

They drove south making good time at first, the only incident being when they reached Blairgowrie, here the road went between the houses. The time now was approaching midday, the lack of any sign of life was eerie and while neither had really spoken so far, the silence seemed to become almost heavy and both occupants were pleased when they left the small town behind.

"Why are the animals alive?" the question from Maggie came unexpectedly. "Dalglish, the chickens, there are animals in the fields they all seem fine, why?"

"The virus affects only humans and certain apes," Mike didn't really want her asking questions and offered no further encouragement for the moment, and silence again descended on the couple as each reverted to their own thoughts. Perth and Dunfermline were reached and then they were circling Edinburgh. "There are half a million people who live here, are they all dead?"

"A handful might survive that's all." Still she didn't open up, she never condemned the people who had done this thing, never even asked about them, just continued to sit quietly in the passenger seat. But Wilkinson was aware that she stole occasional glances at him, at times this made him uncomfortable, his conscience afraid that she would see the guilt that was written across his face.

At these times, he would make a show of peering around either side of the car as the countryside flashed by, in an attempt to divert her attention away from himself.

It was on the A1m south of Newcastle that the problems started. Mike's original plan had been to spend the Sunday evening after releasing the last of the virus in the B&B, then when the virus had completed its deadly work, he would drive over to Mallaig on the west coast. There he would commandeer a boat and sail over to Skye or another of the islands and here he would make his home.

He neither needed nor desired the company of his other conspirators, despising most of them and uncomfortable in their presence. His sudden attachment to Maggie had changed all that and now gave him an unexpected hiccup. Three days earlier on his way north in the BMW, he had stopped en route at services at Washington near Sunderland. Here he had topped up his fuel tank and then given no further thought to the matter, the road trip across to Mallaig being a comparatively short one.

Looking now at his fuel gauge, he was aware that that had been a mistake. The same service area was now devoid of life, and a brief investigation showed the fuel pumps, requiring electricity as a power source would not work.

There was no way he was going to make it to The Manor on what remained in the tank at present, so he needed to do something about fuel.

There were some cars about in the car park area but all locked secured.

Entering the service station building, he discovered two bodies in the staff rest room both of whom had sets of car keys in their pockets.

That was as far as his luck went, when he did eventually find the cars they fitted, both were lower on fuel than his own and he had used up nearly an hour of precious time. Realising that he had to find a better method than this, he continued driving south while he considered ways to solve the problem.

"You gave me the second part of your antidote then, thank you for that."

Maggie's comment came as a surprise and he looked at her expecting something more, again though as with her previous comments and questions nothing followed. He guessed she was still in shock and was slowly making sense of what had happened to her, to the world in the last few hours. Well, he would allow her to take her time and adjust bit by bit, the silence in between times giving him a chance to firm up on his own cover story.

A while later, he explained his new idea for solving their fuel problem, she thought about it for a moment then nodded assent without speaking.

Turning of the A1 near Darlington they entered an area of small villages. Here they looked for and found an expensive looking home with a car parked outside the house. In this case, a Volvo on the current years plate.

Taking a tyre iron from the boot of his car in case of a dog being inside the house, Mike found a partially open window and it was the work of only moments to break in, then ignoring the familiar smells of vomit and faeces looked for and located a set of car keys. Outside, a check of the fuel gauge showed the car was a little over three quarters full and Wilkinson guessed that it ought to get him close to his destination.

They changed their few possessions from one vehicle into another and with Dalglish taking up his customary position on the rear seat they recommenced their journey.

An hour later, he suddenly slowed the car, Maggie still in a world of her own sat up suddenly aware there were bodies on the grass verge. First one then another, then two together, then ahead they saw cars spread all over the carriageway in a variety of positions. The pile up that had happened the morning before and that unknown to him had contributed to both Charles Benford, and before him the trio carrying the antidote to divert. And so to the meeting that fate had arranged for them, had never even begun to be cleared away.

As the hours had passed, drivers becoming increasingly ill and desperate for help had abandoned their vehicles to seek aid of any kind. In doing so they had only succeeded in making the chaos worse.

Those that were not already suffering the effects of the virus were eventually overtaken by it, and that finally resulted in them dying alone by the side of the road.

There was no way through the carnage, and the couple were forced to do a U turn and back track several miles before switching to the other carriageway and now on the northbound, once again headed south.

Another hour and the dog began to whine causing Maggie to break from her reverie and look about her, seconds later she was calling to Mike to stop the car. They were passing under a motorway junction, the road above them running east to west. To the east of them about three hundred yards away was an extra service station area. As they disembarked the car, Maggie peered intently toward it claiming that she thought she had seen a movement over there. Dalglish had followed them out and had relieved himself on the grass verge and now with his nose twitching was looking in the opposite direction to the humans. After a moment of inactivity where they peered, Mike said they should push on. There was no sign of movement and since the dog with its superior sense of smell had never once looked toward the service area, he was sure she must be mistaken. Maggie agreed but asked why the dog was so interested in the other side of the road. Wilkinson glanced first to where the animal was staring, the buildings of a large town plainly visible, then to Maggie. "He can smell death," he said and shrugged. They moved on. Another hour saw them close to Hatfield and they changed cars again for the final run toward the South downs and The Manor. The journey had taken them eleven hours and it was becoming dark when they finally arrived. Mike had planned to leave Maggie outside the walls of the grounds and attempt to approach The Manor unseen on foot. There he would attempt to enter bedrooms and try to locate and steal two capsules. If his search was unsuccessful, he would wait for the rooms occupants and if necessary kill to obtain them. As they came over the final rise toward The Manor it was at once obvious that something was wrong. No lights showed in the building and the gates to the drive were wide open. The electric would obviously not be working but Mike knew that this would have been anticipated and backup generators be on hand.

With a sense of foreboding, he abandoned his earlier plan and turned straight up the drive. Pulling to a stop outside of the front entrance, he barked instructions to Maggie to stay where she was and easing a small automatic pistol from an inside pocket, he entered the house.

The smell hit him immediately the all too familiar vomit and faeces.

Although there were no bodies in the hall or on the imposing split stairwell, they were the only two places free of them. Every door he opened revealed more of his co-conspirators lying dead. Not that he knew many of them, his role although pivotal to the success of the plot had not involved him in much contact with the majority of the conspirators.

Sanders had recruited him, and some boffin type had instructed him in how to administer the thermos buckets. That apart, he had picked up a couple of names and that was his total knowledge of the organisation.

Nevertheless, he knew that these corpses were those of the conspirators.

Sanders and the boffin were both here along with a number of others who though he had not known were involved, he nevertheless recognised. He felt anger mounting in him as he spotted TV celebrities, politicians, industrialists, even an international footballer. So he had been sold out again. Survivors apparently were to have been the rich and powerful, the very people who had screwed up before were to be saved to mess up again. Where were the farmers, the builders, the engineers, the people who would do the real work and rebuild the earth in a sympathetic way?

He found those in the kitchen and work areas below stairs. Some two dozen of them, they had obviously banded together in mutual support and tried to defeat the killer virus. Food and drink had been made easily available laid out on the worktops. A variety of containers seemingly acting as sick bowls lay strewn about, though most of these had been upturned as the occupants had lost their battle against death.

A noise behind him caused him to spin around, gun arm outstretched ready, he had forgotten the woman. She had left the car and had been exploring the house herself. She paused in the doorway looking toward him and said simply, "This is bad for us, isn't it?"

Mike Wilkinson looked at his watch and made his calculations.

It was now almost midnight, he had eight hours left until he needed to take the second part of the antidote. That was no longer possible, having given it to Maggie Keenan more than twenty-four hours earlier in order to save her life. He had no real idea how long after he failed to take the antidote he could expect before the virus would strike him. In Maggie's village, the population had started to fall ill within just a few hours, but he had released the virus less than a quarter of a mile from them, and they had not had the protection of having taken the first part of the antidote in the way Mike had done.

He would count on having at least twenty-four hours before becoming unable to function properly, so had to make the best use of the, say thirty two hours left to him in total.

That some kind of double cross had taken place seemed obvious, and if he was to get his hands on any more of the antidote capsules in time to save his and Maggie's lives, he would have to find out who had done what to whom and fast. In the dark of night it was impossible to see enough in The Manor to obtain any clues of what had happened here. A brief search of the outbuildings failed to locate any generator, though he was sure there must be one somewhere. The best he managed after breaking into a couple of cars was to lay his hands on a torch.

Armed with this, he started to search through the corpse's wallets and pockets. In an attempt to short cut the process, he tried to decide which was the likeliest of the bodies to offer a clue, and finally chose those of the politicians, but only after looking at Sanders unpleasant remains first.

By two am he had found nothing of use and was exhausted. Maggie while aware of the shortage of time, still urged him to rest. Arguing that if he slept for a few hours now while darkness reigned, he would benefit by it later and no doubt make faster time in daylight. Reluctantly, he agreed, and they both settled into the front seat of a car, neither of them feeling like trying to rest among a house full of corpses.

Chapter 24
Zookeeper

Throwing up was stomach achingly painful and the bloody flecks in the vomit were now clearly seen, but at least it was not as inconvenient as the trots. Those attacks came without warning and indeed sometimes without his even knowing that he had suffered one until his own stench assaulted his nostrils and he became aware of the faeces running down his legs.

Eventually, he had stripped naked, and would stop periodically to sluice himself down at the many water points as he walked around the zoo.

The weather was seasonally warm but not enough to protect him from the shock of the cold water, but even this he welcomed as the sudden drop in his body temperature woke him from the dazed state, he had a tendency to gradually sink into.

Noting that for whatever reason, the animals in his charge seemed to be impervious to whatever this virus was that was currently laying the human population of the country low.

Brian Russell had struggled into work that morning as normal, determined that none of the zoo's livestock would suffer from negligence on his part. Unfortunately, his example hadn't been very widespread.

Only three other keepers and one reception girl had managed to join him on duty. Within hours, all of those had been forced to return home, all suffering terribly from the bug. Brian had struggled on alone in his usual steady way. In the early afternoon, he had listened to the radio in the staff dining room and reached the same horrifying conclusion as the programs host. Incredible as it seemed, the entire human population of the world was about to become extinct. Thousands of years of evolution wiped out in just a matter of days, how! It was unbelievable, but true, nonetheless.

Having accepted the truth of what was happening, and perhaps because of his job, he had accepted the knowledge easier than most. Brian did what he always did, his job. He had checked the animals over carefully and all still seemed fine, with the exception of the apes.

Here, the larger species seemed to be reacting in much the same way as their human cousins and were suffering the same symptoms of vomiting and diarrhoea that would eventually result in death. The smaller species in general were as healthy as normal.

He thought carefully about what he intended, if he was wrong and the humans recovered then they would certainly hunt down and kill any of the carnivores that were wandering free. On the other hand, if he didn't do something to save the animals, they would all die of starvation once their human captors were all dead.

He found that the idea of all humankind vanishing from the planet didn't appal him in the way he thought it should. Brian's only family was a sister he hadn't seen in more than twenty years. He knew his neighbours by sight but not by name and outside of the zoo there was no one he thought of as a friend. Even inside the park's perimeter, he had always felt closer to the animals than the humans. He thought about the world his fellow man had created. The disappearing rain forests, the gradual erosion of the Great Barrier Reef, plastic poisoning of the oceans, the hundreds of varieties of creatures in danger of extinction, the list just went on.

So no, while he wouldn't have wanted the demise of all human beings, if something had to happen, he would rather it happened sooner to humans than to his beloved animals.

So he had hatched a plan, release the herbivores first and encourage them to leave the park, then the reptiles and finally the bigger carnivores.

If he retained enough strength, he would feed the latter before opening their pens. Hopefully that way they wouldn't be too quick to leave, thus giving the herbivores more time to wander away.

That hadn't been too successful, the potential prey animals had either stayed within their familiar compounds, or if stepping outside of their confines showed no inclination to leave the park altogether.

He tried driving them away but didn't have the strength to do more than whisper a pathetic, "Shoo, shoo." The animals, used to humans all their lives and to him in particular paid little heed to his weak attempts to spook them.

Judging by the increasing bouts of eruptions from both orifices he knew he was running out of time and wouldn't be physically able to feed the carnivores. His only option would be to undo the gates of the hunters and allow nature to take its course.

The main gates of the zoo park were standing open and once the big cats started wandering about no doubt the prey animals would seek safety as best, they could. He saved Inkosi the great lion until last. By this time, Brian was feeling ever worse, the pain becoming increasingly unbearable.

Not only was he vomiting great blobs of blood and what might be flesh, but he now had barely enough strength left to carry on with his task. He was dying and guessed that he had no more than another hour or two at most, that was why he had saved the enormous cat until last. He knew the strength of the beast, knew how the creature would disembowel him with those mighty rear claws, death would come in seconds. A death that if momentarily painful would be infinitely preferable to that of the filthy undignified way of the virus.

He finished unlocking the security gate and held it wide open. Inkosi was lying about forty yards away his, tail swishing idly as he watched the human's strange behaviour. Beneath the calm appearance the great beast was more tense than at any time in the four years of his life. All of those years spent in captivity, Inkosi was used to being fed by humans. He was used to their smell and associated the smell of this particular human with food.

The lion had no way of knowing it, but Brian had always tried to bring some kind of natural behaviour to feeding times. Along with all the best animal parks, he had adopted methods to try and stimulate his charges.

Hiding food or leaving it in places where they had to make a real effort to obtain it. He couldn't replicate a hunt exactly, but anything was better than the old ways of just hurling lumps of meat into cages of bored animals.

Brian's feeble shouts not only took courage and all of his remaining strength, but they also worked. Attracting the lion's attention, the beast rose slowly to its feet while staring at the man's unusual behaviour. Until, its interest aroused, the great lion advanced toward him. The keeper watched his death approach, the diminishing distance between them matching a similar rise in nervousness on his part. The human licked lips his dry with fear and closed his eyes praying for the animal to hurry and get this over with before the fear totally overwhelmed him and made him run.

After what seemed an age, he felt rather than saw the beasts' immediate presence, followed by the stench and warmth of its foul breath as the great head stopped inches from his own face, the keeper wet himself as he mumbled fearfully, "Hurry please, hurry, I can't take this much longer."

Then as he was falling backwards, the huge animal suddenly caught site of a muntjac deer as it emerged from behind a toilet block and simply barged the keeper out of its way as it charged its prey. The small deer seeing the lion almost too late made a valiant bid for escape, with the predator unused to real hunting in a clumsy pursuit behind it.

Brian left alone and unexpectedly alive tried to rise to his feet but was unable to get any further than kneeling on all fours before throwing up again. This time a mixture of virus and sheer relief. It was another ten minutes before he could finally stagger away to the staff block.

There had to be something in there, something anything would do, so long as it would allow him a more painless way of death than being eaten by lions or the filthiness of the viral disease.

Chapter 25

That First Morning

Surrounded on three sides by trees and having a well-stocked large pond in the rear grounds, The Manor Hotel occupied a pleasant corner site on the outskirts of the city.

Until now The Manor was best known locally as a popular venue for weddings and Christmas parties. With a useful and well-equipped fitness club, that members claimed retained its popularity due to its well managed and rigorous exercise programmes, rather than as jealous non-members said, "Because of the stunningly attractive and scantily clad female staff members."

That first morning the sun, as it often does in May, rose bright and clear and by the time Charles' small group of chosen ones had started to collect in the car park, the temperature was already warm and seemed set to increase rapidly.

Just two days ago, the temperature, the sun and the setting would have heralded the kind of day that makes people feel good. Coats are hung away and shorts, tee shirts and sun hats dragged out. Holiday companies look forward to receiving an increase in late bookings and all seems well with the world. Now! A world had died.

Charles stood inside the reception area watching as the first of the survivors started to arrive. He had been at the hotel for an hour and had not seen a single member of staff scantily clad or otherwise in that time.

Hardly surprising, since if his timetable was roughly correct, there was only about eight hours left before virtually everybody in the country would be dead. He sipped coffee from a machine as he thought about that and was surprised to find that he was relatively unaffected by it. He tried to analyse why this should be so, surely, he should be appalled, he had been yesterday. Yesterday, perhaps that was why he felt nothing at the moment.

Yesterday had lasted months, nightmare had followed nightmare, he had visited dark places in his mind that should never have existed. He had had to make the most awful decisions, had chosen who was to live and who would die, had wrestled with his conscience to make those choices only to find that at times he may as well not have bothered.

Fate had intervened and mocked him, had allowed him to select names and then ripped them away, even that of his own daughter, and she was his daughter.

Deep down he knew that, so he had had to choose again, had to replace. Choose substitutes, "This person is dead so you can live now." What he wondered would those people think if they ever knew that is what they were, second choices, substitutes.

He had killed as well yesterday, twice. The insane thought came, "You go sixty years without killing anybody then you do two in one day."

He could even shrug at his own callousness shown in that thought and then did so as he combined shrug with a wide yawn.

Yesterday, even the word itself was insufficient. "Charles, Charles are you there?" Jilly's voice brought him out of his reverie. "People are waiting Charles, they are frightened," she came into reception as she spoke, looking at her husband, inspecting him quickly.

Was he up to this, how long would his health hold up under this type of strain? She must remember to talk to that nice doctor woman and get her to check Charles over as soon as she could. Her visual inspection finished, Jilly nodded brief approval, he had done as she had ordered, shaved, and showered and seemed to have found a clean shirt from somewhere. He still hardly looked like a superhero, but he was what they had got and she would support him in every way she could, and that meant that he would always look presentable.

"Are you ready, they need you," she kissed his cheek as she spoke.

Charles looked out into the car park, "No let them wait. There's only about half of them here yet. I don't want to repeat myself and I want them frightened, that way they'll be less likely to argue." Jilly looked at him and was about to argue herself, then thought better of it. She knew her husband had a knack of understanding how people would behave in a variety of circumstances, and that he liked to do things in his own time and way. Liked to compose himself, and feel, that as he put it 'his head was ready' before he dealt with any tricky situations.

So she simply nodded her acquiescence and said, "Very well, I'll tell them you'll be with them shortly." As she walked away, Charles continued to stand watching as he once again rehearsed both the speech he had prepared earlier and practised in his mind the body language to go with it. He had thought about these coming hours carefully, had tried to prioritise the various tasks that needed to be done, had been surprised at some of his conclusions and gone over them again to be sure he was correct. He had tried to anticipate how the people would be. How they would react to his orders, they would all have relations and friends who were dead or dying. Many would hold him, at least partly responsible for that situation, by reason of his not being more generous with their particular share of the antidote. Even where they accepted that they could not help their loved ones to live, they would no doubt want to be with them now, if only to bury them.

That couldn't be allowed, there was too much to do, and these first hours were the most important. He needed the people to work now, today.

So he would override all and any objections. The people must do those things that had to be done and their mourning would have to wait until they could afford the luxury.

Using his latest mobile, he called his sons aware that there would now be so few calls being made that his could easily be picked out now, but also aware that it no longer mattered, there would be no one listening, not anymore.

Niall and Robbie gave progress reports, and both promised to be with him within 30 minutes at most. Another coffee, a glance at the time and then he braced himself and walked out to the car park. As far as he could tell everyone who should be here was. He had been watching them closely from reception and was pretty sure the general mood was about where he had expected it to be. People were quiet, standing around in their small family groups and making little or no attempt to speak to any outsiders.

Instead, friends would simply glance across at one another, give an occasional nervous half grin then either look away or more often down at their feet. It was as if they were almost ashamed of being alive, wondering how it had come to be them and yet so relieved that it was.

Of those who might have been expected to be a problem, Rooney, the father who had allowed his own family to die. Almost certainly killed them himself in order to possess the antidote. He stood by himself, a lonely and forlorn figure.

Charles would have to decide the best way to go forward with him; that would be difficult. So, as so often the way with Charles Benford, he chose to put the issue on the back boiler for now.

Continuing his survey of the survivors, he saw his nieces husband Chris the ex-boxer looking decidedly unhappy but subdued. While the other potential troublemakers, the Sanders family had been contacted in the night and their fittest members despatched to go with Niall and Robbie, and so were absent at this critical moment.

No, he decided nobody here would be a major problem, not today anyway.

And if there was, well, the remaining antidote was hidden away so it would be tantamount to committing suicide for anyone to start trouble.

He stayed in the entry portico and made them come to him, as they did so, a rumble of vehicles made everyone look around as Robbie and his helpers arrived in a convoy of minibuses, parking up, and then Robbie himself came across to stand by his father's shoulder, a visual support if one was needed.

The latter addressed the survivors speaking for some twenty minutes.

He gave a very brief resume of everything he knew mixed with an amount of conjecture and even downright lies, then he told them what he wanted them to do. The younger children were to go on the minibuses to a local adventure playground, mother's with children under ten would accompany them. Everyone else was assigned jobs, approx. half of them were to go with the freezer lorries that Niall and his group were bringing.

Right on cue at this point, Niall arrived at the head of half a dozen freezer lorries. The vehicles were to go to local supermarkets and cash and carry warehouses, and load up with as much frozen foods, bread, fresh meat, and fish as possible.

Crews would be leaving to collect more such vehicles and visit the three supermarket distribution centres that lay either in the city itself or within a twenty-mile radius, all of which usually played host to any number of such wagons. Charles made it clear he expected the loading to continue for the next two days with only minimal breaks for food and rest.

Meanwhile, other groups would leave to carry out a variety of other prioritised tasks. A dozen caravans were to be brought to the hotel car park and set up with supplies of gas bottles, as many water barrels as they could find, and large petrol or diesel driven generators. Expecting that they would lose mains water at any time, men would be expected to use the hotel swimming pool for washing, while women and children would take turns using showers in the caravans.

Meanwhile, Niall, Kevin, and Robbie along with small groups of steady reliable people were to be sent off on some particularly grisly tasks that he chose not to mention to the main group yet.

During the early hours, Charles had explained his thinking to his family and the others who he already regarded as his principal lieutenants.

Though much of it was conjecture, he was assuming that they would lose electricity at any moment, he was indeed surprised that they hadn't done so already. That loss would be followed shortly by that of mains gas. Despite his plans for hygiene, he nevertheless hoped that water might last for a longer period but accepted the quality would probably become ever more suspect as time went on. So, caravans powered by calor gas and generators would become permanent essentials as a way of providing hot water and other facilities for the community.

Before he had finished giving his instructions, there was a ripple of movement among the people on the edge of the small crowd who then parted to reveal a small boy. The youngster, obviously the last survivor of his family, and probably coming from one of the houses on the estates opposite the hotel could have been aged anywhere between four and seven years old. Though it was difficult to tell, so dirty and vomit stained as he was. Tears rolled down the youngsters face as his eyes flickered from face to face among the adults hoping to see a familiar face, or at least some kind of welcoming reaction. Such sad figures had been all too common the previous night, wandering the streets appealing for help wherever they could find someone alive to ask.

This morning, with the virus now well into its last phase, those same streets had been eerily empty. The appearance of the boy now seemed to stun the survivors who were still coming to terms with their own situation, and who as a result at first stood immobile simply staring at the lad.

Then, as though the boy's mere presence represented danger, mothers took their own children and drew away from the youngster.

Not so Liz, Charles's twin pushed forward scooped the boy into her arms and holding him close to her turned to her brother defiantly. "Charles, I want you to give this child the rest of my antidote." She stroked the boys head as she spoke, whose sobs gradually lessened under her soothing touch.

"I'm not being dramatic Charles, but I just do not want to live in this awful world any longer, at least not at the expense of children like this." Her brother appeared stunned for a moment as he stared at her for an age.

A long hard stare that made even Liz who was usually the more dominant of the two take a half step back. After a while, he advanced on her, his steps slow and deliberate and eyes blazing. Those who knew him well and were close enough to, could see the rage building inside him, saw it reflected in his face and moved away.

Charles Benford stopped, his face only inches from his sisters. Inside of the man a battle raged, he and Liz where every bit as close as twins usually are and rarely exchanged a cross word over anything. Charles' common sense had told him that in not saving her adoptees, Liz would be heartbroken, and that pain would inevitably turn to anger with him.

Knowing that it must happen didn't make it any easier when it did.

Charles would have denied it, but he was someone who needed the validation of at least his own family, and after his heroics of yesterday needed it now more than ever. In particular, he wanted it from Liz, her attitude to him now, however understandable, cut deep into his psyche. His anger for once overcoming his brotherly love poured from him in a tirade. "Not that easy, you don't. You think you can play God just like that." He snapped his fingers as he spoke. "Because just like everybody else here you suffered a tragedy yesterday. Now you're hurting and you want to ease that hurt by what you see as a noble act. You think that by sacrificing yourself you'll somehow cure the hurt inside you. Or is it just to try to hurt me, because I wouldn't save those you wanted me to, huh. Well, you've forgotten something, the boy needs two doses and you have only one to give. Oh, I know that Phil will be the loving husband even unto death and give his own antidote up to join you, but I won't allow that." He signalled his brother-in-law away as he spoke.

Loyally but aware of the tremendous undercurrents, Phil somewhat hesitantly stood his ground and awaited further developments.

"You see Liz, yesterday I had the power of life and death over people. If I selected you, you lived, and if not, you died, that simple. I had to make those choices, not once but more than two hundred times. But it was exactly that! Life and death, LIFE and DEATH they came together Liz. It wasn't a case of just choosing people to live. By making those choices, I was by default choosing people to die. A name occurred to me, and I would decide whether to include them on my list or not. What that really meant was, you live, you die. It was that bloody simple, live, die, live, die but there was a lot more dies than lives." His voice was becoming higher pitched as he spoke, and his whole body shaking with emotion.

"You know, I think in doing that somehow a piece of me died with every decision. Now you want to throw your rattle out of the pram because you're hurting. Well, if you insist okay, you can fall on your sword but you're not having it that easy. You're not taking Phil with you or at least you're not having his antidote. No, you want to do this, you want the power that I had yesterday, you think you could have done a better job of it than I did, then you must do what I had to do and choose someone to die, as well as allowing this boy to live. Perhaps you should choose between your children or grandchildren, what do you think Liz, do you fancy that?" He held his arm up to stop the protests from Liz and her husband. "No, of course not, that wouldn't be fair, would it? After all I didn't have to choose between my children so I shouldn't make you have to. No, I'll make it simpler for you." Charles had caught sight of Joey's sister, Courtney, with her daughter Cindy. The youngster had become unsettled, so her mother had taken her away from the crowd and was showing her the buses that were going to take them to the play centre. Charles pointed toward them, "There you go Liz, you choose one of them, one lives, one dies. You choose one and you can have the antidote for this boy, mother, or daughter, which one Liz. Come on, which one lives, which one dies."

Liz stared at him disbelievingly quite certain that her brother wasn't really serious in his threat. A look at his face told her she was wrong, this was a different Charles to the brother she loved to the one she had been brought up with, a different man to the one who now shouted at her; almost frothing at the mouth in his rage.

She tried to protest, "Charles you…"

But her twin drowned her out, giving her no chance to finish her appeal, instead shouting in her face, "Well, Liz which one, come on this is what you wanted, the right to choose who lives. This is what you think I got wrong." He was incandescent now, as he continued to wind himself up shaking and screaming at his sister.

His yelling was upsetting the boy in her arms and drawing the attention of Courtney who was aware now that the crowd were looking toward her.

"Well, come on Liz you've only got to choose one, not two hundred. Choose Liz, choose." His voice tailed away and with a huge sigh, seemingly his anger died away with it. "You can't do it, can you Liz. Well, you should thank God for that, and thank him that you don't need to, give the boy to me."

He reached for the lad who tried to draw back from him, but Charles took him gently but firmly from his sister's grasp, who sobbed as she parted with him, without attempting to prevent her brother taking him away.

Turning to his sons, he instructed them to take charge and get the survivors moving, adding loudly, "Don't take any arguments. I want those tasks under way now, anybody wants to argue can bugger off and go their own way, but they'll go without the antidote."

He turned away with the boy still in his arms and walked slowly into the hotel. Liz found him half an hour later after searching the various public rooms and bars in the building. The hotel boasted handsome landscaped gardens, including the large pond. Charles was sat by this on a bench shaded from the sun by a number of willow trees, at any other time an idyllic spot. Her brother had the boy cradled in the crook of his arm. The pillow that he had used to smother the boy was still over the child's face hiding the sightless eyes from the man's gaze.

She couldn't bring herself to look directly at the boy herself as she spoke.

"Oh Charles, I'm so sorry."

"They're wrong Liz, the writers and film makers. I've killed three times now and it doesn't get any easier Liz, it gets harder." His eyes flickered down to look at the boy's body as his voice broke, "It gets so hard Liz, so hard." A sob broke from him as he spoke, his twin sat down beside him, her arm going around him as her cheek came against his and she felt him heave another huge dry sob that caused him to shake.

"Oh, Charles," she repeated. "I am sorry, I of all people should have known what this was costing you. Yet all I've done is wallow in my own misery and forgot what you would be going through. Can you forgive me Bubble?" She called him by his pet childhood name for the first time in nearly fifty years. Her brother responded to its use now by raising his head tiredly, revealing saddened eyes, but before he could speak a cough sounded behind them.

Joey had followed her out and now came around them, "Jilly wants you to come inside Gaffer, she says you need to sleep." His arms stretched out, "Give the boy to me, I'll see to him."

174

Still with a somewhat vacant look about him, and helped by his sister, Charles slowly removed the pillow and stroking the child's lifeless face one last time, passed the tiny bundle over to the younger man, addressing him as he did so, "You know, I wouldn't really have let any harm come to Courtney or Cindy, don't you Joey."

"Course I do, Gaffer, it never crossed my mind otherwise." With that reassurance of his continued loyalty, Joey took the child away. While Charles allowed his sister to escort him to the door of the hotel where Jilly waited for them her face full of concern for her husband.

Liz glanced at her and gave the briefest of nods to indicate that all was well between herself and Charles, then accompanied the couple to the bedroom they had appropriated. In the doorway, Charles turned to them and seeming to have called upon some last inner strength insisted, "Just two hours, then wake me."

"You'll have four and like it, the boys can take care of everything for that time." Past experience told Charles that he couldn't win against his wife whenever she used that particular tone, and anyway he was too tired and worn out to argue, so he simply nodded in acquiesce and entered the room, guiltily aware that he was secretly glad at the thought of the extra two hours of rest.

Chapter 26

Later That Day

He awoke quietly and reluctantly, his body telling him he still needed a lot more sleep, in contrast his mind demanding he get on with what needed to be done. With a sigh of inevitability, he spent a long moment allowing himself to get his head in gear before going over the next part of his plan.

He badly wanted a cup of tea but decided there was no time and as a substitute, raided the mini bar in the fridge for a bottle of orange. How was he going to do this? Looking around the room, he spotted a set of car keys and tried to remember what vehicle he had ended up in last night. The fob said Honda but gave no clue as to registration number.

He squinted hard in concentration and received his reward, ah yes, he remembered a sort of metallic green saloon with a petrol tank half full. That was good, so now all he had to do was to get away from the hotel without being seen.

Opening the door an inch or so slowly and quietly, he peeked out, there was no sign of anyone, he had been half afraid that Jilly would have left someone outside the room to prevent his sleep being disturbed, but the corridor looked all clear, and there was no tell-tale patter of feet to suggest that there was anybody approaching.

Closing the door behind him, he walked quietly down the corridor and through reception without seeing anyone. That was good, though was probably to be expected really, everyone had their jobs to do. Most of those tasks would have taken the survivors away from the hotel for the day and while a few people had work to do around the hotel, none of them would need to be in or around the reception area.

Nevertheless, he stayed in the cover of the front porch as his eyes spanned the car park seeking the Honda. Having located it and with a last look around he walked fast, unlocking the door of the vehicle as he approached, jumped in, and drove quickly away.

He headed to the north of Peterborough, there was a supermarket there that wasn't due for a visit from his work crews until tomorrow morning. En route, he called at his lock up and selected those tools he felt he might need, namely a crowbar and sledge hammer. He was about to leave the lock up that doubled up as an occasional office. When he glanced as he had hundreds of times previously, at the notice board by the door, here a large note bore the words: have you got everything you need. The note was designed to make Charles and his employees, when he had any that is, think carefully about everything they needed before leaving the premises for site.

Seeing it now, he paused for a second then took down a fold away saw bench hanging on the wall, opened it up and using it as a seat sat down in thought. Had he covered everything he could in these first hours. When he had inherited the antidote the previous morning, Benford had identified problem after future problem that the survivors would face. As the various issues mounted up, he had had to accept that he would have to prioritise those tasks he needed to deal with first in those early hours if they were to have any chance to succeed.

He had nearly two hundred survivors in his group, and if his plans worked out those numbers would grow quickly to perhaps as many as four or five hundred within the first twelve months. They would all need food, water, shelter, and security. There would also be a terrible threat to their health posed by the millions of human and animal bodies that would be unburied. Next, it might be supposed that with all the resources of the country at his disposal that food supplies would not be a problem.

Benford thought otherwise. It seemed inevitable that they would lose all power at any moment, followed quickly by loss of a safe water supply. So they would need to find somewhere to live that had access to a natural spring.

It would also need to be in a fairly isolated location so that all human bodies and animal carcasses in the area could be dealt with quickly.

Peterborough was situated on the edge of the fens, an area he felt that without the pumping stations working and with the field drains neglected would eventually revert to real swamp, a consequence of which could be, as in past centuries the place becoming very unhealthy to live in.

From every farm and every allotment, from every supermarket and shop in the country, food was theirs for the taking. But fresh foodstuffs would go off within days and a diet provided by cans and packets only wasn't acceptable. So they had to farm as soon as possible, to ensure a supply of fresh fruit and vegetables.

Fortunately, they had farmers now, but the community needed to move home to a healthier area in which to live. Doing that meant it would take time for those farmers to plant and raise crops on their new land. Benford sighed and rose from his makeshift seat. He was right in his conclusions, he was sure of that, and the most important conclusion he had reached was that their best hope for the future lay in strength of numbers, they had to stick together. The doctors, the farmers, the vets, the teachers, and the builders, they all had to come together and stay together. To make sure that happened there was much he needed to do and all of it fast, then what was he waiting for. Come on, Charles gets with it, now wound up, he returned to the Honda and drove away.

Arriving at the targeted store, he found the sledgehammer acted as a key admirably and entered the premises. Taking a hand basket, he walked around the aisles selecting the goods he needed. A medium sized saucepan was followed by every bottle of green food colouring he could find on the shelves. There were only five of them, and he had hoped for more. No matter, five would have to be enough.

A pair of rubber gloves and then several tubs of 1000 mg oil pills were added to the basket. Looking down at his goods, he gave a grunt of approval and muttered, "This had better work."

He pushed through the rubber swing doors into the warehouse section of the store and located a small office. Here after struggling into the marigolds, he emptied the contents of the colouring into the saucepan and followed them with the oil pills. He stopped when he reckoned, he had at least 1200 capsules.

Then he spent several minutes swirling the contents of the pan around until satisfied that all the pills were thoroughly coated in the green liquid.

Cursing himself, he went back into the store and located another pan and a large food strainer. He drained the liquid of the one pan into the other leaving the oil capsules in the strainer. Cursing again at his lack of foresight, he looked for a way of drying his goods off and for something to put them in other than their original tubs. Unable to think of anything that met with his satisfaction, he settled for tipping them into yet another pan. Then leaving the store and taking both pots and pans with him, drove back to his lock up. The capsules left safe, and the marigolds and other bits dumped, he returned to the hotel. Here, Jilly had discovered him missing and scolded him for going out so quickly.

"Things to do," he muttered. "Now, where's that tea?"

She didn't press him, and he breathed a sigh of relief. He didn't like deceiving people especially Jilly, well, unless it concerned a romance but that was different. This deception though was really necessary. As Charles had made his selections the previous day, he had realised very quickly the confused emotions he would arouse in the survivors.

Gratitude and resentment would be mixed equally in their emotions making his companions feelings toward him ambivalent to say the least.

This mental conflict might well cause individual families to think about leaving the main group. In all probability there would also be those independently minded ones who would underestimate the threats posed to their survival and genuinely feel that they could manage better by themselves.

Farmers especially he knew tended to be an independent lot. Charles on the other hand was absolutely convinced that neither individuals nor small groups could survive alone, and that on the contrary the more people they could bring together the greater the chance of survival for all of them.

He was also convinced that if they stayed together for the first few months, people would quickly come to see the advantages of membership of the community rather than trying to exist as individuals. Charles though was never one to take unnecessary chances and intended to tip the odds his way.

He had demanded a verbal contract of loyalty to the commune as he distributed the lifesaving hypodermics but didn't place too much faith in those promises.

So he had devised his plan. He had told everybody that the antidote comprised not only the two injections, but a follow up pill taken once a month for six months in order to wait out the virus and to maintain their immunity.

So, the harmless oil pills now an unusual bright green colour would become an integral part of the antidote. Charles was certain that no one would take their loved ones away while they thought they still needed the protection the pills gave. By the end of the six months surely everybody would be more settled and see the advantages in being a part of his community, or so he hoped.

Chapter 27

Mike & Maggie's Desperation

Mike allowed the pair to have only a few hours' sleep before again continuing his search for some kind of clue as to what had happened at The Manor prior to his arrival.

Daylight undoubtedly making the task easier to see by, but no more palatable than it had been in the dark last night.

Not just the bodies but the entire house stank beyond belief. This stench together with the cold clammy touch of the corpses proved too much for Maggie who had to run outside for fresh air, and then refused point blank to return to 'that hell hole'. Mike, though irritated by her refusal to help him in their fight for survival, persuaded himself that it was probably for the better, as Maggie who didn't know the real situation might miss some little thing that Mike wouldn't have done.

He gave it six hours, past the time he should have had his second injection of the antidote, then decided that as they were getting nowhere with the searching it was time to adopt his secondary, if chancy, plan of action.

The car they had slept in during the previous night had three quarters of a tank of fuel, so they again swapped their few belongings over and used that one.

Mike droves north to the nearest town but spotting a caravan and camping centre, pulled in to the car park and after smashing his way in, helped himself to a variety of goods. Camping stoves, saucepans, gas canisters and as many sleeping bags as he could cram in, all went into the vehicle before they continued on their route.

Looking now for and finding a good-sized edge of town supermarket, his usual method of opening doors while still effective, on this occasion resulted in an alarm ringing out presumably running from its own power source.

This was both unexpected and irritating but would have to be put up with. It would no doubt eventually go off, and if Mikes worst fears were correct, they would soon have much more to bother about than a bit of noise.

The store had a staff canteen that boasted about a dozen tables and the chairs to go with them. There were toilets at one end of the room separated from the eating area by a small corridor with a door at either end.

There were two cubicles in the gents and three in the ladies. Mike wedged all doors wide open, then piled the dining chairs up in one corner of the staff room and lined the tables up on the other side close to a double sink. Camp beds and sleeping bags were laid on the floor at one end of the room with a now clear express route thru to the toilets.

Under Mike's directions, the camp stoves were set up on the tables with saucepans next to them and spare gas canisters nearby, then they set about piling up as much canned food as the tables could carry. Only tins with ring pulls were collected. Baked beans, soups, rice puddings etc., anything that could be opened and swallowed easily.

Bottles and cans of drinks were situated alongside the beds within easy reach, and more sleeping bags were stored near the piled-up chairs. Now, Mike satisfied they were as prepared as they could be, took time to explain his plan to Maggie.

"So in lay man's terms this thing eats on your insides, it causes vomiting and incredible diarrhoea. You begin to vomit and show blood and then bits of flesh. Eventually, you basically vomit or defecate your insides out and die. What we're going to do is attempt to eat our way out of this, every time we spew up or go for a crap, we eat. Remember that Maggie, get it really registered in there," as he spoke, he tapped the front of her head gently, as though to enforce the message. "Eat, eat every time you let any out. It doesn't matter what it is or whether it's hot or cold just eat and drink, of course. We have to give this thing something to feed on. The virus doesn't live forever, and it may be that if it's got food matter to go at, then it won't attack our bodies. So eat, sleep, throw up, then eat again, hopefully that together with the single dose of antidote we've already had, who knows, we might make it."

Chapter 28

Martin Barnet

Taking a drag on his cigarette, Martin Barnett glanced surreptitiously around the corner. Seeing all was clear, he allowed himself yet another quick swig from the quarter bottle of teachers he produced from his pocket. Leaning back against a wall, he savoured the taste of the golden liquid appreciatively. He couldn't understand Chase's problem with his drinking, it wasn't as if he was a nasty drunk. Actually, it was Martins erroneous opinion that he became quite friendly after he had had a few.

His ex-brother-in-law didn't see it that way though and had made a variety of threats concerning his finding Martin or either of his brothers drinking during working hours. That had really wound Martin up because Chas had also made clear he was going to limit everyone to just two drinks in the evenings as well.

Martin was going through much the same dilemma as his brother Lewis had experienced two days before. It seemed that the whole world was ripe for picking. Anything, everything they wanted was theirs, food, fags, booze, cars, anything. Yet, Charles had made it clear they were going to be very limited as to how much they were to be allowed at any time.

Stupid, the way Chas was behaving, you'd think he was having to pay for it, all stupid gits.

Martin was currently standing in a shopping centre, part of a team of eight men and women tasked with filling up freezer lorries with as much fresh bread and frozen foods as possible. A number of other groups were carrying out similar tasks at other supermarkets and cash and carries around the region.

Charles had particularly emphasised the need for frozen meats and fish, as well as wanting thousands of loaves of bread to be stored in this way. This was the second day of this type of loading work.

Yesterday! Martin shuddered at even the thought of yesterday. What a day of horror that had been, one fright after another in a never-ending nightmare. After they had all met at the hotel and been given their instructions, Martin's team headed up by some mate of Charles had been sent to a supermarket in the south of the city. The streets had been unnaturally almost eerily quiet as the lorries made their way to their destination.

While the mood of the little band of survivors, understandably subdued, did nothing to lift the sombre atmosphere. Martin had wished he had one of his brothers for company, but the three of them had been split up as the duties were handed out. Presumably, Charles, no doubt feeling that the trio could be more easily controlled if each lacked a brother's support.

Surprisingly, the loading had gone well for the first hour. Martin had once been trained as a forklift driver and that skill had been put to good use emptying the large storage freezers in the rear of the premises and transferring the goods to the vehicles.

Then in one of the loading team, some woman whom Martin didn't know had gasped in alarm. Looking up to see what had so startled the woman, Martin saw where three figures had appeared. Two men and a woman, all of whom were visibly suffering the last stages of the awful effects of the virus. No doubt, attracted by the noise of the vehicles arriving, the trio had somehow made their way to the store. All three were covered with dried vomit stains and all smelt terribly of both this and s—t. For Martin and the other survivors, the most awful thing of all was that not one of the pathetic trios spoke. They just stared open mouthed at sight of the eight men and women working as though everything was normal. The three of them had eventually sunk to the floor where they continued to sit staring at the others, still unspeaking. To the survivors there was a sense of accusation about those looks that unsettled them, and one by one they all chose to move away from the area where the dying lay. Martin himself had been the first to retreat to the warehouse proper and stayed with the forklift, those three pathetic bundles both disgusted and frightened him.

Why couldn't they stop at home and die there like everybody else. Being here wasn't right, Martin and his brothers were going to live and that was fine, they had earned their place among the survivors. That day, the day they had delivered the antidote, that day had been another unending effing nightmare with horror following horror. The worst being when he had hit that girl, and then after that what Charles had done.

Martin had seen his ex-brother in laws actions through the rear-view mirror, watched as the life was taken from the girl. He'd wanted to look away, but there was something fascinating about Charles actions that had held him watching spellbound.

That was yesterday, now Tuesday it was different. Today, he felt should be all about the survivors. Everybody had been through enough on that fateful day and now they ought to be left alone to get on with surviving, but instead these three horrors had come along, and their very presence was intimidating. Martin couldn't understand why the others didn't chase them away. That bloke, Charles' mate whose name he couldn't remember but who was in charge of the workers should do something about them, they shouldn't be here.

Towards the end of the shift, he had sneaked back into the store proper to have a quick look at the trio again and was even more unsettled. Two of the three had died and lay where they fell in their own mess. The remaining zombie had disappeared, and Martin had whipped around looking behind him, looking everywhere. The other one must be around close by, there was no way he, was it he? Yes, one of the males was missing and he couldn't have gone far.

Now thoroughly rattled, Martin looked around for his fellow survivors, but there was no one in sight, everyone still avoiding this area. He was scared now, convinced that the missing man was watching him from somewhere waiting to jump out on him. The fact that the poor wretch was in no condition to be a threat to him or anyone else didn't register.

All sense had left the big man and he ran aimlessly, finally ending up back in the warehouse, skidding to a stop as the others turned to stare at his sudden arrival. "You alright?" The leader whose name still escaped him had asked.

"Yeah." Martin had been uncomfortably aware that the others knew he had been alarmed by something and had guessed what it was that had spooked him.

All that had been yesterday, today he had been detailed to a different supermarket and there were none of those spectres left alive now. Not that the lack of life mattered though, these vast buildings devoid now of human life had a really eerie feel to them anyway.

Anyway, today his priorities had changed. Last night, Charles had lain down a number of rules, some of which involved looting, which was ridiculous. Here, they were taking anything and everything they wanted or at least what Charles said they wanted. Mainly fresh bread, meat, and fish and all the frozen foods they could lay their hands on. All this were being loaded into freezer lorries that were apparently to be left running as mobile fridge freezers for months, using fuel that they were just helping themselves to. Yet, according to Chas they were not to help themselves to alcohol or flags. Those were to be collected at a later date only when the foodstuffs had been saved and would then be issued as a limited daily ration. Well, he could stuff that idea, Martin was in a shopping centre packed with booze and fags that were free, and if Charles Benford thought that Martin wasn't going to benefit from that then he must be as stupid as Martin had always thought he was.

Not that the big man was daft enough to let Charles or anyone else catch him, he had waited until he was left for a brief moment then helped himself to just two quarter bottles of whisky and a similar number of cigarette packets. Then exiting the front of the store and turning right along the mall, he had ended up in what had been a food hall. There was a large glass covered area that looked out over neighbouring housing estates and he was pleased to note that a pedestrian door opened to the outside where he could smoke undetected. After that life wasn't so bad, he would work for thirty or forty minutes then slope away for a smoke and a couple of swigs and then back to work. Everything was going fine, although unrecognised by Martin himself, he was gradually becoming drunk. A third quarter bottle had replaced one of the earlier ones and as the alcohol took effect, he became ever more resentful of Charles and his rules. He turned to go back to work when a movement over towards the housing estates caught his eye. His first thought was that it was another of those bloody zombies from yesterday and he was about to head back to the others, but a second look toward where he had seen the movement made him pause. Then he was running, Martin was a big and very overweight man in poor physical condition, and he was well on his way to being drunk. So, his progress was slow but nevertheless determined and he kept his eye on his target all the way, sure of what he had seen, despite the target wandering further away from where he had first spotted his quarry. Totally out of puff, he went over a last dip in the ground and there she was. He had been correct, a girl of about two- or three-years old wandering about aimlessly and crying her eyes out. A survivor, he swept her up, while mouthing anything that came to mind that might serve to quieten the child. Nothing worked but he held her close to him and continued to try to soothe her in his own clumsy way. That was when he saw both the lake and the way to solve the problem of his brother-in-law.

An hour later, the child was in Jilly's arms and finally quiet as Martin made his report to Charles. "I'd just gone outside for some fresh air; I'd been feeling a bit sick like. Then, I just saw the girl wandering about between the houses and the lake. I tried calling to her, but I don't suppose she heard me, then she fell in the water. I knew she'd drown, so I ran across really fast and just dived in to save her without thinking, the waters really deep there, you know." His well-rehearsed tale left nothing out that would help to make sure everyone understood that Martin was a hero.

Charles, certainly seemed impressed as he squeezed the hero's arm and said, "Well done Martin, well done mate." That worthy basked in the limelight, this was wonderful and almost worth the cold shock he'd received when he had held the girl in his arms and jumped into the lake.

The real bonus he knew would be that as long as Charles who adored all children thought that Martin had saved a child's life, he would forever cut him a great deal of slack. The only fly in the ointment was that every time Martin went near the girl, she screamed and tried to back away from him. Even the insensitive Martin knew this would seem pretty strange behaviour from someone whose life he had saved however young she was.

Still from the moment he had arrived back at the shopping centre dripping wet and shivering, he had drunk whisky openly (just to warm him through) and nobody had attempted to criticise him. Yes, all in all it had been a good day's work, if only that girl would just give him an odd smile once in a while, instead of shying away from him.

Chapter 29

Maggie's Departure

At the supermarket, Maggie while she had been kept busy with the tasks given her had seemed to awaken from the black mood that had gripped her ever since she had managed to stop vomiting after receiving the antidote.

Now though she sank again into a morose silence, laying on the camp bed and staring into a nothingness, alone with her thoughts.

Her companion who had given up his own antidote to save her life, found her attitude both annoying and potentially awkward, afraid that if she did too much thinking his cover story wouldn't hold up. So consequently, he felt aggrieved at her attitude. But knowing how crucial morale could prove to be in their attempt to survive, he was desperate to raise hers and tried to involve her in conversations apart from that concerning their own situation.

Being dog tired himself and continuing to receive little or no response, he eventually gave up and slept. Eight hours later and thirty-six hours after he should have taken his second capsule, Mike Wilkinson awoke and threw up for the first time.

He immediately drank a bottle of lucozade and ate a plate of beans that Maggie heated up for him on their camp stove. He kept both down for an hour before the process was repeated, after the fifth bout and assisted by a handful of assorted pills, he managed to gain some respite by falling asleep.

As soon as he was, and pretty sure that if he was to awake, he would be in no condition to follow her, Maggie rose from her own bed and taking the car keys from Mike's jacket, sparing him a last glance and quietly left the store.

As they had left The Manor the previous day, Maggie had tried to keep track of the various twists and turns they took as they had journeyed to the supermarket from where she had eventually parted from Mike.

Despite this act of attempted navigation, she still managed to lose her way twice in the Bocage countryside of the South downs. Only as she was about to give up did she finally spot the pretty cottage that she had used as a marker and managed to find her way back.

Driving as close to the steps leading to the door as she could, she turned to Dalglish who was curled into a ball on the back seat, and calling him, she slipped a leash over his head and made him accompany her.

The animal, disliking the smell of death mingled with that of vomit and excreta whined his objection and attempted to pull back.

It was those same smells together with the awful sights that accompanied them that Maggie dreaded, and she crouched to whisper encouragement to the dog, determined that she would not enter the house alone.

During the past couple of miles, she had been aware of a slight feeling of nausea overtaking her and realised she probably had only a few hours before she would once again be racking her life away.

That she would die she had little doubt, but it was because of that slight doubt that she was now here.

Maggie Keenan was nobody's fool, the daughter of an Irish boxer who had made the Scottish Highlands his home and a Yorkshire mother who had died after giving birth to Maggie's youngest sister, she had inherited all the charm and logic of one and the sound common sense of the other.

Now, though she had never met any of Charles Benford's survivors, she was experiencing the same gamut of emotions that they had.

In the past three days, she had doubted first her sanity, then her sense of reality. Like Benford's survivors, she found the immensity of what had happened to her, to the world was just too enormous to take in. The deaths of her sister and family, followed by the realisation that the entire population of her village were also gone had been too much for her emotions to cope with. As a result, sections of her mind had shut down in an effort to protect her, allowing her body to function automatically, without her brain really absorbing most of what was going on around her.

On the trip south with Mike, she had remained in this trance like state, had seen the empty streets, the immobile vehicles, the lack of any form of human life. Had seen them and knew the why, but without really registering it.

She had listened as her companion had attempted to enlarge on his story of being a government agent, who had been attempting to foil the plotters intentions, but tragically failing. At the time, she had just accepted the tale without question.

It was on their earlier visit to The Manor that she had emerged from the trauma induced trance. The dozens of bodies in the building, many of whose faces she recognised from the media, and who in many cases were obviously with their spouses shocked her into awareness. Mikes frantic need to search those bodies for clues as to what had happened to the occupants helped to concentrate her mind.

As she started to think, it was inevitable that she should also start to question things. It was also just as inevitable that she should reach the conclusion that her saviour had lied to her. Mike Wilkinson was no spook; she was certain of that. The years spent serving behind a bar, listening to men and women talk, telling their life stories, telling tall stories, or just plain gossip, drunk or sober, together they had given her an insight into people that was rarely wrong.

No, Mike was no government agent, but he was certainly a greatly troubled man, and he obviously had intimate knowledge of what had happened in the past days. What about The Manor? Again, the people there were certainly VIPs' but with the exception of a couple of Parliamentarians, they were not government. By the time they had left the place after that first visit, Maggie was somewhat distrustful of her companion and had tried to extract what information she could from him without arousing his own suspicions.

Wilkinson had been guarded in his answers but distracted by his need to find a way of saving the two of them from the virus, wasn't really suspicious of her motives. Perhaps, that combined with his attention thus diverted, his answers had lacked the conviction they needed to support his lies.

So Maggie had returned to The Manor, determined to find the truth of what Mike had been involved in and had made up her mind that if she was to die it would not be with someone who had lied to her. Not that she actually had any idea that Wilkinson was behind or involved in the Conspiracy, just that she felt he was not the man he claimed to be.

So now forcing herself to hold her gorge down at the smells, she steeled herself to touch the dreadful corpses.

Rifling through wallets and handbags, mimicking Wilkinson's efforts of a day earlier, she steadily searched for clues. It was Sir Harmer Evans daughter Rebecah who gave her the lead she needed. Becky had had a bad time of it and had been both terrified and in great pain as she died.

Toward the end during a brief respite from the cramps in her insides, she had sought solace in the arms of her fiancé. TC had rebuffed her, and Becky left with no one to comfort her had instead written a note to her father. There were only a few paragraphs and Becky had had no knowledge of the conspiracy beforehand but what she had written was proof enough that the people here in The Manor were the British end of just such a plot. As she died, the girl had slumped to the floor and in doing so upended the small table where she had deposited the note that now fell underneath her.

Wilkinson, not recognising the girl either for a conspirator or for who she really was had ignored her during his night search. Recognising her the following day and therefore knowing that she hadn't been an active part of the conspiracy he had still ignored her.

Maggie on the other hand had seen the body of someone who had plainly been a lovely looking girl, lying in her own soil. Her legs having been drawn up into the feotal position in her agony, revealed her underwear, leaving her in a somewhat obscene manner. Moved to pity by the sight even amid all this other death, Maggie lacking the strength to move the girl's body had tried to at least make her look more dignified by moving her limbs and straightening her clothes.

In doing so, she had discovered the brief note. Appalled by what she had read, she dropped the note and keeping a firm hold on the dogs lead hurriedly left the building. She thought first of her sister and her family and then of her other friends and relations all now dead in Scotland, then of Wilkinson lying helpless on the floor of a supermarket.

She could return and kill him, punish him for his part in the scheme, though she was still unsure of just what his part had actually been. Instead, she pointed the car north, she would leave the man to live or die as fate decreed. For her part, she would return home to Scotland if she survived long enough, there she would die alongside her family. She would make no attempt to simulate Wilkinson's efforts to survive, and in doing so, condemned to live in a world virtually devoid of other human life.

The cramps started as she joined the M25 and from then on, she had to stop every half an hour or so to throw up. She thought of stopping and finding somewhere to die more comfortably, but she longed for home, and even though she knew she would never make it she preferred to die trying.

She had never been this far south before and had no idea of her best route home. She was pretty sure that she should take a motorway but without a map she had no idea which. Wilkinson had used the A1 on their journey south and she knew that ran from London to Edinburgh, and so to familiar territory. So, she chose this ancient roadway to make her dash for the highlands and home.

Somewhere north of Huntingdon the car ran out of petrol, by that time she was past caring and lacked both strength and inclination to try and obtain another vehicle.

Instead, she started to walk, concentrating on placing one foot in front of the other, then repeating the process again and again, step bring feet together, step bring feet together, step, again, again and again.

Dalglish walked beside her, tail, and ears down, whining softly. She ignored the animal, intent only on going home one staggering step after another.

Chapter 30

Robbie in Scotland

"You're right, it does always rain here."

"Yeah, it does come down a lot. I think, I read somewhere that it's one of the wettest parts of the country, but isn't it beautiful with it?" Robbie risked a quick glance across at Mai Lee as he spoke. Of necessity it had to be a quick look because the rain was absolutely lashing down, lifting the wipers of the windscreen, and making driving along the windy highland road extremely difficult enough, without the added hazard of taking his eyes off the road.

His girlfriend raised her hand to her brow in mock exaggeration as she attempted to see anything other than the rain beating against the car.

"Oh yeah, I see what you mean it's lovely, isn't it? You must bring me here again; I've been missing the monsoons."

He playfully pretended to reach out in an attempt to slap her, "Instead of taking the urine, have you now got that sat nav sorted yet, I've lost all idea of where we are. I'm just driving blind at the moment."

"Yes, I've put the address in, it's just acquiring satellites at the moment, be patient." She watched the screen that was held in her hand for a few more seconds, before, "Ah, here we are, you've got to take the next left." Her words coincided with the machines voice over confirming her instruction.

"Now, tell me the real reason for us coming up here on this, what is it you people call it, a wild duck chase."

"Goose, not duck. And I've told you, Dad thinks that if any of the nuke subs are at sea, and I think there is always one out, then if they stay under water long enough, there's a good chance they could survive. If that is the case, then they'll return to their base at Faslane. Which is a bloody great naval base hiding somewhere around here. Well, it is according to my female navigator." He rolled his eyes in playful mockery, "So please keep your eyes alert." He took his own advice peering hard in every direction before continuing, "When we do finally get there, Dad wants us to leave messages for the crew directing them to us. I don't know how many there are on those boats but probably over a hundred, and a hundred fit young blokes would be a great help to us."

Mai Lee gave an impish grin as she replied, "A hundred fit young men, oh yeeess, I could settle for that."

They both laughed at her saucey joke then resumed their attempts to spot their destination. Robbie, despite the weather condition was enjoying himself. Until the rain had started a little over an hour ago, they had had a good run up to Scotland. He had deliberately chosen the longer route of using the A1 rather than cutting across to the motorways, because he felt the eastern side was prettier. Robbie was guiltily aware that he should be feeling very sombre and all that, but he was a young man going for a drive up to Scotland with a bird he thought was drop dead gorgeous, and since he had his choice of vehicles, he was in a smart BMW. The day had been lovely and sunny in the south as they left, and he was away from all that had gone on over the past two days.

How would one day describe those two days, incredible, horrific, mind numbing. There was nothing he could think of that actually fitted the events of that terrible period. First, there had been his dad's almost unbelievable telephone call concerning the antidote and the killer bug it was supposed to cure. He wouldn't have accepted what his father was telling him as being true from anybody other than the man himself. Even then it took some believing.

Next had been the horrors of the deliveries, and he had missed what were probably the worst of those incidents, all that had been followed the next day by trying to organise the frightened and confused survivors into working parties. Most of them unwilling to commence work until they had visited the homes of friends and relations; desperate to find people alive despite all the evidence to the contrary. So when his father had asked him to go on this mission to the north, combining the visit to Faslane with the leaving of messages painted on to a number of shop windows across southern Scotland, Robbie had jumped at the opportunity and taken his girlfriend Mai Lee with him. He had ignored his dad's advice though on transport. Charles had suggested taking a caravanette so that he could carry plenty of food and petrol supplies, as well as giving him somewhere to sleep. Instead, Robbie had gone with the beamer, much more fun, but he was now realised that dad had been right, the van thingy would have given him a loo and shower etc. As it was, the two of them were going to have to sleep on the front seats of the car. The boot and rear seats taken up with cans of petrol, water, food, paints, and brushes etc.; not only taking up a lot of space but with an unpleasant smell of petrol and paint.

Still, it was good to be away, and Robbie was a natural cheery type so what the hell, they'd manage one way or another.

Another ten minutes and Robbie already hopelessly lost (bl---y stupid sat nav's) had no choice but to pull over, the rain now being so fierce that visibility was nil. This latest downpour fortunately seemed to be the storms last finale and within the hour the rain had stopped altogether. The pair of travellers were now able to move on long before that, and with the improved visibility had made better time than previously. A good highway led to a roundabout that signposted Garelochead to the south of their position, whereas Robbie was pretty sure that it was supposed to have been to the north.

Having more confidence in the local authorities' knowledge of what was where than he had in his map reading skills, he followed the signs and was soon driving through the town's main st that eventually ran alongside Gare loch on one side and some rather upmarket homes on the other. Quite taken with the view, it came as a slight shock to suddenly come across the high security fencing topped with razor wire that announced they had reached their destination. They passed two small entrances that Robbie was pretty sure wouldn't lead to the base proper and he passed them by and after another few hundred yards arrived at the North and main entrance to the infamous Faslane naval base.

Robbie had visited several military bases over the years in connection with building work, so he was well aware of the type of security checks that were the norm before being allowed entry to the camps.

To now drive into a nuke submarine base without anyone attempting to stop him was weird. Not that entry was easy, whatever had taken place on the base during the visit of the killer bug, someone had followed his or her duty to the full and the gates were fully secured.

This was one of the things that Robbie had planned for, and a petrol driven stihl cutter with diamond blade allowed entry after only a few moments work.

Leaving the car and carrying paint and brushes the two of them entered the base and made their way to the waterfront, Robbie was becoming increasingly uncomfortable as they did. It was probably just the eerie quietness of the base, but he had an overwhelming certainty that they were being watched and kept turning around seeking the observer.

His companion was experiencing no such feelings and found his nervousness at first amusing, then annoying, and finally his repeated sudden jerks as he tried to spot their watcher, unsettling.

"Stop it Robbie, you're making me nervous now."

"Sorry, but can't you feel it. I'm sure there's someone else here apart from us." Mai Lee tried to keep a grip and pointed over to the towering blocks of what she assumed were the married quarters that dominated their view to the south.

"It's those places Robbie. They're full of the dead, it just makes for a horrible atmosphere; just paint the message and let's leave."

They figured out where they thought the boats would moor if any returned and painted messages on the sides of buildings in as large as letters as they could manage. Robbie continuing to twist and turn constantly still convinced they were being watched and becoming more irritable by the minute, as a result his nervousness was seemingly infectious. As they finally finished the work both left the paints and brushes where they were and almost ran back to the car. From behind a parked fuel lorry across the way, a pair of eyes followed their every move, ensuring that the couple had left the base before their owner walked across to view what the visitors had written on the walls.

Chapter 31

Geoff Fitzjohn

"Why, I don't get it, why are we doing this?" Tom Hughes panted as he looked up at the guy he was working with. Geoff Fitzjohn dropped his end of the load and stood up straightening his back and sighing at the slight relief it gave him in doing so.

Geoff was far too old to be doing this type of work hour after hour. In fact, he had never been the right age for this type of work. "I don't know, it seems daft to me as well."

He looked down in distaste at the latest body they were carrying between them, then glanced over his shoulder at another couple busily working away in a similar manner.

"I'm pretty sure Niall doesn't know either, but I can tell you this we're supposed to go to two other places after this as well."

"What, doing this same thing?" The others disgust was more than obvious as he spoke.

"Yeah, I overheard Niall speaking last night to that mate of his, the black guy. He said we were going down to somewhere near Chichester and then on to Cornwall. But there's not supposed to be so many bodies at either of them." "Ready to lift on two, two lifts," he commanded and both men heaved the body onto the back of a drop side truck where it joined a growing number of others.

"Well, perhaps we should refuse to go," Hughes tried to inject an amount of belligerence into his voice but couldn't hide the nervousness he felt in suggesting.

Fitz looked over at the speaker, Hughes looked to be around the same age as his own, sixty-three years maybe even a little older and was plainly feeling the hard work. Both men along with four others had left Peterborough on that first day with hardly a chance to say goodbye to their families, or to mourn their dead friends and relations.

Looking back on it now, Fitz wondered how he had come to agree to go, leaving his family behind at such a time. He assumed it must have been a combination of the fear and confusion they all felt that had allowed them all to be bullied into acquiesce by Charles Benford.

Whatever it had caused them to comply, they had driven over to a stately home on the North Norfolk coast near Wells on sea. The house stood at the centre of a large estate that included both shops and a hotel, as well as farms and any number of houses.

Once arrived, Niall had set them to work, systematically clearing the bodies from all the buildings. Off the estate, a commandeered JCB had been used to dig a mass grave, or rather a mass pyre that was to be lit as soon as all the bodies were in place. The work was heart-breaking as well as grisly. Fitz particularly hated handling the children. He was a father and grandfather himself and there was an unforgettable indecency about casting a child's body onto a heap of others like so many sacks of vegetables. It wasn't right, it would never be right, but then what did that matter now. A world had died, and now little would ever be right again.

Nevertheless, although he had never been a religious man, Fitz muttered a little prayer to himself every time they added another body to the pile.

"We must be needed in Peterborough," Hughes continued, his moaning breaking into Fitzes' thoughts. "And anyway, we should be with our families at the moment, not doing something as pointless as this."

The two men had walked back towards the row of smart red brick terraced homes that Fitz guessed must be two hundred years or more old. Once, no doubt very much sought after but now acting as just so many mortuaries.

Fitz braced himself to face the now familiar smell of death again as he entered the house they were working on before replying to his companion. "We had our second injection yesterday morning, now we have to take a capsule every month for six months. Are you going to go back to Charles, the man who has those capsules, and who saved our families and tell him where to shove his orders? Because I'm not."

Hughes ignored the comment since the answer was obvious and turned instead to the next corpse. This one, a woman probably ten years older than his own wife, and who had evidently lived here together with her husband who they had deposited onto their makeshift hearse earlier that morning.

"I'd still like to know what we're doing this for though," and he continued, "You reckon we've got to do this in other places as well, it doesn't make any sense."

Fitz let him drone on, he couldn't see any sense in what they were doing either, or although related to Charles by marriage, he wasn't a great lover of their self-appointed saviour/leader. Not that that Benford had ever done him any harm, and the two had always rubbed along well enough when they met, but there was just something about the bloke he wasn't keen on.

Now he owed his life to the man, and not just his life but his wife's and son's as well. So, now he would be forever indebted to someone he didn't completely trust. "Lift," he commanded, and the woman joined her husband again. Fitz thought again of his own wife Betty and longed to be back home with her. She would be missing him as well, the two of them rarely apart for more than a few hours.

"Oh come on, let's get on with this pointless shit and get home."

Further down the row of houses, Niall looked towards the two men, he guessed what their conversation would be about and sympathised with them. Like the others, Niall wanted nothing more than to be back home with his own family. When his father had informed him of what he wanted done, Niall had come close to refusing him. Charles' blunt refusal to even explain why he wanted the tasks carried out hadn't made things any easier. In the end, it was remembering an earlier conversation of that morning that had made the son acquiesce to his father's wish.

After all the antidotes had been distributed and before Charles had despatched his lieutenants to pick up the freezer trucks and buses that they required, Charles had taken time to explain more fully some of his thoughts about the dangers facing them and how he proposed to deal with them. His father had spoken for more than an hour, listing all kinds of hazards to come, so many that now Niall could recall only a few of them, as Charles had reeled of problems with food, water, power and heating supplies, diseases of all kinds, wild dog packs, changing landscapes, and climate, river flooding's etc. and explained why and how these things would become problems. Niall had marvelled at how his father had been able to visualise these things while simultaneously he had battled to put together a list of those chosen to survive. Not only that, he also had had to plan how to both distribute the antidote to those people, while at the same time avoiding those trying to take it from him, both friend and foe.

It was this then, coupled with a lifetimes trust in his father's judgment that had finally overrode his desire to remain with his partner and their children and sent him off on this awful task.

Awful hardly covered it, some of these people had been dead for nearly four days now and for people, who in most cases had hardly ever seen a dead body before, and even then, normally only when that body had been prepared by a mortician. What they were faced with now was horrific.

His father had suggested that they might find as many as a hundred bodies on the estate and thought it would take no more than a single day to deal with them. Well, this was day three and the count was already at one hundred and seventy-one.

He thought ahead to their next destination, a marina near Chichester and a Manor House on a headland in Cornwall. Charles had assured his son that both places would have been almost deserted at the time the virus struck, so would contain only a handful of corpses between them. Well, he hoped his dad's guestimate of those would be closer than this one had been. Either way, the question in his head remained, why?

He knew that dad was planning to remain at The Manor hotel for about three or four days. While the village of Kingsthorpe was cleared of bodies and prepared for the survivors, they would then live at Kingsthorpe for some weeks, perhaps even months, while they were busy gathering all the various types of supplies, they would need for the future.

Charles reckoned that their local knowledge of the shops, supermarkets and garages etc. would allow the acquisition of those supplies a lot faster if it were done in Peterborough than it would be in a strange area where they possessed little or no local knowledge of these places.

At the same time as the stores were being put together, other members of the community would be in the peak district preparing the villages that were to be their permanent homes.

So again, why was dad so determined to have these other places cleared of bodies now? He half grinned and half sighed to himself as he reflected that no doubt, all would be clear in time, he hoped.

Chapter 32

Fish and Chips

"I have an idea," Debbie Freeman turned to look at her husband Dave, who knowing that tone of voice from years of experience recognised that it meant some sort of problem for him. So, promptly dropped his head and tried to sidle towards the door as if he hadn't heard. "No, don't mess about Dave, this is a good idea and it's something you and I could do for everybody quiet easily."

Resigned to his fate, her husband shrugged his shoulders and with an exaggerated sigh and trying to put as little enthusiasm into his voice as he could manage, replied with a simple, "Well."

Used to his ways, Charles Benford's older sister put her arms around her husband of forty-five years and gave him a peck on his cheek.

Taking his hand, she drew him to the window of the hotel bedroom they were living in until the move to Kingsthorpe took place. "Look at them, Dave." In response to his wife's instruction Dave glanced outside to where a minibus had just drawn up, disgorging a work crew returning from yet more loading up of lorries. A half dozen men and women all looking tired out after a twelve-hour shift, though Debbie knew that it wasn't just the physical work that was draining people. Morale amongst the survivors was low and dropping by degrees every day. The arrival of a young man the previous evening, the first natural survivor to have joined them had raised spirits temporarily. Since his arrival though, he had done nothing but lay on a bed recovering from whatever personal trauma he had been through. This understandable but immediate disappearance of the man meant that the slight rise in morale his arrival had triggered didn't last long. For a short while, hope had been raised that there was a real chance that things weren't as bleak as first thought.

Maybe loved ones living away had survived, more people would come in, the young, the fit, surely there was hope. This young lad had survived, then there was the girl saved from drowning yesterday, it showed there were survivors, so there must be a chance for their loved ones.

The hope was no more than a temporary blip, both reality and the long faces that reality brought with it had soon returned. Obviously, everybody was in mourning and fearful of what the future held for them. Though in Debbie's opinion it wasn't these major dramas that were pulling people down during the working day, no, those type of nightmares came in the dark as she lay in bed and thought of the people that she had lost, of the world she'd lost and of what horrors awaited her children and grandchildren in the years to come. And as those fears arrived in the dark, she like everybody else had to deal with them in whatever way she could.

You worried, you talked to your partner or whoever and because there were so few answers to anything you eventually fell asleep, then come the morning, you put a brave face on for other people, and got on with things.

It was the daytimes that ground the people down, little things, mainly the unnatural silence, wherever you went, everywhere you went, there was no noise except those that you or your companions made. There was obviously no traffic, no aeroplanes overhead, no distant sirens, no radios or other music playing. Machinery didn't hum, even nature seemed to have taken against them. It was May and the weather was lovely with no wind, therefore, to rustle through the tree branches, birds seemed to have sensed that something was terribly wrong and had absented themselves, and even the dogs no longer seemed to bark.

Even the noises the people made themselves weren't right. Everybody insisted on communicating with one another in whispers as though to talk in a normal tone risked offending the dead. They could have played music, but no one did. Everyday idle gossip, the sort that goes on all the time between friends was totally absent. Most communication between people was confined to a series of grunts and monosyllables.

After just a short while this quiet would grow oppressive and Debbie was sure this was one of the main reasons for the despair that could be seen on the faces of so many members of the community.

She explained her plan to her husband who despite his earlier reluctance listened closely and gradually allowed himself a half smile. Finished explaining she paused and asked, "Well, what do you think?"

Her husband reached out and pulled her to him for a little hug, "I used to think I had married the clever one in the family, now I realise it was the one who likes to make me work."

She gave him another peck on his cheek and muttered, "But." This time Daves grin lit up his entire face. "Why not, let's give it a try, you'll have to talk to Charles, and we'll probably need a mechanic to get it started, but yeah let's do it."

Now full of enthusiasm, his wife crossed to the door, "I'll go and ask Charles now and see if it's okay, be back in a minute and we'll work out the details."

As she walked away her husband allowed himself another private smile and wondered, how long it might be before Debbie realised that for the first time in her life, she was going to ask little brother for permission to do something that she wanted to do. Well done, Charles, the thought entered his mind, wish I could find the secret of how to do that sometime.

A crew of twelve were working in the Tesco supermarket the following day, loading yet another lorry with provisions when a racket of doo dah doo dah rang loud and clear from the car park. The sound repeated and again demanding investigation from the workers in the store.

Emerging outside, the twelve were confronted by the open doors of a large van bearing the logo 'something's fishy' on either side and accompanied by the marvellous smell of fish and chips cooking.

A beaming Dave yelled, "Come on then there's fish or sausages and plenty of chips but we are only here for twenty minutes, then we're off to Asda and Waitrose. Plenty of people wanting fish and chips, so come on let's be having you, beats stale sandwiches and pork pies that are going over."

Debbie was proved correct, as the two visited the various sites of their fellow workers. The stir they created in the survivors was immediately noticeable. Men and women sitting around in the glorious May sunshine commenting on and even laughing at the welcome and unexpected treat.

A treat that only days before wouldn't have warranted a second thought, but today brought a welcome air of near normality with it. Later that evening, the van was parked outside the survivor's hotel where the younger people that had missed out during the day could go and get a pile of chips served in of all thing's newspaper. It caused Sean to fall about laughing and calling, "Come and see Mummy, come and see, Auntie Debs is putting her chips in newspaper, it makes them taste good though." He added as he savoured a particularly chunky one.

By the end of the evening, a very tired Debbie turned to her equally exhausted husband with a grin a mile wide, "Well, that went really great, didn't it?"

"Yes, you're a very clever wifey, now tell me how having retired from a chip shop that I had run for most of my working life, two years ago, a very nice shop I might add, with a staff that knew what they were doing and between them did most of the hard work,

"I now find myself driving about in a mobile van having to work my unmentionables of. Not only that but I'm doing it in a van that I've stolen from Bill Purdy an old mate of mine, huh." He finished in mock reproach as he gave his wife a hug.

She brushed his cheeks with her lips as she replied, "Have we stolen it, I don't think we can actually steal things now, can we? Because surely we now own everything between us." She paused to think about the unintended truth behind that statement and causing an immediate sobering of both their moods. Then more seriously now continued,

"Anyway, Charles suggests that we train Sally and Mai Lee up in how to use the van so that we can share shifts. Charles seems to be really tickled by the whole idea." Then after thinking about her last sentence added, "I'm pleased about that, I wanted to do something for him, something to show our support if you understand what I mean."

"Yeah, I know what you mean, and I do agree with you. But don't you worry about doing things for your brother, I've known him long enough to know he won't be slow to ask for what he wants." Husband and wife looked at one another in silent agreement. Debbie's brother had never been shy of inviting people to join his schemes in the past, sometimes with disastrous endings financially, that was before the plague had come and the world had changed. Though the way Charles had taken charge of the situation and expected everyone to just follow his lead regardless had all the hall marks of his past behaviour. Thoughts of what some of his ideas might consist of now caused both to cease their joking and make their way inside the hotel for a well-earned rest.

Chapter 33
Little Hero

Sean was enjoying himself, for three, or was it four days, he had played in the adventure centre with the other children. In the past, he had only ever gone there as a special treat. He loved the equipment, tubular slides, soft ball pit, climbing apparatus cat walks, was that the right word? Anyway, it had all been great.

Then he had discovered for the first time in his young life that you can have too much of a good thing.

He wanted a change, he had been on that swing, slid down that slide and that tunnel a hundred times, climbed that frame so often he could have scaled it in his sleep. Then he heard that this was the day they were all going to move to Kings something and that they were all going to live in caravans and have horses and dogs and all sorts of things. Sean was determined to see this wonderful place as quickly as possible, especially if he could get to see it before Affy and Endy, his older sisters.

He begged his Grampa, Charles first, hugging him and telling him how much he loved his Grampa, then asking for what he wanted. It worked as he and Grampa both knew it would, and having received Gramps consent, if he could persuade someone to allow him to accompany them, he could go. So his uncle, Robbie who Sean knew had just returned from a trip somewhere was the next to suffer his nephews charm offensive.

Robbie only last night having returned to the hotel after carrying out his Scottish mission for his father was spending the day towing the last of the sixty plus caravans needed to house the entire survivor population across to Kingsthorpe and grinning to himself at his five-year old's nephews serious offer of help in the task, allowed him to go along.

Sean was particularly intrigued to drive along the empty roads, his sisters kept telling him that everybody in the world was dead except them. And Sean knew they were right because he had checked with his mummy who knew everything, but he didn't really understand what that meant. The five-year-old had been brought up in a world of TV where people were regularly killed in one film only to appear in another days later. He played games with his friends in which people were killed and simply counted to one hundred, or in Sean's case only to ten because he ran out of both fingers and patience after that and then you came alive again. It was all very well, Affy telling him that did not happen in real life, but Sean could still not really accept the concept. So, the boy found it intriguing that there was no traffic on the roads, no pedestrians walking about, and had tasked himself to spot one or the other before the day was out.

The child chuckled as he watched the lady walk funny and then fall over.

He liked the way she simply fell flat on her face without making any attempt to save herself, just sort of went plonk. He thought he might try and do that tonight in front of his friends, they'd be sure to find it funny as well and he'd be the gang leader for the evening.

Robbie and his passenger had been on a flyover crossing of the A1 when Sean had seen the woman some thirty feet below them. So consequently out of Robbie's eyesight, his uncle heard his nephews laugh but was distracted by thoughts of his own, so it was moments later before he asked him what was so funny. When the boy told him about the funny lady and the way she walked, he assumed at first that he was referring to something from his past and took little notice for a while longer. It wasn't until the child announced, "I told Affy that not everybody was dead," that Robbie pulled over onto the grass verge and questioned the boy.

"Sean, when did you see this lady?"

"Just now."

"You mean just a few moments ago?"

"Yes."

"Where did you see her?" He couldn't keep the urgency from his voice and was aware that his questioning was bringing a cloud to his nephew's face. The child was afraid that he had said something wrong. "Where Sean, where did you see her?"

"Near Extra." The word was used as the name of the service station area that Maggie and Mike had paused near on their way south a few days previously, and where at the time Maggie had thought she had seen movement. Robbie gave his nephew a speculative look. Sean had a vivid imagination and loved to play games, but! Making a U turn in the road was not an easy thing to do with the caravan attached but Robbie managed it and drove back the short distance to Extra. If his nephew had really seen a woman then she must be another of the one in twenty thousand who had a natural immunity to the virus. They had already had three others come in from the local areas and this one would bring the total population of the group up to 197, as each one arrived, the rise in the community's morale was amazing. Each newcomer's very existence seeming to promise that there was still a functioning world out there and that their own little group of survivors was not the only hope for humans.

They reached Extra, and Robbie slowed peering about him, "No, not here it was over there on the bottom road." Sean pointed over toward the A1.

Twenty minutes later, Robbie, doctor Showandra and Charles were gathered around an unconscious Maggie. Robbie's father was puzzled by her very existence and explained his reasoning to the Doctor.

"She hasn't had the antidote, so she should have been dead at least three days ago, unless she is one of the lucky few. But if she is one of those then why is she now ill." Continuing himself before anyone else could answer, "Or does this mean that the other survivors might still go down with the bug."

"I don't know," Ursula Showandra shrugged. "This is all beyond anything that I or any other GP has ever experienced. The only way we'll know is if she pulls through, and right now that doesn't look very likely."

Charles reached into his pocket and extracted a small package. Five days earlier, when he had won possession of the antidote, the box had been designed to hold two hundred doses of two. At that time, four complete double sets and three other single syringes had been missing.

Charles himself had left two complete doses behind with the bodies of the conspirators for the authorities to find. That had left him with 191 complete doses and three single capsules.

He had combined two of these to make up a whole and had wondered what to do with the odd half dose. The obvious thing seemed to be to give it to someone and allow the individual to take their chances.

Charles had felt unable to do that, had found the very idea of it repulsive. Fortunately, for him the decision had never had to be made, Joey's sister, Courtney was seven months pregnant. Charles knew that the virus would remain alive for the best part of a month at least, if Courtney was to give birth prematurely while the virus was still active, would her baby have inherited sufficient immunity from its mother? Unable to be sure either way, Charles had decided to hold onto the single remaining capsule in case of need. He now reversed that decision and passed the antidote to the doctor and nodded toward Maggie, both Ursula and Robbie looked at him in question, both aware of the reasons for his having retained the last of the capsules.

He simply spread his hands, "No matter what plans you make in life you still have to win the battles as they come up, she needs the antidote now."

Charles gave a forced smile as he spoke and watched as the Doctor with a nod of assent injected the lifesaving medicine into the unconscious woman's stomach.

The feel of clean, soft sheets around her and voices whispering softly in the distance were Maggie's first waking sensations, followed gratefully by an overwhelming feeling of relief. A dream, or rather a nightmare. All just a dream, in her waking moment she even managed a sigh of contentment, then that blessed sense of well-being was slowly but surely eroded away.

She failed to recognise the room, it didn't have the look of a hospital and it certainly wasn't her own bedroom. If anything, it looked more like a hotel room and the voices now approaching closer sounded English when they should have been Scots. Reality returned, Mike Wilkinson, the virus, the dead. They were all real and she felt her heart drop and with that the questions started. So, where was she and who were the two women in hospital whites entering the room and smiling reassurance at her as they saw her awake. According to Wilkinson, other than a few traumatised and highly vulnerable survivors, everybody ought to be dead by now.

Dr Ursula Showandra looked very much alive and almost cheerful as she despatched her assistant to fetch Charles Benford, then introduced herself to her patient. Simultaneously, seising Maggie's wrist to check her pulse and then shoving a thermometer in her mouth in the old-fashioned way to take her temperature and evidently finding both acceptable, grunted her approval.

Maggie for her part had shrunk away from Ursula in slight alarm, but gradually relaxed as the doctor went about her tasks in a professional, even friendly way.

Charles arrived within minutes and introduced himself, and the three of them spoke for more than two hours. Questions and answers flowing freely from both women. Charles more content to listen to Maggie's story, interjecting only occasionally to ask a question, or to answer one himself when Ursula Showandra was unable to. Jilly interrupted them halfway through to bring in tea and sandwiches and insisting that Charles should break off the interrogation long enough to allow their guest to refresh herself. Jilly's naturally cheery attitude going a long way to relax the Scots woman still further.

Finally, Charles sat back in his chair and summed up, "So, we think that this Mike Wilkinson, did you say, was a part of the conspiracy, possibly even the person tasked with releasing the virus. He is now somewhere in the south downs area attempting to ride out the symptoms, and we assume that all the others involved in the plot are now dead, am I right?"

"Yes, but you can't just leave him there, if he recovers, he will come after you, I am sure of that." Maggie was desperate, she wanted these people to understand, as she now believed just how dangerous Mike Wilkinson was.

Dangerous beyond the obvious, yes, they knew he had probably released the virus and so, of course he was a killer. But they needed to understand that if he did survive the virus, and she was sure he would, then there was a single-minded determination about the man that she knew would drive him to track down the person or person's that had destroyed the conspirator's plans and take revenge on them.

She was aware of the man Charles staring at her as if reading her thoughts. "If I send men to kill this Mike, are you willing to go with them or can you give them directions to this shop where he's holed up?"

"I, yes, that is no..." she was flustered didn't know what she thought or wanted, "you, you need to kill him but no, I don't think I can go with them. All I want is to go home, my home that is and die. Please, just let me go and be with my family, that's all I want now."

Charles contemplated the woman slowly, in deep thought. He had no intention of sending people to kill this, Mike Wilkinson. Not for any reason of mercy, more simply because he had no intention of ordering a murder, however richly deserved. Besides, without a second antidote the bloke would surely die anyway, Maggie would certainly have done so without that second shot of the antidote. He also had no intention of allowing this woman to go home and commit suicide and was now busily gathering thoughts and ideas in order to persuade her otherwise.

"O Maggie, here's the deal, I have a young grandson who right now is the hero of the hour, having been the one who spotted you. His mates all think he's the bees' knees and he's walking around with his little chest sticking out thinking one hell of a lot of himself. At the same time, there are nearly two hundred people out there whose morale rises every time we get another survivor come in. I'm not keen to now see that morale plummet because we lose you, and I certainly do not fancy having to tell young Sean that he wasted his time." He raised his finger to stop her interruption and continued. "I also have a job that I need doing that you are far better equipped to do than anybody else we have here."

Seeing her about to interrupt him and guessing she intended to still insist on leaving, he continued loudly. "Look, I really do need this job doing, it's going to make a big difference to the people here, so I'll tell you what I'll do, if you agree to stay here for six months and do this job. Afterwards, I will give you a vehicle with enough petrol to get you home, and I'll ask the doc to give you something too." He paused, embarrassed and not sure how to put what he was thinking. "Well, you know, to make things easier for you when the time comes. You can also," he added lamely, "leave your dog here if you want and we'll give him a home. Do we have a deal? I should warn you," he continued attempting a wry grin, "that if you say no then I'm giving you the job of telling Sean before you leave." Maggie still looked dismayed at his pressing her to stay. The last days had been so traumatic that it was difficult to think with any degree of cohesion.

Nevertheless, frightened, and emotionally drained as she was, Maggie was no wimp and behind the look of dismay, she was thinking deeply as she studied Benford. He had openly admitted that he had possession of the missing antidote and had given her the same garbled story that he had told the other survivors. Which wasn't much, something about overhearing a conversation, a now dead hero, and the death of three conspirators one of whom had died at the hands of Benford himself but only after being tortured. As he had spoken, her mind had drifted back to picture Mike Wilkinson. He had had a hardness about him that this rather eccentric sounding little man lacked. If the two ever met, she reckoned Charles Benford would last a matter of seconds, then again though this man had got hold of the antidote somehow and had used it to save this group of people, she could only try to imagine the strength of character that it must have taken to make the decisions he had had to take. There was also something about both Ursula Showandra and Jilly as well that emanated a calmness and a confidence in their situation. She liked them both instinctively, though she had never met either of them until today.

So, while she was still sure that Mike Wilkinson would come to kill Benford she still found herself asking, "You promise not to try and prevent me leaving when the time comes?"

"You have my word on it," he assured her and looked expectantly at her.

She gave him a hard stare resenting his resistance but too weak to argue further said, "What's this job you want me for?" Charles explained his plans and as he finished as though on cue Sean walked through the door and took up a position half hiding behind his grandfather's leg and looking shyly at her.

Maggie smiled at the little boy's timidity and as she caught Charles eye gave the merest of nods. Charles couldn't hold back a slight grin in response, both knew she was staying.

Maggie would never know that for the last ten minutes as Charles had been talking to her, his wife had been listening outside the door, holding Sean in check, and had gently ushered him into the room at just the right moment to tip the odds in her husband's favour.

Chapter 34

Public House

It was his sister Debbie's idea of the fish and chip van that had prompted Benford's idea of the pub.

Prior to the arrival of the 'death', Kingsthorpe had boasted a handsome free house pub restaurant that enjoyed a well earnt reputation for excellence. The restaurant at first had been of no interest to Benford yet but the idea of a pub was. Somewhere, the people could get a little taste of normalcy, and yes occasionally even have a little too much alcohol if it helped to relax them.

He knew that the existing beers would go off eventually, but spirits and red wine would keep for years. Later, once they had settled permanently over at Hardworth, he knew several the group who were capable of brewing a whole range of drinks, beers spirits and wine. Maggie's arrival, an experienced and good-looking pub land lady and her agreeing to stay for at least six months had therefore been a real blessing to him. Though not so much to his youngest son-in-law Dean Davids and his family.

Charles first marriage had produced two sons, Niall, and Robbie. While Jilly's had given her a daughter, Kelly. Shortly after their own marriage, another daughter 'Lucy' had come along. Twenty-one years later and eight years ago, Lucy had married Dean, a cockney and to her parents delight in the following years had in her turn produced three lovely grandchildren for them.

Dean, a fencing contractor had moved to Peterborough when as a child his family had come north from London as part of the city's expansion.

A family run pub had always been a dream of Dean's parents, and Dean himself had come to fancy the idea as much as them.

When the idea of opening the pub up had first occurred to Charles, it was the Davids family he had had in mind to run it. Maggie's arrival had given him someone far better equipped to do the job of landlady, and meant that Dean could

211

spend his time doing what he did best, security fencing. Dean unfortunately made no attempt to hide his disappointment at losing out and became yet another of the survivors to be less than happy with his father in law.

Chapter 35
Ernie Digby

"Clarrie, Clarrie," Ernie's voice was weak, in part because he had spent more than twenty years deliberately speaking in such a manner, and in part because he had been calling for his daughter for days now and his throat felt as though it was on fire.

"Clarrie, where are you, are you their love?" His voice trailing away to nothing denoted his despair. Ernest Digby was in trouble and knew it.

Twenty-one years ago on his seventieth birthday, Ernie had laid down on his bed and declared that having lived the three score years and ten that the good lord had allowed him, he was now ready to die. Since then, he had resolutely refused to leave his bed despite pleas from both the few members of his family still alive, and his doctor, who warned him repeatedly that he would almost certainly die if he did not get up and take some exercise, Ernie ignored them all. During the next twenty-one years, his daughter Clarissa had waited on him hand and foot. Clarry saw to his every need. He used a bedpan for his bodily functions that Clarrie had to empty. She shopped, cleaned, washed, and shaved him daily and gave him a bed bath twice a week. Between them, they had even developed a method whereby she could change the bed linen without his having to get out of it. Obviously, she also had to do the cooking, not that Ernie ate much. His diet consisted of bread and milk for breakfast, and chicken soup for his midday and evening meals, accompanied by two rounds of bread. Other than two packets of crisps a day this was Ernie's sole intake of food, never varying even at Christmas.

The constant work involved in looking after her father had gradually ruined Clarries health. She had never been a strong woman and her divorce shortly before her father's retirement had affected her confidence badly. Not that Ernie seemed to mind about his strange lifestyle, he had his TV complete with video and DVD players and now in his 91st year appeared set to go on for many more, though for how many of those years – Clarrie was now well into her sixties – could last was another matter.

But then the nightmare had started, Ernie could not be sure exactly when, but thought it must have been about a week ago. The news had carried a report of a strange illness that had started over in the Pacific but quickly spread to Europe and then the UK. After that it was Bedlam, the first deaths had been reported by grim faced broadcasters, some of whom in the way of journalists seemed to be almost milking the moment. But then as TV staff were themselves affected and therefore making things very personal, television programmes became very sporadic and within two days had ceased altogether.

Clarrie had held out quite well to begin with but eventually complained of feeling nauseous and then started throwing up.

When the pain and sickness became too bad, she had come into her father's room and begged him to help her.

Ernie seeing the state his daughter was had been frightened. Clarrie was his rock, she looked after him, not the other way around. She had no right to become ill like this, she knew he wasn't well enough to help her, she had no business worrying him like this. Ernie had pulled his covers up over his head and refused to listen. At one point as she persisted in her entreaties, he had even begun to sing la la la la la as loud as his weak voice box allowed in an attempt to drown her out. Unfortunately, singing and hiding under the covers couldn't hide the smell. She stank of shit, and from underneath his hiding place, he screamed at her to get out and leave him alone.

He heard her continuing to throw up a few more times and thought she called to him but made no attempt to answer, then she had gone quiet.

That had been some days ago as far as he could tell, and since then he had been totally incommunicado. The television had never come back on, there was a phone in the house, but it was downstairs, so it might as well have been a mile away as far as Ernie was concerned.

Clarrie did have a son and two grandchildren, but they lived in Australia.

Other than them they had no other relations left now, while friends had been non-existent for years. Ernie in desperation had finally made a valiant effort to rise from his bed, but twenty-one years of immobility had allowed muscle tissue to waste away and Ernie found he was incapable of moving little more than his arms and neck, and so he continued to just lay where he was.

Since he had no idea of what was happening in the outside world, the irony that he was one of the 20,000 to 1 survivor was lost on him.

For days now, he had survived on the bottles of squash that were on his bedside cabinet, but without any food. Occasionally, he thought that he had heard people's voices outside and once had definitely heard a vehicle drive down the road. Every time he heard such noises, he had tried to yell out, but his thin reedy voice had sounded inadequate for the task, even to him. So Ernie lay in his own soil hoping against hope that Clarrie would miraculously recover and come to his aid.

All that had only been the beginning, the real nightmare for him were the dogs. When her family had emigrated, Clarisse's grandsons had had two Staffordshire pups. Clarrie an animal lover had decided to keep them herself as her last visual contact with her family. They were seven years old now and had never had any reason to develop a relationship with the human at the top of the stairs whom they smelt but never saw. Ernie had heard them moving about for days now and could sense their growing distress at a lack of food. About four days ago, they had come upstairs for the first time, and he had heard them drinking from the toilet bowl. Later, there had been a strange scratching sound that he had eventually puzzled out as being the animals scratching at Clarrie's bedroom door that she tended to keep closed. Two days ago, well he thought it was two days, it was increasingly difficult to keep proper track of time without his TV, the biggest of the dogs had stuck its head around the door. The animal had stood for several minutes just staring at Ernie who had shouted and yelled in his tinny voice until the dog had gone away. Since then, one or other of them had been back a number of times, each visit had lasted a little longer than the previous one as the dogs grew bolder or more desperate.

On the last occasion, the bigger of the two had actually entered the room and paced around his bed never taking its eyes from him. He had tried everything he could think of to shut the bedroom door that was normally kept wedged open. Rolling to the edge of the bed and reaching out ineffectually, then resorted to throwing pillows and anything else within reach in an attempt to shut the damn thing, but nothing had worked.

Finally, realising what would become inevitable, he had in desperation thrown the last of his drink away in the hope that he would die of thirst before the dogs had worked out that there was only one source of food available to them.

Chapter 36

Stevee Lenton

Stevee closed the bedroom door carefully and tip towed away. He didn't know why he was being so careful; his parents were both dead as was his sister. Yet somehow, it seemed right to be as quite as he could.

At only eight years old, Stevee didn't really understand death, he had cried as his family died one by one, but that had been fear as much as anything else, fear of what was going to happen to him, was he going to die as well.

If he didn't die, then who would look after him. Stevee liked to think of himself as grown up. Two years older than his sister, and bigger and heavier than other boys of his age, he had always been the leader of their group. The one the other boys of his age looked up to, but playground games hadn't prepared him for anything like this. He felt so lonely the world seemed such a big place now and Stevee had no idea of what to do.

The first day he just sat around reading comics and looking through his dad's naughty books from the shed. He knew they couldn't, but he still sorts of expected his mum or dad to wake up. They must have known he needed them, children need their mum's and dad's. But it didn't matter how many times he glanced toward their bedroom door, it still remained resolutely closed.

He lived from the house cupboards at first, cereals, cakes, and biscuits mostly, until the smell of his own family eventually drove him away from the only place he had ever known as home.

Still looking for comfort from adults, he tried the neighbour's houses first, ringing bells and knocking doors, but was met with only a stony silence and Stevee was too afraid to enter the buildings alone.

Instead, he walked the streets looking at every house trying to see any signs of life, sometimes calling out, "Anyone, is there anyone there, hello, anybody, please, is there anybody there?" Somewhere a dog barked in reply, but he couldn't tell where the sound had come from and besides it had sounded big and Stevee wasn't really into dogs. At the corner of school road was Singh's shop, Stevee was banned from here having been caught stealing sweets some months ago.

Nevertheless, overcoming his fear, he somewhat gingerly pushed against the door and surprisingly found it open, again disappointingly there was no answer to his shouts. A door at the rear of the shop he knew led up to where Rajeev Singh and his family had their living quarters.

Stevee looked at it is longing for some sound of life to come from behind it, he would even welcome Singhy himself coming through the door and shouting at him. Anyone, any one at all, but no such luck, there was no one and he knew there wasn't ever going to be. In the end being too afraid, he chose not to go through the door.

Anyway, he didn't need to, everything he wanted was here. The boy was hungry and so he started on the crisps first then moved on to chocolate bars and biscuits, washed down with three cans of coke. For a while fear changed to euphoria as he realised, he could have anything he wanted. He managed to get into the till and stuffed the contents into his pockets, ten-pound notes, twenty pound notes, all of it. For the first time in his life he felt the tremendous thrill of being rich. Having pocketed the cash, he then did the same with sweets and chocolates, involuntarily checking over his shoulder in case anyone was watching, and all the time continuing to cram a variety of goodies into his mouth.

Then the overindulgence hit him, and he ran outside to be sick; terrified, the vomiting itself rekindling memories and terrifying him into thinking that whatever had killed his family was going to do the same to him.

After thoroughly purging himself, he felt better and going back into the shop he helped himself to cigarettes. He had smoked before down the park with older boys. They had thought it funny to watch him puff away, especially when it made his head spin and he had had to sit down.

That paused him for a moment as he thought about his mates. He supposed they must all be dead as well, and he felt the loneliness return, and with it the fear.

He slept on the shop floor that night afraid of every sound that came from the dark, and aware that there were bodies just up the stairs. A cat appeared the next morning, a black and white one and deciding he preferred cats to dogs, he fed it a tin of tuna and gave it some milk, enjoying the sight of the animal lapping with its tongue and the way it jerked its head when eating the lumps of tuna. He had never had a pet before, so all this was new to him and he enjoyed its company. He especially liked the way it rubbed itself against his legs and jumped onto his lap if he sat down. He played with it during the morning, trying unsuccessfully to teach it a variety of tricks. Like all cats though, the animal would do only what it wanted rather than what the human wanted.

Nevertheless, delighted at its company, Stevee rewarded it with another tin of tuna. For himself, he'd had enough of crisps and looked around for something different.

A packet of chocolate biscuits later, and he decided to take a walk out. Not sure what to do about the cat and not wanting to lose it, he carried it in his arms for a while, evidently against its will, and its struggles eventually became too much and he had to drop it. Pleasingly though the animal seemed content to follow him around, albeit slowly. He wandered the streets aimlessly not looking for anywhere in particular and eventually found himself outside a supermarket. Again, the doors were unlocked and he wandered inside. The thoughts of having such a big shop full of stuff, that was now just for him was both exciting and yet also intimidating.

At the deli counter there were cold cooked chickens and he gorged on these for a while, wondering if the cat would eat meat, he turned to offer some but the animal had disappeared. Alarmed, he looked around the aisle for the creature without any luck. He widened his search, becoming ever more desperate as he felt the loneliness creeping over him again and he began to panic. His wanderings had taken him into the rear of the store and opening the door of what turned out to be an office, he was confronted by the body of a man lying face down over a desk, and screamed aloud at the sight. Slamming the door shut, he ran from the store and didn't stop until he was back at Singh's shop. The floor was no more comfortable than it had been the first night and he slept badly. Every time he closed his eyes, he kept seeing the dead man in the store. Why this particular corpse should upset him amongst so many others he didn't know and it never occurred to him to wonder about it.

Eventually, sometime in the early hours the cat returned and snuggled up to him. Relieved beyond measure at the animals return, he cried like the child he was, until his gentle stroking of the animals fur soothed the boy himself and he fell into a deep sleep.

Breakfasting again on biscuits and coke, he felt the urge to do something more than just wander the streets. Not wanting to lose the cat again, he wondered whether he should try to lock it indoors. Eventually decided against it, the animal seemed to know where to return to; whereas locking it in might upset it and encourage it to leave him any time it could. Trying to carry the animal about with him was just as difficult. In the end, he trusted to his instinct and let it wander at will. Stevee had thought about things while he had been eating and knew exactly where he was going to go to today. Webster's cycle shop had always fascinated him with its amazing collection of machines. Especially attractive to him was the shiny blue mountain bike that had dominated the front window ever since last Christmas. The price tag of more than four hundred pounds had meant it would never be his but now things were different, he could have anything he wanted.

This time his luck was out, the door to the shop firmly locked against him barring his access. After the open doors he had found everywhere else he had been, Stevee felt almost affronted by this new set back and in frustration threw stones against the window as hard as he could, all to no avail. Realising he needed something bigger than stones, he looked around, and spotted where a few houses along the road from the shop, a front garden wall had been allowed to collapse, offering a number of loose bricks as ammunition.

Picking up a couple of the bricks, he returned to the shop and using all his strength hurled one at the widow, and immediately had to jump aside as the reinforced glass bounced the missile straight back at him.

Now somewhat more carefully, he tried several times just as fruitlessly and was about to give up when on what was supposed to be his last throw he saw a hairline crack develop running diagonally across the glass.

Encouraged, he threw harder than ever and was rewarded by seeing the window suddenly collapse in front of him. He cut his hand on as hard as he entered the store and nearly cried as he saw the blood. He wanted his mum now more than ever, wanted a cuddle from her, wanted someone to treat his wound and kiss it better. But there was the bike in front of him and as he ran his good hand over the shiny metal, he felt better and the cut in his hand didn't look so big now. He licked the wound for a moment and it seemed to be alright, perhaps he could find a plaster for it later, for now he had something more exciting to do. Easing the bike of its stand, he very carefully this time carried the machine through the broken window and out on to the road.

The bike was bad really bad, faster than Gavin Lamberts had been and definitely more brill. He really badly wanted some other kids to see him on it, to see what he had, but there was no one to impress and without someone to share his delight the loneliness soon returned.

The bike didn't seem quite so good now and being hungry he cycled to the supermarket again. Avoiding that part of the store where the office containing the body was, he dined on cold chicken again, though this time it tasted a bit funny. What he really wanted was his mum's egg and chips, or a pizza that would be nice. There was plenty of those in the supermarket but he had no idea of how to cook them, and they tasted horrible uncooked. He tried holding them on a fork above a fire, that didn't work, the base burnt, before that the toppings melted and slid of and he burnt his hand slightly. He ate more crisps. Outside the temperature grew hotter during the afternoon and he cycled to the park. There was a paddling pool there and he spent an hour splashing around and washing the bike, though the machine didn't really need it.

The days passed like this, doing nothing really and achieving less and with Stevee becoming ever more bored. Oh, he could have anything he wanted, that wasn't the problem. He broke into toy shops and helped himself to whatever he fancied. He even returned to school and broke nearly every window in the building. Remembering happier days, he visited a couple of McDonald's, the sight of all those burgers and chips had him salivating. Then the realisation that he had no way of enjoying them had him almost weeping with frustration. He tried a couple of muffins but they tasted funny and he spat them out. A visit to a KFC, and a pizza place followed just as disappointingly. Worse, nothing held him for more than a few moments. There was just nothing for him to do. He would have loved to use his wii but that wouldn't work. He had tried other things as well, TVs, kettles, toasters for pop tarts, but just like the lights nothing seemed to work. He guessed that for some reason the electric wasn't working, probably because there were no grown-ups he supposed.

He had even crept home one day, the smell when he opened the door was terrible and he almost turned away without entering, but home was home and was at least familiar. So forcing himself to go in, he tried to switch on the kettle in the kitchen, disappointingly the electric didn't work here either. But he did pick up his mum's laptop, that did switch on but didn't seem to have all its functions and after the battery went flat, he threw it away. He was still sleeping nights at Singh's shop, although there was a bad smell in there as well. He had thought of trying somewhere else to live and rode the streets exploring the various housing estates for a likely place.

His mum had always said how posh the Florence Nightingale estate was, and certainly the houses looked smart from outside, so maybe here was where he should stay. Other than the long grass, that was everywhere now, one house in particular looked well-kept and choosing this one he approached the front door cautiously. For some reason, he was suddenly nervous at the idea of entering someone else's home without permission.

Before his hand could make contact with the door handle, there was a faint sound of scuffling from within and then something huge slammed into the door from the inside, this was followed by a series of terrifying barks and snarls from what was obviously some kind of devil dog attempting to get to him. Stevee frightened out of his wits ran as fast and as far as he could even forgetting his bike in his mad rush to get away from the beast.

He picked up another bike on his way back to Singh's and never again dared to approach any houses other than those he was familiar with.

Tommy, the cat would still visit every night to be fed but tended to disappear again during the day. Stevee never did find out where the cat went, though when it returned it would more often than not be filthy and occasionally smelled of fish.

His own diet hadn't improved any either, cakes, biscuits and chocolate for the most part, washed down with cans of coke or red bull.

The chickens in the supermarket had become inedible after a few days and while he had opened some cans of beans and sausage they weren't as nice cold as they had been when his mum cooked them for him.

He attempted to build fires and tried to heat things up but as with the pizza the flames were either too hot for him to get near enough to cook. Or as soon as the flames died down enough for him to get closer, the fuel he was using being mainly paper would burn through and the heat would be lost leaving the food still cold.

He cried most nights, the loneliness at times totally overwhelming and his fear of the future terrifying. He didn't know why he was afraid of the future so much, just knew instinctively that he couldn't go on like this.

There was a smell everywhere he went now, even outside. A smell that he associated with dead people. Certainly the body in the supermarket was getting worse, the stench permeating throughout the store and mixing with that of rotting vegetables. Rats as well, he didn't like rats and he was seeing lots of them now. They ran about everywhere, and with no humans and few dogs to control them the rodents became ever bolder and wouldn't run from Stevee even when he yelled and threw stones their way. If the cat was about she would hiss at them but even then the bolder rats would still be slow in leaving. There was a dog about as well, a big black one. Stevee had seen it around on several occasions and always tried to avoid it. He had never liked dogs and he certainly didn't like the way this one looked at him, though he did notice that at least the rats would disappear if they sensed the animal was around.

But what frightened him more than anything else was the tummy pains, he felt ill all the time and was often sick. Not like Mummy and Daddy had been just before they died, this was different he wasn't bleeding like they had, and he felt so hot all the time. He tried holding his hand to his head to see how hot it felt. His mother used to do this and say whether he had a temperature or not. If he had, it meant a day of school, and that was good.

But sometimes it also meant a visit to Mrs Judd, the nurse and that was bad. Now he didn't know if he had a temperature or not or how hot his head was supposed to be. But he would have liked his mum to be here now to look after him, he would even welcome nurse Judd if she could appear and make him feel better.

Toilets had become a problem as well, before his mummy had died she was forever telling him off for not pulling the chain, and for not washing his hands after he had been for a wee as well as a poo. Well, she couldn't tell him off now even if she had been here, because there was no water and the chains didn't work either, or rather they worked the first time he used them but never again. After the one in the shop had become too foul to keep using, Stevee had taken to using public toilets wherever he could find one. Supermarkets, schools and so on, then as he began to feel poorly they were too far away for him to travel to and he had started squatting in corners.

By then the smell of decomposing bodies had driven him away from Singh's shop and he had taken to living in the shopkeeper's garage.

For no real reason, perhaps just boredom, he decided that his family ought to have had a funereal. He had never been to one himself but his mummy's auntie had died last year and she and his dad had both gone to her funereal. He had heard them talking about it and it seemed that the old lady hadn't been buried but burnt. Dad had said, "Well, she ought to get used to it because it's going to last an eternity for her." His parents had rowed for days after that remark, but Stevee remembered it now. Not the eternity bit, he wasn't sure how long an eternity lasted for but the burning bit. He knew that he couldn't bury his family, even the thought of seeing them now was frightening, but he could burn them or rather he could burn the house around them.

He gathered lots of old newspapers and bundles of firewood loaded them into a supermarket trolley and wheeled them around to his old home. The house was only a few hundred yards from the store, but so deteriorated was his health that he found even this short distance exhausting and almost gave the venture up.

Eventually arriving at his destination, he became confused for a moment when he found the front door wide open. Then realising that as he had left it that way there was no longer anyone around to close it behind him as there would once have been. Even after these weeks or months that thought brought him to tears again and he sat on the front garden wall for a time as he composed himself.

Finally bracing himself for the awful smell, he gathered a bunch of the newspapers and braved entry into the house. Not prepared to go too far in, he screwed the papers up into balls added the firewood on top and lit the pyre.

Outside again, he remembered that people said prayers at funerals and muttered the only one he knew from school assembly and waited for his home to burn down. It never happened, there was a lot of smoke for a while then nothing.

He crept back cautiously, afraid that there might be a sudden explosion like there was in some films. The fire had scorched the floor a bit and one side of the cabinet in the hall way, and that was it.

The failure to cremate his family seemed to have a really demoralising effect on Stevee. It was as though his family were confirming that he was not only on his own but also a complete failure. He was not the one that ought to have survived.

He lacked both the will and the strength to try again and returned to his garage. As autumn was now pulling in, the mornings and evenings were turning cool and he spent more and more time just lying in his sleeping bag.

He knew he should get up more, he seemed to be forever hungry and he really should make an effort to eat better food. If only he didn't feel so bad. But even the thought of getting up exhausted him now. He would leave it a little while and perhaps try a little later.

Stevee fell asleep waking only intermittently over the next few days. The cat stopped visiting him some days later when the boy was no longer able to feed it.

Stevee Benton died of a typhus related disease five months after his family had died from the virus and just six days short of his ninth birthday. No one knew he had died and no one cared.

Chapter 37

Sean's Joy

"Go on, go on you can do it." Sean jumped up and down in excitement as he urged half pint on. The dogs intended prey was a furry toy rat. A memento of the pied piper pantomime he had been taken to see last Christmas. Every child in the theatre had been given the toys but now six months on the novelty had long worn of. So having rediscovered it, Sean was now enjoying himself enormously having hidden the toy behind a stack of firewood and was now busily urging the dog to find the rat and kill it.

Life for Sean just seemed to get better every day. The world had come to an end and that had made all the grown-ups sad, and for a while their fears had infected the boy as well, then childish resilience had taken over and Sean now thought that things were perfect. First of all he was a hero, having saved Maggie's life. She was now doing what gramps had asked her to do and was preparing to re-open the Kingsthorpe village pub, gramps said that was good for morale, whoever he was.

If Sean wandered round to the pub, Maggie would make a fuss of him and give him various treats and allow him to help her. He thought Maggie was really pretty and had decided he would marry her when he grew up.

When he had told his sister Affy of his intentions, she had laughed and said, "Don't be silly she's really old, certainly far too old for you." Well, that didn't matter because by the time he married her he would be older as well.

Anyway, when the day arrived he'd teach Affy a lesson by not inviting her to the wedding. Then two days ago, his daddy had bought the dog home, a Jack Russell cross, Mummy called it and that was confusing because if it was called Jack Russell then why didn't people use its name instead of calling it half pint.

Mummy said that gramps wanted everybody to have a terrier, and it seemed that was also a Jack Russell, in their homes from now on to keep rats away otherwise they would become an epidemic.

That was why Sean was now busily attempting to train the animal to do its job, and so far with great success. Sean prided himself that he wasn't as stupid as Affy was always saying he was. Before starting the training, he had rubbed chocolate sauce all over the rat and even though the dog had licked all the stuff off straight away, half pint had still been able to find the toy every time so far.

But there was even better to come, he and Affy had overheard Mummy and Nanny Jill talking last night and Nanny had said Gramps wanted as many people as possible to volunteer to have a pony when they moved to their new proper home, at some place where Sean had never been yet. It wasn't Kingsthorpe, which was a new home to them but this was another new home they were going to when it was ready.

Then he would have a pony of his own and gramps had already said he was going to have chickens and Sean and the other children were going to collect the eggs every day as well as feed the chickens. But best of all, although Gramps kept saying there was going to be a school soon, so far there was no sign of it. Instead, Sean and his friends spent most of the time in the grounds of a house in Kingsthorpe, the house had its own swimming pool and another little pool that was really hot and bubbled a lot. Inside the house, the furniture had been removed and the rooms equipped instead with a variety of toys and games for different age groups. This was where the under elevens spent their days but only after they had carried out the tasks appointed to them. Since most of these little jobs concerned animals, the children generally enjoyed them. Yes, as far as Sean could see this end of the world thing was pretty good, although he did still miss his friends from school.

Chapter 38

Sandy Dawson

"Whoa, get in there," he accompanied the command with much waving of his arms as he urged yet another of his cows to enter the cattle truck. The bovine, reluctant to enter the strange smelling space tried to turn away.

Only to receive a sharp rap on her rump from the farmers hand and further encouragement to obey his wishes from his border collie worrying her lower legs. Loudly bellowing her indignation, she finally obeyed the man's command and stumbling somewhat on the wooden ramp entered the vehicle.

The man wiped sweat from his brow as he secured the tailgate and for the umpteenth time and cursed Charles Benford roundly. The weather was hot and getting hotter and Sandy Dawson had lots of work he should have been doing. Instead, Benford insisted that Sandy and his family assisted by several others, few of whom knew anything about farms or animals and so in his opinion were totally unsuited to the task, should abandon his crops and leave all his normal work.

Instead, he was to spend his mornings delivering water to a number of other farmers animals. Although, since those other farmers were presumably dead, he supposed that animals anywhere now all belonged to the community. So it was his job to keep them alive make sure they had water and enough pasture. Milk those cows in pain from their heavy udders, that weren't being milked often enough since their human carers had died. Then he would round up as many as he could into transports so that they could be taken by others in the community to Hardworth.

Here Tom Bradbury, who had also been ordered to leave his own farm, and assisted by his equally mocked up crew would settle the animals into their new meadows and take over responsibility for them. Of course, only the best breeding stock were supposed to be sent off in this manner.

Those not selected were to be killed, some for food the remainder out of mercy. Sandy didn't agree, he had a good farm here and with now having the pick off any animals in the area he wanted, along with unlimited plant and equipment, he couldn't see the point of leaving it.

Benford as usual overrode him, insisting that the fans weren't suitable in the long term. The man seemed to be obsessed with supposed long term dangers. The fens would flood, the water supplies would become unsafe and present a danger to health, a whole list of arguments.

Sandy had fleetingly wondered about leaving the others and taking his own family away, certain that he could look after his own. Only the antidote stopped him doing so. He needed those capsules for himself and his family or they would all die, and there was no way Benford would give him the capsules in advance. On top of that, Sandy himself along with all the other survivors had supposedly given his word that he would stay with the group for the next fifteen years. While he was prepared to go back on his word if he felt the need, he wouldn't feel comfortable about it. So he would go along with Benford's wishes for now at least. Perhaps, just see how things worked out. But that didn't mean that Benford wasn't still being a bloody idiot.

Chapter 39

Puzzled

She had chosen what had been the master bedroom of a very select five bed detached house. The twenty first century stone and slate built property was cited on the highest piece of ground in the village of Kingsthorpe.

The building had been selected to serve as temporary offices for the survivor's administrative work. Liz had opted for this particular room as being large enough for both herself and Dawn Porter to carry out their, what Charles referred to as 'intel work'.

The view across the valley to the west where the outskirts of Rockingham forest could be seen was lovely and as usual when that thought occurred to her, she would remember guiltily and tear her eyes away to look out of the smaller south facing window.

From here, she could see the work crews loading up their vehicles with whatever they needed for their days work, not that their needs amounted to much. When you spend your day looting, food and drink are both easily available. That was what most of those people she was looking at would be doing again today.

Not food, they had collected enough of that in those first four or five hectic days. Freezing as much as they could, and loading tins, packets and bags into vans and lorries of every size. Those vehicles were now parked in the streets of a number of neighbouring villages, their contents carefully recorded and listed by dawn or herself, in their 'intel work'.

These would all be moved eventually over to Hardworth. The intention being that these would see them through the first year or two. While their own farms were established, or so Charles hoped.

After that initial food collection was over, the survivors had been allowed a couple of days to mourn and then bury or burn their dead as they wished, then to return to their homes to collect whatever clothes or personal effects they wanted in their new world.

Though that hadn't been easy, Liz still cringed as she remembered the row between Charles and the great majority of the survivors, including even members of his own family. Her twin determined that the dead could and must wait until more important work was complete. It was that word 'important' that lost the argument for Charles. Liz knew that it was probably a slip of the tongue rather than intent, but to his listeners coming from someone whose own family group were mostly safe it sounded about as offensive as anything could be.

With Niall, Robbie and others of his closest lieutenants were absent on working trips, Charles had been forced to back down. At first, begrudgingly but as his anger slowly evaporated common sense kicked in and he had apologised for his unthinking words. Liz, Debs and Jilly along with the other women in his family had spent hours talking the survivors round and settling things down. So when a week later, Charles announced that it was time for the community to take the first of the six antidote pills they needed. The not so subtle reminder of their indebtedness to him restored his position completely.

So now peace restored, everyone was back to the tasks assigned to them. In the case of those she was currently watching, that meant loading ever more lorries up with all types of supplies. Clothing, bedding and cleansing were the priorities now for the crews she was looking at.

Others, farmers, engineers and those from a medical background were spending their time selecting the supplies needed for their specialist kills.

While those from the construction industry were engaged in preparing homes over at Hardworth house, concentrating especially on installing heating and sanitation facilities. The ltater being mainly based on using septic tanks. Many of their proposed homes already had these, and it wasn't too major a job to install them where they didn't already exist.

Heating was different, existing systems could be relied on to take the community through their first winter, but eventually fireplaces and chimneys would need to be built in almost all of the houses, and this would take more time.

It didn't end there either, drinking water, electricity etc. would all have to come later.

As she thought about all these things that needed to be done and the pitiful numbers of survivors available to provide them, Liz's face clouded over with doubt, could they really manage to do these things.

Chapter 40
Endia

If her young brother was pleased at the change in life the virus had brought about, his eldest sister Endia was anything but. Endia had fallen an early victim to the virus the only one of Charles Benford's family to do so. The antidote had saved her of course but contracting the bug had meant she was out of it during the critical period during which her grandfather had been dispensing the miracle cure.

That had also meant that Endia hadn't been able to plead for Craig Keeble's life. Craig was the prize catch at school, ever since he had started at her school in year ten all the girls had fancied him. He was good looking, brilliant at sports and top of the class in most subjects.

Everything about him was 'bad'. And if all the girls fancied him, it seemed that Craig liked most of them just as much. In the following terms, Craig had been out with probably every pretty girl in the school, even some from the year above him, and then finally one day he had asked Endia out. Of course all the other girls were jealous and made snide remarks about Craig, claiming that they would never go out with the creep; blithely ignoring the fact that most of them had already done so, or if their own romance with him had been too recent to deny, would boast that they had of course been the one to finish it, not him.

Others like Nicole Hamilton made remarks of how far down Craig's list Endia must have been, considering he had only just got around to dating her as they were all about to leave school for university.

Endia had ignored all the jibes, Craig had explained how she was the one he had always fancied but had thought she was too far above him. He was sure that the beautiful brown haired girl reputedly to be also the cleverest in the year would have nothing to do with him.

He looked so sincere and handsome as he said this, Endia knew he had to be telling the truth, and had kissed him there and then in full view of a seething Nicole Hamilton.

Prior to the arrival of the virus they had been dating for six weeks, Craig assured her that was two weeks longer than he had ever dated any girl before, so that proved how he felt about her.

With university coming up, Dad would have gone mad if he had known that his Endy was serious about a boy, so as usual she hadn't told anyone in the family about her romance. Affy of course knew, she had been seeing a lot of Craig but not just how much, or of how Endia really felt about him, then this horrible plague had come and she had lost the boy she loved. If only she hadn't been so ill herself, and she had been ill really ill this time. It wasn't as her mum said at the time 'alcohol', yes, she had been out with Craig the night before, although her parents thought she was with Siobhan and Kirsty. And as usual Craig had kept buying her drinks, and Endy understood why he was trying to get her tipsy. But she was sure she wasn't tipsy at all, in fact was sure she had only had about five or six alcopops or whatever they were he was pouring down her. When she was sick it must have been the burger she'd eaten or as she later discovered the virus.

But food poisoning or virus she had been asleep at the critical time.

When she woke, she had called Craig's house and texted him time, and again without answer. Desperate she had wanted to go round to see him but she didn't know where he lived. He had always insisted that his family wouldn't let him go out with girls, so apart from saying he lived at the nearby village of Elton none of the girls knew anything beyond that.

Endia had been beside herself with grief and cried herself back to sleep, her parents thinking that her distress was all due to the virus in the same way as everyone else, had allowed her to rest.

Craig wasn't her only cause for grief, there would be no university now and no career, Endy had wanted to be an architect. Now what would she do, like a number of the survivors Endy was still having trouble coming to terms with the reality of their situation. She wasn't stupid, she knew what had happened to the world and that things could never be the same again, but how to translate what that meant, into anything except her own immediate world escaped her. University gone, Craig gone, her friends gone, her home gone, career gone.

Fashion, TV and cinema, celebrities everything about her social circle, every dream she had ever had for success, all had disappeared in a single night.

Now there was nothing but a void in front of her. How did she make plans for a future when the only certainty about the future was that there was nothing. She had overheard Grampa, Charles talking to her dad. Grampa was explaining that it would be thousands of years before the world's population would recover to a level sufficient to maintain anything like a semblance to their old life. Before then a lack of numbers would mean that it was only a question of how far back mankind would slide before a recovery could begin. So that was great, she was to become a cave girl, her greatest achievement to be able to light a fire using two sticks, or something equally archaic.

Oh how she hated all this, it was stupid, everything about all this was stupid how could it have been allowed to happen. There were governments, armies, intelligence agencies and police forces all supposed to be alert, to be looking out for the public safety. What good were they if a whole world could be killed almost overnight? Stupid, stupid stupid, all so stupid. The girl sighed loudly bringing herself back to reality and a happier thought struck her; there was one bright spot.

Davie Abbott, she felt the familiar tingle as she thought about the newcomer. Davie was one of the growing numbers of survivors joining the community. He and Endia had hardly spoken yet but she judged him to be about her own age. For the first ten days after the virus had struck, the survivors had worked like trojans in carrying out all the urgent works Charles had insisted had to be done 'NOW'.

During those ten days there had been a sort of revolt among the people, it hadn't affected Endia, so wrapped up in her own problems was she that she didn't know what exactly had taken place or been said. But her grandfather had finally given in to the survivor's pressure and allowed a couple of dozens of them to leave each day and to go and attend their dead.

This usually meant visiting relations homes and if time allowed, even perhaps close friends as well.

Here, inevitably discovering only corpses, momentos would be collected if desired, and then the homes burned around the bodies.

The return of one such burial party just over a week ago had brought with them the blond blue eyed and tall, Davie Abbott in company with a young boy of about six or seven. The younger lad had been suffering from a bad cough when they arrived, so both youths had been quarantined for a week before being allowed into the community a couple of days ago.

Endy was spending a month in the kitchens, her grandfather wanted young people like herself to spend some time experiencing different types of work before deciding where their future lay. Members of the community could eat at home if they wished or go to the canteen. Food was provided here for sixteen hours a day and most of the survivors ate at least two meals a day here. As the stray survivors, those who had had a natural immunity to the virus had first started to drift in to the camp at Kingsthorpe, Charles had made an impassioned speech to his own chosen ones, he had pointed out that 'they' had all had their closest loved ones with them. They had the love and support of spouses, parents, or children etc., but these newcomers were alone, even though most had joined up with others they were still comparative strangers to one another.

There had been tears in her grandfather's eyes as he had begged his people to welcome these new arrivals into their community fully. Finishing an impassioned speech with, "Please, don't let them be alone anymore, if you see someone sitting alone invite them to join you and your group, welcome them, befriend them, above all look out for them."

The survivors had responded well. New arrivals would find themselves invited to sit with would be friends in both the dining room and pub. They were befriended at work and in some cases a single individual might even find themselves offering a room in a family's home.

Endy had spotted the good looking Davie on the first day he had been allowed to enter the community proper. His attraction for her increased by his younger companion's assertion that Davie had saved his life, that he would certainly have died if the older lad hadn't looked out for him.

That had interested her in him, but at first her duties in the kitchen had offered her no chance to speak to the youth.

Since then, their paths had crossed only at a distance, but today she had asked Nanny Jilly to allow her to have an early break. Endy had noticed that Davie tended to take his lunch early and she intended to invite him to sit at her table, and then hopefully, mmm, well, maybe life here wouldn't be all bad.

Chapter 41

Wilkinson Awakes

His eyes watched the seconds hand ticking away, another two minutes and he would have lasted three quarters of an hour since last throwing up.

Already he had exceeded his previous best by seven minutes and was determined to maintain a constant improvement. Still watching the clock face, his hands groped for the box of matches in his pockets, he had promised himself that his next meal would be heated.

It would only be a can of beans but it would still be the first hot food he would have had in, how long would it be, weeks he supposed. When he felt stronger, he would have to find out how long he had been fighting the virus. His mind diverted for a moment as it grappled with the problem of just how he was going to achieve that, then just as quickly dropped the thought from his mind, he had other more important things to do at the moment.

However long his struggle against the virus had lasted, the entire time had been a never ending nightmare. Life, if it could have been called that, had consisted of non-stop vomiting and defecating, either throwing up or feeling shit running out of him unable to stop the flow until his bowels had emptied themselves. Afterwards the pain would come, gripping, gut wrenching pain. But it was the pain he was using to try and save his life.

He was using the pain to remind him that as soon as he had finished spewing or whatever, he had to then force himself to eat in order to replace what his body had just rejected and so give the virus something to feed on.

Opening cans, bottles, packets of anything that his stomach could begin to tolerate, his whole being revolting against the very idea of having to make any more efforts to digest the unwanted foodstuff. Baked beans, rice, tinned fruit, cans of beer anything that came to hand was swallowed fitfully, painfully. He would eat, drink, and gasp for breathe at the effort required to do this most simple of functions, only to then start the cycle again, his entire being felt as if he was on fire, his stomach muscles bruised beyond belief causing him unbelievable agony.

It wasn't possible to ignore the pain but Wilkinson's SAS training had taught him how to manage it, so he had focused his mind and carried on fighting the microbes that were trying to kill him, steadfastly refusing to give in.

For most of the time he was barely conscious, aware only that he had to keep eating and drinking. Eat, drink, throw up, then eat and drink again, never allowing the bug to defeat him, wouldn't allow the bug to defeat him.

At some point, he had vaguely realised the woman had gone but at that time wasn't even able to recall her name.

Neither was he aware that he had twice had visitors. Two survivors, a middle aged woman and a teen aged boy who had found each other among the thousands of dead in the housing estates surrounding the supermarket where Mike Wilkinson lay. Intent on gathering supplies, the two had heard noises emanating from the rear of the store and nervously investigated the source.

Even to people who had become used to the smell of death, the stench in the enclosed staff room was appalling.

Wilkinson laying in his own vomit and perhaps worse, was thrashing about in his delirium, shouting it seemed to some unknown person in an unintelligible language. Looking at the foul spectral figure both visitors took fright and ran.

A different kind of fear, the kind inspired by a wish to survive, made them return days later, perhaps recognising in the man a toughness that they could hope to recruit in their own fight for life.

One look at the grey faced emaciated form lying on the camp bed, stinking of vomit and faeces convinced both that this thing that hardly looked human could hope to survive for longer than a very few hours. The two had gazed crestfallen for a few moments more, then both continued on their desolate way.

He kept the beans down followed by a can of fruit and then slept. He would not rush, content to allow his recovery to be gradual, small meals followed by long sleeps to build his strength.

He did not know it yet but Wilkinson had been fighting for his life for six weeks. In that time, his muscles had relaxed, his whole body lacking exercise becoming ever more lethargic.

On the third or was it the fourth day of consciousness, he heard the patter of rain on the roof followed by the sound of thunder in the distance.

Forcing himself to walk the sixty feet to the door of the store, he stood in the deluge allowing the water to wash away the dirt and excrement that he had been too weak to remove himself.

The rain seemed to refresh him more than the food and sleep had done. A change of store clothes gave him a further boost. From then on, he went outside every day especially if he heard rain, and he changed his clothing regularly. His morale now so much higher, his physical recovery quickened. He started to do light exercise, cleaned up the staff room where he still lived and turned his thoughts to the future.

The woman had gone and would be long dead by now. He wasn't sure why she had left, had he perhaps talked in his delirium revealing his part in the plot, or had she just chosen to die elsewhere. Either way, it did not matter now. She was gone and Mike had survived, just as he had survived Iraq, Ireland and Afghanistan. Mike always survived, but now what to do. Perhaps it was the absence of the woman, but somehow the idea of going to Skye no longer appealed in the way it had.

All his life he had felt left out, ostracised by those around him and over time had become used to it. So much so that he had long been convinced that he was the ultimate loner, content with his own company, immune to any feelings of loneliness.

Over the following weeks as he slowly recovered his strength, he tried to analyse this change that had come over him, he didn't actually feel lonely and had no real interest in finding any other survivors. He just felt there was a hole in his being that had never been there before.

For a while he assumed that it was the absence of the other conspirators.

Had they still been alive then perversely he would have gone to Skye in order to be away from them. Now they were no longer there, he had no reason to leave.

That conviction lasted no more than a couple of days before he realised that it wasn't the case.

It was only as he wondered what had gone wrong for them that he finally found the answer he was looking for.

He had no purpose, all his life Wilkinson as most others did, had always had somebody telling him what to do. Either as in the Army by a superior giving him orders, or as in Civvy Street the need for money, for shelter, transport or whatever in order to live. People need to do certain things, go to work or sign on. Shop, clean house, maintain transport, manage income, arrange holidays a thousand and one things to occupy oneself.

Wilkinson had virtually nothing to do, except live from day to day. He opened a tin of food in the mornings, another later in the day and again in the evening. He took whatever he wanted as and when he needed it. He had no need for money, no need to obey any rules, just live.

That wasn't enough, he knew that eventually he would need to plan a way of life, he couldn't exist forever on tinned food and bottled drinks.

He would have to grow food and raise livestock, find somewhere to live more permanently. That was exactly what he would have done had things worked out, and he was sure that was what he had wanted. Now he needed something more, he wondered what had happened to the others, what had gone wrong for them. Whatever it was had also cost him the woman. They hadn't been able to obtain the antidote they needed, so that forced Mike and Maggie to this store in an attempt to survive, and then to her leaving him. He wasn't particularly resentful of this but curious.

What had gone wrong for those two hundred intended survivors? He had met Roberts on the Sunday and collected his dose of the antidote. He hadn't met the other assassins on the day but was pretty sure he knew who they were. He also knew that whoever they were, they like himself would have had to meet with the same trio of spooks responsible for meeting the aircraft carrying the antidote in order to obtain their own doses of the lifesaving syringes.

Wilkinson was equally aware that among the couriers only Roberts himself knew what the three of them were picking up. His associates had remained in the car as the two conspirators briefly exchanged a few words. Roberts was a few years younger than Mike but had seemed steady enough if somewhat understandably nervous.

They had parted with a final hand shake and gone their separate ways.

Mike to release the deadly virus and the other to make his way back to The Manor with their precious cargo.

A journey that should have taken no more than ten hours at most. So what had gone wrong, whatever it was had cost the other conspirators their lives and wrecked Mikes own plans.

It was enough, Mike would find out what had happened that had cost the conspirators their lives, if only for his own interest. What then? He didn't know, he might be tempted to kill whoever had been the prime mover.

Not that he had any particular grudge against anyone, it wasn't anything to him who survived, as long as he did. But he somehow felt that someone should pay for what he had been through in the past weeks, and for those people lying dead at The Manor. Mike, had he supposed been on their team, so to speak. So yes, that's what he would do, find whoever had stolen the antidote and then perhaps kill him or her, he'd make his mind up about that when the time came.

He felt a lightening in his mood, in his whole being really. Just the idea of having a mission in life again made all the difference. Mike Wilkinson opened yet another can of beans and for the first time in weeks actually enjoyed his meal.

Chapter 42

More Hopes Destroyed

If Charles Benford's granddaughter Endia was mourning the loss of her university place and subsequent career, she wasn't the only one frustrated at the change in their personal futures. Marie Sanders was twenty seven years old and married to Garry Sanders. They had enjoyed a fantastic wedding six years before, courtesy of her father in law Tom. The big mechanic come scrap dealer had always been good at making money and as the head of his family took great pride in helping his son along.

Tom had provided the deposit for Garry and Marie's four bed detached house. In the following years, Marie who considered herself as having incredibly good taste had spent every penny she could on making her home the envy of all their friends. New kitchen, new bathroom, Georgian style conservatory and landscaped garden. Garry had worked long hours increased his mortgage and taken on loans from wherever he could.

At times he despaired, knowing no matter how much money he gave his wife she would always want something more. His father had tried to warn him about Marie before they married, pointing out to his eldest son Marie was too high maintenance for anyone less than a prem footballer.

Garry had ignored the warnings from his father and others and hidden the loans from everyone especially his wife and father.

Marie herself was oblivious of the strain her husband was under in his attempt to keep her happy and continued to lust after one of the new houses in West Deeping, the ones with Granny flats adjoining. Not that she had any parents to move in with her. Marie's father had emigrated to Australia with his new wife years before and the only contact from him had been the occasional Christmas or birthday card. Since he never enclosed his own address contact had been lost when her mother had announced they were moving to Spain with some new boyfriend Jorge or something similar. Marie had just turned sixteen and recently met Jason a really 'bad' agent for something or other who had promised to look after her and get her some modelling work. Her mum had hit the roof and said she had to come with her to Spain. A strong hint that Jorge had tried it on with Marie, put a stop to that and Marie had been left behind. A few weeks later she had been left behind by Jason as well.

After the most awful two years of her life during which she had been involved on the fringe of drugs and prostitution without ever quite having to get her hands dirty, she had met Garry.

One look at his dad's Merc and the five-bedroom house they lived in, she decided that this had to be better than where she was.

Then this bloody bug had come along to spoil her plans. She had been amongst the first to fall ill and had only to close her eyes to relive those few hours of knowing they were all going to die. Garry, as always, had looked after her even after he had started to vomit himself.

Then her father in law had somehow produced a miracle cure, 'some bloke he knew'. Within hours, she and Garry had recovered and a world had died. Then the nightmare had started again. The world really had come to an end, there was nothing left but survival itself. Then it seemed that some old fellow named, Charles Benford considered himself to be in charge of the survivors. Since he also had the antidote, both the hypodermics and the monthly capsules they needed, her father in law had pointed there wasn't a lot of room for argument. The old bastard hadn't made any effort to hide his pleasure at his daughter in laws distress in her change of circumstance.

Now it seemed that this Benford bloke expected everyone to work, really work, that is actual physical work. During her drop out period as she now tended to think of it Marie had spent a few weeks on a hairdressing course.

Nothing had ever come of it because she had dropped out after those first few weeks and that was it. Marie had no other work skills, she wasn't even a good cook, with her figure to think about, who wanted to be eating anything other than fruit and salads.

With no skills to speak of, Marie had been faced with helping out in what was termed the enabling department. A euphemism for the labourers who as far as she was concerned were landed with all the rotten jobs. So inspired by overhearing a couple of women complaining about their appearances, she had lied and claimed to be a hairdresser. Charles ever a flirt who liked to see women at their best, and mindful of the need to raise morale had equipped a room in the main house as a salon and left her to get on with it. She hadn't fooled the women for more than the time it took her to make a complete mess of her first two customers, and she soon found herself clearing tables and doing other people's laundry.

All that was bad enough but what really drove her mad and made her hate Charles Benford was her home. She was living in a bloody caravan, 'only a temporary thing', she was assured by her husband, houses needed to be converted, wood and coal fires for heating needed chimneys built, cess pits dug and generators provided for electricity (and that was strictly rationed). When all of that had been installed and it became their turn on the list they would be assigned a home.

That word, assigned, really grated on her, that she Marie who had such impeccable taste should be 'assigned' a house. And what sort of house would it be.

She'd seen the sort of places they were working on and they didn't suit her. Oh, a lot of people liked cottages and village life and good luck to them. Marie preferred modern and that's what annoyed her so much.

After she had got over the initial shock of the virus and its consequences, Marie had gradually realised that she could have any house she wanted. Anywhere in the country, any size, she could have whatever she wanted.

Not just her, they could all have their ideal homes and why shouldn't they. There was no ownership now, so why should they live in some old pokey place miles from anywhere when they had their pick of the best.

Yet, here they were living almost communally, and Marie actually shivered at that thought, in bloody caravans.

She had got on to Garry and his father about it. Garry had tried to sweet talk her round, Tom never long on patience had simply told her not to be stupid, and she had another fall out with her husband about that as well.

No, this was all bollocks and she wasn't going to put up with it, Garry was going to have to do something or she was off. Off where, to whom? As she considered the problem, the helplessness of her situation really came home to her and Marie Sanders looked out of her caravan window towards the hen house from where she was expected to collect eggs every day and sobbed.

Chapter 43

Some Progress

"Have you seen Sean when he tries to collect the eggs?" Jilly chuckled at the memory as she addressed her husband. "He seems to think that he needs to grab hold of a hen then force an egg out of them in some fashion. There are chickens squawking and hopping about, feathers flying, little half pint outside the wire chasing around barking and Sean diving around having the time of his life." She paused to see what effect she might be having on Charles, any mention of his grandchildren would normally bring an immediate interest from her other half and she badly wanted to divert his attention away from work. He was working too hard and too long and seemed to be really worried about something. Obviously, there was plenty of things to concern him, but for the past couple of days there seemed to be something especial occupying him.

For his part, Charles looked at his wife fondly, fully aware of what she was trying to do and guessed why. But this time Jilly was wrong, Charles was preoccupied but not really worried as such, in fact just the opposite.

Things seemed to be going well. The move from Kingsthorpe to Hardworth was progressing with about a third of the population now at the new location. Kingsthorpe was still serving as a collection centre for the lorry loads of supplies still being collected from their home city, but there were less numbers of the people working on these duties now and more on the long term needs at Hardworth.

Their numbers were increasing steadily and the people seemed, if not actually happy, at least to be accepting life as it was now.

So yes, things did seem to be progressing fairly well and Benford was one of those who while never a pessimist was always guarded and trying to look ahead for any gathering clouds.

There were plenty of those, the chief of which was the lack of numbers in the community. From the time of his winning possession of the antidote, he had been all too aware that there was simply not enough people available to prevent mankind sliding so far back in time, they may never recover.

Twenty first century life needed so many varied skills and resources from around the world, with so many of these interdependent on one another that millions of people were needed for even simple things to be manufactured. Rubber, plastics, nylon rope, paper even, the list was endless. How long would it be he thought before anything like those everyday items were again produced for use in Britain.

They needed people and they needed to learn new skills or rather they needed to learn old skills that had long ago all but disappeared.

Benford felt that by cannibalising the machines and resources of the twenty first century, they could perhaps gain a hundred and fifty year period in which to learn how to manage without those same things.

Electricity and clean water were the twin keys. If they could learn how to produce power from the elements, wind, water and sun, and an ability to provide clean water for drinking and hygiene, then he believed that they could limit the slide back in time to some bastardised medieval period.

Of course it wouldn't be Charles himself or any of the current population that would achieve this ambition if it was achieved. For a moment, he wondered just how many generations would pass before the survivors did run out of 21st century supplies. If the country had say two weeks supply of petrol and gas in stock at the time of the death, supposing that the population was, NO not was, HAD BEEN around sixty million, then if they could build their own numbers up to, what, say around a thousand and collect and save around a half of those stocks then in theory they would have enough for two and a half thousand years.

Of course, he didn't kid himself that they could hope to collect anything like that amount, and he had no idea how long petrol might remain good for. But surely a hundred and fifty maybe even two hundred years shouldn't be too much to ask for. Two hundred years, that would equate to about eight generations. Well, a lot could change in two hundred years and during eight generations, and he couldn't control it for good or bad but he could and would lay the foundations for success.

A lot a squawking outside interrupted his thoughts and back to the present, evidently Sean was still egg collecting, so enough day dreaming, there was work to do.

Chapter 44

Wilkinson Investigates

He started by going back to The Manor, the weather was hot and had been throughout his recovery, so the stench of the place was intolerable.

Either he or someone had left the front door ajar allowing rats and other carrion to enter and feast on the rotting bodies.

One particularly large cat gave him a hard stare, reluctant to leave TC's body, Mike returned the cats look for a moment before turning away from the corpse with a half-smile, muttering, "I never did support your lot," and retreated to his car. From the boot he took out a set of disposable overalls and a face mask, donning these he entered the building again and started his search.

He worked steadily for several hours, one body after another. The unbelievably grisly task at first requiring every ounce of his determination to continue, became gradually merely unpleasant as he grew more used to his macabre work.

Wallets, purses, notebooks, any and every scrap of paper with writing on it were read and addresses entered into his own files. During this work, he made another puzzling discovery, there were more than two hundred corpses here, a careful count revealed a total of two hundred and thirty nine, knowing that there were seven people involved in the release of the virus and in picking up the antidote meant that there would have been at least forty six people more than there was antidote for. Very odd but nevertheless, he decided that particular riddle could wait for the time being and continued his search.

Wilkinson had little hope of finding any real clue that might give some idea of what had gone wrong for the intended survivors. Instead, he concentrated upon identifying the corpses and then discovering their antecedents and addresses.

If he was to solve the puzzle then he would need every piece of information on the chosen ones he could get. Who they were, where they worked and who they knew, especially who they knew.

Mike would bet that whoever it was had stolen the antidote, he or she would have been known to one or more of the plotters.

Perhaps, someone who had not been included in that final two hundred plus, but who was aware of the existence of them. Even more likely was that the culprit was someone who had been included as a survivor, but who was determined to possess more of the antidote, wanting the luxury of choosing his own group of people to survive.

The more he thought about it the more likely he felt this latter idea would turn out to be correct, so he needed to find out who was missing from among the dead.

Someone who should have been there but wasn't, and that should lead him to the guilty one. It wasn't much to go on especially as if the idea was correct then that would be increasing the numbers selected to survive again by at least one. Nevertheless, he had plenty of time and nothing else to go on so back to the search. Now though, he was becoming aware of other needs.

As far as he could figure, September was approaching, some three to four months since he had released the virus.

During that time his body had been subjected to the most appalling viral attack imaginable. He had lost half his body weight and though he didn't know it, his internal organs had suffered long term irreparable damage.

Wilkinson had survived the virus but he could sense that he would never make old bones, so he was keen not to waste any time.

The mild summer weather continued into the start of autumn but the nights were beginning to turn cool. Mike had again searched The Manors numerous outbuildings and finally located the generator that he knew must exist.

Now with light and heat available, he cleared a room over a garage of old newspapers and other debris. Bringing in a bed, table and chair he made the room comfortable for somewhere to live, while he conducted his investigation. A camping gas cooker provided his means of hot food and it was while heating yet another can of baked beans that Wilkinson broke down.

It was nothing important at first, he just became bored of his diet, cans of beans, cans of spaghetti, cans of Irish stew, ham, rice pudding, fruit, cans, cans cans. There was no bread, no fresh vegetables, no meat, all fresh and frozen foods were long since spoilt. Oh, he could go out into the surrounding countryside and kill something and no doubt find some vegetables that hadn't yet spoilt, but that would take time, and that time would come from his search and so put him behind in discovering who had stolen the antidote. Those thoughts made him think further, Mike had gone into the conspiracy willingly enough, knowing that he was saving the planet and, if he was honest because he disliked his fellow man. The idea of living off the land appealed to him, his special forces training had equipped him to survive quite happily and he was content with his own company. Training and planning was one thing, reality quite another. Everything he now realised was down to him, if he wanted fresh food, he would have to grow it. Mike would have to plant the seed, tend it, harvest it, grind corn for flour, breed livestock.

Anything he wanted, he was going to have to provide, and the quiet! He had never needed noise, who did, but this quiet was deafening. It was one thing to sit alone at a bar, or by a riverbank, an outside table at a café, or a walk in the country; prior to the plague, almost anywhere you went, however peaceful, there was always background noise.

Traffic, background music, half heard conversations going on around him, livestock mewling, children playing. Noise was everywhere, but not now.

In the countryside, the fields were full of dead cattle, cows, pigs, and sheep. The virus had left them unharmed but as Charles Benford had predicted, wherever animals were secured in fields and pens dependent on humans for water they either found a way to break out of their surroundings or they died. As he journeyed around, the only signs of life he saw were rats and birds, both types disappearing as soon as they heard the sound of his vehicle approaching.

There was nothing it seemed unaffected in some way. He spent hours every day doing things he needed just to survive. Surprisingly, he was still getting water from some taps, but it tasted funny, sort of acidy, so he used it only for washing purposes, and that needed heating. Drinking water came from bottles, he had the generator for electricity, but that in turn required fuel.

The list was endless, and for what. Now the same instability that had made the Special Forces RTU, took him over. Mike looked down at the plate of beans and in sudden anger threw them across the room, not content with just those he hurled the table after them and picking up the chair raised it above his head and smashed it onto the floor jarring his arms painfully as he did so.

The chair was followed by everything within reach as the frenzy overtook him. Until turning to look for his next target, he caught sight of himself in the mirror, Mike was a man who frequently lost his temper, an individual who when thwarted could fly into a terrible and violent rage.

With bulging eyes and flaring nostrils he was an intimidating sight and in other circumstances, he enjoyed the look of fear his rage engendered in others.

There was nothing intimidating about the man who stared back at him from the mirror now. This man was unshaven, his hair unkempt, a man still two stone lighter than normal, a pathetic man with tears running down his face, and he wasn't even aware that he was crying. Mike peered closer, trying to recognise this stranger who looked back at him, licking salty lips and breathing harshly. He looked around him at the destruction he had just wrought and thought of the blank future he faced, he had leant against the wall and now slid down it until his bowed head rested against his knees and cried.

How long he remained like this he had no idea, but when he did finally arise, he carefully tidied the room, removing the breakages and sweeping up the debris. His living quarters attended to, he addressed his own appearance, washing and shaving, then changed his clothing.

He looked again in the mirror, his hair was to long but apart from that and looking thin, he was almost his old self. But now in him was a terrible determination to find who had stolen the antidote and in Mike's twisted mind, by stealing the antidote, the thief had also stolen Mike's future. So yes, he would find the guilty one no matter what or how long it took him, and then there would be such a reckoning.

Chapter 45

Son's Concern

Transferring her pub activity from Kingsthorpe to Hardworth hadn't been easy for Maggie. After moving from the hotel in Peterborough, all of the survivors had lived in the former village, except of course when away on work duties over at Hardworth or elsewhere.

But present in the village or not, the one pub had been enough to serve the entire population.

Knowing that the existing stocks of draught and bottled beers would soon go off, and that these would be followed shortly by the white wines going the same way, Maggie had entertained huge doubts about the whole idea when Charles had first voiced his proposal of her opening the pub.

Benford had overrode her objections claiming that the survivors boasted two or three keen home brewers already who would soon learn how to brew larger quantities. In between times they would manage with what beers they had and red wines and spirits that wouldn't go of.

She needn't have worried, from the very first, the pub was a great success. Bringing along with the chip van parked outside the premises a sense of familiar normality to the people's lives.

Maggie was careful to limit everyone to just three alcoholic drinks a day and to no more than four visit's a week, not a popular rule with everybody but still rigidly, though at times with difficulty enforced.

With her experience and charm Maggie made the bar somewhere people felt at ease and where new arrivals to the community could be welcomed enthusiastically by the existing population.

After the move to Hardworth it was intended that with the population growing as it was, the survivors should be spread around four local villages, three of these of which had existing public house premises.

Unable with their existing resources to staff all three of the inns, eventually Maggie and Charles had selected the building closest to Hardworth house itself to be the first pub, with another small bar in the canteen attached to the Stately house itself. If the population continued to grow, a second Inn would be opened in the largest of the villages, this to be run by Charles' in laws, Harry and Peggy Chambers who were currently helping Maggie part time.

It was in one corner of Maggie's then that Niall waited for his brother to arrive. The pub was officially closed at this time of day but it had become a regular occurrence that what might be termed as staff meetings were held here. Maggie ever obliging would usually provide some soft drinks and ensure a degree of privacy when she sensed it was called for.

Robbie had asked for this particular meet and Niall had an idea he knew what his brother wanted to discuss.

When their father had first produced the antidote all those weeks ago, people had obviously asked where and how he had obtained it.

Charles had never really given any details. Only ever saying that he had overheard a conversation that he wasn't supposed to, and that had led to an incident where four men had died, one of them being the real hero who was responsible for their survival. If pressed, he would also intimate that one of the terrorists had died at his hands and then only after being tortured in some way by Charles himself, the speaker would usually break off at this point as though choked up by the memories of what had obviously been a traumatic experience.

At the time people glad simply to be alive and with their families, had just accepted this briefest of stories, and not wanting to upset their rescuer further refrained from asking him any more questions.

Inevitably though as time passed and the survivors settled into their new lives, a growing sense of curiosity arose. This inquisitiveness was further enhanced by the steady flow of newcomers to their population, these arrivals while glad to have joined the community that would give them a better long term chance of survival, didn't owe their lives directly to Benford and his antidote in the same way as the originals survivors did.

Just as inevitably, having lost friends and loved ones to the plague, individuals wanted to know how come this guy had managed to save his own family and friends. Where had this magic serum come from, how had Benford come by it, inevitably the question asked most of all was, had he been a part of the conspiracy that had wiped out an entire world. Charles himself still avoided giving straight answers to the questions.

Continuing to be able to do so because so many of the original population having known him for so much, or all of their lives, didn't believe for a minute that he would have been one of the conspirators.

But even amongst his own relations there was some mutterings. That same old strange mix of gratitude and resentment was still simmering, especially amongst those who felt that they ought to have been given more of the antidote.

Benford had saved their lives and the lives of their nearest and dearest, their husbands, wives, sons and daughters, but not brothers, sisters, mother's, father's. Now as the weeks passed, his foresight and leadership continued to keep them safe from the dangers that most of them had never thought of, let alone planned how to cope with. Gratitude and common sense demanded that they should accept what they had and give thanks for it. Grief however wasn't that easily dealt with, and the occasional suspicions of a newcomer sometimes found fertile ground among the population.

This then was the subject that Robbie wished to discuss with his brother. The scurrilous rumours were becoming both more frequent and vicious. Robbie was afraid that it could only be a matter of time before at least some of the people started to believe in the adage that 'where there was smoke there was fire'.

Niall as aware as his brother of all the loose talk was just as keen as Robbie for his father to clear the air and give out more information on how the antidote had been obtained.

"But he won't do it, Rob. I've asked him time and again what happened that day and he doesn't want us to know." Niall shrugged as he spoke, both brothers were aware their father who usually despised stubbornness as a form of stupidity could nevertheless dig his heels in as determinedly as anyone when he chose to.

"All he ever says is that he overheard something he shouldn't have and as a result four men died. One of the four was the real hero and died at the scene, the other three were all part of the terror group. These three also died in whatever incident took place, and at least one of them was at Dad's hands and only after he had been tortured, also by Dad if you can believe that."

Niall finished his precis of their father's well-rehearsed story with yet another shrug. Both men like most of the original survivors knew the story by heart, having heard it many times over the past weeks, and both men still found it just as difficult to believe that the man they had loved and respected all their lives could torture and kill a man in cold blood. Then again, they both knew about the girl knocked over in the road during the delivery of the antidote and of the small boy at the Castle hotel the following day.

So their father was obviously quite capable of killing when he felt it was the right thing to do. Neither brother would ever admit to holding any doubts about their father's innocence regarding the conspiracy, but he wasn't making it easy for them to convince others to the same degree.

Frustrated, the meeting broke up with nothing decided other than to ask their father yet again.

Chapter 46

Further Investigation

Someone was missing from The Manor, someone who had been included in the numbers. Someone chosen to survive had double crossed his companions and stolen the antidote for his or her own purpose. It was the only thing that made sense, that idea was what he had been working on for the last couple of days and that's what he would continue to do.

Only now he changed tactics, he started to visit the homes of the dead conspirators, searching through telephone contacts, addresses, Christmas card lists, not sure of what or who he was looking for but convinced that he would know it when he saw it.

It took weeks and he travelled widely around the home counties in his search, but he was in no hurry now, he had a purpose and he would see it through, however long it took. But he was no detective and not a terribly good organiser, so his research was haphazard and, in the end, it was the sight of his own name that gave him a clue. He was back at The Manor and searching again through the various papers he had found there.

He was glancing for the umpteenth time through the diary of politician Lou Amphlett's wife, when he spotted a short list of three names with a lot of doodling around it. He could picture the woman in a thoughtful mood writing the names down and then absently scribbling anything as she pondered those names. The three were his own, plus a Trevor Pearce and Steve Bent.

Pearce, he knew, was a fellow assassin, one of those who like himself had been chosen to release the virus. There was to be six flasks, or was it eight, increasingly his memory seemed to be at fault since his illness. No matter six or eight there was to be three assassins, of that he was certain.

Mike for some reason had been sure that the three were himself, Pearce and Crispin Sterry Brown. So why was this Bent guy on a list of three names with himself and Pearce? He tried to think back why he had thought Crispin was one of the killers, and couldn't come up with anything. What if this Steve Bent was the third man and not Sterry Blunt, Crispin's body wasn't in The Manor and he was certainly a leading plotter so where was he?

Excited, he ran the thought along, Crispin was definitely a plotter but he wasn't here. If he wasn't an assassin either, then he was likely to be the double crosser.

When he considered Crispin's character, he was only surprised that he hadn't thought of him earlier. He briefly considered the other two names as well as possible suspects. He knew Pearce, a keen sailor had planned to take his boat and go with his girlfriend to the states. The pair of them had been due at the airport in Scotland to meet Roberts at the same time as Mike himself had been. Their late arrival had meant that though he had caught a brief glimpse of them as they climbed out of a black range rover, he had had no chance of talking to the couple.

But the speed at which the virus had spread confirmed that Pearce had released his flasks of the killer bug, and he would hardly have done that unless he was in possession of the antidote. No, he was pretty sure that Pearce had carried out his duties as arranged, and as the man had never seemed to care much about anybody else. No, Mike couldn't see Pearce stealing the antidote. Steve Bent he didn't know, had never met him and until now had never even heard of him before, but if Bent was the guilty one and had stolen the antidote then Crispin's body ought to be here at The Manor. So he would begin by pursuing that line, and only if that came to nothing would he look further at Steve Bent.

Chapter 47

Captain Tim Burton

"Still nothing from the Bagration sir, that's forty eight hours now without any contact."

"I know number one," Commander Tim Burton's sigh and tone of voice did little to hide the disappointment he felt at the lack of response from the Russian sub.

Turning toward the third member of the trio taking part in the pow wow, lieutenant commander William Marshall, Burton asked, "Take me through the time frame again bones."

"Billy Bones," Marshall studied his notes for a moment, not that he had any need to already knowing them of by heart, then replied to the submarine's C/O, "Using the day that the state governor of Hawaii first became aware of the viral outbreak as day 1, it runs like this. We and the Kansas receive notice that there is a serious worldwide problem, possibly even an act of terrorism on day three.

"Day four, the MOD advised us to stay under until further instruction." He paused for breath or perhaps to clear the emotional lump in his throat. "By day nine there is no contact with the outside world other than the Kansas. On day fourteen, the Kansas puts into Norfolk Virginia and investigates the situation. We know," he added as an aside, "that all personnel that went ashore at that time were wearing protective suits and all the normal safety precautions were taken. Despite those precautions, less than twelve hours later the Kansas reports its crew falling ill, and certainty that the virus is both airborne and aggressive, and of course still very much alive. That same day the Bagration having heard all the radio talk makes contact. Like us, ever since the virus first hit, they had remained submerged, and like us they continued to do so. That was fifty eight days ago or in other words, making today, day one hundred and two."

Burton interrupted the doctor and continued the narrative himself. "Then four days ago, day ninety eight, Commander Koenig informs us that he has to surface and that he was approx. one hundred miles south west of lands' end at that time. Since then, we have had just two contacts from them, both in garbled Russian, and completely incomprehensible to us and then nothing."

He looked at both Marshal and his first officer Andy Holt to see if either disagreed with anything that had been said.

Both men gave slight nods in affirmation without speaking. As far as Andy Holt was concerned, there was little to say. The Resolution was a nuclear powered sub, she could stay down for weeks yet, but sooner or later they would have to surface and if the virus was still as aggressive as now then it would mean death for all of them. Like many of the men aboard, the sub including the other two men now in the captain's office was married with a family. So like all the other crew, he was desperately worried about what was happening to his loved ones. There had been that chaotic week as whatever this killing bug was had hurtled around the world killing it seemed every living thing in its wake. Andy like the others had been beside himself with worry. Within days all crew members on the surface ships that they had been accompanying were dead.

Commander Burton had ignored cries from the last few requesting to be taken aboard the sub. Even when his own crew headed by both Holt and Marshall had added their pleas to the unfortunate men, Burton had remained adamant, sure that only by staying submerged and isolated could they hope to survive long enough for the virus to burn itself out.

Hawaii had been more than fourteen weeks ago and, in the time since, they had added very little to their knowledge of the virus. Crew members of the ill-fated USS Kansas had discovered that animals for the most part seemed unaffected by the bug itself, though not to other dangers, and they believed that there was evidence that some humans had survived, though dismally very few.

The Resolutions own crew were not happy that the skipper hadn't sailed immediately for home. Men naturally wanting to discover what had happened to their own families, hoping against hope for the best while at the same time fearing the worst.

Burton wouldn't have it, the skip had charted the progress of the virus.

Starting in Hawaii, it had spread around the globe in an ever widening circle so that the UK had been amongst the last countries to be hit.

According to the Bagration's radio operator, for some reason both Greenland and Iceland had remained virus free for a further three weeks before finally succumbing just as badly as everywhere else.

Bill Marshall had insisted that even in the age of supersonic aircraft, no virus could travel at that kind of speed. There had to be some kind of human assistance and if that was so and the virus was human made, then it could be supposed that those humans would want to survive the epidemic they had released and would have designed it to die out after completing its terrible task.

The Greenland and Iceland blips he believed were just that blips. The bug had just taken longer to spread to those northern places. Marshall's theory was so mind blowing that no one really accepted it.

Andy himself went along with the idea that it was a manmade virus and probably released as a terror weapon, but no one would actually plan to wipe out all mankind surely.

Even the most crazed terrorist would want his own kind to live, would want their own creed to win out and become dominant. So people would survive, it was simply not possible to visualise anything else.

So Andy, along with all the others aboard clung to the hope that his own family would survive somehow, and if they did then they would need him now.

They should be going home as fast as possible and if the virus was still live then, so be it, they would die along with their loved ones.

But in the end, he was a naval officer and obeyed his commanding officers orders.

As the submarines commander and with a heavy heart, Tim Burton had set aside his own feelings and put the survival of the boat and its crew above all else. The viral outbreak had started in the Northern Hemisphere during May, just as spring was turning to summer.

USS Kansas had been north of the equator and the virus only about a fortnight old when its crew had become exposed to its deadly effect.

Burton had promptly turned and headed for the Falkland isles and the colder temperatures of the southern hemisphere, in the hope that the virus wouldn't last as long as it might in the warmer north. Some seven weeks after the initial outbreak, the Bagration had made further contact with them. The Russian sub had been well to the north of its Brit counterpart and was heading for home waters.

Burton had agreed with his opposite number, commander Koenig to follow along and had sailed north in the hope that the virus may have run its course.

Then had come a couple of garbled messages, something about the crew planning mutiny but most of it delivered in a mixture of Russian and broken English and almost indecipherable. They never knew exactly why the Russians had surfaced and opened all hatches, but that the virus was still active was proven beyond doubt.

So the British sub had turned around once again and sought the safety of colder waters. Burton brought the meeting with his two subordinates to a close without mentioning his own fears of a similar mutiny amongst the resolutions crew.

The men were getting more restless by the day, questioning how were they going to know when and if the virus was over. What was happening to their families, why was there no word from the admiralty. The answers to these were all painfully obvious and discipline was slipping accordingly. Nevertheless, the three men agreed that they would continue to stay submerged for as long as possible in an attempt to wait out the deadly bug.

Sipping a fresh coffee after the other two officers had left his tiny cabin, Burton reflected again on that last decision. Yeah, stay down as long as possible. What then? Sooner or later they would have to surface and face what they all inwardly knew. The world was gone, at least their world was gone. Families and friends, all dead, as much as the thought was unpalatable, he knew it to be true. Then what would they do, the whole base of his authority would be gone. He would have no right to demand that the crew continue to follow him, though no doubt many of them would. He knew he was a popular and respected commander, but what could he promise them, every avenue of thought seemed to lead to a dead end.

What the hell was he doing, Burton jumped to his feet suddenly recognising the way he was slipping into depression. He was an officer in the British Royal navy and the commanding officer of this boat. Whatever they eventually faced out there, he would do his duty as he saw it at the time. He led an excellent crew and between them they would overcome whatever problems presented themselves as they met them.

Chapter 48

On the Hunt

Now with both a purpose and a plan, he enjoyed a new sense of wellbeing, his old self coming to the fore again. Mike Wilkinson had been SAS for a while, he was tough, confident and self-reliant and a man who could plan a tactical campaign.

Fuel had been a constant problem for him, there were plenty of petrol stations around but no electric to work the pumps. So now, he visited a number of garages collecting as many jerry cans as he could. Then he drove around the countryside until he found a farm with its own diesel tank. The tank was new and in an effort to avoid theft was again electronically operated. He made no attempt to be clever, the tank had a gauge on its side showing the level of fuel inside, Mike simply drove a spike into the side of the tank about half way down the level, then as the diesel erupted from the hole, he offered the cans in turn under the flow.

Running out of cans before the flow stopped, he forced his spike back into the hole in a futile attempt to halt it, failing, he ignored the problem.

When the fluid fell below the level of the hole it would stop anyway and he would repeat the operation when he needed to. A visit to a caravan centre fixed him up with a large camper van. Diesel and supplies loaded, Mike felt once again able to turn his attention to finding the antidote thief.

It still took time, as far as he remembered there had been no mention of his quarry in any of the paper work that he had found in The Manor. Indeed it was only his absence on the list of names of the bombers that had drawn his attention to the man.

He seemed to have a dim memory of hearing that Crispin lived somewhere near Guildford and as a starting point made his way there.

The telephone book didn't show any number for Crispin but there was a Mr and Mrs Sterry Brown listed. Whatever Crispin's father had done for living, he must have been successful at it. The mock Tudor house Mike pulled up outside of was impressive by any standards, it was also empty.

No bodies and no smell of death made a welcome change. Mr Sterry Brown also boasted a good wine cellar as well as several bottles of good malts and equally good brandies. Mike sampled a couple of both as he settled into a deep leather armchair to study the families address book.

An hour later, he arrived outside of a modest block of flats, Crispin apparently leased the penthouse. A crowbar gained him access to both the block and Penthouse. That same putrid smell of death that he had become so acquainted with permeated the hallways and stairwells of the block.

Though again, there was an absence of bodies inside the apartment itself. Mike was becoming increasingly excited by this, taking the lack of either Crispin's or his parent's corpses as further possible evidence of the formers guilt. Bastard had obviously double crossed the others and saved his own family and friends. No doubt setting up his own commune somewhere, where!

Once again it was an address book that provided his next clue. He recognised a number of names of some of the leading figures in the British security services. Though once again, his detection skills let him down, there was nothing in the apartment to indicate where Crispin and his family may have gone. Mike had found a safe in the bedroom, nothing very special just the sort of thing that could be found in any hotel room and it was the work of less than an hour to gain access to it and less than another ten minutes to rifle the papers inside, still nothing. It was another two days before leafing through Crispin's notebook, he spotted two names and distant memory recalled and linked Rebeckah and Sir Harmer Evans as father and daughter. He also clearly remembered the girl's body being at The Manor, but not the fathers.

That in itself was incredible, Sir Harmer's was a name he knew. Wilkinson had never met Sir Harmer Evans, but the knight's name was legendary among the Special Forces people and it seemed impossible that such a pillar of the security world, a man who had risked death on repeated occasions in the service of his country, would then betray that country in such a way. But with the body of the girl, his only daughter being at The Manor, it would seem certain that Evans himself however unlikely must have been a part of the conspiracy. Mike was becoming ever more confused though, if Crispin and Evans had double crossed the others how come Rebeckah had died.

A rethink was needed, after some thought his next theory went as: if both men had been involved in the plot, and that now seemed certain, then if Crispin had been the double crosser then perhaps it was Evans that had headed up the search for him.

That made more sense, because then the daughter would have been with the others at The Manor, while her father would have remained somewhere he could control the search for Crispin or whoever else was in possession of the antidote.

It took a while and involved visits to a number of ministry buildings until he eventually found an address for Evans, in Canterbury and he drove the eighty miles across that same day.

Surprisingly, Evans office wasn't difficult to enter and the familiar smell of death hit him straight away. A corpse lay on a chaise lounge with half its head missing and a revolver lying on the carpet next to it suggested that Sir Harmer, if that's who the corpse was had chosen to cheat the virus and taken his own way out.

Charles Benford's name and address didn't take any finding. Harmer Evans had been a tidy man and there was only the one piece of paper on his desk. Fingering it, Mike Wilkinson studied the information for a moment excitedly wondering about the man whose name was printed there. Charles Benford, not Crispin Sterry Brown. He sat puzzled, was this the man who he was looking for then, was this the thief. If not, then who was he?

The name meant nothing to Mike, but from the evidence this was the last thing Evans had been working on before blowing his brains out.

Knowing that without the antidote both he and his daughter would inevitably die, Evans wouldn't have wasted his last hours on anything but hunting whoever was in possession of it. So whoever this guy was, he must be his quarry, or at least know must be able to lead Mike to his him.

So how had this guy got hold of the antidote or even know of its existence. However he had gained possession of the antidote, Charles Benford must think he was a real cute bastard to have survived the virus.

Mike gave the slightest of nods in acknowledgment of the fact before muttering, "But your luck just ran out," then tucked the paper into his pocket before heading for his car.

As he drove north toward Peterborough a memory came back to him. A memory from months before, of his journey south with Maggie. The thought of her, her womanly smell, that sexy mature figure, the smile that lit her face up. At least it did prior to the arrival of the death, still stung in more ways than one. Putting aside the disappointment of losing the woman, Mike dimly remembered her yelling at him to stop, convinced she had seen movement at some service station. He was pretty sure that was somewhere close to Peterborough. At the time Mike had been sure she was mistaken about seeing anything, now it seemed she may not have been. It was dark by the time he reached the city but with the aid of a map, he drove straight to Benford's former home. He held no hope that the man would still be living there, but he needed some kind of starting point in his search and this seemed as good as any.

There was no sign of life at the house and the front door took little kicking in. The all too familiar stench of death assaulted his nostrils as he entered the house and for once, Wilkinson was uncharacteristically visibly shaken when he recognised the remains of what had once been Crispin Sterry Brown. Reluctantly, he took time to inspect the body looking for any signs of violence. While reasonably sure, the former spook had died as a result of contracting the virus, Mike needed to know for certain. He had never been a fan of Crispin but he did have a certain respect for the man's abilities, and if Crispin had died violently at the hands of this Charles Benford, then it made the latter far more dangerous than Mike had anticipated. Satisfied that it was the virus that had been responsible for the corpse and not Benford, Mike spent the night in the camper while waiting for the daylight he needed in order to better search the house for any intimation of where the occupants might have gone.

When he could finally carry out his search, the result left him more frustrated than ever. There was no indication as to whether Crispin and this Benford bloke had been in it together and then turned on each other with Crispin coming out the loser. Somehow, Wilkinson couldn't see that happening. Looking around, this was the home of a nobody, one of the little men that Mike had spent years in the army protecting.

No way could someone like this have even known an upper class prick like Crispin and certainly not gain the better of him. No, they weren't in this together, couldn't have been. His utter certainty of this still provided little help. There was nothing here to suggest where Benford and his band of survivors might have gone and Wilkinson had run out of ideas.

He tried to imagine what he would have done if he had found himself in the same situation as Benford. That didn't really help, Mike had been trained to survive alone in some of the most desperate situations imaginable. But nothing in his past, nothing in his makeup had ever included having to consider the welfare and care of two hundred others.

Mike himself could survive anywhere, but what facilities would two hundred others need. What sort of people would they be, what age groups and what skills would they have. He tried to imagine who he might have chosen to save. That was difficult, Mike had few friends and he continually found himself listing types and occupations of people rather than names of real individuals. His limited imagination and bigoted opinions didn't allow him to visualise how others might behave in such fraught circumstances. Frustrated, he could think of nothing better than to drive around the area in ever increasing circles, visit every village around in the hope that the survivors would surely stay close to the area they knew best.

They would need food, clothing, and equipment of all kinds. They needed to generate electricity that would mean fossil fuels, they needed to plant crops for the future and to raise animals. Staying local to the places they knew would make sense, so surely if he threw out a wide enough ring he must make contact sometime. With no more promising idea than that, and having already just travelled up from the south without any contact with other human beings, he started his search by travelling around the villages and farms to the east, then slowly swinging anti clockwise toward the north.

His plan was to visit anywhere within a twelve mile radius of the city centre on his first circuit and increase by another ten miles on every subsequent one. Sooner or later he must come across some signs of life, two hundred people scavenging, and that's what they would be doing, would leave all kinds of traces. He would find them, it was just a matter of time.

Kingsthorpe lay to the west of Peterborough, so was in the last but one section of his first search area. He reached the village on the third day and was already becoming frustrated at the amount of time this was going to take. His arrival was from the higher ground to the north of the village afforded him a clear view of the entire parish.

Just behind him was a major fork in the road and seeing that Kingsthorpe was plainly deserted, he took the right fork towards his next intended search section.

Mike had no way of knowing that he had missed the last of the survivors leaving for Hardworth by more than a month, and so continued his fruitless wandering.

His search method idea of ever increasing circuits around the area had seemed simple enough at the time it had occurred to him, putting it into practice wasn't so easy. While the villages to the east of Peterborough were fairly sparse, the road layout serving them was poor and confusing and involved constant reference to his map. On the other hand to the west of the city, the villages were far more numerous than he had expected but the road system still as confusing. He had a sat nav in his vehicle and surprisingly it still worked. Presumably, the satellite continuing its work until instructed otherwise. However it still seemed of little help and frequently inaccurate. After a fortnight, he was still within a twenty two mile radius of his starting point and apparently no nearer to discovering his quarry then he had been at the beginning.

He stopped for supplies at the smaller village shops where forcing access was easier and continued to obtain diesel from the farms he passed.

Finally on the seventeenth day of this fruitless searching, his patience ran out and he decided to return to Benford's house. He would go through the man's papers and photos carefully, see if he had had a favourite part of the country that he visited a lot. If he had, then maybe Benford had chosen to move to there.

It was probably a flimsy hope but would at least make a change for a few days, he could always resume his search pattern from where he left of later on if need be. His route into Peterborough this time took him past a supermarket and it was only by chance that he happened to glance in that direction in time to see that something had been painted on the window of the store, writing of some sort, but too far away to read from where he was.

For no conscious reason that he could fathom, Wilkinson turned into the access road and drove up to the shop front. He didn't need to exit the car to read in large white letters, 'SURVIVORS GO TO THE VILLAGE OF KINGSTHORPE', then in smaller letters, 'you will find help there'. He stared, trying to reason what this meant. Reference to his map showed he had been to Kingsthorpe early in his search though he had no sense of memory about it. Though, evidently, he had seen no sign of life there.

Was this just a case of one or two survivors seeking to join with others or was it the group he was looking for. Either way, he had obviously missed any sign of them and would have to visit this Kingsthorpe again.

Then what? Time enough to decide that, if and when he knew if this was what he was looking for. Half an hour later, he was again looking down at what appeared to be a deserted village. Kingsthorpe was little more than a hamlet of some fifty to sixty upmarket homes ranging from seventeenth century stone cottages to twenty first century imitations of the same. There was a stately manor and what was still a nice looking pub restaurant. As he looked again, he started to notice that Kingsthorpe while empty of life nevertheless had a sense of recent habitation about it. There were no cars parked on the roads but some of the houses on the far side of the village had five or six parked in their drives, more than the size of the buildings suggested they needed, as though someone had moved surplus motors from point a to point b to get them out of the way. The pubs gardens had been tended until not too long ago, as had The Manors. He drove through the main street slowly, seeking some kind of clue. He found what he was looking for on the village notice board opposite the church yard. All other notices had been torn down leaving only one, again headed SURVIVORS, it went on to explain to any such that the community had moved on. There was over two hundred of them, they were organised with among others doctors, teachers and farmers. The notice went on to explain that Kingsthorpe had only ever been intended as a stop gap while they prepared their permanent home more than eighty miles away. Survivors were urged to make their way to Woodall services on the M1, here they were promised members of the community would visit the services every day for two hours between noon and two pm in order to guide any refugees to their base. Everybody, they were assured would be made welcome and cared for.

He should have felt elated at finding his quarry, but strangely wasn't. These were obviously the group of people who had somehow wrested the antidote from Roberts and the others. If they were more than two hundred strong as claimed then their recruitment campaign that they were evidently running must be working. He found himself admiring that.

Individuals would stand little chance of surviving in the long term and for this Benford guy to have prioritised contacting them in this way spoke well for him. Not that the humanity aspect of the effort impressed him, just the imagination and leadership that it showed in itself. Benford's scalp might turn out to be more of a prize than he had expected after all.

The drive to Woodall took two hours and he decided to change vehicles, parking his mobile home some miles away and picking up a nondescript car. That simple operation took some time to organise, car batteries now being very flat he had to locate a set of jump leads long enough to reach from his own vehicle to the car. Subsequently, he was much later approaching the service station than he had planned on.

Arriving on the northbound side, he parked his car among a couple of dozen other abandoned ones, and explored the area.

Painted signs directed survivors toward two caravans, one of which was locked, the other having a sign inviting visitors to enter and make themselves at home. With the added assurance that they would be contacted between noon and two pm either that day, or the one following.

Inside the caravan was a variety of food and drink, medical supplies and clothing. He touched nothing and left, closing the door as before. Back at the camper van, he slept well, better in fact than he had for weeks.

He breakfasted then returning to the services took up position on the highest part of the roof he could access and hid himself behind a parapet wall. If his watch was right, he had about two hours to noon.

Chapter 49

Surgeons and Butchers

"He wanted you to do what?" Stephen Lamb looked at his fellow doctor Ursula Showandhra in open amusement. Ursula didn't share the feeling, she had had a tiring day and one she could well have done without.

Their small community, though boasting quite a number of different skills and trades had no butchers or slaughter men. This had been no problem until now, the community had farmers and a number of shooting enthusiasts for whom the despatching of chickens, rabbits and other small game was a regular occurrence.

Likewise, fishermen would gut and clean their catches themselves and deliver them to the kitchens. There was though, no one with the skills needed for the slaughtering and butchery of larger animals. For the first few weeks that hadn't mattered, the community had lived off the frozen meat and other foods that had been stored back in those hectic first days after the virus had struck.

As the days passed and the stocks become lower, Charles had decided that it was time they learned how to deal with larger animals. A bullock had been chosen as their first victim, but how it was to be done and by whom were the pertinent questions.

Reggie Koniev was the son of restaurant owner, Maria, and not the sharpest of people. After leaving school and having no wish to work with his parents, he had tried a number of jobs, failing at all of them.

Eventually, following the premature death of his father seven years before, he had finally given in and joined the family restaurant team.

Disappointingly, Reggie had not measured up to either his father or brother, Pyotr, as a chef or restaurateur and he was eventually relegated to general kitchen hand.

Then had come the 'death' and Maria, only a casual acquaintance of Charles Benford had been chosen to survive along with her family due to her experience in catering. Especially in catering for large numbers, and because Charles had mistakenly assumed she would have at least a basic knowledge of butchery.

Reggie had overheard the conversation between Charles and his mother when she had disillusioned him, and immediately volunteered himself for the post of slaughter man cum butcher, when the time came.

Charles who hated to see animals frightened or ill-treated had tried to absent himself from the building selected as the community's slaughterhouse, until hearing from Joey that Reggie's equipment had included shotgun, axe and baseball bat. Conscience had overcome his squeamishness and he had hurried to the warehouse.

Entering just in time to be splattered in blood as Reggie went desperately about the business and made a complete hash of it. To Benford's horror, the animal was still alive, though it seemed its back legs were broken and the crazed creature lay thrashing about on the floor amid its own body fluids. For once panicking, Benford had seized the shotgun and approaching as close as he dared, fired both barrels at the animals head killing it instantly.

Ashamed and guilty, he had waved the others away without speaking and blundered outside to throw up.

Afterward as was his way, the community leader had diagnosed the mistakes made and put together a plan of how to kill humanely and then butcher efficiently.

The day following, a small and disparate group gathered at the slaughterhouse site, they included Reggie, who Charles had noticed had despite the previous day's disaster been unshaken by all the blood and gore. So, as he had declared himself still prepared to carry on as designated butcher and in the absence of anyone else volunteering, Charles had accepted the others offer.

Big Tom Sanders was also present along with one of his sons. Charles could never remember the younger man's name and simply nodded to both men.

Doctor Showandhra and veterinary Darrell Firman were also present, Ursula herself a vegetarian had initially objected to being involved in the task, but had eventually given in to Benford's persuasion that it was in the communities interest as well as the animals that the slaughter and subsequent butchery should be carried out as painlessly and efficiently as possible.

They started by the vet injecting the animal, as yesterday another bullock had been chosen. Obligingly after only a short delay, the creature collapsed to the floor without any fuss. Then doctor and vet having agreed on method, Reggie was shown where to position a .45 revolver just behind the animals ear and fire the weapon. The noise deafening in the enclosed space and bringing grimaces to the faces of several of those present.

Tom Sanders and son now came forward securing a metal bar between the rear legs of the beast and tied to it with a rope. This rope in turn, linked to a steel cable that passed over a gantry the two men had erected some four metres high. The cable then ran to the back of a recovery truck normally used to rescue broken down vehicles.

By driving the truck forward a few feet, the animal was pulled firstly in to the gantry and then raised up until it hung by its splayed rear legs.

Doctor and vet then advised Reggie and his assistants, in this case Neill Hughes, a former employee of Benford's and Stewart Wright, Niall Benford's friend, how best to go about removing the animals hide. After this how to then remove organs and offal prior to butchery of the meat.

The whole operation took all day and was carried out in almost complete silence by a thoroughly subdued work crew.

Satisfied that the task, while not expertly done was at least just about humane and therefore passable.

Charles and the doctor finally felt able to leave before its grisly completion. The community's leader explaining that he had further requests to make of the doctors time and skills.

Now as her colleague Stephen smiled at her story of the bullock and the part she had played in the slaughter, Showandhra took some consolation in informing her fellow GP of Benford's latest additions to the ever-growing list of duties he expected them to take on.

During the past months since the death had first struck, the small communities population had been kept busy stockpiling supplies and moving home, firstly to Kingsthorpe and then on to Hardworth House.

During that time those people in the medical team were eight, of those ranging from trainee nurse through medical students to the two doctors. After grabbing a couple of van loads of basic medical supplies, had all pitched in with the other survivors emptying shops and loading lorries. With the people now all settled into the villages around Hardworth and the winter months approaching,

Charles had decided that it was time to establish more of those institutions that make a community. The under elevens had already been attending school since shortly after their arrival at Hardworth. A pub, a proper restaurant (not just the day time canteen) and a mobile chip van had been added, all of which helped to bring a degree of normalcy to their otherwise very abnormal situation.

Benford's next intended step was the establishing of a school for the older children, this in turn to lead to a system of further education for those who warranted it and skills training for others.

A hospital cum health centre was also to be up and running as soon as possible, the intent being that this was to cover all of the community's medical needs.

"So," Showandhra announced to her colleague, "you and I are not only now become surgeons. We are also to organise both a dentist and an opticians, even though we don't actually have either. We are also to train all medical staff, nurses, paramedics etc. Don't relax." she warned the other GP. "He also requires us to teach in both upper and lower schools biology, he calls it, but I think he means sex education at least to the older kids. Oh, and just in case we get bored, he wants every member of the community to learn first aid to a high standard. We to do the teaching of course, and now it seems we are to train butchers."

"Hang on," Stephen Lambs face showed how appalled he was. "Never mind the butchery bit what was that you said about us becoming surgeons, you have explained to him that you and I are general practitioners and the difference between us and consultants."

She smiled at his discomfort, getting her own back for his previous amusement at her having to take part in the slaughtering earlier.

"He knows that Stephen but as he said if someone needs their appendix removed, then the choice is between one of us trained doctors. Or would we prefer Charles to ask a carpenter or a brickie or something similar to that to try their hand at surgery." Lamb shrugged his shoulders in silent acknowledgment of the point and she continued.

"It doesn't stop there, Tina was a nurse consultant and she is now to take over as a GP freeing us up for these other duties. You have to admire his optimism though, and you never know the way he's trying to bring back the good old days. If we become very good surgeons, he might introduce Knighthoods and peerages next to reward us."

Chapter 50

Service Station

By his estimation they arrived early, a land rover towing yet another caravan pulled into the car park and circled around to park alongside the hostess van. Before their arrival, he had been slightly surprised to have watched twice as lorries roared by on the motorway heading north. The sound of the heavy diesels so strange after these months of silence. The vehicles had been too far away to see the drivers or even into the cabs but as they drove by at some speed, he closed his eyes and for a moment it felt almost as if the past months had never happened and life was back to how it had been. Almost against his wishes, he found himself wondering where they might be going, where they had come from and what they were carrying. As ever, he quickly forced himself away from any hint of nostalgia and instead forced a grim smile and asked himself, was he that bored that just the sight of other people doing what would have been such a forgettable task before the 'death had come' would so intrigue him now.

Down below, two men and a woman had exited the vehicle along with a couple of dogs, the sight of the latter caused him a wince of alarm. Would the animals be trained to pick up a strangers scent and so give his presence away before he was ready? While one of the men opened the door of the caravan designated for visitors and checked inside, the other two had started a cursory walk around the area.

Wilkinson cursed as they paused when they saw his vehicle, the woman seeming to refer to a piece of paper, presumably a list of the registration numbers of the cars that had been abandoned here for the past months.

After careful checking, she called to the first male and all three gathered around the car. Evidently, these people were well organised and had listed all vehicles in the services car park so that they would know if they had had any visitors. One of the men was placing his hand on the bonnet and then the wheels, feeling for any trace of heat, trying to assess how recently it had been used. That wouldn't do them any good, the vehicle would be long gone cold by now. But they would still be aware that someone had been on site and maybe still was. As if in response to his thought, the three had a quick conference and then started to walk around the area shouting loudly but nevertheless in a friendly tone.

"Hello, anybody around. Hi there," almost every variety of greeting was tried followed by assurances that the trio meant no harm and that everybody was welcome.

The shouting excited the dogs who added their own noise to that of the humans, and then slowly worked their way across to the building where Mike was hidden. Fortunately, none of the three humans seemed to have any affinity with the animals and paid little attention to them other than trying to get them to cease the barking.

In the next half an hour, he was given a short version of the history of the survivors. The information came in short staccato bursts, shouted by the three searchers. By piecing bits together, Wilkinson gathered that there was now more than three hundred of them. Their villages, he noted the plural, were situated some miles away, they had a school and hospital, electricity, gas and clean water. Most surreal of all, if he hadn't miss heard then they also claimed to have a pub and a fish and chip shop.

As he listened, the anger inside him started to grow again. He had expected to find a band of frightened survivors struggling to stay alive, grateful for any help that they could get, especially from someone as well trained in survival as Mike Wilkinson.

This bunch however inept they might be in locating him, showed no sign of being fearful or of struggling. The talk of pubs and fish shops, surreal beyond belief in the circumstances. Mike hadn't made any particular plans for when he had located his prey, expecting to play it by ear according to what he found. Yesterday, he had thought that perhaps he would observe for a while then if it seemed suitable just approach whoever turned up at the services and accompany them back to their base. Once there, he would identify his principal target, presumably Charles Benford and make plans to kill him.

Now the very matter of fact way these three were behaving offended him beyond belief. He and a few others like him had all but destroyed mankind, killing billions in a matter of only days, in doing so they had created a new world, a better world. A world that would be cleaner, purer, a world fit for the future. In recent days, as he had travelled the country in his pursuit of Charles Benford and his group, Wilkinson had noticed a growing change in the countryside. Despite the presence of thousands of animal carcasses in the fields, other beasts had escaped the confines of fields and barns and were surviving, in some cases even thriving. Wild life no longer hunted by man were increasing in numbers. Vegetation was taking over the bricks and mortar of buildings and the tarmac of roads.

Nature was taking back what was hers and if allowed would slowly create a new Eden.

Yet, these morons below were continuing with their pitiful lives in much the same way as before, forcing themselves on to the land, shaping it in the way that they wanted it to be and not as it should be. His hand caressed the butt of the pistol that snuggled in his shoulder holster, he was tempted to kill these three simply because they were there, and their very presence in being so offended him.

With effort, he controlled himself and settled down to wait the others out.

He needed time to control himself and to make plans, needed to sort his mind and decide exactly what form his vengeance would take. The death of Benford would no longer be enough. These people were challenging the work that he had started those months ago, on a wild Scottish moor when he had released the virus. That was work that had very nearly killed him.

Now they had to be punished. Below him, Jerry Hunter called his two companions over to confer. Jerry was a former RSPCA inspector, one of two in the survivors group and contrary to Wilkinson's opinion, had noticed the behaviour of the dogs. In particular, the way they kept hanging around the tall building overlooking the parking area, neither had he missed the parapet wall that offered cover for anyone seeking to hide from watchers below.

Jerry was reasonably certain that at least one person was currently watching the three of them, and wasn't at all surprised at the cautious behaviour. Back at Kingsthorpe, there had been a slow trickle of survivors that had made their way to the comparative comfort and safety of Charles Benford's people, with the move to Hardworth house that trickle had gradually become a torrent. Benford was adamant that fuel was the key to their future. Fuel powered the generators that provided electricity, it ran the freezer lorries that contained the frozen foods that would see them through the winter. Fuel powered machines of all kinds, agricultural machines that allowed relatively few members of the community to feed the remainder and so allow others to become builders, engineers etc., all of whom in turn also required fuel to power their machines.

So teams of seven or eight people were constantly leaving Hardworth, and travelling to all parts of the country seeking petrol tankers and bringing them back to lorry parks that were scattered around the area.

Jerry had never counted them but he knew that there were at least two hundred tankers now in storage. He also knew that as they were emptied, the idea was that they would then be used to empty the storage tanks at petrol stations, farms, marinas anywhere that had stored diesel or petrol would be raided in the years to come. Charles reckoned that if they systematically collected every drop available, there would be enough to last the community for a possibly a couple of hundred years.

But salvaging tankers wasn't the only task of the teams that left Hardworth to collect them. Even more importantly, they posted notices everywhere they went, on supermarket windows, chemists, petrol stations, D I Y stores etc., anywhere that survivors might go to for supplies. The notices gave information on the Hardworth community and directions on how to find them, and they came, not every day but certainly at least a few every week. Usually in two's and three's, and normally in quite odd combinations. The last arrivals had been a seventeen-year-old Muslim boy accompanying a rather well spoken English woman in her mid-forties and a former Catholic nun in her late sixties. Survivors who had managed to find someone else always seemed reluctant to then leave that other, no matter how odd the company.

They would make their way to the service area on the motorway as instructed. Here they would find the supply caravan well equipped for their immediate needs. Every day a different trio from Hardworth would be taken off their normal duties to conduct what was called a circuit tour.

This consisted of driving around a number of storage dumps where the community stored a variety of supplies. The dumps were left with gates or doors closed but never locked. Charles Benford's attitude being that if other survivors outside of their own group needed any of the goods, then they had an equal right to them.

The duties of those on circuit tours at these places was simply to monitor any signs of visitors, so that these people could be contacted and possibly recruited. At midday, Jerry or whoever else was on duty would call at the service area and wait for two hours for any new arrivals.

If there were any visitors, they would be asked to remain in the caravan that would then be swapped with the one towed by their hosts, this one to be left for the next visitors, while theirs with the newcomers still aboard would be taken to a small compound just outside of Hardworth itself.

Here, they would be visited by a doctor who would check them out physically and then request that they remain in quarantine for a few days before being taken into the community proper.

Jerry himself had never actually brought anybody in so far, but had been present when others had arrived. He had been struck by the behavioural similarity of such people with those of the animals he used to rescue in his former life. Nervous, shy, bewildered with a determination to please and a defenceless look in their eyes that drew pity from everyone.

It wasn't unusual for some visitors to take time in making contact with the Hardworth community. The host caravan occasionally showing signs of having been used overnight or of supplies having been taken, then nothing more for a day or two as the visitors plucked up enough courage to approach their would-be hosts.

So, Jerry followed the recommended procedure for this situation, shouting the announcements as they had, pinning a note to the table inside the caravan, assuring the visitors of a friendly welcome, then making a show of topping up the supplies available in the van, before leaving after the allotted two hours. Mike Wilkinson watched them leave, still seething with anger at what he had just viewed, that these fools would ignore the opportunity that he had given them to change their ways was unbelievable. Well, he would punish them, he knew that now with a cold certainty. He would visit death on them, not just this Benford but as many of them as he could.

But first, he would make them suffer, make them fear his unseen presence.

That meant he needed to learn as much about them as possible, learn everything he could, then perhaps join the community before making his final plan for retribution.

First though, he needed to locate their base. He dismissed trying to follow them, with such few other vehicles on the roads that would be impossible.

But they were unlikely to have travelled far from their camp to the services, and the way their population was apparently growing it shouldn't take too much finding.

Chapter 51

Chris and Kerry

"Chris, we have to go to these people we don't have any choice, we certainly can't carry on like this." Kerry spoke as calmly as she could trying not to get Chris going again. Not easy, after weeks wandering around the countryside, they both had had enough. Enough of roughing it and more than enough of each other. "We're not living Chris this is just existing, no electricity, no running water, no baths or showers, no proper food. Look, Chris you're just not this type of person, living rough off the land, repairing your own cars, building a house, raising animals it's just not you Chris." She tried to soften the blow a little, it would make life easier later if he wasn't sulking. "You're better at other things, you're an organiser, a cook, sorry I meant chef, you're a chef." Her hands came up in a gesture to placate him, not that Chris was violent but he did sulk so.

For his part, her boyfriend glared at her exasperatedly with hands on hips like a woman. "I've told you, we can't join these people they will want to know how come we survived, both of us I mean. It just wouldn't have happened. Any way, it's not too bad here." He looked around the cottage they had commandeered. It had taken weeks of driving around the country looking for the right place. What was the right place? As far as Chris was concerned, this was it. A stone built cottage that had been modernised but retained an open fireplace, was a reasonable distance from other homes and more important with no corpses (the occupants presumably on holiday at the time of the death) to have to eject before moving in.

There was a mini market in the next village along the road with plenty of canned food on the shelves and that suited him fine. As far as Chris was concerned, he had become an expert forager in the last months. He could hole a cars petrol tank and drain it out and into his own vehicle in less than a half hour. Isn't that how they had managed to drive around the country in order to find this place. Kerry was unreasonable to expect all of life's previous luxury's, no they were doing alright. With that certainty in mind and a single glance at the black look on her face, he stormed out.

He had converted an outside shed into a bar stocked with wine and spirits taken from the mini market, so Kerry could go and hang herself for all he cared.

Kerry watched him stalking away, knowing exactly where he was going and sighed. She supposed it wasn't all his fault, he wasn't a bad bloke as it goes, she had certainly known worse, but they couldn't carry on like this, living out of tins, drinking bottled water and using the same stuff for strip washes. Having no electricity they went to bed every night as darkness fell, and with the winter coming that would be early evening time.

Oh Ron, why couldn't it have been you who found the antidote instead of Chris. No, that wouldn't have any good either, he was married and wouldn't have swapped his wife for Kerry, face it, he never had.

No, Chris would come back in later and if he was drunk, he would want to climb on top of her. Well, she would use that moment to have another go at him about finding these survivors. Whoever they were, they had left signs on a number of supermarket doors up and down the central area of England giving directions on how to find them. They seemed organised and even if they weren't, it would just be nice to be with other people.

She would try and persuade him to go with her but if kept on refusing then sod him, she'd go without him.

After all, his only reason for not going was he thought that these people would twig the two of them had been together before the 'death' had come and realise that was next to impossible.

Well, she was pretty sure that any survivors would have better things to think about and he was just being stupid. No! Like it or not, the two of them were leaving here tomorrow and were going to join these other survivors.

Chapter 52

Eye Opener

Now in the right area his finds came thick and fast. Benford's survivors had taken over an entire industrial estate just off the motor way. Wherever they could they simply bulldozed anything they didn't want to keep into one side or corner of the premises, then brought in their own goods.

Sometimes in containers other times in lorries, vans and trailers. All these were first marked clearly with a combination of letters and numbers presumably for future reference, then the various units were stored in lanes that left room for future unloading and access.

Elsewhere, he found a disused airfield and a few miles away two separate sports fields all three of which had been taken over as lorry parks for tankers.

Twice, he came upon areas of fields that were obviously being farmed, one for livestock, the other for crops. The harvests had been taken in already but he stopped and managed to pick up some late vegetables and that evening with the help of some cans of stewing steak ate better than he had in weeks.

The next morning, he found Hardworth or rather found where it was. Hardworth itself was a very grand stately home surrounded by a deer park, and set in what must be thousands of acres of farm and moorland.

He couldn't see the house itself, according to the map that appeared to be at the centre of an area containing four villages of varying size and all of which he discovered were being used by the community.

Further investigation suggested that the survivors were gradually fencing the entire area in. A task that as far as he could figure meant constructing some fifteen miles or more of fencing.

On the second day of his exploration as he drove around a shallow bend, he suddenly found the road he was travelling was blocked. The highway having been dissected with two huge metal gates.

Again as with all the storage facilities, he had found the gates were closed but not locked, meaning he supposed that while animals could not get in or out, adult humans could do both.

As he finished inspecting the gates, he saw a vehicle approaching from the other direction. Hurrying back to his vehicle, he turned it around with some difficulty on the narrow road and drove swiftly away. Checking his rear view constantly, he could see no sign of pursuit and finally felt confident enough to drive towards his next objective.

Mike had noticed that a column of smoke seemed to sit permanently over the town of Chesterfield, about ten miles to the east of his position. Every afternoon the column would seem to grow in size and intensity, gradually dying down during the night and early the following morning, before rising in intensity again the following pm.

There were also several other smokes rising to the west. These were smaller and scattered and seemed to be progressing in an arc around the survivors' base some eight to ten miles distant. It was these later columns that he decided to investigate first.

He was lucky, his approach to the nearest column of smoke took him across high ground to the west of Hardworth. He ignored the A road that he thought would attract the survivors vehicles, and instead looked for farm tracks and minor roads to use for his purposes. Eventually, he found a private road that seemed to lead to a recently ruined farm. The road more of a dirt track really twisted and turned, snaking its way up a hill that gradually afforded him a fine view of a wide valley below him.

The valley cris-crossed by fields, marked out by dry stone walls and down in the bottom of the valley where a road ran along its length, he could see human activity. Leaving his vehicle in the open gateway of a grass field, he ran across the track, leapt a series of stone walls until crouching down behind a slight rise in the ground to observe.

Some four hundred yards distant and a hundred feet lower than his present position a farmhouse burned. Not a huge blaze as yet but grey smoke billowed from several broken windows, suggesting that inside furniture burnt steadily. There was no sign of life around the buildings, until he noticed two vehicles turning left out of the access road that lead to the burning farm about another three to four hundred yards further away from Mike.

He watched as the vehicles that he could now see were towing four wheel trailers turned on to the road proper. He drove for barely a hundred yards before again turning, this time up a shorter drive towards yet another farm, this one consisting of a stone built detached house that formed one side of a square, the other three sides being taken up with a variety of barns, cattle sheds and what may have been pigstys.

The two vehicles came to a halt in front of the house and as at the service area on the motorway, two men and a woman decamped the vehicle again accompanied by a couple of large dogs.

Making himself as comfortable as he could, he took up position and for the next two hours watched as the two men visited the various buildings, occasionally carrying something back to the vehicles and placing whatever they carried on to the trailers. At other times, they turned towards the woman and presumably spoke to her, who seemed to be writing down whatever it was they dictated.

The search of the outbuildings took little more than an hour, during which the dogs bounced about sniffing and barking until cuffed to silence by the larger of the two men. Finally, the trio approached the house itself, from around the left side of the house that was out of Wilkinson line of sight. Two large gas bottles were loaded onto the rear trailer. Apparently satisfied that they had salvaged everything they wanted or had at least recorded the existence of, the search part of the trio's visit was ended.

Below him, Jilly Benford's nephew, Colin Chambers, in charge of the salvage operation watched as his mate went around the house breaking the panes of all the lower windows. Colin followed behind pouring generous amount of aviation fuel through each of the broken panes.

When searching for an easy accelerant for the hygiene burnings, petrol and diesel being too valuable to the community, Charles Benford had hit upon the idea of using aviation fuel as being extremely flammable but of no use to the survivors for any other purpose, as being an effective way of starting the blazes needed to sanitise the immediate area of their homes.

His wife, Colleen in turn followed her husband dropping small pieces of burning cloth through the windows and then moving smartly away before the ignition took place.

From this range, Mike Wilkinson could only imagine rather than hear the whoosh but within moments the familiar smoke was soon pouring out and the visitors drove away to their next objective.

Approaching the scene of the larger fires to the east was more difficult. The pall seemed to hang over one of the residential areas of Chesterfield.

This meant that to get close enough to see anything, he would have to enter the streets of a town that he was unfamiliar with and risk running into the survivors. As it was, he didn't need to, entering Chesterfield from the west was like entering a bomb site. Every house showed signs of recent fire, some only lightly with windows blown out and scorched roof tiles. Others had been so badly affected that walls had collapsed, exposing the burnt interiors. He had no need to see more, it was obvious, Benford's people were burning the town presumably in an attempt to prevent the diseases that would emanate from the thousands of unburied bodies. Though, if that was the purpose then some of the properties that were only lightly scorched were going to need a second visit.

It also seemed that as in the more rural areas they were again salvaging anything of use, or at least recording the existence of such items in preparation for the future before carrying out the burnings.

He would have liked to get closer to the work crew but the presence of yet more dogs that might pick up his scent prevented that.

As it was now early evening, he turned away intending to head back to his camper and away from the area of burning. He spotted road signs for the A61 Sheffield. Without looking at his road map, he was pretty sure that this would save him a few miles and followed the signs. Too late he realised that he was running alongside one of the industrial estates that the survivors used more heavily than most, and there at just the wrong moment were three vehicles carrying what looked to be about a dozen people leaving one of the premises. He couldn't avoid them as they were heading south on the same carriageway that he was driving north on.

Instead, he floored the accelerator and sped past them aware of heads turning to stare at the stranger.

He needn't have worried, as usual there was no pursuit and he relaxed after covering a couple of miles. But he was intrigued, the small convoy and its occupants represented the largest group of people he had seen away from Hardworth. He tried to remember if the building he had seen them leaving had any signs outside indicating its former use. Memory eluded him but he had a feeling that the place had been fairly small.

One of those factory units that could employ perhaps up to a dozen people that could be found on industrial estates all over the country.

Checking again that there was no sign of his being followed, he swung around and retraced his route, stopping when he guessed that he would be about a quarter mile away from his target. Warily, he advanced on foot toward the building. There was a wire fence around the perimeter that contained a building some thirty metres square, at some time in the past there had been a company logo or name painted on the side but that had long ago faded and there was little on the outside of the building to show what the place had been before the 'death had come'. There were no vehicles outside the premises and no sound emanating from the interior, so he advanced to the gate. As usual with these people there was no lock barring entry on either the gate or the door to the building itself. By the fading daylight, he could make out that there were lights hanging from the ceiling that were connected to a cable leading from a hole drilled through the rear wall. A quick walk around the perimeter revealed a sizeable generator that obviously provided power, it took only moments to start it and he returned to the door. Inside, the building was now fully illuminated and he stood amazed at what was revealed.

Two, four wheel wooden horse drawn farm carts stood side by side. One was obviously ancient and was as dilapidated as could be expected. The other not yet complete was in the process of being newly constructed.

It was plainly obvious that the new one was being built to match the old one as near as possible, using the original as a template.

Wilkinson approached the twenty first century version and ran his hand over the various surfaces. All four wheels were complete as was most of the superstructure. Only the driver's seat, the rear board and the horse coupling were left to be finished, and they were all laid out on trestles, obviously still being worked on.

Looking around, he spotted other current projects. A number of wooden barrels, the staves held by metal hoops, none of which were very impressive looking were ranged along one side of the workshop.

In the corner, farthest from him was stacked a number of sticks, upon closer examination these turned out to be bows of about four feet in length. These, though not exactly long bows, actually looked the part. One that had been left with a string attached to one end, he strung with some effort and was then surprised at how much strength it took to draw the bow to its fullest extent. To the side of these weapons there were yet more wheels were under construction along with a variety of household utensils.

Wilkinson sat down puzzled, until now everywhere he had gone these people had been hoarding all the comforts and amenities of the 21st century. The dozens, maybe even hundreds of petrol tankers, vehicles of all shapes and sizes, including dustcarts, fire engines, ambulances and mobile cranes. Farm machinery, construction machinery, lorry containers marked with everything from toilet rolls to men's trousers to canned foods were parked in buildings and fields all around the area, a whole fleet of freezer wagons on the car park of what had formerly been a sizeable factory, some with engines still running. And more vehicles arrived at these storage sites every day.

The place he now found himself in was a complete contrast with all of that. These utensil's and equipment were more reminiscent of the fifteenth and sixteenth century than the twenty first. His attention was now drawn towards a desk in the corner, adjacent to the one containing the bows. A number of working plans quiet professionally drawn were open showing details of what looked like a water mill. He perused them for some time, certain that these had been drawn recently and were for a new project rather than the details of some ancient monument. Still deep in thought when he finally rose, he turned right rather than left out of the door, his route taking him around the opposite side of the building to the earlier one. Rounding the corner, he fell full length on his face, cursing he looked for what had tripped him and found himself facing an old fashioned horse drawn plough. Except this didn't look old, though on closer inspection, he found that while the wooden parts were all new, the metal plough share itself was clearly original. For the first time in years, Mike Wilkinson found himself actually being excited about something that didn't involve sex or violence.

During the next few days, he discovered more sites, both storage and workshops. The latter for both metal and woodworking, the former for every sort of household supplies imaginable.

Remarkably, he was also was seen at least twice as he drove around the countryside, vehicles suddenly rounding bends coming from the opposite direction leaving him no time to evade them. Yet, nobody tried to interfere with him, on the second occasion a passenger actually waved a hand in greeting.

Finally, after another week, he left the area altogether and drove up to the lake district, an area he had always loved.

Late autumn had turned to winter now and the nights that had been chilly before were becoming increasingly cold. Early snow covered much of the countryside in a crisp white blanket, making that most beautiful of the former national parks even more spectacularly lovely.

He spent the days happily fishing and shooting while he tried to gather his thoughts.

A fortnight ago, his plans had been to destroy Benford's community, blow the petrol tankers and they would lose their electricity; that would all but cripple the survivors. Then he would join them via the procedure of the service station, identify and eliminate Benford, and finally disappear leaving the weakened and demoralised community to fend for themselves.

The workshops had changed that, they had puzzled him. On the one hand, the survivors were desperately storing everything imaginable, as though they were determined to live forever on salvaged goods.

Against that were the work shops where all manner of old type tools and equipment were being manufactured, even if some of them were of a rather iffy quality. And the farms, as he had explored the countryside around Hardworth, he had become aware that there were a number of active farms still being worked. As far as he could tell there were three mainly arable farms that might include some chickens and other fowls, plus a similar number of farms for livestock at least one of which was purely for horses of all types and sizes. It all seemed to equate to an attempt to return to a lifestyle more approximate to the late nineteenth century than the twenty first. He thought long and hard about these various efforts and attempted to square the circle.

He tried to put himself in the survivors' position and think as they would. Finally, he came to approximately the same conclusions that Charles Benford had reached months ago when he had first won ownership of the antidote.

No matter what they did, the survivors and their descendants must sink back into the dark ages and beyond. The world they had been born into had been a global community, billions of people working together for mutual if not equal benefit. Go into any supermarket, look at any motor vehicle or any large piece of machinery, and you looked at a minor representation of the world's economy.

A motor car used components from dozens of countries, those parts were transported by boats, trains and aeroplanes that in turn used resources from many more, while the raw materials for these involved yet more.

These things required millions of people each performing their small part in creating a supply chain that had been the main structure of life in the twenty first century before the death had come.

Now no matter how much equipment and supplies the survivors gathered and put into storage, they would eventually run out. When they did, there would be no way of renewing the majority of them. Given the paltry numbers of survivors currently around the world, and their chances of continuing to survive, it would be thousands of years in the future before population levels reached anything like the numbers required for overseas trade and manufacturing. In western Europe, when the Roman Empire collapsed, it had taken twelve hundred years to reach similar levels of civilisation again, and that had been with a starting population of millions rather than hundreds. Wilkinson had learnt a great deal in the past months including that the original plotters had vastly underestimated the dangers the survivors faced. He now realised it was very possible that human beings would become extinct. The twin keys to survival were, as in the past, power and technology. Electricity and fuel provided the means for that power and technology to exist and even thrive, and in doing so increased human strength and speed immeasurably, allowing one individual to do the work of many.

Benford by collecting as much fuel as he could, it seemed was buying time for future generations. He would salvage everything he could and put it into storage. While at the same time the survivors would learn all the old skills that their ancestors had learnt and their fathers forgotten.

Even more importantly, the survivors were expanding on their revitalising of old skills by attempting to find other ways than the use of fossil fuels to generate electricity. The plans Wilkinson had seen of the water mill had been for the grinding of flour, but the drawings had made plain that it was also hoped that with some adaptation other machines could be used for generating electricity. During his travels since then, he had also seen rough sketch plans for other wind powered machines as well. Some years ago, he had dated a mature student from Oxford, a history of architecture buff, who had dragged him around a number of churches, castles and stately homes. It had always struck Wilkinson that without electricity the various palaces and manor houses were just so much bricks and mortar, a complete waste of money, how could such places be comfortable without power. In his opinion, the occupiers would have been better off in a small warm hovel. It seemed that Benford was of a similar opinion as Mike.

Despite himself, Wilkinson found he was getting more and more interested in the survivors' community, this for him is what the whole thing had been about. He and other people like him had killed the world, killed the billions who were destroying nature with their greed and thoughtlessness.

Afterwards the intention was that the favoured ones, people like Mike himself, would live out exactly the sort of life that Charles Benford was apparently planning for his group.

Mike realised now that that would never have happened, those involved in the plotting were too political to be true conservationists. They would never have been able to cooperate as a group long enough, or even care enough about the future of mankind to do the things that had to be done, those very things that Benford's group were valiantly trying so hard to do now.

So Mike was suddenly unsure of what his next move would be, a few days ago he had planned to bring the whole thing crashing down around Benford's ears. He would blow the various storage facilities to kingdom come. He knew a place near Hereford where there was explosives to spare and then a quick visit to his former base and, boom!

Without their stores, without their fuel tankers, Benford's community would never last, and Mike would have his revenge. His plans had taken no account of his growing admiration for the survivors and their leader. Wilkinson still didn't know what had happened that day when Benford had found himself in possession of the antidote, but whatever the details were, the man could only have had hours to: (1) take in the enormity of the situation, (2) realise the full extent of the ongoing dangers to any survivors of the virus, (3) decide just who he would select for survival and (4) put his subsequent plan into operation. All of that would have been against a background of being hunted by both the authorities (assuming they had knowledge of the antidote) and of Wilkinson's fellow plotters.

Those plans had obviously taken into account that the only long term hopes for humanity to continue to exist would be to learn many of the old skills that western civilisation had long ago given up.

All this excited Mike, this is how the future was supposed to be, this is why the world had been destroyed. He could totally empathise with the survivors' leader, and he recognised the huge contribution the skills his SAS survival training would be to the community.

The following morning when the trio on circuit tour duty arrived at the service station they found a Mike Wilkinson waiting for them. Barney Rogers a friend of Charles Benford since childhood was heading the team that day and immediately went into the standard routine. Despatching a team member to go straight to Hardworth with the news of the arrival.

Then keeping a reasonable distance from the visitor, he explained the procedures regarding a limited quarantine. Having obtained Mikes acceptance of this, they all settled down to wait out the statuary two hours in case there should be any other arrivals that day. While still maintaining the distance between them, Barney and his remaining companion chatted with Mike explaining more about their growing community.

The visitor grew ever more excited as his hosts explained their peculiar mix of 21st century cum medieval lifestyle that they enjoyed. So rapt did he become that he eventually relaxed enough to admit that he was the guilty party that had been driving around their stores and workshops recently. In answer to their question, "Why hadn't he come forward before this?" He simply replied that he wanted to be sure before joining the others. Barney and the others accepted this and admitted that he wasn't the first that had had similar reservations, although he had taken longer making his mind up than most.

Finally with a glance at his watch, the team leader announced that it was time to hitch the caravan up and return to Hardworth. Mike settled onto the caravan seat for the journey, aware that his stomach was fluttering in much the same way as it used to do during his time in the SAS when setting of to go on an active service mission.

Presumably out of consideration to their passenger lurching about in the back, his hosts took their time getting to Hardworth. When they did arrive, his ride was parked in a pleasant looking meadow that contained another half dozen caravans, though he noticed that these were separated from his own by a wire fence some four feet high, and fifty yards apart.

After dropping the four corner steadys and connecting the caravan to both water and power supplies, Barney shouted to him to make himself at home but not to leave the segregated area until his return with Dr Showandhra.

He was back less than forty minutes later accompanied by an attractive Asian woman whom he introduced as Dr Show. Barney then retired and the Dr alone entered the caravan, and having finished introductions, she spent some fifteen minutes carrying out a fairly detailed examination. At the end of which, while still talking over her shoulder, she stepped outside the van. As she was in mid-sentence, Mike felt compelled to follow her.

The woman had turned to her left after exiting and he went to do the same. Too late he sensed rather than saw the baseball bat swung hard and low that whacked against his shins. The cause of the blinding pain in his legs was followed by a flurry of other blows, this time from the fists and feet of Chris Porter the ex-boxer and Charles Benford's foreman Joey Sharp. The force and fury of their blows reflected the human losses of friends and family that both men had suffered as a result of the virus.

Only when Wilkinson had fallen unconscious did Charles commanded stop the beating, though it didn't prevent Chris from spitting copiously on the unmoving man.

Ursula Showandhra had turned at the sound of the first blow and Mike's subsequent gasp of pain. Her attempt to intervene and stop the beating was prevented by the strong but gentle arm of Tom Sanders, and his softly spoken but still strongly commanding of, "Whoa there my love, he's got this coming and more." As soon as the beating stopped, Tom's arm relaxed slightly and the doctor managed to break free and stooped over the still form.

"What are you doing," she shouted towards Benford, "What the hell are you doing?"

Charles nodded his head towards the woman as he barked a command to the others, "Bring her away," and to Ursula herself, "He gets no treatment doc, none at all. This shit is one of those who spread the virus, and he will pay for it with his life in the morning."

"What! How, how do you know who he is?"

Benford sighed heavily before replying, "Maggie, this bloke has been driving about for the last weeks spying on us. Dave Green spotted him a month ago and Stewart Wright a couple of days later and both got long range photos of him. You know that some of the survivor's drive around checking us out before they come in, and that's okay, but this fella was doing it for days, positively stalking us. It seemed weird, so on a hunch I showed the photo to Maggie, they weren't the clearest of shots but despite that she clocked him straight away. His name is Mike Wilkinson, at least that's what he told her and he's one of them alright." His tone mollified somewhat as he continued, "He even used the same name to Barney, obviously he couldn't know that Maggie had lived and was with us. He's one of them alright, and he gets no medical treatment."

With that final order, Charles strode away leaving the doctor open mouthed at the change that had come over the man compared with his usual behaviour.

Chapter 53

This Is Wrong

Mike woke to pain, pain everywhere, in every joint every muscle. That was his first awareness, the second was that he was gagged with something that tasted awful and the third was that he couldn't move.

Through the waves of agony, he forced himself to focus, he needed to work out where he was and what was happening to him. Memories came back somewhat blurred, the service station, approaching what was his name, Barney something, then the quarantine caravan, a woman doctor, rather attractive he remembered, then nothing except pain. He worked out that his hands and feet were tied and that he had then been laid in a foetal position on his right side with a short rope joining those, securing his hands and feet together to prevent his even slight movement. The main centre of pain seemed to be his ribs where he guessed at least two were broken and his left arm that he thought was also broken similarly in a least two places.

"He's awake." Mike opened his eyes for the first time since regaining consciousness and looked toward the sound. A big man, big and heavy was looking at him and there was no mistaking the hatred in the man's eyes. There was something wrong with the man though, he was plainly a big man, Mike would have thought at least six three but somehow he seemed shorter. Then as his eyes focused better, he realised that Mike himself was laying inside a cage that was in turn inside the back of a van that had the double rear doors open. The big man was standing outside of the vehicle, so was only visible above the knee. A police van, the thought came to him. They were using a former police van of the type sent to transport prisoners to the police station after being arrested, as a prison cell.

"Robbie, I said he's awake."

"Yes, I heard you, just leave him as he is, dad doesn't want him talking to anyone or anyone to him. He's not to have food or drink either." Mike had tried to view the second speaker but couldn't swivel his eyes far enough around, and any attempt to move his body even slightly brought unbearable pain.

There followed a conversation between the two guards that Mike could only hear snatches of. In the morning, drawing lots, and dad's on his way, nothing very clear and certainly nothing to give him a great deal of info of what his position was. He was pretty sure they didn't treat their other visitors this way, so did that mean they knew who he was. He couldn't see how, so perhaps they were simply suspicious. He had been hanging around for a while and he knew that he had been seen on more than one occasion. The amount of time he had taken before coming forward to join them may have aroused suspicions. That must be it, there just wasn't anything else that it could be. He started to rehearse what he would say when they removed that bloody awful tasting gag from his mouth. In these situations, the first few words were all important, you needed to convey puzzled innocence with righteous indignation, if you could get across a sense that at the same time as those two that you also understood why the others were suspicious, then so much the better.

But first he had to be allowed to speak, he was good at thinking on his feet and could spin a tale. Once they heard of his SAS training and realised the asset he would be they would soon warm to him. Having worked out an idea of what to say, he concentrated on controlling his hurting body, he needed to manage the pain in order to think and speak clearly. Finally, he started to make grunting noises in an attempt to attract the guard's attention, it took only seconds for the big guy to appear and Mike increased the tempo of his noise, managing to convey a sense of urgency and he hoped appeal to the sounds, his eyes attempting to fix the other man's to his.

His efforts were wasted, Tom Sanders had lost a lot of family to the virus and would have been quite happy to have entered the cage and killed his prisoner with his bare hands. The thought of doing so had indeed been in his mind ever since he had heard who this p---k was and it was only his growing respect for Charles Benford that had held him back so far. No amount of eye contact from Wilkinson was going to warm Tom to the man.

The same SAS background that Mike was so proud of, especially his resistance to torture training quickly convinced him that he was wasting his time with this guy and he fell silent deciding to save his strength for a more receptive audience.

His chance came sooner than expected. It was late night now and quiet, that silence was broken by the sound of a vehicle pulling up somewhere very close to hand and then the sound of barking dogs and a shouted command that immediately quieted the animals.

A man appeared in the van doorway, at first glance there was nothing very special about him, late fifties, sparse grey hair, and a couple of stone overweight. Not at all terribly prepossessing but as soon as he looked at the man's face, Mike knew this was the man he had once thought to kill, Charles Benford.

Eyes met and held, Wilkinson's unsure, Benford's betraying no emotion whatever, as his hand reached beyond the door and pulled another figure into view, a woman, Maggie! This time Mike couldn't prevent his surprise, Maggie alive and well, how the hell had she managed that. Then he realised what this meant for him. The pub in Scotland, Maggie dying until he gave her the antidote, his garbled explanation followed by the drive south for more of the life saver, then the disaster of The Manor, the woman wasn't stupid she would have worked it out. Combine that with the knowledge that Benford must have picked up when gaining possession of the antidote and they must know!

Neither spoke for a moment, then well, Maggie didn't reply verbally, simply gave the merest of nods, then both stared in unblinking accusation at Wilkinson. He couldn't meet their gaze and his eyes dropped, he ached to lick his lips in nervousness but the gag in his mouth prevented that.

After a moment, Benford turned to the guard and commanded, "I'll be back shortly, tell Joey to get another vehicle and meet me here in a half hour." With that he turned and led the woman away.

Mike was shaken, he was in great pain and very well aware of the danger he was in. He had received no medical treatment so far and no food or water either. Wilkinson was well aware that all this was in direct contrast to the sort of kind behaviour that Benford and his people seemed to usually show. More than ever he needed to be able to communicate, if he couldn't. Mike thought again of those accusatory stares and of the looks that his guard had been giving him. No, they weren't about to show any mercy to him. He had made a mistake when he had gone to the services and contacted the survivors, he should have stayed with his first plan and destroyed the lot of them.

Given the never ending pain he was in it was difficult to figure time. He tried to concentrate on what to say when they finally removed the gag. Should he make a last desperate effort to convince them to keep him alive, that they risked cutting off their collective noses to spite their faces, or accept what was probably inevitable and be defiant, let posterity know what and why he did what he had done and then die for his beliefs.

His thoughts were disturbed by the sound of a vehicle pulling up and the larger guard commenting, "Here's Joey." Wilkinson heard the sound of a car door slam and then of the visitor walking across and joining the other two and exchange greetings but couldn't strain around to see the new arrival. But the pain of trying to do so forced another groan from him.

One of his watchers, he couldn't tell which, sniggered at the sound and muttered, "Bastard." Apart from that one expletive, their voices were kept low and came as no more than an inaudible murmur. He already knew though that the arrival of this Joey guy meant that Benford would soon be returning and then what.

The community's leader hadn't enlarged on what he was returning for or why he needed a vehicle, but it didn't take much working out that it was something to do with Mike, and presumably nothing good.

Beyond the open doors of the van, the sounds of his guards continued with an occasional face peering around them to stare momentarily at the prisoner. On one occasion, not recognising Joey as one of his attackers of earlier, the face seemed new to him. But he nevertheless guessed the young man's identity, and Mike tried to make eye contact with him, tried to communicate in some way. His effort failed or was simply ignored, the younger man, another who like almost everyone else had lost people he cared about to this man wasn't about to empathise with him.

A while later and the guards seemed to become restive, Mike still with no way to be sure of how much time was passing was nevertheless certain that Benford had now been far longer than he had said he would be, and wondered what that might mean.

Chapter 54

A New Society

Charles was being delayed by arguments, the first had been Dr Showandhra. The doctor had seen Wilkinson attacked earlier, but having had her back turned to the incident while she berated Benford for the violence, she had missed the worst of the incidence.

She had then been hurried away from the scene by Joey, so had no sure way of knowing how bad or even how many and what type of injuries the man had suffered.

After discovering who the recipient was, her first thought had been, "Good, couldn't have happened to a more deserving cause." Then inevitably, the Hippocratic oath she had taken all those years ago troubled her enough that she decided that she ought to at least have a look at the wretch. The guards had turned her away without allowing her even a glimpse of Wilkinson, and now aroused at her brusque treatment she had gone straight to Benford.

Charles had assured her that the man was fine, 'just a few bruises is all' and she had allowed herself to be fobbed of, but after finishing her evening surgery her thoughts had turned again to Wilkinson. Earlier that day when she had carried out her assessment of the man prior to his being quarantined, she had quite liked him. At his best, Mike could be both charming and with his height and build an imposing figure.

Ursula Showandhra was no foolish young girl and fully accepted that Wilkinson was who Charles said he was and consequently a mass murderer, and as he put it an evil bastard.

But two wrongs etc., and he was still a human being, so she had again asked Charles to be allowed to check the prisoner out. To her surprise, and for the first time since the doctor had met him, Benford had lost his temper with her.

Refused her request and shouted at her to stop pestering him with this stupidity. He had almost instantly calmed down and apologised but was still adamant in his refusal to allow her access to Wilkinson.

No sooner had Charles ushered the doctor from his door than Terry McFall asked to see him. Terry was son in law to Debbie Freeman, Charles' older sister and was a solicitor prior to the coming of the virus.

Terry had learnt of Mike Wilkinson's presence from his mother in law, and wanted to know Charles' intentions, pointing out that even in their new circumstances the rule of law must always be paramount in any society.

Charles' face adopted an unusually hard look and he gave a deep sigh before rubbing his chin vigorously with his right hand. He was feeling really pissed off with everything at the moment, and especially of his treatment of Ursula Showandhra. An inveterate flirt all his life, he had been slowly but surely working his charm on the doctor, at least he thought he had been. Now he was sure that even if he hadn't cooked his goose for good with the woman, he had certainly suffered a setback.

Now this.

Although, Terry was nephew in law to Benford, the two met only infrequently. Christmas some years, weddings, funerals etc., so the younger man didn't know the older one to well. Had he done so, he would have recognised the gathering storm beginning to rage inside Charles.

That now came bursting out, as in a quiet but intense voice the older man marked his card.

"You understand this, you will never be allowed anywhere near our legal system as long as I'm alive." McFall tried to interrupt but Benford gave him no opportunity. "People like you, lawyers and politicians screwed our system in the past. You took what should be mankind's most precious invention, a justice system and wrecked it. Your greed made it unavailable to all except the very rich. You turned it into a game where it was acceptable to get the guilty off scot free, and where the innocent had to plead guilty because they couldn't afford representation, you allowed terrorists and cheats to abuse our legal and benefit systems just as long as you picked up your fees. You conveniently ignored the fact that fear of the expense involved in fighting a case caused thousands of people to either plead guilty wrongly or to drop a case altogether. But at least you lot were honest in one thing, you never claimed to be administering justice, only the law. And you used the word certainty to justify doing so. Certainty, you said was all important, even more so than justice. Well, that won't apply here," his tone softened slightly, "Look Terry, I believe that people know when they're doing wrong, it's why they try to hide their actions when doing so. Now in a small community like ours, I believe that we can provide justice rather than simply apply the law. I also believe that it's a government's duty to do so, and that's what I am," he added, "Whether I like it or not, I am the government here. As such, I believe that it's a government's duty to provide three things as an absolute minimum, shelter, food and security; that last includes the security of having access to a justice system that can be relied upon. Our government's lost sight of those things years ago resulting in all kinds of social injustices. We are going to do things differently here or at least we are going to try to. So our legal system will be based on the principal that that if you do wrong knowingly then you're guilty and the injured party will receive justice. And that system will be available to everyone equally and will try to administer fair play at all times, and that means anybody tainted by involvement in the previous system will have no place in ours."

McFall, though affronted by Benford's tirade and somewhat intimidated by his wives uncle was prepared to fight his corner, "So, what about this fellow you've under lock and key, does he have no rights under your system?"

"No, he doesn't," Charles was shouting again now, but lowered his voice somewhat as he explained what was known about Wilkinson from his contact with Maggie. "I saw his face when he recognised Maggie, he's guilty alright and your own common sense tells you that." Charles paused to study the others face and saw he was correct in this and so continued, "I might add that he is also the only new arrival who didn't ask as one of their first questions, how did we all come to survive?"

"He didn't ask because he knew very well how we survived."

"Look, any other time I would agree with you and it's my intention that of course everyone will get a fair trial. But this is different, this is if you like a left over from the past and not a part of our new world. I have no intention of allowing this man or any of the other maniacs who killed seven billion people to get a platform. If we try this man, he will be found guilty but as with all these loonies, he will use his trial as a platform to try and justify his actions, and in years to come there will always be some fools that will be taken in by his arguments. Look at the revival of 'Hitlerism' in Germany in recent years among the ignorant, that's not going to happen here. This man will not get a chance to make a speech in any way at all.

"There is another point as well that you and everybody else needs to know and will be announced in the next couple of days. Putting this bloke to one side, we are developing a problem that I am sure you will be aware of. As with any society we have some people who are becoming a nuisance, pushing the boundaries if you like, even though so far there hasn't been anything serious. What's going to happen when there is a real incident, someone goes too far and commits a real crime. What are we going to do with them?"

"Fine them, tell them off," he made no attempt to hide his sarcasm. "Maybe put them in some kind of prison and use up valuable resources guarding and looking after them. They're all non-starters for obvious reasons but we need some way to discourage unacceptable behaviour and to punish it when we fail to do so. What form can those deterrents take, extra work? Loss of privileges like the pub etc. Maybe we should bring back the stocks, minus the rotting fruit of course, or banishment maybe." He paused for breath and to collect his thoughts before continuing, "Do you see what I'm trying to say Terry, our society is different to the one we were all brought up in. Here everybody has somewhere to live, somewhere to call home and to raise a family, we all have food and clothing. There are no great inequalities, so there are no excuses for crime, at least not for gain. So everybody should be responsible for their own behaviour, none of this passing the buck because you didn't have the same start in life as the bloke down the street. No, each of us owe a responsibility to the other members in the community and if we do wrong and harm the community there has to be a price to pay. So as you know, I have raised a small part time body of responsible behaviour officers or RBOs. Yeah, I know they are already being called police but they are not meant to be quite like that. In the days to come, I also intend to appoint a panel of magistrates as well, and I'll call the people together to discuss what type of punishments we might think appropriate, and at that time you can voice an opinion, but you cannot stand for office.

"Now, please go Terry, I'm very tired and I still have a long night ahead of me. We will talk again soon, I don't want you involved in our laws but I appreciate that you are a clever and very capable man. I've been toying with an idea recently and have finally made my mind up on what I want to do with it. I need someone to do a new job, it will be very important to the future of the community and it's a role that I think you would be perfect for. So we'll talk again in a couple of days but for now please just go."

After Mc Fall's departure, Benford sat trancelike for a while before finally rising from his seat, and crossing the room opened an old oak cabinet and brought out a bottle of Balvennie malt and a glass.

He had a job, no more of a duty to perform shortly and knew that it would be easier to do it if he was at least partly drunk.

He also knew that getting to that point wasn't going to be easy, his emotions were so hyped up by today's events, he felt he could drain a barrel of whisky and still feel nothing but anger and despair.

That wasn't like him and he knew that he only had to sit for a while and contemplate life in general to put himself in a more positive mood.

Of course, a few glasses of his favourite malt wouldn't hurt either.

He spun his chair around to face the window, he couldn't see anything out there in the dark of the night, but he knew that when the next day dawned it would reveal the new world they were building, and that they were building it as well as they reasonably could.

Another sip of Balvennie, a glance at the calendar, and he allowed his mind to drift over the past eventful months.

They had come a long way from that dark day when he had to decide who was to live and who not. No, as always he wouldn't allow his mind to contemplate the other side of who lived. Only the living mattered now, it was the living who were building this new world of theirs, the dead could do nothing and so were irrelevant.

Still reflecting, he took another sip of the amber liquid, but yeah they were doing okay.

Those first three days had been hectic, loading freezer wagons one after another, attending to livestock–at least those earmarked as their future breeding animals–and clearing the dead from the houses intended for the community's use. That last had been the most awful, there were so many corpses to bury and in so many locations. Seven months into the work and they were still a long way from achieving the corpse free zone they felt was the minimum area they required for their good health.

The community had lived at the hotel, some in the rooms, some in caravans for those first few days while the houses at Kingsthorpe had been cleared and prepared for their use.

At the same time, work crews had been despatched to Hardworth house their intended long term home to clear the dead from both there and the surrounding villages.

Another crew had been despatched to do the same job in three further locations. Charles allowed himself a grin at that thought, had those other clearances been a mistake. There were certainly those who thought so when it came out where that crew had been to and what they had been sent to do at such a crucial time.

All three locations had been at the coast, two in the south and one in the east. Having cleared the dead and either buried or burnt the corpses, the buildings concerned had been secured and then left until very recently.

Meanwhile at Kingsthorpe, the loading of lorries had continued endlessly.

Not freezer wagons now, but the biggest juggernauts with solid sides, those and any container lorries they could lay hands on.

All of these were loaded with every type of commodity imaginable, tinned and packet foods, cleaning supplies, clothing, furniture, liquid gas bottles, camping gear, tools and equipment of all types, stationery and other office supplies, medical equipment, pots and pans the list was endless. Once loaded, the lorries were parked on the streets of the surrounding villages awaiting their final move to Hardworth house.

Eighty miles away over at Hardworth, tremendous works were being carried out. Charles had consulted with his sister Liz's son in law, James Forsyth, an architect and with a number of the builders among the survivors. They had agreed the modifications the houses intended for the community's use would need. That is what they would need in order to suit what would have to become their new lifestyles.

Heating for instance would have to revert to solid fuel, meaning the construction of chimneys in any house that didn't already have them.

That in itself would be the work of months to prepare enough homes for everybody. Toilets were another problem, existing sewers would work for a period, toilets being flushed with buckets of river water poured down them. Though septic tanks would be the more long-term answer and fortunately quite a lot of the proposed homes already used this system.

Clean running water wasn't possible for the time being, but a major reason for the move to Hardworth was the presence of natural springs in the area. These would provide drinking water, though it would have to be provided in barrels for a time until a pipeline could be constructed, and work was currently being carried out on that, though not as fast as he would have liked. Meantime, bathing would have to continue via swimming pools where the same water could be recycled, and drinking water came from bottles of the supermarket shelves.

Because of these practical problems and the delays they imposed, caravans were still to be used as a stop gap. There they had been fortunate that there was a large site close to Hardworth and the facilities there were being utilised. Seven months on only some thirty homes had been converted and moved into. These provided housing for only about half of the original population, let alone the new arrivals.

That last thought was certainly a positive one. The community was growing, indeed numbers had almost doubled and was increasing if not daily then certainly on a weekly basis.

At the time of the 'death', Benford had estimated that some three thousand people would have survived the virus by virtue of their natural immunity. But those three thousand would have been spread across the whole population, both men and women and of all age groups.

His mood that had lightened slightly for a time darkened again. Those with a natural immunity would have numbered amongst them children of all ages. How old would a child need to be to survive alone in this new world. Before he could prevent it, his mind flicked to the thought of a baby laying in a cot crying until, no! Again the golden rule don't do this, don't go down this path. Think of the positives, but it was too late his mind was back to that day. 'The choosing', during the last months whenever the thoughts of that day had surfaced or anyone had spoken about it, Benford had attempted to switch off. He had tried consistently to blur his memory about it, perhaps hoping that it might fade away beyond recall, but now it was back with startling clarity.

Choosing, choosing, who lives, who dies, pictures in his head, Harry and Peggy's faces at the loss of their daughter, Dawn Reed as she told him that her daughter, no his daughter, Gemma was abroad and therefore doomed. Thoughts of family made him realise that he hadn't had contact from any of his own brood since this bastard Wilkinson had arrived, that was surprising his sons especially would have been as keen as anyone to lynch the murderous sod.

He forced himself to interrupt the flow of despair and took another swig of the malt and thought of what he had to do. Yeah, he was ready his head nodded in agreement with his intent. Oh yes, he was ready for the prick, a last swig and he would go and visit Mr Mike Wilkinson and enjoy it. Well, certainly enjoy it a damn site more than Wilkinson would.

The bottle emptied, he headed for the door, pausing to replace the chair that Terry Mcfall had sat in, back to its proper place.

That paused him, Mcfall and his upholding the law, cheeky sod coming here and making demands of him. Well, Charles had marked his card on that. Justice is what mattered most not law, and justice is what Wilkinson was going to get.

Justice as represented by a bullet in the head. Charles reckoned he was just about drunk enough now to administer justice alright.

His hand froze on the door handle, drunk enough. "God forgive me," he muttered, "What am I about?" He sat down heavily and slumped in the seat.

Through the alcohol induced fug in his brain he tried to rationalise, what was he actually doing. Wilkinson deserved death, that wasn't in question and Charles believed totally in a legal system that sought to place justice first and foremost. So Wilkinson was going to die and he was going to die without having a platform for self-justification. All of that was right and just, what wasn't right was that the execution be carried out by a drunken man. It shouldn't happen that way, not because of any rights that Wilkinson possessed, he didn't warrant any. No, the execution had to be carried out by a sober man because that's what a justice system deserved.

Any legal system could only retain its integrity if the organisers, the people behind it, those whose authority it carried, believed in it themselves.

If he didn't respect it and treat it accordingly then how could he demand that anyone else should. If Wilkinson deserved to die for his crimes, then the executioner appointed by the legal system to carry out the sentence should do so because he or she believed the sentence to be correct.

In that case, the individual should be sober and confident in the justice of the act and not in need of Dutch courage. Otherwise all that he had just spouted to Mcfall would be just so much B-----Ks.

How drunk was he? He tried to recall how much whisky there had been in the bottle. As near as he could guess, he reckoned that he must have drunk the equivalent of at least four doubles, certainly more than he had ever had in a single session for years.

Charles wandered through into the kitchen and made a strong black sweet coffee. He reckoned that the drink along with the sobering effect of his recent thoughts ought to put him right, and only when he was sure that he was acting for the proper reasons would he carry out the sentence he was determined on.

To allow the coffee time to work its effect, he sat down and allowed his mind to drift again.

Christmas was only a fortnight away and the survivors were going to celebrate it in the traditional way, that is as a community coming together with carols and feasting and a nativity play put on by the younger children.

Hardworth had been a popular tourist destination in happier times and had a huge indoor restaurant area. The survivors normally ate here communally but in shifts, food being cooked by the housekeeping department. Jilly who ran housekeeping along with sister in law, Debbie, Niall's wife Judy, who had been a sous chef in one of the local hotels and Maria Koniev a former restaurateur, had promised a spectacular dinner for everybody in one sitting. That was to be followed by the children's nativity play and then there would be singing and dancing. The carol service was to be the evening before and was open to everybody whatever their religion or lack of, it was to be a traditional Christmas day in the fullest sense.

A few weeks before, Joey's sister, Courtney, had agreed to have her baby that had born back in July, the first child to be born to the community, christened.

Every one of the survivors had been invited to attend the ceremony.

Conducted first in the traditional Christian way and followed by blessings given by Muslims, Hindus, Buddhists and Jews. A barbecue in the former deer park had followed, again accompanied with music and dancing. The weather had been kind for October and people had actually laughed and enjoyed themselves. Of course, the laughter would still often come to an embarrassed end as people remembered the past, but the improvement in mood was there and had stayed. Since that day there had been occasional smiles that had been guilt free, and since the announcement of the Christmas celebrations excited talk of how great the day would be.

Last month had seen the final capsules of the supposed antidote distributed and taken. This final ending of the fear of the virus could have triggered an exodus of the original survivors, but it had passed almost without mention. It seemed that finally the people had reached accommodations within themselves and accepted this new way of life.

Benford rose from his seat, his mood had lightened despite what he was about to do and he felt able both mentally and physically to carry the task out in an appropriate manner. With a muttered, "Come on you bastard," he left the building.

Wilkinson lay wracked in pain, he seemed to hurt from every bone, every joint and every muscle in his body. He had both vomited and wet himself.

The vomiting had been the worse, with the gag in his mouth, he had thought he must drown in his own mess. But he had brought up only fluid and had thus managed to exit most of the awful stuff, though enough had remained to make his mouth taste as though he had been eating excrement. Along with his physical deterioration, his morale had also plummeted, his much vaunted SAS training had been twelve years ago and was at least partly forgotten. His guards checked him every few minutes to ensure he was unable to even attempt escape, other than that they totally ignored him. He had lost all idea of time but knew from the occasional snatches of conversation that he overheard that Benford was hours late now. With the delay had come visions of all kinds, none of which were good, and Mike was beginning to lose hope. He tried to concentrate on one final aim, if he was going to die, he wanted to do so with some kind of dignity and there was none in laying here tied like an animal in his own waste. He had to remain conscious, had to keep alert and when Benford finally came, he needed to make eye contact with sufficient intensity to get the man to allow him to speak. He might not be able to save himself, he wasn't even sure that he wanted to. But he needed to validate his actions, needed to keep his dignity if he was to die.

Despite the pain, he must have slept because he was aware of being woken by the sound of a vehicle pulling up, followed by muffled conversation. Hands closed the doors of the van and he couldn't see who those hands belonged to. This wasn't what he wanted, he needed to see Benford or whoever had just arrived in order to make some contact with the man.

The vehicles engine started and they pulled away. Whoever was driving wasn't hanging around, they travelled at speed taking corners uncomfortably fast and causing Wilkinson to slide on the van floor and scream aloud in pain despite the gag. The journey lasted for around ten minutes and he was bounced around more than ever.

The last part must have been on an unmade road or at least over very rough ground. Finally they stopped, he heard the driver's door open and seconds later the rear ones opened revealing Charles Benford's face. Mike was ready for him and his eyes stared at his captor in challenge, then turned to fear as he saw the gun in Benford's hand pointing at him and the look in the other's eyes as he took aim. He tried to yell NO but only managed an oomph sound as Benford pulled the trigger, and heard him swear as he missed his target from six feet. The bullet passed through the floor of the van, inches in front of Wilkinson's face and showered him in hot metal shards. He shook his head in denial, he needed to talk, Benford must allow him to say something, he couldn't simply be murdered like this. The gun pointed at him again and he could see the panic in his killer's eyes as he fired and missed again.

Ludicrously and in a state of panic now, Benford actually apologised for the miss and made a visible effort to steady his shaking hand before pointing the gun again. Mike was thrashing about on the floor as much as his bonds and injuries allowed him, desperate to make some contact with the gun man.

The weapon fired for a third time and he felt a searing pain in his abdomen, the fourth shot tore through his shoulder as Benford totally freaked out now fired again and again. Mike Wilkinson was past feeling anything after the sixth shot.

Finally the weapon clicked on empty and the killer dropped his arm and staggered away to lean against the side of the vehicle. Benford was still in this same position breathing deeply as Joey pulled up. His instructions had been to remain outside of the entrance to the rubbish tip where Charles had chosen to take his prisoner for execution. Joey hadn't been told of what was to happen when they arrived, just to follow the gaffer with a second vehicle and wait for Charles to call him.

Hearing the gun shots, Joey had realised what Benford was doing and knew that his former boss and now leader would need him. Joey had been a teenager straight from school when he first met Charles, and over the years had become entirely devoted to both the man himself and Jilly.

He knew that while Charles liked to portray himself as a hard bitten man of the world, he wasn't. Oh, the gaffer had an inner hardness that he could call on when needed, but that was exactly what he had to do. Call on it, hardness didn't come naturally to him and whenever he had to call on it, it always left him like he was now, thoroughly drained.

The younger man looked into the rear of the van and gasped on seeing the torn and bloody form of what had once been the mass murderer Mike Wilkinson.

He closed one of the doors, shutting out the awful sight and trotted over to his own vehicle. Benford insisted that any vehicle that left Hardworth compound must be equipped with first aid box, emergency rations of food and water for three days and a couple of gallons of fuel. It was the latter that Joey now reached for. Taking out one of the two jerry cans, he returned to the prison van and emptied the contents inside and out of the vehicle making sure that the corpse inside received plenty of the liquid.

Charles had pulled himself together as Joey had been about his work and now thanked the younger man and instructed him to go back to his own vehicle. Joey took time to assure himself that the Gaffer was himself again before complying and handing over a box of matches muttering, "You'll need these, just open the door boss, stand well back and flick the match in," and walked away.

Charles took a long last look at Wilkinson's corpse and whispered, "I don't know how your maker will deal with you, but I'm pleased at being the one that sent you to him. I hope you rot in hell forever." On the last word he struck a match and flicked it inside the vehicle, stepping back smartly as the conflagration started with a whoosh. He caught up with the younger man and grabbed his arm.

"You never talk about this Joey, not to anyone. I don't want that piece of shit remembered in any way at all, as far as I'm concerned he never came to Hardworth, he never even existed okay."

"Boss." The single word served as assent, and the two returned to what was now home.

Epilogue

While Charles Benford had been getting drunk enough to execute Wilkinson, his eldest son had Chris Simpson pinned up against a wall of the swimming baths that the males of the community used for hygiene purposes.

Simpson had arrived at the refugee service station accompanied by a stunning blonde about a fortnight before, and been released from quarantine just five days prior to Wilkinson's arrival.

Claiming to be a chef, he had been assigned to catering while his stunning companion was spending a few days in different departments until she found the right niche.

Neither of them being very good liars their original story of having met on the road only a few days before their arrival at Hardworth had soon fallen apart and suspicion had soon followed.

After the community's arrival at their new home and with his ex-brothers in law in mind in particular, Benford had appointed a number of the younger fitter men and women as part time behaviour-officers and as he had explained to Terry Mcfall, planned to appoint some of the older, wiser heads among the people as magistrates.

The idea being that anyone causing a 'nuisance', a euphemism for any kind of bad behaviour that caused inconvenience to others, could be dealt with and discouraged from repeating such behaviour easily and quickly.

Without arousing particular attention to themselves, Niall and Robbie had waylaid their target after his shift had finished and were now questioning Simpson as to how both he and his girlfriend had both survived the 'death'. "Don't give us any bollocks about being immune to it, or not knowing one another. Your girlfriend has already said openly that she has known you for years. Then the chances of any individual having natural immunity is one in twenty thousand, that means that for a couple to both have it is four hundred million to one."

Niall finished speaking and shook his prisoner violently.

"For you both to have survived you must both have had the antidote. That means you or at least one of you must have been a part of the conspiracy and that means you're going to be tried and hung."

There was an air of real satisfaction on Niall's face as he said this. He only ever had to close his eyes to again re live that awful night and if this bloke had been a part of that then he wasn't about to give him any sympathy.

Simpson was panicking and close to wetting himself, "No, you don't understand. Look, Niall isn't it?

"Look Niall, it's true Kelly and I know each other, and yes we had the antidote, but we're not part of the conspiracy. From what I understand, I got the antidote from the same place as you got yours."

Both brothers glanced at each other momentarily, then misunderstanding what Simpson meant, Robbie dived for him in a welter of fists and boots screaming, "You lying bastard, my father got our antidote and he took it from three terrorists, so you can hang, you c—t," and continued to flail at his victim who rolled around the floor trying to avoid the worst of the kicks aimed at him.

Niall jumped in somewhat reluctantly and eventually managed to drag his brother off the other man as Simpson shouted to be heard.

"I know, I know, listen to me, I know how your father got the antidote and he left a little behind, enough for two people and that's what I took."

On the final word, the speaker pulled himself up to sit with his back against the wall gasping and groaning simultaneously. "Oh bloody hell there was no need for this." He groaned again in pain, while the brothers both lost for words simply gaped at one another.

"Ask your father if he left enough antidote behind for two people, he'll confirm what I'm saying."

"Are you telling us that you know how dad got the antidote," it was Niall who spoke in an almost awed voice at the idea that they might finally get to know what had actually happened that day.

"Yes, I came along, I suppose just after your dad left," Simpson paused to see how that went down or if he was about to get kicked again.

"So, what happened?" both brothers shouted together.

Relieved that it appeared he might still be alive tomorrow and taking a deep breath Simpson, spoke, "Well, it was like this."

CPSIA information can be obtained
at www.ICGtesting.com
Printed in the USA
LVHW081923220122
709124LV00011B/254

9 781398 402485